"With a crash, the elephant broke through the boughs."

THE SPIES ABROAD;

OR,

The Perils of the Gold Coast,

BEAUTIFULLY ILLUSTRATED.

COMPLETE.

LONDON:
"BOYS OF ENGLAND" OFFICE, 173, FLEET STREET, E.C.,
AND ALL BOOKSELLERS.

THE SPIES ABROAD;

Or, The Perils of the Gold Coast.

"'DEMON!' CRIED JACK, 'I WILL HAVE YOUR LIFE FOR MY FATHER'S!'"

No. 1.

THE SPIES ABROAD;

OR,

THE PERILS OF THE GOLD COAST.

(A Sequel to " The Spies of The School.")

CHAPTER I.

REACHING PORT—UNMASKING A VILLAIN—A DESPERATE POSITION.

" LAND HO ! "

The look-out man on board the "Lapwing" had, one very hot morning, after a short and prosperous voyage, sighted the coast of Africa.

Immediately the greatest excitement prevailed on board the ship.

Mr. Spencer, Jack, Marian, and Harry Rawlings hastily left the breakfast table, and, crowding on deck, leant over the taffrail.

Before them was a low-lying sandy shore, on which a line of white surf showed that the waves were continually breaking.

Graceful palms and other tropical trees abounded.

They were somewhat disappointed to find that the town of Three Points consisted only, as far as they could see, of about a score of native huts, a large wooden warehouse, and a dwelling-house adjoining, while in the centre of the huts was a house built in a square shape, with a flat roof, and painted white.

Ormsby did not make his appearance, though Mr. Spencer was anxious to put several questions to him about their new home.

When within half-a-mile of the shore, the captain dropped anchor, the yawl was lowered, and several deal packing-cases, containing goods, and two puncheons of rum, were hoisted out of the hold.

Jack and Harry watched the proceedings carefully.

The cases were directed to " Vandervelde, Merchant, Three Points, on the Gold Coast, Africa," while the rum was labelled, "For W. Blunt," at the same address.

They were informed by the mate that the goods would be landed first, and that the yawl would come back for them and Ormsby.

" Are you not going ashore ? " asked Jack.

" What is the use of landing in a forsaken sand-hole like that ? " replied the mate.

" My father would, no doubt, be glad to receive you at my late uncle's place."

" I don't know nothing about him," continued the mate, brusquely. " We're going on farther as soon as we've got rid of you."

With this discouraging answer, Jack was obliged to be content.

The goods were put in the boat, and they awaited her return, when Ormsby appeared from below, explaining that he had been transacting business with the captain.

Their baggage was now placed in the yawl, they took their seats aft, and the sailors pulled for the shore.

No parting cheer greeted their ears, the captain and crew of the " Lapwing " looked at them apathetically, and a general chill seemed to have fallen on everybody.

" It is strange," remarked Mr Spencer, " but I feel dull and gloomy instead of high-spirited, as I ought to be, now the voyage is over."

" You will be all right presently," replied Ormsby, with a grin he could only half conceal.

" It is a small place."

" Yes," said Ormsby, dryly.

The conversation languished. Marian admired the beautiful palms, and Harry looked at the dusky natives, men, women and children, about fifty in number, who had assembled at a landing stage, built on piles, to stare at the ship and watch the incoming boat.

" It is not often they see a ship, I should imagine," observed Jack.

" The ' Lapwing ' is the only one that trades here, and she only comes once in three months—that is, four times a year," replied Ormsby.

"Not much trade?"

"Nothing considerable."

"Then we shall have to wait three months before we can return!" exclaimed Mr. Spencer. "Why did you not tell us that before?"

"I thought I did. You will find the time pass quickly enough," said Ormsby.

As they drew near the shore, they were enveloped in a cloud of mosquitos, which bit their faces, hands and ankles severely.

The wind, which was blowing off the shore, carried minute particles of sand into their eyes, while the sun beat down on their heads with tropical severity.

Altogether their first impressions of African soil were the reverse of agreeable.

When the boat reached the stage, they landed, the sailors piled their trunks in a heap, and saying farewell, began to row back to the ship.

Half-an-hour afterwards, the captain raised his anchor, set sail, and put out to sea.

The emigrants were left alone on a foreign strand.

There were no means of returning to their own country.

No boats, save and except a few canoes of primitive construction, more like coracles, were to be seen on the beach.

The natives, pure-blooded African negroes, with thick lips and flat noses, large ears and woolly hair, stared at them in silence.

They did not seem to have energy enough to offer a water-melon or an orange for sale.

"Well, here we are, at last!" exclaimed Mr. Spencer. "Whose house is that in front of us?"

"It is a tavern, frequented by the niggers living here and others coming from the interior; the name is the 'Trader's Rest.' It is kept by an Englishman, who was a sailor, by name Bill Blunt," replied Ormsby.

"And those houses at the extremity of the village?"

"One is the warehouse of Mynheer Vandervelde, a Dutchman, who is a great friend of mine; the other is his dwelling-house."

"Are there no other Europeans?"

"None. Vandervelde does what little trade there is to be done here."

"Where are we to go?" enquired Mr. Spencer.

"Just where you like," answered Ormsby.

The farmer regarded him as if he had suddenly gone crazy.

"Where is my brother Robert's establishment?" he demanded.

"He did live here," said Ormsby, "but the little place was burnt down five years ago. I was a sailor then, and made his acquaintance by touching here."

"I understood you all along that he was dead and had left me his property?"

"He may be dead, for all I know."

The truth all at once dawned upon Spencer and the others.

They had been tricked for some purpose by a villain.

There could not be the possibility of a doubt that they were the victims of a cruel deception.

Choking back his rage—concealing his chagrin, Spencer spoke again.

"Why have you brought us here?" he asked.

"Because I was paid to do so."

"You have deceived me by the concoction of an infamous falsehood."

"I had to make up a story, or you would not have come."

"What are we brought here for?"

"To die, I expect," answered Ormsby, brutally. "I am going to Vandervelde's. You can go to the 'Trader's Rest,' if Bill Blunt will take you in; if not, you can camp in the woods. There is no law against trespassing here."

"Who is your employer?"

"Find out; it is none of my business to inform you."

Mr. Spencer could control himself no longer.

He rushed at Ormsby and seized him by the throat, when a fierce and determined struggle took place between them.

The negroes did not attempt to interfere, though they began to chatter like a lot of monkeys up a tree.

Jack and Harry felt their blood get up to boiling pitch.

As for Marian, she trembled violently, and, girl-like, burst into tears.

Suddenly, Ormsby's long black beard and whiskers came off in Spencer's hand.

It had only been fixed on as a disguise.

"Garner!" cried Spencer. "Now I can see it all. Miserable assassin! I know who your rascally employer is without further query. You have been paid by Squire Rawlings to do all this!"

He still held him by the collar.

"Let go your hold," said Garner, for it was the man who had acted as Mr. Rawlings' bailiff, and who had tried to take Harry's life.

"Not until I have satisfaction out of you."

"Fool! what would you do?"

"Pound you to a pulp. You come to us disguised, and bring us to this barbarous spot under false pretences, either to leave us to perish, or to become the helpless prey of our enemies, who, for what I know, may arrive here at any moment."

He saw how grievously he had been hood-winked, and his just anger knew no bounds.

At that moment he could have killed the villain.

Blinded by passion, Spencer rained a shower of blows on the rogue's face.

The blood spurted in all directions.

Garner put his hand in his pocket, and drew a pistol, which he fired point-blank at the outraged and incensed farmer.

The ball entered his side, and he fell with a deep groan of anguish.

Harry caught him in his arms before he reached the ground.

In a moment, Jack, pale and ghastly, advanced to Garner.

The latter presented the revolver at him.

"Stand back!" he shouted. "Stand off, or I'll drop you. It is not my wish to shed more blood than I can help."

"Demon!" said Jack, "I will have your life for my father's!"

"Stand back, I say, or I'll send a bullet through you!"

He retreated rapidly while talking.

Marian seized her brother's arm, clinging to it convulsively.

"For heaven's sake, be calm!" she cried.

"How can I?" asked Jack.

"He will kill you and Harry. I shall be left to the mercy of the world."

"We are betrayed."

"Let us put our trust in Him in this awful hour of trial. He will protect us. No, Jack, you shall not follow him."

Had it not been for Marian's clinging embrace, Jack would have undoubtedly pursued Garner.

He did not then consider the consequences of such a rash act.

None of his party were armed; their rifles, shot-guns, and pistols were in their baggage.

They had not thought it requisite to get them out before landing.

Garner, without more ado, retreated rapidly to Mynheer Vandervelde's house, inside the portals of which he soon disappeared.

"Another time," said Jack, bitterly, as he turned round and went to his father.

The farmer was much hurt, bleeding profusely from the wound in his side, to which he pressed his hand, while beads of perspiration gathered on his brow.

"I'm afraid I'm done for, my boy," he murmured. "What a fool I was to listen to that villain's lies."

"We'll be a match for him yet, father," replied Jack.

"I fear not, on this desolate coast. Squire Rawlings is after Harry, his son after

Marian. I must have been mad not to see through it."

"The spies are with them as well, I expect," remarked Harry.

"For myself I do not care so much," continued Spencer, "but what will become of you three?"

Before Harry or Jack could reply, a tall stout man, who seemed a very Hercules for strength, pushed his way through the crowd of listless negroes.

It was Bill Blunt, the proprietor of the "Trader's Rest."

He had heard the shot fired, and had come down to the landing-stage to see what had happened.

When the yawl had delivered his puncheons of rum, he did not know that any passengers had come in the "Lapwing."

Why should anyone come to such a place?

Rumour had it that Blunt had fought a man in a drunken quarrel in England, and durst not return.

Anyhow, the fact was that he had settled at Three Points, lived by himself, and managed to make a living somehow.

"Avast there!" he exclaimed. "What is all this to-do about? Who is shot? What for? Who did it? Who are you folks? What are you here for? There's a lot of questions for you to answer. Don't speak all at once. I'm Bill Blunt, an English sailor. I keep a saloon in this sand-pit. You can trust me, for I'm square."

"Tell the gentleman all about it, Jack," said Spencer.

As quickly and succinctly as he was able, Jack informed Blunt of the circumstances which had brought them to the Gold Coast.

It was a long story, though he tried to cut it short. At times, Harry helped him out.

While he was listening, Bill Blunt was engaged in attending to Spencer's wound. He stripped aside his clothes and tied a bandage round it, as well as he could.

To stop the bleeding was the first thing, the bullet could be looked for another time.

"I understand," cried Blunt, presently. "There are a good many villains in this place. Garner sha'n't touch you any more, nor shall this Squire Rawlings, if I can help it, though he may come here in his yacht."

"Will you be our friend, sir?" asked Jack.

"That I will. I'm not a chap to see my countrymen in distress and not lend a helping hand."

"Heaven bless you!"

"Look at this pretty young lady, too; she's crying her eyes out. You shall all four come to my diggings. It isn't much of a shanty to boast of, but I'll make you welcome. I don't think the guv'nor is mortally wounded. We will pull him through."

"Can you protect us against Garner and his friend Vandervelde?" enquired Jack.

"Rather. If Vandervelde said a word to me, I'd have him burnt out to-morrow."

"How?"

"The niggers here love me. I can do what I like with them. You see, they live principally on suction."

"On what?"

"Suction. When they aren't sucking a melon or a cocoanut, they come to me for rum. I accommodate them to a certain extent on credit, then I send them out to get ivory and gold dust to pay me," said Blunt.

"Did my uncle, Robert Spencer, ever live here?" asked Jack.

"He did; I knew him well. Vandervelde has got his buildings now—through fraud, I have always suspected."

"Is he dead?"

"That I can't say."

"He did not live here recently?" continued Jack.

"Not he," answered Bill Blunt. "It is six years ago since he went on a journey inland, to visit King Makolo, and arrange for a monthly consignment of dust and ivory. He has never been seen or heard of since."

"Then he may be alive, and we may hear of him?"

"Why not? Stop your talking for awhile. We must attend to the guv'nor, and get him to bed."

"We have money, sir, and can pay you for your kindness."

"That's all right; I'll take what is my due and no more. When I want it, I'll ask you for it. You have a friend in me, my boy, and it's lucky for you."

With these words, Bill Blunt raised his voice.

"Congo!" he shouted, "come here."

A gigantic negro, nearly eight feet high, left the crowd hard by and walked up, his black skin shining like polished ebony in the sun.

"He's as big as an elephant and as strong as a horse, but gentle as a lamb," continued Blunt.

"Me Congo, sah!" said the negro. "What me do?"

"Take this wounded man up in your arms and carry him to my house. Now, miss, you, please, take my arm. You two youngsters follow on behind. I killed a fine sheep this morning, and I'll give you as fine a piece of fresh meat, in the shape of a leg of mutton, with yams, as ever you tasted in the Old Country."

Congo started first, carrying Mr. Spencer as easily as if he were a child, Marian dried her tears, and accepted Blunt's escort.

Jack and Harry followed in their wake.

CHAPTER II.

NEWS FROM THE SLAVE COAST—OLD CALABAR—A NEGRO FIGHT—ARRIVAL OF THE "CASSANDRA"—THE SPIES COME ASHORE.

A GOOD dinner and a night's rest did wonders to recruit the strength and energies of the emigrants. Bill Blunt was kind and friendly. He extracted the ball from Mr. Spencer's wound, and Marian nursed her father tenderly, but it threatened to be a long time before he would be able to leave his bed.

Blunt advised Jack to go along the coast to Cape Coast Castle, which was about a hundred miles off, and there claim the protection of the British consul.

Two causes, however, were in operation to prevent this course being taken.

They could not leave Mr. Spencer, and the very next day a negro elephant hunter of great repute, named Old Calabar, came into Three Points, saying that Bonna, the slave-dealer, was making a raid on the Gold Coast.

Bonna's name was a terror.

Whenever he took the field, the country he entered became disturbed and demoralised.

Trade was put a stop to, for he seized both black and white men alike.

Jack, Harry, and Blunt were seated under the verandah, while Old Calabar was relating some of the atrocities of Bonna which had come to his ears.

Some rum, in a bottle, stood on a table, with glasses and water. The hunter and Blunt helped themselves as they felt inclined.

"How is it," asked Bill Blunt, "that King Makolo lets the slave-dealer come into his territory?"

"Him give him present of plenty cloth—Bonna give lot," replied Old Calabar.

"Do you think they will come down to the coast, here?"

"Can't tell—dunno."

"We've got a poor lot of niggers; they ain't worth stealing."

"Bonna know you got shot-guns—perhaps keep away. White man know how to use gun better than black man. Who that nigger there? Him fine buck fellow."

Calabar pointed to Congo, who was standing near the verandah, in the forlorn hope that he would be asked to have a drink, for he had done no work lately, and was in the miserable condition of having neither credit nor money.

"What you got to say about this nigger?" he asked.

"Bonna coming this way. Me tell him about you. Perhaps you worth two elephant tusks and double-handful of gold dust—eh?"

"Me crack 'um skull, if talk like that," said Congo.

"Take six niggers like you to crack 'um skull," retorted Calabar.

"Bettee you two, four drinkee of rum."

"Me see you on that."

Saying this, Congo went into the house, presently returning with a couple of thick, rough cudgels, cut from the wood of the tamarind tree.

He handed one to Old Calabar, and, keeping the other for himself, took up his position on the sand outside.

In a moment, he was joined by Calabar. Both were naked, excepting the loin cloths they wore, and each had an equally determined aspect.

"What are they going to do?" asked Jack.

"Fight it out in a kind of singlestick way. They know I don't allow them to use knives, though they've each got a carver hidden away in their cloths. You will see some fun presently in the way of hard hitting."

"Will they hurt one another?"

"Not they. A nigger's head is the hardest part of his body. One of them will haul his wind when he has had enough," replied Bill Blunt.

"Don't they have rifles?"

"Some do, but they sell everything for 'm. Old Calabar got one. He's artful, an has left it in the bush, for fear of temptatio"

"Iow do you supply his wants? Has he g money?" continued Jack.

"L brought in a lovely elephant tusk. I valu it at one pound. It is really worth a good al more. He intends to drink it

out. When its value is gone, he'll dive back into the bush and get another, or some dust. He don't mean to leave the coast until Bonna's raid is over," said Blunt.

"What a funny way of doing business," laughed Jack.

"I tell you, niggers is all suction—when they can get it," Blunt added. "Look! Vast heaving! They're at it, hammer and tongs. Watch 'em."

The boys did so, and were vastly amused, for the two skipped round one another, holloaing and shouting, while they struck at random, having no idea of the science of guarding or countering blows.

Whack after whack resounded in the still air, while the perspiration ran from them in streams.

At length, Old Calabar had to give in to his taller and more muscular opponent.

He threw down his stick in token of surrender.

"Me give you best man and payee for the rum!" he exclaimed.

"No good to 'sult me," said Congo, proudly. "Me worth two you."

They did not appear to bear any malice. Congo followed his defeated opponent to the verandah and helped himself to a couple of glasses of the rum, to which of course his victory entitled him.

He was about to take another, when Old Calabar stopped him by laying his hand on his arm.

"No more," he said; "we fightee for two."

"Fightee for four," replied Congo.

"You liar and t'ief!"

"So you, more'n me. You bad nigger; no drink fair."

They would have come to loggerheads again had not Blunt interfered by telling Congo that he could help himself at his expense.

This amicable arrangement settled matters.

Congo soon went to lie down under a palm tree. Old Calabar continued his potations until he went to sleep in his chair. Blunt repaired to the kitchen to see after his domestic affairs, and the boys were left to their thoughts.

Marian was in the sick room talking to her father, and fanning his fevered brow.

The situation they were placed in weighed very heavily upon their minds. With the farmer dangerously wounded, they had lost the head they relied upon for guidance, and they did not know at what moment they might be attacked by their enemies.

There was no one to help or protect them at Three Points. If any crime were committed, the inhabitants had to avenge it themselves, or repair to Cape Coast Castle for redress.

In the case of anything very serious, the consul sent a gunboat to inquire into the matter.

Garner had not shown his face outside Mynheer Vandervelde's dwelling since his entry therein on the previous day.

"I wonder what will be the end of this?" said Harry. "It is all my fault again. If it had not been for me, you and yours would not have been involved in this trouble."

"I am not afraid," replied Jack. "If I could leave this moment, I would not do so."

"Why not?"

"Because I mean to get even with Ormsby—I mean, Garner—for the injury he has done my father."

"We are in the midst of great danger," continued Harry. "I think we ought to unpack the gun-case and arm ourselves."

"By Jove! you are right. What a numskull I must be not to think of that before. Come on," replied Jack.

They repaired to the room in which their boxes were placed, and opening the one containing the guns, took out a couple of rifles and the same number of pistols, as well as two knives, and belts containing a plentiful supply of cartridges.

Then they loaded their weapons, and returning to the verandah, took their seats again, feeling more secure.

"We can sell our lives dearly now," remarked Jack.

"Yes," said Harry; "being armed puts us on equal terms with any foe, black or white, and it strikes me we shall have to look out for Bonna and his slave-dealers."

"There will be danger nearer home first," exclaimed Jack.

"How so?"

"Garner did not decoy us here without there being a pre-arranged plan between him and Squire Rawlings. Garner has been leading a vagabond life. He has been here and seen Uncle Robert. It was he who invented the plan to entice us to the Gold Coast, but the yacht won't be long in following."

"I fear not," replied Harry, who saw how forcible his friend's reasoning was.

"Boom!"

Suddenly they were startled by the loud report of a cannon.

It came from the sea, and looking out on the bay, they saw that a yacht had anchored close to the shore.

Almost immediately the report was answered by the discharge of a gun, three times in succession, from Mynheer Vandervelde's house,

"That's a signal," said Jack.

"It is answered by Garner," exclaimed Harry.

"How do you know?"

"I ought to, for I have been on board that vessel."

"When? Explain."

"I know every line of her; it is the 'Cassandra.' Every rope is familiar to me. By George! she hasn't been long in tracking us."

There was no doubt that Garner had answered a preconcerted signal.

As soon as the three shots had been fired, the yacht lowered a boat, which was rapidly propelled to the shore.

Garner left Mynheer Vandervelde's house and advanced towards the landing-stage, as if to meet the occupants of the boat.

Jack sprang up impulsively.

"Where are you going?" asked Harry, anxiously.

"To return that villain's shot," replied Jack.

"Take care. Two can play at that game."

"Exactly; and that is why I am going to try it. Didn't he shoot my father? Hasn't he beguiled us to this land of peril and death?"

"Keep calm."

"I will not."

Throwing off the hand Harry laid on him, Jack ran down the steps of the verandah.

He was closely followed by his friend.

Garner and he soon came within fifty yards of each other.

"Go back to your den," shouted Garner, "or I'll drop you."

"Will you?" replied Jack, presenting his pistol. "If you don't return, I'll put an ounce of lead into your vile black heart."

In an instant Garner quailed.

He was a loud blatant bully, but a rank coward at heart.

"Do you hear me?" continued Jack. "You go back, or I'll be the death of you."

Seeing that Garner hesitated, Jack fired at him. Not being an experienced shot, he missed his aim, but Garner took to his heels and ran into the Dutchman's house.

"Ha, ha!" laughed Jack. "That shows the fellow is afraid of me. Now we wil' interview the people in the boat. No dou' we shall meet some old acquaintances."

"You are right," replied Harry. If my eyes do not deceive me, Peeping om and Knowall Dick are sitting in the tern sheets."

They were standing on the sand, little way from the landing-stage, which the "Cassandra's" boat was quickly approaling.

A few niggers were grouped r nd them,

"THE NEGROES THREW THEMSELVES FURIOUSLY ON THE BOYS."

attracted by curiosity. Several large land-crabs crawled lazily about among the dry seaweed and the pretty shells with which the land was everywhere strewed.

It soon became apparent that the spies were in the boat.

If his father had been able to assist him, Jack would have tried to prevent them and anyone else belonging to the "Cassandra" from landing.

This, however, would be an impossible task for Jack and Harry to perform alone and unaided.

Should they succeed in repulsing the spies, they would go back to the ship for assistance. The yacht was fully manned, and the Squire would send an overwhelming force against them.

While they were waiting, the colossal negro, Congo, came up to their side.

"Plenty white men come to Three Points!" he exclaimed. "They friends ob yours, sah?"

"No; I am sorry to say they are enemies," answered Jack.

"Massa Blunt friend. Why not ask him to call out 'um Gold Coast Rangers, sah?"

"What are they?"

"Twenty-five niggers lib here, all able to carry a shoot-gun musket. Massa Blunt arm them to keep off oder tribes and slave-catchers."

"Indeed! That is a good idea."

"When any danger come," continued Congo, "Massa Blunt blow 'um horn, sah, and the Rangers all turn out. Me general."

"You?"

"Yes, sah, after Massa Blunt, ob course. Him admirable ob de Gold Coast Rangers. Me only de general," said Congo, drawing himself up proudly.

"Can you fight?"

"We fight like debbels. You see."

"I must speak to friend Blunt about that. It is too late to stop this boat coming any nearer," replied Jack.

He was very glad to hear that Blunt had provided some means of defence for his little settlement in case of need.

Still he had not much faith in the courage of the negroes.

They fought tolerably well, though, he had heard, when led by a white man, and liberally dosed with rum.

Anyhow, they would be better than nothing in an emergency, should one arise, either with Bonna's slave-hunters, or Mr. Rawlings, Charlie, and the crew of the "Cassandra."

When the men ran the boat alongside the landing, they shipped their oars, but did not move. Only Peeping Tom and Knowall Dick got out.

They wore the same uniform they had on in Suffolk when they first announced their intention of going to sea, but their appearance was more martial, not to say piratical.

In their belts were stuck a brace of pistols, and by their sides hung a midshipman's dirk, or small sword.

Sharp as needles, they did not fail to catch sight of Jack and Harry. Nothing daunted, smiling impudently, they walked up to them.

"You here?" cried Peeping Tom, simulating surprise. "Who would have thought it!"

"Quite unexpected," said Knowall Dick.

"Ah! yes," drawled Tom. "How do you like the town?"

"I should like it all the better if you had stopped away," replied Jack. "What do you want here?"

"Got a letter of introduction to a Dutch party, by name Vandervelde."

"You are a pair of rascals," exclaimed Jack, "and you have come here with a vile purpose."

"No, indeed, nothing of the sort," replied Tom.

"Wouldn't dream of injuring a hair of anybody's head," remarked Knowall Dick. "Intentions strictly honourable to all, 'pon honour—quite pure, I assure you."

While they were talking, Harry had carefully picked up a good-sized land crab, holding it by the back, so that it could not bite him.

Getting behind Tom, he held up the crab, and let it tightly fix its largest claw to one of his ears.

"Oh, lor! what has got hold of me? Take it off! Is it a snake? Something is biting my ear like mad," he yelled.

Dancing wildly up and down, he put up his hand, which enabled the crab to grasp his finger with the disengaged claw.

The spectacle amused the negroes immensely.

"Yah, yah, yah!" they laughed. "White man got his dinner now, hanging on his ear."

Knowall Dick went to his friend's rescue, but it was with some difficulty he managed to liberate him from his troublesome assailant.

"Confound it!" said Peeping Tom, when it fell to the ground and scuttled away, "how did the beastly thing get there?"

"They climb up your back in these parts," replied Harry.

"Well, are you going to tell me where Mynheer Vandervelde hangs out?" asked Tom.

Before anyone could make any answer, Old Calabar stepped up.

"I'll guide you," he exclaimed, "if you gib me a dollar."

"Done with you," said Peeping Tom.

"Clear out ob de way, you niggers," cried Old Calabar, shouldering the crowd right and left. "Follow me, sah! Me good guide!"

The spies walked after him, without saying anything to Jack or Harry, whom they suspected of playing them the trick with the crab. They saw that their protestations of friendship were not believed in, and were careless about keeping on the mask any longer.

Watching them, Jack saw them enter the Dutchman's house, the door of which was opened by Garner, who shook hands with them.

Old Calabar also went in, and did not come out again for some time.

"Did you notice that the spies greeted Garner?" said Jack. "Does not that show that he is a paid advance agent?"

"I never doubted it," answered Harry.

"Calabar, too, seems to be on friendly terms with the enemy."

This observation was overheard by Congo.

"Him bad, treacherous nigger, sah," he hastened to exclaim. "No good me know of him. He pretend 'fraid ob Bonna. No such t'ing. He um friend. Don't b'leeve anyt'ing him got to say; he awful liar, sah."

"I never trust any man until I know him," answered Jack; "and with regard to him I don't like the look of his face."

"That bad ole man, sah, got de debble in him."

Jack nodded, and taking Harry's arm, walked back to the verandah, where they resumed their seats, it being the only cool shaded place they could find in which to escape from the burning sun.

It was fully an hour before Peeping Tom and Knowall Dick emerged with Calabar from the Dutchman's house.

They got into the boat, and were rowed back to the "Cassandra," while Old Calabar walked towards the palm trees, and disappeared in the bush.

"There is something up," observed Jack.

"Calabar has made a short stay," said Harry.

"The black rascal is in league with Garner and the rest. He has gone into the bush for some dark purpose. Squire Rawlings won't be long in opening the ball. What a position ours is, with father laid on his back."

They looked gloomily at one another, as well they might.

Just then Marian tripped lightly on to the verandah, wearing a smile on her lips.

"Father's sleeping nicely," she exclaimed, "and does not seem to have so much fever. I have squeezed some berries for him, and the drink cools him. What is that ship in the harbour?"

"Only a trader," replied Jack.

He did not think it advisable to let her know the real character of the vessel.

If she knew Charlie Rawlings was close to her she would be terribly alarmed.

"Will they not take us?" she queried.

"Father can't be moved. It might kill him."

"True, I had forgotten that; but, oh! I shall be so glad to get away from this horrid place. My mind is full of dismal forebodings."

"Cheer up! All will be well," said Jack.

He was trying to impart a feeling of hopefulness, which he was far from experiencing.

Marian stayed for half-an-hour, when she went upstairs again to the sick room.

Scarcely had she gone than Bill Blunt made his appearance.

Jack pointed out the ship to him, and related what had happened.

"Thunderation!" exclaimed Blunt; "that's quick work. It is a planned thing. I have been in the back getting some 'sudden death' ready for your dinner—that's fowls killed one minute and cooked the next. You can't keep anything in this climate. I didn't see the ship. Old Calabar bolted, too! That's queer. When he brings in a tusk, he generally drinks it out. He's as great on suction as the rest of 'em."

"Congo was telling me about your Rangers," said Jack.

"My Gold Coast Rangers? They're good as far as they go. If I blow my horn they'll turn out night or day. I wish there were more of the black-skinned rascals."

"What are they armed with?"

"Muzzle-loaders. Shove in the powder, ram down the wad, chuck in bits of iron, lead, stones, anything—old style. I'll have a couple to do sentry duty to-night. Rely upon me to protect you as far as I can."

"What do you dread?" inquired Jack.

"A raid on the place by Bonna," answered Bill Blunt, "the object being to carry off you and your friend to sell into slavery, or kill in the bush. If the Squire had you slain here, it would come out sooner or later, and be a subject for consular inquiry, d'ye see?"

"I know the Squire would not hesitate to murder us in secret," replied Jack. "Will you help us?"

"All I can. There's my hand on it, as an Englishman," exclaimed Blunt.

CHAPTER III.

THREE days elapsed after the arrival of the "Cassandra" at Three Points, and those on board held no communication with the shore.

Neither did Garner quit the house of the Dutchman, where he had taken refuge.

It was so calm that scarcely a ripple disturbed the bosom of the sea.

The "Cassandra" lay like "a painted ship upon a painted ocean."

Just before the sun set, in a flood of golden splendour, Garner appeared at a window in Mynheer Vandervelde's house.

He waved a red flag in the air.

The signal was answered by the firing of a gun by somebody on board the yacht.

At midnight, when all lights ashore were put out, a boat was lowered.

It was propelled rapidly to the landing-stage.

In it were Charlie, Peeping Tom, and Knowall Dick. They landed, and the boat remained alongside.

Charlie seemed in excellent health and spirits. As he walked with his companions towards the dwelling of Mynheer Vandervelde, he laughed and chatted gaily.

They were evidently expected at the Dutchman's, for Tom had no sooner rapped on the door with his knuckles, than it was opened by Garner.

"Here you are!" he exclaimed. "Nothing like being punctual. Mynheer is in the back room waiting for you with Calabar, who has just come in from the bush."

"Is everything all right?" asked Charlie.

"Right as rain, if you have brought the stuff with you."

Charlie significantly touched a canvas bag he carried under his arm.

A jingling sound resulted. It was full of sovereigns.

"Then all will be well. Come," said Garner.

He conducted them to the rear of the house, where, in a room looking out on a garden, they found the Dutchman, who was a fat, good-tempered, bluff old fellow of sixty or thereabouts, seated before an open window.

By his side, paying attention to some schnaps on a table, was Old Calabar.

There was no necessity for a lamp, as the beautifully serene starlit sky afforded plenty of light.

It was of a dim subdued character, just the kind suitable for conspirators.

"How you was?" exclaimed the Dutchman to Charlie, as Garner led him forward. "I drink your goot 'elth several dimes."

"Thank you very much."

"Die schnaps bottle was on the table. Ach! it is for all."

"Presently," replied Charlie. "Business first. Take this as an earnest of my good will. It contains one hundred English pounds."

He handed him the bag, which Mynheer dropped into one of his capacious pockets.

"Enough. That will do!" he exclaimed. "I pay Calabar meinself."

"There is more where that came from."

"It is goot enough, I say," answered the Dutchman. "Sit down, all of you. Now we can dalk. Calabar, von old black rascal, shall begin. Ach! he is an old fox, with a woolly head—ha, ha!"

Calabar emptied his glass and looked at Charlie.

"I have seen Bonna!" he exclaimed. "He has had a battle with King Makolo, and beaten him. Now he is only three miles inland from Three Points, with one hundred fighting men."

"When will he attack?" asked Charlie.

"This night, in about two hours."

"Very well," said Charlie. "These friends of mine, Tom and Dick, will point out Harry to him. He is not to be killed, but carried off as a slave."

"They shall come with me," remarked Calabar. "I will see to it. What about the other white boy, Jack?"

"Leave him here to take his chance. I don't care about him."

The spies and Calabar nodded their heads.

Their task was to see that Bonna, the king of the slave-dealers, secured Harry and ran off with him into the interior.

That was one part of the plot.

"Now for your task, Garner," continued Charlie.

He had carefully mapped out his plan of campaign.

"What am I to do?" enquired Garner.

"You will go to Blunt's, after the attack has succeeded, and seize the girl Marian, take her along the shore, westward, for about ten miles, and wait. Presently I shall go on board our ship, and we shall sail away to meet you, when we will take you and Marian on with us."

"I am to attend to the girl only."

"That is all you are required to do. Execute your work well, and your reward is assured."

"There will be no slip or hitch, I promise you," replied Garner, with a grim smile.

"I have nothing more to say, except that I will send the boat back to take off Tom and Dick, when they can assure me that they have seen with their own eyes Bonna carry off Harry into the bush, on his way to death or life-long servitude," said Charlie.

It was a carefully concocted plan.

If news of the affair reached the authorities at Cape Coast Castle, no one would suspect those on board the yacht of having any complicity in the slave-trader's raid.

Having drunk another glass of the fiery Schiedam, in which the Dutchman delighted, Old Calabar shut his eyes.

He showed unmistakable signs of being sleepy.

"Wake you oop," cried Vandervelde. "What shall the matter be with you? Too moch schnaps taken hein!"

"'Pears to me I was going off," replied Calabar. "I haven't had much sleep las' three days and nights. Been runner after Bonna."

"I thought you niggers could do without sleep a week at a dime."

"Me gettin' old. Not so young as was once. It all on account ob old age."

"Wake oop and walk in the garden. It was schnaps taken, I say."

Taking the hint, Calabar stepped out of the window which opened on to the ground and disappeared.

He pretended to go at a sharp pace, but doubling behind some trees, returned in his tracks, and concealed himself near the window.

Being an artful old fellow, he wanted to hear what was said in his absence.

"When the attack begins," exclaimed Charlie to Vandervelde, "what shall you do?"

"Nodings," replied the Dutchman, "nodings at all. Bonna knows me. I have had dealings with him, and he will not touch me."

"Won't Blunt think it odd if you do not come out and fight?"

"He is aware that I only fight to protect meinself. What for I want to get killed! Ach! I have worked in this blace for years to send money home to Amsterdam. Next year I go pack to spend my money, and enjoy die rest of my life."

"A bullet in your body would spoil all that," remarked Charlie.

"What you dink, eh? That was drue.

Well, I trink your 'elth, and hope your plans coom off all right. Perhaps we never meet again. Ach! it is a funny worlt."

"Anyhow, if an inquiry should be set afoot about this night's work, I feel sure I can rely on your silence," said Charlie.

"For sure!" replied the Dutchman, slapping his pocket. "I have a oondred goot reasons for silence, here."

"Can we trust Calabar as well as we can you?"

"I cannot say. The niggers on this goast are all liars and thieves. Dey would sell their soul, if dey had got one, for rum. As Blunt says, dey was all suction."

"If Calabar was to go to Cape Coast Castle and pitch a tale to the consul, I might get into a scrape."

"Ya, it would make droubles."

"Do you think he would do such a thing?"

"Dere is nodings a tarn woolly-headed African nigger will not do, except say his prayers."

Charlie turned to Peeping Tom, with a cold-blooded look in his eyes.

"When Calabar has given Harry to Bonna," he said, "put your pistol to his ear and blow out his brains."

"Wouldn't that come under the head of murder?" asked Tom.

"It's no sin to kill a nigger in a free fight."

"Oh,! if that is the case, I'll soon settle his hash."

"Do so. He is best out of the way. Eh, mynheer, what is your opinion?"

The Dutchman removed a cigar he was smoking.

"Ya," he replied, "it was petter like that. You are a clear-headed young mans; but, mein Gott, you dispose of your enemies in a quick way. I should not like to offend you."

"Fear not," laughed Charlie, "I regard you as a friend."

Old Calabar had overheard every word of this conversation, which was of such importance to himself.

Grinding his teeth together, he shook his head and rolled his eyes.

"Me ti'nk me know a game worf more than dat," he muttered. "White man make use of me, then shoot—no good that."

Waiting a little while, he presented himself at the window and walked in.

Charlie was taking leave of his friends to return to the yacht, for he did not see the use of paying people to do his work and take a hand in it himself.

He particularly impressed upon Garner the necessity of being careful with Marian, as a stray bullet might strike her.

Then he departed with a diabolical smile on his thin lips, feeling sure that his plans were so well laid, that nothing could go wrong.

The spies accompanied him to the beach, and saw him on board the boat.

"Be sure," said Peeping Tom, " we will see to your instructions."

"Oh, yes , we always do our duty," said Knowall Dick.

" Stick to me, boys."

"We will. You are something like a friend," continued Tom.

" A regular brick, I call him," added Dick.

" You will find me so," cried Charlie, with a self-satisfied smile. " Once let me get Marian in my power again, I will persuade her to marry me, and—"

"So handsome!" interrupted Peeping Tom. "If I were a girl, I couldn't resist you."

"Quite a gentleman, too!" remarked Knowall Dick. "Everything combined. Good looks, manners, and money,"

" You flatter me," replied Charlie. "But as far as the money goes, I shall have plenty of it when I have disposed of that impostor Harry. He, as you two fellows know, is trying to usurp what really belongs to me."

" May you soon come into your own."

" Thank you. I have an indulgent father ; you shall not want for anything. I will take you round the world in the yacht."

" Glorious! " said Tom, rubbing his hands.

"Magnificent!" cried Dick.

" Ah ! wait a week or two until we round the Cape of Good Hope and get into civilization again, I'll show you how to enjoy yourselves."

Saying this, Charlie stepped into the boat.

" Give way, my lads," he said.

Off shot the boat, bounding like a cork over the surf.

" In two hours," he added, " she will be sent back for you."

The spies retraced their footsteps to the Dutchman's.

" Splendid fellow, isn't he ? " said Peeping Tom, alluding to Charlie.

" Princely! " replied Knowall Dick. " It was the chance of a lifetime when we came out with him."

" It will make men of us ; and how we do and will enjoy ourselves."

" The best part of it has to come, my dear boy."

When they reached the house, Garner was waiting on the threshold.

He had an anxious look on his face.

" Thank goodness, you are here ! " he exclaimed. " The fun is just going to begin."

" How ? Where ? " queried Peeping Tom.

" Old Calabar has received Bonna's signal, and replied to it."

" Bonna here ? "

" Yes. The woods are full of his men. You may expect the fighting to begin every moment. Keep close."

They entered the house and repaired to the back room. Their business was to keep quiet until Calabar called upon them to act.

The time had not yet arrived.

The night had hitherto been calm with starlight, but storms soon arise in the tropics, and in an inconceivably short space of time the sky became overcast.

Ominous flashes of lightning darted athwart the dark expanse.

Loud rumblings of distant thunder out seaward were heard.

"We are going to have a storm," remarked Vandervelde. " Do you hear the sea hiss ? I can. When it makes dot noise, look oud ! '

" Look out for what ? " asked Garner.

" Hammer and nails—poker and dongs. Wait a bid. You see what shall come."

Peeping Tom and Knowall Dick did not care much about the storm. They were more interested in the night attack.

Each one in his heart wished it was over.

Half-an-hour elapsed, and it was a period of suspense.

Suddenly there was a report of a musket.

Scarcely had its reverberation died away, than it was followed by half-a-dozen more.

Then the loud blowing of a horn was heard.

Bill Blunt, Jack, and Harry had not been caught napping.

" Ha! " cried Mynheer Vandervelde, " the ball was begun. Ach ! we shall have some blood spilled to-nide."

" Blunt has called out his Rangers," said Garner.

" What good the poor niggers 'gainst Bonna ? " asked Calabar.

" Not much account, that one sure ding," replied the Dutchman. " Bonna's men knock the stuffing oud of them in no time."

A few minutes elapsed, and then the firing became hot and heavy.

The air was filled with hoarse cries, groans and shrieks, the latter coming from the wounded in the affray.

It was clear that Bill Blunt was making a stout defence with his Gold Coast Rangers, and that Jack and Harry were backing him to the best of their ability.

After a while the firing slackened.

Only a few desultory shots were heard.

" Now is the time," said Old Calabar. " Come with me."

Garner, Peeping Tom, and Knowall Dick followed him out of the house.

They were armed to the teeth.

When they were gone, Mynheer Vandervelde shut and bolted his door.

"They vas off!" he muttered. "Goot riddance! Now I once more schnaps taken, and go to mein shleep, for I was tired like one leedle tog, and der firing not wake me."

Calabar wended his way carefully.

The negroes, whom Blunt called his Rangers, had been beaten off by the slave-traders, leaving half their number on the ground.

Some were taken prisoners, the rest had taken refuge in the bush, leaving their homes to the mercy of the invaders.

Bonna, a tall, thin, sinewy man, was waiting for the arrival of Calabar before he stormed the house of Bill Blunt.

This had been previously arranged between them.

How it had fared with the brave defenders of the "Trader's Rest," nobody knew at present.

Finding that the negroes were dispersed, and that the village was practically at his mercy, Bonna retreated behind some palms, and uttered a sound resembling the cry of a jackal.

The next minute, guided by the sound, Calabar and his friends stood beside him.

"Ha!" cried Bonna, "I have kept my word. Where is the white boy I am to take for a slave?"

"I have come to show you," replied Calabar. "Be careful of him, for he is worth his weight in gold."

They were conversing in the Ashantee tongue, which was not understood by Garner or the spies.

"He shall be the apple of my eye. The Great Spirit hears me," said Bonna.

"So doing, may you always prosper."

"I like a white slave. It is easy to sell them to the kings and queens up the country," remarked Bonna.

"True!" answered Old Calabar. "I have remarked that a white slave, if he is young and good-looking, takes the fancy of the women. Would you like some more?"

"Ha, ha! Can a man have too much of a good thing?"

"Yes; I have drunk too much rum, also have I eaten more honey than was good."

"Well, I will have some more young whites. Where are they?"

"There—close to you," said Calabar, indicating the spies by an inclination of the head.

"Those two!" cried Bonna, in surprise. "I thought they were your friends."

"Bah! I am my own friend. I will give these two. You shall compensate me when we halt in the bush."

"Good! You are a man I should like to have for a neighbour. I will give the order to storm the house."

Bonna was about to address a few words to his followers, who were impatiently waiting for orders to advance.

They knew that Blunt kept a goodly store of spirituous liquors, and they were all panting to get a share of what they called "white man's makee laugh, ha, ha!"

Suddenly the door of the "Trader's Rest" opened, and a man, carrying a lantern in one hand and a white flag in the other, appeared.

"Don't fire!" he exclaimed. "I am the African's friend. I come with words of peace to Bonna."

It was Bill Blunt, who had become alarmed for the safety of himself and his premises, after the dispersion of his Rangers.

As well as he could, he had fulfilled his promise to Jack Spencer and Harry Rawlings, but he was not prepared to be shot, and have his house burnt over his head.

That was taxing him too far.

He could not be expected to give up everything for perfect strangers.

Bonna gladly stepped forward to meet Blunt, to whom he had no wish to do any harm.

In his visits to the coast, he had always been on friendly terms with him, and if he could get what he wanted without fighting, he did not want to sacrifice the lives of his men.

Already he had lost many in his fight with King Makolo, and this night more than a score had fallen beneath the deadly fire that Jack and Harry had poured upon them from the upper windows of the "Trader's Rest."

A wounded man was counted as one killed, for Bonna never paid any attention to a man after he fell.

He had no knowledge of medicine or surgery, neither had he any time to spare, or any conveyance for sick or wounded.

"We wish you well," said Bonna. "These are our terms. Let some of my men go into your house. You have a white boy there I want for slavery. Then we stop and drink rum together, shake hand all round, and go away when the morning shall break."

"Do what you like, but don't burn or ruin anything," replied Blunt.

Bonna called six of his men, and told them to follow Old Calabar and the spies.

As for Garner, he did not ask for any help.

He knew that when Calabar had done his work he would have no difficulty in dealing with Marian.

So he waited behind until the firing, if any took place, should be over.

Calabar found the lower part of the house deserted, but he was guided upstairs by a light to a room, in which were Jack and Harry.

In an inner room, Mr. Spencer was lying on his sick bed, watched over by Marian.

What the end of this terrible thing would be, she was afraid to think.

"Follow me," Calabar said to the Ashantees who were close at his heels.

They rushed up the stairs, and saw Jack standing by the side of Harry, each with his rifle in hand.

"Charge! seize them! No firing—no knives! Break their heads, if you like," cried Calabar.

The spies discreetly threw themselves on the floor when they saw the rifles.

It was well for them that they did so.

In a moment two shots rang out, and two of the foremost Ashantees fell.

The four others ran at the defenders of the room.

Two shots were now fired from pistols, and a third negro sank to the floor.

Rushing to close quarters, the remaining three, headed by Calabar, who was not deficient in courage when his blood was up, threw themselves furiously on the boys.

Jack ran his knife into one man, who, as he was stabbed, dealt him a fearful blow on the head with the butt-end of his gun.

Groaning horribly, Jack sank to the floor in a pool of blood.

The two remaining negroes quickly succeeded in disarming Harry, whom they held for further orders.

When the firing and shouting began in the passage and the outside room, Marian fell into a dead faint.

Mr. Spencer, though terribly anxious and alarmed, could render no assistance either to her or to the boys.

He was unable to move in his bed without help, and in this crisis he was as helpless as an infant in arms.

Seeing that all danger was over, the spies got up from their rather inglorious position and advanced to the room.

"That's the one!" cried Peeping Tom.

"Bind him tight and see that he has no arms about him, for he is a desperate kind of a chap," said Knowall Dick.

Calabar had provided some rope for this purpose.

While the process of pinioning was going on, Harry looked at the spies with ineffable scorn.

"I did not think you had sunk so low as to lend yourselves to a trick of this sort," he said.

"We always do our duty," answered Peeping Tom.

"Regardless of consequences," said Knowall Dick.

"We were schoolfellows together," continued Harry. "If you could not do me a good turn, you need not have done me a bad one."

When Calabar had bound Harry's arms behind him, he ordered one of the remaining negroes to take him to Bonna.

Suddenly Peeping Tom drew a revolver from his pocket, and aimed it at Old Calabar.

The venerable Ashantee, however, was fully prepared for this manoeuvre.

Quick as lightning he knocked the pistol up, the bullet going through the roof.

Snatching the pistol from him he turned sharply upon Knowall Dick.

The movement enabled him to be just in time to floor him, with a blow on the side of the head, before he could plunge a knife into his back, which he was about to do.

Seeing him sink on his knees, he again turned his attention to Peeping Tom, who was rushing at him with his dirk.

He could not avoid receiving a stab in the arm.

This favour was rapidly returned by a blow from Calabar's fist, which sent Tom sprawling on his back.

Kneeling down before he could recover himself, Calabar bound him as he had done Harry, and handed him over to the care of the remaining Ashantees.

To treat Knowall Dick in a similar manner was the work of but a few moments.

Almost before they could realize what had happened to them, the spies were placed side by side, Calabar holding the end of the rope with which he had bound them, so as to prevent the possibility of escape.

"Me not dead yet," he observed. "White boys plot well, but this ole post got ears. Very kind ob you to want to kill the ole man, only he not tired ob 'um job yet—yah, yah!"

The old fellow laughed to himself and chuckled as if enjoying the joke intensely.

Not so Peeping Tom and Knowall Dick.

Surely Calabar did not mean to make prisoners of them for any length of time?

"What is the meaning of this outrage?" demanded Tom, angrily. "I shall complain to Mynheer Vandervelde."

"And to Bonna, too," chimed in Dick.

"What for you shoot and stab me?" asked Calabar.

"Oh!" replied Peeping Tom, "that was only a bit of a joke."

"Just a little lark," added Knowall Dick. "Undo my arms, there's a good fellow. It is possible to carry a joke too far."

"I'M GOING TO BE MASTER HERE!" CRIED GARNER."

No 2.

"Yes; I like a lark as well as anyone," continued Peeping Tom; "but it must not go too far. I'll give you that pistol of mine and my dirk."

"He can have my knife, if he will only make haste and let us go. The boat will be waiting for us," said Dick, impatiently.

Old Calabar grinned till he opened his mouth so wide that he showed the blackened stumps that had once done duty as teeth.

"Joke not ober yet," he remarked. "Come 'long of the ole man."

"Where to?" enquired Peeping Tom.

"Come see Bonna. Tell him all 'bout it. How 'um laff."

Calabar gave the rope a jerk, and led the way downstairs.

Their minds were ill at ease, but they did not, even then, dream of the dread reality of the calamity that had befallen them.

It was one they had brought upon themselves by their treachery.

Harry had gone on before. Jack was lying senseless on the floor, looking as if he were dead and totally disregarded by everybody.

Going down the stairs, they were passed by Garner, who was going up in search of the hapless Marian.

He had a pistol in each hand, so as to be prepared for any emergency.

It was so dark that he could not see that the spies were bound, and though they thought they recognised him, he was gone before they could call out.

He alone could have rendered them any service.

Garner would, in due course, meet Charlie, and could have told him of the fate to which they had fallen victims.

They were halted in front of Bonna, who had continued in the same spot, talking to Blunt in an amicable manner.

Harry Rawlings had arrived a few minutes before them.

"These are the three I promised to bring you," said Calabar.

"Tie them to trees," replied Bonna; "we shall not march till we see the full face of the sun."

"Who is to watch them?"

"You. I will send you a flask of rum. Watch them well; my arm is long, and I never fail to punish the guilty."

"I will serve you," said Calabar, "but I journey not with you to the interior."

"Why will you leave us?"

"I have business of my own. Ivory is coming to the coast; I want to intercept it. When you have held your palaver and done your drink, I shall deliver your slaves into your hands, and you will see me no more."

"Good. It shall be as you say."

This dialogue was spoken in Ashantee. Blunt gathered the meaning, as he was more or less used to hearing it talked, but he did not offer to interfere.

Calabar produced what was left of the rope he carried, and placing the spies and Harry with their backs against a tree, ran the rope round them, so that they could not move an inch.

Harry made no remark, for he saw that Bill Blunt had been obliged to abandon him to his fate.

He could not reproach him, because he had done the best he could under the circumstances, and it was not likely the man would utterly ruin himself for people he had known only a few days.

It was possible that he might have been killed, as well as robbed and burnt out, if he had not made terms with the slave-trader.

The spies, on the other hand, were terribly upset when they saw that no attempt was being made to liberate them.

"Mister Blunt, I think that is your name," cried Peeping Tom, "do you see that my friend and I are being treated as slaves?"

"That's none of my business," replied Bill Blunt.

"Surely there must be some mistake! Ask Bonna; you have come on terms with him."

"I have heard all about you," continued Blunt. "Didn't you come ashore to make a slave of the other poor lad? And you've succeeded."

"But we belong to the yacht."

Bonna smiled as he took in the situation.

"B'long to me now," he exclaimed.

The hearts of the spies sank.

Old Calabar sat down on the ground and lighted his pipe in a phlegmatic manner.

Bonna and his warriors followed Blunt to the house.

As they approached, a man was seen emerging from the door, carrying what looked like a bundle in his arms.

It was Garner, who had found Marian insensible by the side of her father's bed.

No one attempted to intercept him, and he rapidly disappeared in the darkness with his fair prize.

The negroes, who were quite half-a-hundred in number, squatted outside the house, with Bonna in their midst.

Blunt was not slow in providing them with tin pannikins of liquor, which they very quickly emptied.

As they became exhilarated, they sang a song of victory.

At length, the storm, which had been threatening so long, burst with tremendous violence.

As the Africans were not overburdened

with clothes, and the night was very hot and sultry, they hailed the rain with satisfaction.

It was like a refreshing bath to them.

Blunt plied them with rum until daybreak, when Bonna led his men into the bush, laughing, singing, and shouting.

The three boys were placed in the middle of the band, and, wet and weary, were compelled to tramp through the jungle growth, going they knew not whither.

Calabar went to Vandervelde's house; the negroes of Three Points, who had hidden themselves, returned to their homes to weep over and bury the bodies of their friends, while Blunt went upstairs to see what had happened.

After passing the bodies of the Ashantees who had been killed when led on by Calabar, he came to Jack's room.

The latter was recovering from the knockdown blow he had received, but his ideas of things in general were not very clear.

He recognised Blunt, however, in an instant, and staggered to his feet, his face stained with blood. His strength was not sufficient to allow him to stand up. If Blunt had not caught him in his arms, and conveyed him to a chair, he would have fallen again.

"What has happened?" he asked, faintly.

In a few words, Blunt told him all that had come within his ken, adding that he was very sorry to have had to make peace with Bonna, but when his Rangers fled, he could not help it.

"Poor Harry! Heaven help him!" exclaimed Jack. "Go into the next room. My father—my sister—how are they?"

"I hear no sound," replied Blunt.

"Go—see, for pity's sake."

Blunt opened the door, and advanced to the bed.

Mr. Spencer was so quiet that he fancied him asleep, though that would have been strange, as the lightning was flashing, and the thunder roaring loudly.

He placed his hand on his heart.

There was no movement.

Mr. Spencer was dead, killed by the shock of the night attack, and the abduction of his daughter.

"Your father is dead, and your sister gone!" cried Blunt.

Jack uttered a startled cry, and became insensible again.

With great solicitude, Bill Blunt undressed and put him to bed, but before long he was in a high state of fever, his brain wandering, unconscious of all around him.

CHAPTER IV.

IN THE POWER OF A VILLAIN—THE WRECK—MUTINY IN THE CAMP.

WHEN Marian recovered from the swoon into which she had fallen, she found herself reclining on a bank of earth beneath some trees.

Standing over her was Garner.

She easily recognised the man, and began to dread the worst.

The storm which had been raging had partially decreased in violence on land, but it was terrible at sea.

Thunder crashed, lightning flashed, and the waves beat against the shore in huge masses of white creamy surf.

"The yacht will have a rough time of it. I'm glad I'm not aboard of her," muttered Garner.

He fell into a reverie while watching the sublimity of the storm, from which he was roused by Marian.

She was anxious to know her fate.

"You are Squire Rawlings' man, if I mistake not?" she said.

"Yes, I am employed by him," he replied.

"What has happened?"

"The slave-dealers have captured your lover, and carried him into the interior. You will never see him again. Your brother got knocked on the head, but he is not likely to die."

"Horrible! And what are you going to do with me?" she inquired, trembling violently.

"Deliver you to the young Squire, that is my task. We shall meet the yacht about ten miles lower down. It is a long walk for you, but I have no means of conveyance."

Marian's tears fell fast.

Separated from her brother and Harry, she became very miserable, feeling that she did not care what became of her.

"Come, get up," exclaimed Garner. "It is best to march in the cool nighttime. You will be able to sleep on the yacht to-morrow."

With a weary sigh, Marian rose and walked by his side. She knew that it would be worse than useless to resist.

A thin rain continued to fall, the thunder gradually died away, but the lightning flashed incessantly in the distance.

Out at sea the waves were running mountains high.

Nothing was to be seen of the yacht "Cassandra," though her lights should have been visible.

Perhaps the captain had deemed it prudent to stand out, for fear of being wrecked in the dangerous shallows.

The journey was a slow one.

Marian soon got footsore and weary; he offered her his arm, which she was glad to accept.

When the ground was stony and difficult, he took her up in his arms and carried her.

It was impossible to gaze at Marian's pretty face without becoming interested in her.

Garner had often thought her very lovely, but knowing that Charlie was her sweetheart, he had refrained from loving her.

Now the feeling came over him, too strongly to be resisted. He suddenly bent over and imprinted a kiss on her lips.

She uttered a slight scream.

"Forgive me," he said, "I could not help it."

"Beware!" she cried. "If you do that again, I will tell Mr. Rawlings when I see him, and he would not think much of shooting you."

"That is a game two can play at," said Garner, bitterly. "If Charles Rawlings or his father presented a pistol at me, I would soon draw my own, and we should see who would go down first."

Marian almost wished that Charlie and Garner would quarrel over her and shoot one another.

"Do you think I am worth running so much risk for?" she asked.

"I would risk anything to get your love," he rejoined.

"You know I could not give it you, because I love another—him who has been carried away into captivity."

"Forget him."

"That is not possible while memory lasts."

"You can never see him again. He'll die up the country of the fever, or be flogged to death."

"I will think the matter over," replied Marian, who wanted to make a friend of this man, if she could.

"Come back with me to Three Points," said Garner, whose passion grew upon him every minute.

"What for?"

"I will play the young Squire false. We will find shelter at the Dutchman's house."

"No, I cannot consent to that," she answered.

Rather sullenly Garner continued the journey.

At length day broke with its usual tropical splendour, though there was no diminution of the force of the waves.

As they rounded some rocks, Garner uttered a loud exclamation of surprise.

The shore was strewed with wreckage, interspersed with which were the bodies of several recently drowned men.

Huddled together were some others who had escaped from a watery grave.

Looking closely at this group, Garner had no difficulty in recognising Squire Rawlings and his son Charlie.

The other men, four in number, were those of the crew of the "Cassandra," who had been saved.

The beautiful yacht was a wreck.

She had been dashed to pieces.

It was a wonder that anyone had escaped.

Caught in that terrible tempest, she had been driven along like a straw by the wind.

Human skill was not of the slightest avail.

The captain had died at his post.

By the furious blast the mate had been swept overboard.

So disconsolate were Squire Rawlings and Charlie at the terrible misfortune which had befallen them that they scarcely looked up at Garner's approach.

It was a calamity that stunned them.

For a time they were incapable of rousing themselves.

They had no means of getting away from this horrible coast.

They were entirely at the mercy of the natives and the wild beasts.

Their cartridges and most of their weapons had been engulfed by the waves.

Garner was as much alarmed as the others, for he had depended upon the yacht to take him back to England.

"What does this mean?" asked Marian, who could not understand it.

"Mr. Rawlings' yacht has been wrecked," replied Garner.

"He is not hurt; I can see him and his son on the shore."

Garner whispered in her ear—

"Rely upon me."

"For what?"

"Safety. I am your friend, and will protect you. This occurrence has altered the state of affairs."

"Thank you," answered Marian.

He pressed her hand, and gave her a significant look.

Charlie advanced to meet them. His clothes dripped water, showing that the wreck had not long taken place.

"Glad to see you again, Miss Spencer," he exclaimed. "I wish I could give you a better reception."

"You have been wrecked ? " she remarked.

"An hour ago. The hurricane did as it liked with us. Father is a good deal bruised, and I am knocked about a bit."

"You must not grumble; your life is saved," said Garner.

"What have you to report ? "

"Harry is Bonna's prisoner. Jack Spencer is disabled, and I have brought the girl as ordered."

"Good. What has become of Harris and Wilkins ? "

"Peeping Tom and Knowall Dick, as they call them ? "

"Yes. They were to have come on board after pointing out Harry to the slavers."

"Did the boat come for them ? " asked Garner.

"It did, and waited an hour, after all the firing was over," replied Charlie.

"Then I should say that Bonna did a smart stroke of business and collared them, too."

At this suggestion, Charlie could not help smiling.

He had no feeling even for his so-called friends.

"What a good thing that would be ! " he exclaimed.

"I don't think they will find much fun in it."

"They'll get used to it in time."

"What shall you do now you have lost your ship ? "

"Make a camp here for a time, I think," rejoined Charlie. "That rock over there makes a good shelter. Get all the chests and boxes you can find and make a kind of house. There are only four men left, but they will help you. Miss Spencer will come with me."

"All right," said Garner ; "I'll soon knock up some kind of a shanty."

He beckoned to the men, who joined him at once, glad to have someone to direct them what to do.

There was one named Dawson, and another Matthews. Garner had known them in Harwich, and they shook hands with him.

The tide was still coming in.

Aided by the wind, boxes, barrels, and chests were continually being washed upon the sand.

These contained all kinds of liquors and provisions, which, being in tins, could not be injured by the water.

Timbers, sails, and pieces of wreckage were cast on the shore.

Picking these up, the crew placed them, one on top of the other, near the rock, making a square room.

Sails were stretched over the top, and some canvas, placed in a corner, made a rough bed.

Some biscuits and tinned meat were found by Garner, with a bottle of dry sherry, which he set out in the room for Marian.

It was a shelter for her, at any rate, and would protect her from the heat of the broiling sun.

"Very good ! " said Charlie, as he led Marian to the spot. "Nothing could be better. It is quite a lady's bower."

He told her to take some food and rest, of both of which she stood greatly in need.

Then in an angle formed by the rock and the boxes, he arranged a seat in a shady place, to which he conducted his father.

The Squire was unusually dull and taciturn.

"This is a great misfortune," he observed.

"We shall soon get over it, father," replied Charlie. "Our lives are saved. Marian is once more in my power ; Harry has disappeared, let us hope for ever."

"Misfortunes never come singly, my boy. We shall have something else, before long."

"Keep up your courage," cried Charlie. 'It takes a lot to frighten me. Sit down here with a tin of biscuits and a bottle of wine. We shall not starve. I will go and look after the men."

Garner was talking earnestly to Dawson, while the three others were fishing the boxes out of the sea, as they drifted up.

"Now then," cried Charlie. "Wake up, my men ; bustle about."

Garner looked angrily at him.

"Who are you talking to ? " he demanded.

"Why, you, of course. If the yacht is wrecked, you are still my men. I employ you, and shall have to pay you some day, so I want my work done ! "

"Do it yourself ! "

"Eh ! What ? This is rank mutiny ! " exclaimed Charlie. "Dawson, stand by me —Matthews, and you two others ! "

Dawson deliberately turned his back on him.

Matthews and his companions went on with their occupation without taking any notice of his appeal.

Seeing that he was deserted by his men, Charlie quickly drew his revolver and endeavoured to shoot Garner.

Owing to having been immersed in the water, it missed fire.

He tried the next chamber.

The result was precisely similar.

With a fierce cry he threw it to the ground.

"You thought you would rid yourself of me, eh ? " sneered Garner.

"What is your design ? " asked Charlie, impatiently. "You may as well tell me first as last."

"I'm going to be master here," replied

Garner. "Dawson and the rest will back me up. You and your father have got to be the servants, or you can quit the camp and live in the bush the best way you can."

"Are you mad? We can never consent. My father would die sooner than give way to such as you."

"And let me add," went on Garner, ignoring his words, "that you are to keep away from that girl. I won't have you speaking to her."

"You rascal!" yelled Charlie. "I will not submit to this!"

"Ha, ha!" laughed Garner; "you cannot help yourself. No, my young cock-of-the-walk, we meet on a level now."

"What do you mean? I am a gentleman, you are a low scoundrel."

"The Wilds of Africa, my lad, isn't England. I'm master here, and if you won't believe it, take that."

Garner lifted his hand as he spoke, and gave Charlie a stinging blow on the side of the face.

Staggering towards the rock, he shouted—

"Father, help! Mutiny! Garner has struck me, and says he is master."

Squire Rawlings quickly came out from his place of shelter. He could see in a moment that he was betrayed by his men.

"If we will not be Garner's servants, we are to go. Will you consent?" continued Charlie. "If you do, your spirit is not like mine."

"Where are we to go? If we seek Three Points we are likely to meet with scant welcome there. Blunt would not entertain us, and the Dutchman would quickly show us the door, now we have no money. I told you our troubles were not over. We must submit to Garner, I suppose."

"I would rather die."

Garner was again talking to Dawson.

Presently he called out—

"I've been talking to the men, and they say they would rather have your room than your company. So clear out at once, before we do either of you any hurt."

"My good fellow!" exclaimed Mr. Rawlings, "we are willing to live peaceably with you, if you will let us stop."

"Can't do it," was the stern reply.

Charlie was beside himself with passion. He drew a knife from his belt and brandished it in the air.

In vain the Squire endeavoured to restrain him. With the utmost fury depicted on his countenance, he ran at the mutineer.

Attacked so unexpectedly, Garner was somewhat taken aback.

He also drew his knife, and met the savage onslaught as best he could.

Although it was a boy fighting with a man, the boy had considerably the better of the frantic encounter.

Garner was soon wounded, and bleeding profusely.

The courage displayed by Charlie seemed to frighten his opponent, who was a coward at heart.

He kept retreating, so as to get near the rock, which he thought would give him some advantage if he could get his back against it.

Unhappily for him, he did not see a large packing-case, which was directly in the backward course he was taking.

Naturally, he fell over it, and fruitlessly struggled to recover his balance.

Uttering a wild cry of triumph, Charlie sprang upon him, and seized him by the throat.

"Help! help!" he gurgled, despairingly.

Dawson and the others held aloof, either alarmed at the impetuosity of Charlie or startled by the suddenness of the whole affair.

There was no assistance for Garner, who was completely at his opponent's mercy.

Raising his knife, Charlie did not hesitate to stab the wretched man.

The blade penetrated his heart, and, with a horrid death-rattle, he expired without a struggle.

Springing up, with his knife streaming with blood, Charlie shouted—

"Now who is master? Come on, Dawson—come on, any of you, or all; I am ready to fight you to the death."

None of the crew appeared at all anxious to accept the challenge.

"We give in, sir!" exclaimed Dawson. "We didn't mean it. He it was as put us up to it."

"If I have any more disobedience or insolence," continued Charlie, "I will treat you all as I have Garner."

The men were completely subdued, and went on with their work of snatching what wreckage they could from the sea.

Soon afterwards they dug a hole in the sand and buried the bodies that were lying about. From an aperture between two boxes, Marian had watched the deadly affray with breathless interest.

When it was over, she covered her face with her hands, and shed bitter tears. True, she had one persecutor the less, but a spirit of lawlessness was around her. Blood was being shed like water. Her father she did not know was dead, but she feared he would die. Jack was in danger, and Harry had gone to be sold into hopeless slavery. No wonder she was dismayed and heart-broken at her forlorn position.

CHAPTER V.

TREATMENT OF THE CAPTIVES—ARRIVAL IN ASHANTEE—SOLD TO THE KING.

BONNA was a man of luxurious ideas. When travelling, he rode in a kind of palanquin or sedan chair, the poles of which were supported by four carriers at each end.

His followers surrounded him in the form of a hollow square when on the plains, and when traversing a forest, they kept as good formation as they could.

Behind the palanquin marched the three boy slaves, tied together by a rope.

Immediately in their rear was a negro of the name of Damara.

He held a whip, with which he urged on the slaves if they lagged or halted.

The first part of the journey lay through a thick wood, which, if they had not followed a beaten path, would have been impassable.

Through the wood the rate of progression was not more than two miles an hour.

Wild beasts roared, and snakes hissed, but no one was attacked.

About midday, a halt was called, near the borders of a small lake, which, however, the negroes did not bathe in.

This was owing to the water serpents.

The slaves were allowed to sit on the ground, a permission they gladly availed themselves of, as they were footsore and weary, and their backs ached with the lashes they had received on the journey.

Damara gave them some biscuits out of a bag which they had taken from the "Trader's Rest," and, what was more precious, a can full of water.

Hot and stagnant as it was, they drank it eagerly.

"Sleep now for six hours," said Damara, as he walked away.

Up to this time Harry had not been able to speak to the spies, although he had one tied on each side of him.

What with falling over roots and picking their way through the forest, their time had been fully occupied.

Looking reproachfully at Peeping Tom, Harry exclaimed—

"You have done a nice thing for me and yourselves, too."

"Oh, dear!" whined Tom, "I wish I had never come to Africa."

"It was all right on board that beautiful ship of Squire Rawlings'," said Knowall Dick, half crying.

"You have met with your just deserts," returned Harry.

"The Squire meant to rid himself of you," remarked Tom. "It was a neat trick to get the Spencers and you to come over here."

"A dastardly plot, I call it," replied Harry.

"You stand between him and the property."

"If it is mine, why should I not have it?"

"That is true enough," answered Tom; "but your chance is a poor one now."

While they were talking, Bonna had come up silently, and was looking at them. Like most of the leading men on the Guinea Coast, he could speak English through coming into contact with white traders and sailors.

"What your names?" he exclaimed.

They started at the sound of his voice, which was deep and guttural.

Each one told his name.

"Harry," he said, "you pretty, handsome boy. Me sell you to King Makolo's daughter, Princess Matabele. She want good-looking white boy slave to hand her drink and fan away flies. You play any music?"

"I can play a whistle, that's about all," replied Harry.

"Play—me listen."

Harry happened to have a small whistle in his pocket.

Producing it, he played the "British Grenadiers," and the "Last Rose of Summer."

Bonna condescended to express his pleasure and satisfaction.

"Very good!" he exclaimed. "Matabele like you. She will give a hundred ounces of gold for such a slave."

"I sha'n't have to work in the fields?"

"Oh, no; live in a palace. Perhaps Matabele fall in love and take you for her husband."

"I should not care about that kind of distinction," replied Harry.

His mind reverted to Marian.

"If so, one day you be king," added Bonna.

"Now, why you others called Peeping Tom and Knowall Dick?"

"I can see everything," answered Tom.

"And I know everything," replied Dick.

"Ha! that very clever. If able to do that, King Makolo give two hundred ounces of gold dust for each. You find out everything for him."

"We can do it. Our education in spying is complete."

"THE SQUIRE AND CHARLIE WERE COMPELLED TO OBEY ORDERS BY DAWSON."

"Ha! Now you, Tom the Peeper, tell me what I got in my hand?"

He had put it down suddenly and closed it.

"Nothing," hazarded Tom, pretending to look narrowly at it.

He was right.

Bonna's broad face expanded with a smile.

"That capital. Now, Dick the Knower, what I going to have for dinner?" he asked.

Knowall Dick had seen Damara skinning a monkey.

"You're going to have roast monkey and baked yam," he answered.

"Ha! that so? Me sell you two dear. King Makolo will be pleased," he cried. "Me glad to get rid of you. Perhaps you know too much—see too far, and tell me when me going to die."

"So I could, if you particularly desire to know," said Dick, boldly.

"No, no; that's enough!" said Bonna, hastily.

He was very superstitious.

Beginning to tremble violently, he walked away to hide his agitation.

When he was gone, the spies smiled at one another.

"I say, weren't we lucky?" said Peeping Tom.

"I frightened the old wretch," replied Knowall Dick.

"All the better. If he is afraid of us, he will be more friendly disposed towards us."

"That is so. The real test will come when we are sold. Who is this Makolo?"

"King of Ashantee," exclaimed Harry. "He is rich and powerful. What with my music, and your supernatural attributes, we ought to have a good time."

"If King Makolo does not find us out to be humbugs," answered Tom.

"What would he do in that case?" asked Dick.

"Cut our heads off, bury us alive, or some other equally cheerful performance."

"That is not a cheery look out."

"Bonna will crack us up to get money, and we shall have to keep up the deception," said Peeping Tom.

"I am sorry you spoke now."

"Well, I'm not. It has given us a chance."

It was very apparent that they had made an impression on Bonna.

When the column again moved forward, Damara spoke civilly to them, and threw away his whip.

During the rest of the journey, they were well fed and not illtreated.

It took them some days to reach the city, which was of considerable extent.

The king's palace consisted of a number of huts, all standing in gardens which were fenced round by a palisaded fence of bamboo.

The slave-dealers halted outside the city.

A messenger was despatched to the palace, blowing a horn and beating a drum.

Hundreds of people turned out to see him.

In a short time the messenger returned with a dozen soldiers, armed with old flint-lock muskets and spears.

Their captain held a brief conversation with Bonna.

Then the latter told Harry, Peeping Tom, and Knowall Dick to accompany him to the palace.

King Makolo had been graciously pleased to say that he would look at the young white slaves at once.

Their hearts began to beat anxiously.

They had a trying ordeal to go through.

They found the king, the principal officers of the Court, his wife, the princess, and the bodyguard grouped together in a garden under an enormous awning.

The royal personages were seated, the others standing. Black slaves fanned the king and his family incessantly.

A murmur of approval ran through the select throng as Bonna and the boys stood before them.

Evidently white slaves were considered fashionable in Ashantee.

The king and queen were growing old and grey.

Her majesty and the princess wore striped cotton loose gowns, broad gold bangles encircled their wrists and ankles, gold hoops were in their ears, and each had a large ring in her nose.

King Makolo had on sailor's pumps and white duck trousers, an English admiral's cocked hat, and a major-general's red coat, trimmed with gold lace.

A huge chain of gold encircled his neck, and a very large diamond was in a ring on his finger.

"O king, great and mighty," exclaimed Bonna, "I have brought you three wonders from the Western regions across the great water."

"It is well that you have thought of us," replied the king. "We fought your men and chased them for entering our territory without permission."

"It shall be peace between us. Such is my prayer."

"Yes; we desire peace. What can these white slaves do?"

"The handsome one plays on a tube of metal and makes sweet sounds. I thought you would buy him for the princess, your daughter."

"Let us hear what he knows," replied Makolo.

Producing his humble instrument, Harry threw all the taste and feeling he could into half-a-dozen tunes.

The king and his suite nodded their heads to the "Campbells are Coming," they couldn't keep their feet still to an Irish jig, and when he played an Highland fling, the Prime Minister was so carried away by his feelings, that he began to dance.

This enraged his majesty.

It was a gross breach of Court etiquette.

He gave the minister a box on the ears and knocked him down.

Everyone then exclaimed—

"O, wise and mighty king, it served him right!"

The minister retreated to the rear. He was overwhelmed with shame and confusion.

"I will buy the white slave," cried the princess. "How much do you want for him, O Bonna?"

The slave-dealer quoted his price.

Now ensued a lively bit of bargaining. The princess tried to get Harry cheaper, but Bonna would not give way.

He knew his trade too well for that.

At length the sale was completed, and the king began to inquire about Peeping Tom and Knowall Dick.

He was much struck by their names and the qualities attributed to them.

"I will try them," he exclaimed. "You must wait till the sun goes down, Bonna. I will give Tom the Peeper and Dick the Knower till that time to find out who stole my gold bowl."

Peeping Tom bowed profoundly, as did Knowall Dick.

"When was it lost, your majesty?" asked Tom.

"Yesterday. It is as large round as my head. Someone took it from my table. If you fail to find it, I will have you buried alive, head downwards."

"Rest assured we will find it, O king," said Tom.

"Has your high and mighty magnificence any other commands to give us?" asked Dick.

"Not at present. Bonna shall be my guest. Tom the Peeper and Dick the Knower are to go about where they like, but not out of the city."

The king rose.

Long shouts of "Long live King Makolo!" arose from every throat.

The audience was over.

Taking Bonna by the arm, the king led him into the palace to drink and talk with him.

Princess Matabele conducted Harry into her quarters.

He was soon an object of interest to her and her dusky maidens.

CHAPTER VI.

BONNY, THE BLACK BOY—THE SEARCH FOR THE GOLDEN BOWL.

WHEN King Makolo went away to enjoy the seclusion of his palace, and the spies were left alone, they looked at one another in a downcast manner.

"Here's a go," said Peeping Tom. "We've done another sweet thing for ourselves by pretending to know and see everything."

"I call it anything but rosy," replied Knowall Dick. "Our young lives will come to a premature end at sunset."

"I fear they will."

"We are too good to live long," continued Knowall Dick. "But, candidly, I don't want to be an angel yet, do you?"

"Not much," replied Tom. "To be buried alive, head downwards, is an awful thing to reflect upon."

"If we find the golden bowl, we are saved."

"True; but how is it to be done?"

This was a poser, and Dick could not answer the question.

The task which had been set them was almost an impossibility.

At the end of the garden, near a house which looked as if it belonged to a distinguished person, was a grove of orange trees.

They were laden with the ripe yellow fruit, scores of which had fallen to the ground.

"Let us seek shelter and suck oranges, and think," continued Tom. "Hang it all! this sun is too fierce for our heads."

"I wonder how the niggers can stand it?" asked Dick.

"It's owing to the wool on the top of their heads, which acts as a mat."

They walked to the trees, and sitting down on the sandy soil in the shade, quenched their thirst with the oranges.

They enjoyed the feast all the more because there was nothing to pay for it.

While they were thus occupied, and looking gloomily at one another, a black boy, about fourteen years old, came up and looked at them.

He was so fat that he looked nearly as broad as he was long.

A pleasant smile played around his coarse features, and he seemed as happy as a butterfly on a fine day.

"Me speak English," he exclaimed; "born at Three Points. Know Massa Blunt, Massa Vandervelde. Slavers steal me. Sell me to king."

"We don't want you here," replied Peeping Tom.

"Got to stop. King Makolo sent me."

"What for?"

"To keep a watch on you. Go where you like in city. Not outside. Me like you. Be your friend."

The spies saw the advantage of having a friend in the distressing circumstances they were placed in.

"All right," said Peeping Tom. "If you stick to us, we will not be ungrateful, and you will find firm friends in us."

"That good enough. My name Bonny," replied the black boy. "When you going to find that bowl?"

"Presently," answered Dick.

"You know where it is?"

"Certainly; but we are in no hurry."

"Everybody says you see all and know all. Berry good gift to have."

"Of course we do," said Peeping Tom. "But the thing is so easy to us that we never put ourselves into a perspiration about it."

"You find the golden bowl?"

"I have told you so."

"When the king heard what you could do, and gave you the order," exclaimed Bonny, "all the people stare."

"It was enough to make them."

"Abomey nearly have a fit," added Bonny.

"Who is Abomey when he is at home?" asked Peeping Tom.

He began to prick up his ears.

It seemed as if he might extract something from the black boy which would be of use to him and his friend.

"Abomey is king's head-man. Great power. Fond of money and gold. Got heaps!" answered Bonny.

"Ah! you mean he is a kind of Prime Minister, manages the affairs of State and all that?"

Bonny nodded his head.

"What did Abomey do when he knew the golded bowl was to be looked for?" asked Knowall Dick, winking at Tom.

"Me watch him," said Bonny. "Old beast often beat me with bamboo stick. Me hate him. King Makolo give him slap when he dance."

"Oh! that is the chap!" cried Tom. "I know him now."

"Well, me see him feel very bad, and go home, so me follow. He go into his house, and give plate of rice, plate of chicken to his idol."

"His idol?"

"Yes; all Ashantee men hab idol. When idol gib 'em what they want, they make present ob food. If not gib, beat with stick."

Peeping Tom burst out laughing, so did Dick.

"That is a funny idea of religion," remarked Tom.

"Never mind; it is the custom of the country. Ask him something more. I've got an idea," said Dick.

"So have I."

"Proceed," said Dick, winking again.

"Where does Abominable live?" enquired Tom.

"Abomey live there," replied Bonny.

He jerked his thumb towards the other side of the orange trees, indicating the house which they could see within a stone's throw.

"Will you show us where his old idol is?"

"Yes; me show you. Me friend Do all for you. Like Englishman. Jolly fellow, Englishman. Hurrah! three cheers! Ro'st beef! Me talk English."

The black boy laughed till his sides shook.

"Now then, young ebony!" exclaimed Peeping Tom, "control your feelings."

"Me can't."

"Perhaps I shall have to make you."

"Plum pudding—ba! ha! Me speak English—yah! yah! Jolly fellow, Englishman. Teach Ashantee to drink rum."

"Who does that?"

"King does—Abomey does. Him drink rum, now, allee samee as Englishman does."

"How do you know?"

"Me see him."

"Come and show us where he is, and if he talks, tell us what he says," exclaimed Peeping Tom.

"Me do that—yes, sir."

"We must not be seen or heard, understand that."

Bonny put his fingers to his lips.

"Quiet as a mouse," he said. "Make no more noise than a snake in the grass—no."

"If you do, I'll punch your head."

"No punch. Me friend. Me like jolly Englishmans. Come on; all right. Hurrah! three cheers! When you find the gold bowl?"

"Plenty of time. That's as easy as shelling peas."

"Peas! What they?"

"I'll put it another way. It's as easy as peeling an orange," replied Tom.

" Nola says you no good."

" Who is Nola ? "

" Him medicine man—what you call priest. Nola go to dig hole to bury you to-night.

" Bless him ! " cried Knowall Dick. " What a kind man he must be ! "

" Why doesn't he like us ? " asked Peeping Tom.

" He say you so much white humbug."

" He'll find that he's mistaken."

" Yes. I want you to be friend of king ; then he give you gold chain, house to live in, and make a fuss ob you."

" That's the ticket, young ebony," said Peeping Tom. " Take us to Abominable's house. We must go quietly."

" Crawl on hands and knees ? "

" Yes."

" What for ? "

" He's got the bowl," said Peeping Tom.

Bonny jumped half a foot from the ground.

" How you know ? " he asked.

" That is our business. Abomey, or whatever you call him, is the thief. What do you say, Dick ? "

" It is either he, or one of his relations," replied Knowall Dick.

" Who told you that ? " enquired Bonny.

Tom put his mouth to his ear, and replied, " The Spirits."

" Things in the air ? " asked Bonny.

" Yes, they tell us everything."

Without more ado, Bonny led the way to Abomey's house.

There was no such thing as a door, so they entered on their hands and knees, without having the trouble to knock.

In the front room they saw Abomey standing before a hideous idol carved out of wood.

It was quite six feet in height.

Two diamonds shone in its eyes, and a collar of gold was round its neck.

On a table by its side was a dish of rice, and another containing a roasted fowl.

Abomey had his back turned towards the intruders on his privacy, and consequently did not see them.

Both Dick and Tom thought that the head-man, as Abomey was called, knew something about the golden bowl, if he did not actually have it in his possession.

A large basket of fruit stood near the door, which had been presented to the minister by some obsequious person who wanted a favour done.

Behind this the spies crouched.

Abomey seemed to be in a bad temper with the idol, for he took away the rice and meat, throwing the plates to the ground with such force as to break them.

Taking up a stick, he beat the idol over the back as if he were chastising a living person.

Peeping Tom thought the idol sounded hollow, and made a mental note of the fact.

At the same time Abomey poured out a volume of what seemed to be abuse.

" Him use bad words," said Bonny. " Swear at idol."

" What for ? " asked Tom.

" For letting you two come here."

" Tell us all he says."

" He swear he break up idol, burn it to ashes, and buy another from Nola, if idol lets you know where the bowl is."

" Very good," smiled Tom.

He felt sure he was on the right track now.

Presently Abomey retired into another room, where he threw himself on a bed of scented grass, and went to sleep.

" Stay here, you," said Peeping Tom.

Knowall Dick and Bonny nodded, and Tom proceeded to the idol on tip-toe, so as not to awaken the head-man.

If possible the idol looked more hideous when one was close to it than when at a distance.

Its fat cheeks, flat nose, and large open mouth were uglier than a gnome's mask in a pantomime.

Out of mischief Tom picked up a bone of the fowl, which had fallen on the floor, and put it in the idol's mouth.

It dropped right down as if it had been swallowed.

The wooden effigy was evidently hollow.

For what purpose had it been so fashioned?

As it was not made of boards, but cut out of a solid block, it must have been done with a particular purpose.

So much labour would not have been bestowed upon it for nothing.

In one of Peeping Tom's pockets was an English penny.

He dropped this into the idol's mouth and listened.

There was a momentary pause, and then a metallic chink was heard.

The penny had struck something that was hard and solid like itself.

Going to the back of the idol, Tom examined it, and was not at all surprised to find that a board fitted in.

This was made to take out.

A little nail was inserted for that purpose.

Pulling at it, he had the satisfaction to find that it yielded easily.

When it was removed, Peeping Tom, to his delight, saw a large golden bowl standing on a shelf inside the idol.

In it were a quantity of rings and precious stones.

Tom at once drew it out.

Abomey was the thief who had stolen the bowl, though, owing to his high position, not a single person about the Court thought so.

He was the last one they would have suspected.

"We are saved!" cried Tom, incautiously.

"Hurrah!" exclaimed Knowall Dick, with similar imprudence.

Abomey awoke instantly.

Springing to his feet with considerable alacrity for a man who was close upon sixty, he rushed into the outer apartment.

Seeing Peeping Tom, who had now joined Knowall Dick and Bonny, he feared that something had happened detrimental to his interest.

One glance at the back of the idol settled that question.

The golden bowl was gone!

Uttering a loud cry of mingled rage and fear, he snatched up a gun which stood in a corner.

Shaking with fury, he pulled the trigger and discharged the contents.

The boys had taken to their heels.

Fortunately the bullet did not strike them, and they vanished behind the orange trees before he could load again.

To discharge a gun in the precincts of the royal palace was a very serious offence.

The guards, who were in personal attendance on the king, came running out into the garden.

"Who fired?" asked one.

"Abomey," replied Bonny. "We have found the bowl in his house."

"It is wonderful!" cried the guards in chorus.

"We are going to the king," continued Bonny. "Arrest Abomey. He will be wanted directly, and you will be rewarded."

The guards hastened on to the head-man's house, eager to execute the commission.

Abomey had been in power for some years, and he had made more enemies than friends.

For nothing at all but the love of inflicting pain, he had caused high officials to be beaten with many stripes.

At their cries he had only laughed.

He had squeezed a great deal of money, too, and rich gifts out of all classes and conditions.

Consequently, the fall of such a man could not fail to be a popular event.

The spies, guided by Bonny, went direct to the king's pavilion.

King Makolo and Bonna were still together, smoking a mild fragrant tobacco out of native-made pipes, and sipping rum and water from horns.

Peeping Tom and Knowall Dick advanced ahead of Bonny, carrying the bowl between them.

"Ha!" cried the king; "you have found my treasure!"

"We only live to execute your majesty's commands," replied Tom.

"Where was it?"

"Inside Abomey's idol. These rings and stones were also there."

"Mine! mine!" exclaimed the king. "I have missed them from time to time. Abomey—he shall die. Ho, there, guards!"

"He fired a gun at us, and the soldiers have gone to arrest him," said Tom.

"Here he comes!" cried Knowall Dick.

Abomey was seen coming along, dragged between a dozen soldiers.

Some people of the palace followed at a respectful distance, anxious to discover the cause of the disturbance.

Among the latter was Nola.

A thin, spiteful, vicious, half-starved-looking fellow was the high priest or medicine man.

He had a score of inferior priests subordinate to him, they all living in a building called the Temple.

As the Ashantees were grossly ignorant, this man exercised a great deal of influence in Court circles.

He was a friend of Abomey's, and an enemy of the spies.

It would not suit his purpose that they should gain an ascendancy which would throw him into the shade.

If he could accomplish their ruin and disgrace by any means, he intended to do so.

The Temple was not far from Abomey's house, and a quick-footed slave had carried to Nola the news of the head-man's arrest.

It was with wonder and rage that Nola learnt of the discovery of the bowl.

He did not suspect that Abomey was the culprit any more than other people.

It came upon him like a revelation and a great shock.

The white slaves, in his opinion, were in communication with spirits, and were able to exercise a power, the subtle essence of which he could only dream of and guess at.

His view of the case was that they should be put down at once, so he determined to use his priestly powers in two ways.

To save Abomey, if possible, and do the spies all the harm he could.

"Ah! wretched man," said the king, "have we raised you to a high and powerful place in order that you shall rob us?"

Abomey fell on his knees.

"Pardon! mercy!" he cried, extending his hands.

"You shall die. Guards, call the executioner."

"No, no; pardon! I have served you well and faithfully. Spare me in my old age!" screamed Abomey.

"The executioner, I say!" shouted the king.

That functionary was already on the spot, fancying that his services might be required.

King Makolo was an absolute monarch. He despised such trivialities as going through the form of a trial and hearing witnesses.

The executioner always carried a long wooden sword, hard edged, but so sharp that it would cut a man's neck through at one blow.

He advanced towards Abomey, who, mute with fear, bowed his head, awaiting the fatal stroke.

At the same time, Nola neared the king.

"Will King Makolo listen to the words of Nola?" he asked.

"Am I not always glad to do so?" said the king. "But, first, let justice be done to this old villain, who is like an evil scent in our nostrils."

"It is of him I would speak."

King Makolo frowned, but paid attention.

"I said to Abomey, knowing that he was rich and powerful, that I wanted a bowl of gold for the Temple," went on the priest. "I can only think that in a moment of forgetfulness he took your majesty's. He did wrong, but with a good purpose. Let him live. Do not sacrifice Abomey because two white slaves come here to bring distress on us."

"How do you know they will do so?"

"It has been revealed to me, O king. I can tell you that they are in league with bad spirits. How else should they get the power to do as they have done?"

"Bad spirits!" repeated the king, shaking his head. "I do not believe that, yet I will give Abomey his life. Take him away. To-morrow I will see what to do with him."

Abomey could scarcely credit his good luck. Grovelling at the king's feet, he attempted abjectly to kiss them.

King Makolo, however, would not permit this. He kicked out with such force as to send him sprawling down the steps of the pavilion.

Nola quickly picked him up, and led him away towards the Temple, where he intended to hide him, lest the king should change his mind.

It was, so far, a triumph for him.

"Do bad spirits tell you things?" asked the king of Tom and Dick.

"Don't you believe it," replied Peeping Tom.

"Let us assure your majesty that your priest does not tell the truth," added Know-all Dick. "We have nothing to do with bad spirits."

"Very well; I will buy you," said the king.

"I think I ought to raise my price," exclaimed Bonna, who had not yet spoken; "but, as you are a friend, I will stick to the bargain."

The king sent for his treasurer, who paid the slave-dealer the amount of gold dust agreed upon.

The king bade the spies sit down, and sent for some food for them.

Every now and then the king turned his head to look at them, as a man is apt to do when he has bought a new horse or invested in anything new.

He was apparently pleased with his new purchase.

Knowing that the king was very wealthy, and could afford to lose money, Bonna produced a dice box with three dice in it, and handed it to him.

Then he took out another box, with the same number of dice.

"What's this?" asked the king, who knew nothing of gambling.

"Something I bought from some sailors at Cape Coast Castle. You throw them out of the box on the floor. I do the same with mine, and the highest number wins."

"Ha! very good. We play together. What for, gold dust? I win back all I pay you. Ha, ha!" said the king.

"I'm agreeable," replied Bonna. "We will see which has the luck. But I cannot stay long. I must be off directly. My men wait."

A little explanation and a trial throw made the king well acquainted with the dice.

Peeping Tom had been watching Bonna's countenance narrowly.

He was a capital judge of character, and could read faces pretty correctly.

In this instance he felt sure that the slave-dealer was about to play some trick on Makolo.

"Dick," he whispered, "there will be some cheating going on directly, mark my words."

"I'll watch it," replied Dick.

"The king is our boss. We must stick to him, and if I see anything wrong, I will expose it."

"Look out."

"Who's afraid? We've done with Bonna. Keep still. They are going to start."

The two Africans settled down to the game with evident zest. Bonna was a very smart trader, and loved to make money, because at Cape Coast and at Benin he knew what money would buy. The dice he had bought of a Jew who sold a variety of European knicknacks.

To them there was a secret attached.

This, however, he had not revealed to the king, as it would not have suited his purpose.

The fact was, the king's dice were loaded with lead on one side, so that he could seldom throw so high as Bonna, as the lead was put in the king's high numbers, which, consequently, fell downward instead of upward.

All the courtiers had retired after the expulsion of Abomey, except the treasurer, the executioner, and the black boy Bonny.

Bonny, being the king's page, took up a large fan, and stood behind his royal master.

When Bonna staked so many ounces of gold, the royal treasurer covered it, and the game began.

King Makolo stood a very poor chance with his opponent, who won nearly every time.

"Who is going to win, you, Dick the Knower?" asked the king.

"You are going to lose," replied Dick.

"Ha! you sure of that?"

"Just as certain as I am of my existence."

"No use more play; I shall lose all. But how do you know that?"

"I know it, but you must ask Tom why it is so," replied Knowall Dick.

"Tom the Peeper," cried the king, "why shall Bonna beat me always?"

Peeping Tom had been watching the dice fall very carefully.

He saw distinctly that the slave-trader always turned up the high numbers, and the king the low.

"Because the dice you are playing with have lead in some of the holes," said Tom.

"Ha! can you see that?"

"Yes, your majesty. Have them examined."

"Seize him; he is a cheat!" exclaimed the king, angrily. "Is everybody going to cheat me?"

The executioner firmly grasped Bonna, who tried to make his escape. There was a struggle, in which the slave-dealer was thrown down and held by the throat.

Meanwhile the treasurer took up the dice, and, with a knife, knocked by a stone, split them into pieces.

It was as Tom had said. The king's dice were plugged with lead, and it was apparent that he was the victim of a clever imposture.

"Take all the money I have paid the wretch," said the king. "He shall not have an ounce."

The treasurer did so with great glee.

"Now kill him—cut off his head. Send out my soldiers, and bring in the heads of all his men."

In a moment the executioner sprang up.

His heavy sword was whirled through the air, and ere Bonna could make any attempt to save himself, the weapon descended, and his head rolled from his shoulders.

The treasurer hastened to despatch the officer of the guard.

In less than an hour, the whole of Bonna's men were shot, and their heads brought into the city and stuck on poles.

While this was going on, the king drank some more rum, and went to sleep as tranquilly as if nothing had happened.

Tom and Dick glided away, unfavourably impressed with Ashantee justice.

They were at the mercy of a man who could put them to death in a minute, should his drunken temper so incline him.

The spies went into the garden.

Seeking their favourite spot, under the orange trees, they saw Nola about to enter the house of Abomey.

He darted a snake-like vindictive glance at them.

"That fellow is no friend of ours," said Peeping Tom.

"Not he," replied Knowall Dick; "but we have been lucky so far. The king believes in us, and so long as his sable majesty is our friend, we are safe."

"I wonder how Harry Rawlings is getting on?" said Tom.

"By Jove! here he is," cried Dick.

Harry was advancing towards them.

"Hullo, you fellows!" he exclaimed. "I've just got let out for a run. How are things?"

"All right with us," answered Tom.

He related what had happened.

"This is a lively kind of place," continued Harry. "My cheeks ache blowing that confounded whistle for the princess and her maids. I am to be her husband, she says."

"What an awful lookout," replied Tom.

"Shall you do it?" asked Dick.

"I shall make a bolt first."

"Where for?"

"The coast," rejoined Harry.

"Good move. Perhaps they won't watch us so much in a few days, and if there is any opening, we will go with you," exclaimed Peeping Tom.

They passed a pleasant hour in conversation, when the treasurer came from the king and decorated each of the spies with a gold chain, and conducted them to a house which had been set apart for their use.

They were provided with a good supper, palm wine, and plenty of fruit. If it had not been for the anxiety they felt for the future, they would have passed, comfortably enough, their first night in Ashantee.

But troubles loomed ahead.

"'GIT UP, DAB,' CRIED SAMBO, CRACKING HIS WHIP."

No. 3.

CHAPTER VII.

JACK SPENCER RECEIVES NEWS OF THE WRECK OF THE YACHT, AND TURNS THE TABLES ON HIS FOES.

THANKS to a young and vigorous constitution, and the care bestowed upon him by Bill Blunt, the fever soon left Jack Spencer.

In a week he was able to get up and sit in the verandah.

He knew that his father was dead, and had been buried by Blunt; also that his sister had disappeared; that Harry and the spies had been carried into captivity; and that the "Cassandra" had left her moorings in the bay.

All this set him thinking in a very melancholy manner.

What to do, he knew not, and his spirits sank so low that at times he wished he had died of the fever.

But it is said that when things get to the worst, they are sure to mend.

It was so in his case, for events of importance were on the eve of occurring.

The negroes who had escaped death at the hands of the slave-traders, were very much incensed against Vandervelde and Old Calabar.

It had leaked out that Calabar had been seen in confidential communication with Bonna, and that the Dutchman had encouraged him.

After much discussion, the blacks determined to wreak their vengeance on both of them.

One of their number came to Blunt, informing him of what they were going to do, and warned him not to interfere.

He would certainly have done so if he had dared.

It was early morning, and Jack was enjoying a cool breeze, which came from the sea, as he sat under an awning in front of the house.

The negroes were gathered together on the sandy shore, talking and gesticulating excitedly.

Blunt came to Jack, who was wondering what had happened to cause such a commotion amongst the blacks.

"What's up?" he asked. "Are the niggers going fishing or hunting?"

"Neither one nor the other," replied Blunt. "They are on the war-path."

"Not against us, I hope?"

"No. They intend to kill old Van and Calabar. Their dander is up, because of the raid the other day. Rightly enough, they put it down to the Dutchman."

"Are you going to allow it?" enquired Jack.

"How can I help it?" answered Blunt. "I am as powerless in the matter as you are."

"This is an awful country to live in," said Jack, shuddering.

"You may well say that," answered Blunt. "Human life ain't of much account here, and that's a fact."

The blacks now began to move in a body towards the Dutchman's house, shouting and clapping their hands.

Some flourished knives, others held up shot-guns, which were loaded with bits of lead and small stones; others again had axes, with which they evidently intended to cut down the door if access was denied them.

Their approach was soon noticed by those inside.

Vandervelde and Calabar appeared at an upper window with rifles in their hands, and fired two shots at their assailants.

Two negroes fell dead.

This only served to inflame further the passions of the blacks, who returned the fire, driving the defenders back.

They then rushed towards the house in a tumultuous mob, howling and screaming at the tops of their voices.

When the door was reached, it was found to be strongly barred.

Strong arms wielded the axes, the door fell in, and the blacks poured like a torrent into the building.

What happened after that, Jack and Blunt could only guess at.

More shots were fired, showing that the Dutchman and Calabar were selling their lives dearly.

Loud shouts for help arose, and terrible cries filled the air.

Then all was still.

The negroes came out. Smoke and flames arose, indicating that the house had been fired.

"They have killed the Dutchman and the traitor nigger," said Blunt.

"I hope they won't turn their attention to us!" exclaimed Jack. "But I do not think we need be alarmed, as we have done nothing to offend them."

"They will come and demand free rum, I expect."

Blunt was right.

As soon as the negroes were satisfied that the flames had got a secure hold on the building, they came to the tavern and asked to be supplied with drink.

It would have been dangerous to refuse them, as their blood was up.

Jack watched the dry wooden house burn. It was rapidly destroyed, as if it had been so much tinder.

In less than half-an-hour it was reduced to ashes.

The terrible tragedy was over.

After receiving some drink, the blacks returned to their homes, as if nothing had happened, and Jack began to breathe freely again.

While he was watching the glowing and smoking embers, he noticed a man coming towards him.

He was a white man, and he came along the seashore

When he got close to Jack, he made a bow and a scrape with his foot, exclaiming—

" I ax your pardon, but if this 'ere place is Three Points, perhaps you are acquainted with a young gentleman named Jack Spencer ? "

" That is my name," was the reply.

" Then I may tell as how I've got a message for you."

" From whom ? "

" A lady as says she's your sister."

Jack's heart gave a great leap.

" Speak ! " he cried; " do not keep me in suspense ! Is she safe and well ? "

" Ay, sir, she's well enough in body, but kind of distracted in mind at being kept a prisoner. My name's Dawson. I was one of the crew of the yacht, ' Cassandra,' which belonged to Mr. Rawlings."

" Does it not now ? " asked Jack.

" It don't belong to anybody, because it's gone to Davy Jones' locker."

" Wrecked ? "

" Yes, sir; a week or more ago, on the shore, a matter of ten miles from here."

" The Squire ! his son ! are they alive ? "

" They were saved, so were four of the crew, including myself," replied Dawson. " The young Squire, Charlie, as they call him, has been going on more like a madman than a sensible being."

" What has he been doing ? "

" You shall hear, sir," continued Dawson. " First of all, he kills Garner, the man who brought the young lady to him."

" Garner dead ! Then there is a scoundrel the less in the world."

" Some liquor was saved from the wreck. Master Charlie has been drinking that, and he falls foul of me and my mates. Three of 'em he shot, just for a lark, as he called it. I concluded it would be only prudent to bolt, but before I did, I axed the young lady if I could do anything for her, and she told me to come on here and see if I could

find you ; if so, I was to tell you how she was circumstanced."

" I cannot find words to thank you," replied Jack. .

" There's only Mr. Rawlings and Charlie to guard her," Dawson went on, " and if you want to rescue her, I'll show you the spot and lend a hand."

" Bravo, my friend. You are made of the right stuff."

" I can't a-bear to see a female in distress, sir. I'd always strike a blow in defence of a petticoat."

" An excellent sentiment. You shall have some refreshment and a rest. We will start in the cool of the evening, and surprise the villainous father and son in the night."

" Thankee for me, sir," said Dawson. " I'll own that I'm a bit hungry and tired."

Jack took him to Blunt, to whom he communicated the good news.

The latter was very glad to hear it, for Marian's pretty face and gentle manner endeared her to everyone with whom she came in contact.

He volunteered his services for the rescue expedition, which were accepted willingly.

The afternoon soon passed.

When the sun had sunk in its fleecy bed, they armed themselves and started along the seashore.

The silence of the night was only disturbed by the sound of the phosphorescent waves as they beat upon the beach.

Jack hoped to be able to fall upon Mr. Rawlings and Charlie as they were asleep.

Being desperate men, he apprehended they would make a determined resistance if they were not taken unawares.

Bad as they were, he did not want to kill them, rather wishing to make them suffer the horrors of captivity, as they had made others suffer.

He intended to punish them for all their villainy, if he could only succeed in taking them alive.

Three hours sufficed to bring them to the spot where Marian was held in captivity.

While Jack and Blunt halted under the shadow of a rock, Dawson crawled on his hands and knees over the sand to reconnoitre.

With the noiseless movement of a snake, he approached the hut, which had been made of boxes.

The Squire and Charlie were stretched on some sail-cloth, side by side, and wrapped in a sound slumber.

He returned to the others with this welcome information.

They had brought a coil of rope with

them to secure the prisoners, and, with pistols drawn, they advanced.

It was arranged that Blunt should seize the Squire, Dawson should grasp Charlie, and that Jack should bind their hands behind their backs as expeditiously as possible.

Everything turned out as well as they could wish.

Father and son were secured and bound before they could fathom who their assailants were.

When they were raised to their feet, they saw Jack, and their countenances fell in a moment.

No explanation was necessary now.

Jack did not stay to speak to them. He ran into the hut to find Marian. She was sleeping, but her sleep was troubled. Cries and sobs broke from her. Jack lifted her up in his arms and kissed her.

"Help! help!" she cried.

For the moment she thought it was Charlie who had disturbed her slumber, and a look of horror and loathing crossed her countenance.

"It is I, Marian!" exclaimed Jack. "Don't be afraid."

"Thank heaven!" replied Marian; "but the Squire—Charlie! where are they?"

"In safe custody; they can't harm you."

"I thought you would find me. Oh! Jack dear, this is almost too much. I feel faint; my head is so dizzy."

"Lean on me—that's it. You'll be all right presently."

"How is father?"

"Alas! he is dead."

"Oh, heaven! And Harry, have you any news of him?"

"None at all. I have been ill with an attack of fever, or I should have tried to find out something about him. I shall hear of Bonna's movements in time. We are sure to have a runner from the interior come into Three Points, sooner or later."

"Did Dawson tell you about me?"

"Yes; he is outside with Blunt," replied Jack.

He led her out of the hut. By this time Mr. Rawlings and Charlie had recovered their scattered senses.

The expression of their countenances was a study for a painter of the diabolical school.

Their features were distorted with rage, their eyes full of malignity, the corners of their mouths twitching, and their hands quivering.

"What is the meaning of this outrage?" asked Mr. Rawlings, savagely.

"Yes; explain your conduct," said Charlie.

Jack laughed in a sarcastic manner.

"It sounds rather funny to hear you two talk of outrage," he replied. "Have you not had my friend Harry carried off into slavery? Did you not kidnap my sister? And yet you talk glibly of outrage."

"I demand to be set at liberty," cried the Squire.

"I refuse to comply with your demand."

"What do you intend to do with us?"

"Keep you in custody. Your friend at Three Points, the Dutchman, is dead. No one will take your part."

"You shall repent this!" Mr. Rawlings cried, furiously.

"Bah! That for your threats!" cried Jack, scornfully, snapping his fingers. "Step out—march. We are going back to Three Points."

The Squire and Charlie were compelled to obey orders by Dawson, who struck them with a stick over the shoulders.

Marian walked between Jack and Blunt.

Jack asked her how she had contrived to keep Charlie at a distance, and she told him that it was only by threatening to destroy herself if he annoyed her.

His persecution had been incessant and persistent.

"It is all over now, dear," said Jack; "the tables are turned."

"If we could only find Harry, I might be happy once more," replied Marian.

"That will be done in time."

"You will protect me—I know it."

"With my life," rejoined Jack, earnestly.

"And so will I, miss," said Blunt. "I'll be a second father to you."

At this allusion to her unfortunate parent, her tears began to flow, but after a time she partially recovered her spirits.

When they arrived at Three Points, Marian was given the best room Blunt's house afforded.

Mr. Rawlings and Charlie were securely locked in an outhouse, and Jack retired to rest, conscious of having done good work.

His enemies were in his power.

He determined to make them feel it.

CHAPTER VIII.

THE PRINCESS MAKES LOVE TO HARRY, WHO REJECTS HER AMOROUS ADVANCES—
RAGE OF THE PRINCESS—HE IS PUT IN THE CAGE—HE ESCAPES—A FIGHT WITH
A PYTHON.

HARRY had not been many days in the service of the Princess Matabele before she became passionately in love with him, and showed it in every way.

Instead of having him wait on her, she made her women fan him and supply his wants.

When he played on the whistle, she would sit at his feet, and look up lovingly into his face. The ebony-hued princess, however, made no impression upon Harry.

He turned away from her with a secret loathing.

Her complexion, black as ebony, her woolly hair, thick lips, flat nose, and projecting ears, only inspired him with disgust.

At length, things came to a crisis.

The princess was tired of looking at him with languishing eyes, and as he did not propose to her, she resolved to ask him.

It was evening. The sun had gone down, after a tropically hot day. The princess and Harry had been enjoying a siesta in her garden pavilion, which was nicely shaded by trees and creeping vines.

"My own love!" exclaimed Matabele, sitting down by the side of Harry, who was lying on his back, "it is time for me to speak."

"About what?" asked Harry, in a drowsy tone.

"I like you more every day. You are the light of my life, the sun of my heart, and the inmost joy of my soul."

"My princess, I am glad you are satisfied with me."

"It is my intention to make you my husband. I have spoken to King Makolo and my mother. They have no objection. To-morrow, Nolo will make us one, in the Temple. Are you pleased?"

"M'—no," Harry stammered. "It is too great an honour."

"What does my beautiful bird say?"

"I am not worthy of the affection of so great a princess nor so mighty a king."

"That is for me to decide!" exclaimed Matabele. "Of course the moon cannot approach the sun in power and dignity, but I am content to raise you up and make you my equal."

Harry rose to his feet. He had feared this moment all along.

Marry the Princess Matabele, he would not.

How would she take his refusal?

Perhaps she could be as hard, cold, and cruelly relentless as she was at present soft, amiable and loving.

"My mistress," said Harry, puzzled how to get out of the dilemma, "I cannot marry you, because my religion is different from yours. You worship idols, but I am a Christian."

"Then I will become a Christian," she replied. "Teach me about your religion. If you have a fetish, I will worship it."

"Your illustrious father would not like that."

"Bah!" she said, "I control my mother, she controls my father. Everything goes as I will it. Be mine to-morrow?"

"I cannot."

"Why, O joy of my heart?"

"Because I don't want to!" exclaimed Harry, who was goaded nearly to madness by her persistency.

"What!" she cried. "Don't you like me?"

"I like you all right," replied Harry, "but not well enough to marry you. It is best to be candid with you."

Matabele's face changed in an instant.

Her woman's pride was scorned. She saw his meaning, and became a fury. He was her slave, and he had rejected her advances. This humiliated her terribly. She thought she had only to ask and to have. It was a surprise, indeed.

Fire flashed from her eyes, her nostrils dilated, and she drew her breath in short quick gasps.

Her power was absolute. If one of her women offended her, she could have her beaten or instantly led to execution.

Raising her hand, she gave Harry a blow, which made him reel.

"Wretch!" she cried, "am I to be despised because my skin is not so white as yours?"

"Pardon me," said Harry. "As a mistress or a friend, I respect you."

"Is not the daughter of a king good enough for a slave?"

"I cannot marry you. Listen to me: I love one of my own race."

"Ha! if she were here, I would have her put to death."

"Surely you will make some little allowance for me?"

"No. I am a lioness when aroused," replied the princess. "You have been too well treated. But, by my idol and the fetish I carry about me, I will be revenged."

"What have I done?" asked Harry.

"Insulted me. I can hate as well as love. In the middle of the city is a wooden pen, called the cage. In this are criminals placed before their execution. The people prod them with sticks, jeer at them, and cover them with garbage and refuse. To the cage I will consign you."

"I don't care," said Harry, trying to look indifferent.

"A little bread, a little water, is all you will have for three days."

"I can survive it."

"Ignorant fool! that is not all," answered the princess. "If you do not alter your sentiments at the end of three days, you will be killed by the executioner."

"Then I shall have no more trouble."

"I will invent some horrible torture. You shall suffer for hours before you die."

Harry was silent.

"Do not my threats frighten you?" cried Matabele.

"No," replied Harry.

"Are you going to change your mind—to hold me in your arms—to kiss me, and go to the Temple to-morrow, and marry me?"

"Never! I can only die once, and I can see that life with you would be a living death. Do your worst; I defy you."

Harry said this boldly, and folded his arms.

Come what might, he was determined to be true to Marian.

The princess spoke to one of her women, who ran out of the pavilion and made a loud outcry.

In less than a minute, a dozen soldiers made their appearance on the scene.

"Take the white slave and put him in the cage!" exclaimed Matabele.

Seized roughly by both arms, Harry was dragged away.

They took him out of the palace grounds, and conducted him through the streets, arriving at last at a structure made of bars of wood, and about six feet square.

Opening a door, the soldiers pushed him in. The door was then closed and fastened by a chain and bolt.

There was no covering, no protection from the sun or rain, and the bars were so close together that a prisoner could only get his arm through.

Not even a stool or a heap of grass invited repose.

Standing up like a wild beast caged, Harry saw that he was surrounded by a crowd of men, women, and children.

This increased in numbers every moment.

The news spread like wildfire that a white slave had been put in the cage.

It was rumoured that he had committed some horrible crime in the palace.

The populace regarded him as a monster of the deepest dye.

Those who were possessed of decaying vegetables and doubtful eggs, did not hesitate to throw them at him.

The Ashantee boys got long bamboo rods and poked him from one side of the cage to the other.

His position was truly deplorable, for he was utterly unable to defend himself.

A perfect babel of abusive sounds arose, but this he little cared for, as he did not understand the discordant jargon.

Undoubtedly the Princess Matabele had her revenge.

Harry was suffering a martyrdom for the sake of his beloved Marian.

His cap had fallen off, the European clothes he still wore were torn, and he was covered with the refuse thrown at him.

Perspiration streamed from every pore as he ran from corner to corner to avoid the bamboos of the boys.

In about an hour, the adult portion of the population had enjoyed enough of the amusement, and they went away.

Some girls and boys remained. The former pinched the prisoner whenever he came near the bars; the others goaded him.

At length, Harry succeeded in snatching a long rattan from a boy, which enabled him to act on the defensive.

Driven to madness, he dealt some of his tormentors blows which made them keep at a respectful distance.

At length the children went away, leaving Harry alone.

He sank exhausted on the floor, panting for breath.

He was not long in that condition before Peeping Tom and Knowall Dick came by that way.

They were taking a walk of exploration through the city.

King Makolo had given them no new task to do, as his majesty had been drinking rum in large quantities ever since he had put Bonna and his men to death.

He had an easy faculty of getting drunk, but he did not find it so easy to get sober again.

Perhaps there was no great difference in this respect between his sable highness and a white man.

"Hullo!" exclaimed Peeping Tom, "this is the cage that Bonny told us about. They put criminals in it, and shy things at them."

"There's some poor beggar there now," replied Knowall Dick.

"So there is, by Jove!"

"Let's throw something at him. Where's a stone?"

Dick had not far to look for one.

Picking it up, he threw it at Harry, hitting him on the leg.

"Bravo our side!" cried Dick.

"How's that, umpire?" asked Tom.

"Middle stump. Out with a duck," Dick replied.

Harry sprang to his feet with a yell of pain.

"Hang you all, you black imps," he exclaimed, thinking the stone came from his native tormentors.

"Why, it's Harry Rawlings!" said Peeping Tom.

"What's he done to get into this disgrace? We must ask him," observed Knowall Dick.

They went close up to the cage, peering at Harry curiously.

He looked a very ragged and dilapidated specimen of humanity.

"It is kind of you to visit me," he said. "Who told you I was in limbo?"

"Nobody," answered Tom.

"Did you come on me by accident?"

"Entirely. What have you been doing?"

"I wouldn't marry the Princess Matabele. That's all," rejoined Harry.

The spies whistled.

"Wouldn't I if I had the chance!" exclaimed Knowall Dick.

"Ah! it is different with you," replied Harry. "Because you are not in love and engaged, as I am to Marian Spencer."

"That would make no odds to me," said Tom.

"Charlie has got her by this time," observed Dick.

"Do you mean to tell me that, under any circumstances, you would be false to your vows to a girl?" asked Harry.

"One does not pick up a princess every day," said Peeping Tom. "See what you have done for yourself."

"Never mind. I don't care so long as you have come. I am not guarded. Lift the chain and put that bolt back."

"What for?"

"To let me out."

"My word, you *have* got a nerve!" said Peeping Tom. "I wouldn't do it on any account."

"Why not?"

"We might get into the same fix as you are. No, no; we have got to look after ourselves, old fellow."

Harry looked deeply depressed on hearing this.

"We are old schoolfellows," he said. "You might do something for me. I will run into the bush and take my chance."

"Can't do it," replied Peeping Tom.

"Too much risk about it," said Knowall Dick.

"Lend me a knife, then, to saw my way through these bars."

"I don't mind that," answered Tom. "You are welcome to my knife. Here it is, old chappie."

This was something gained.

Harry received it through the bars, and stuck it in his belt.

The possession of it gave him renewed hope, for he thought he would now be able to escape from his thraldom.

"Don't take your own life with it," observed Knowall Dick.

"I'm not that kind of a fellow," answered Harry. "My object is to get back to Three Points, if I can, and join Jack Spencer."

"If you do, think of us," said Peeping Tom.

"I am afraid I can't do much for you. It would take an army to get you out of this place."

"Well, do your best. We must be off now, or we may be noticed talking to you. Good-bye," replied Tom.

Saying this, he and Knowall Dick walked rapidly away, evidently thinking more of their own safety and well-being than they did of Harry's.

They were always selfish to the last degree.

In a minute Peeping Tom came back to the cage. He had picked up a bamboo rod which one of the playful Ashantee youths had dropped.

Dick stood still and looked on.

"What do you want?" asked Harry. "Have you forgotten anything?"

"No."

"Want to lend me your pistol, perhaps," said Harry, hopefully.

"It isn't that," replied Tom. "I picked up this bamboo, and I could not resist the temptation of returning to have a prod or two at you."

"You little wretch. "If you do—oh!"

Just then Harry received a poke, which doubled him up and took his breath away.

A second prod behind straightened him again.

Peeping Tom laughed till the tears ran down his cheeks.

"I say, Dick," he cried, "this is fun. Come and have a poke. It beats 'baste the bear' into fits."

"Can't, I'm engaged," answered Dick.

"What in?"

"'HA!' CRIED JACK; 'THE TWO SPIES!'"

"There is a water melon ground outside this house, and I have just cut a beauty, all juice."

"Give me some of it."

"You will have to make haste, then."

Reluctantly, after giving Harry one more poke, Peeping Tom gave up the sport, being beguiled by the superior attractions of the water melon.

He rejoined Knowall Dick, and they went away together.

It was now quite dark, and under cover of the gloom, Harry could begin his work.

A slave had brought him some corn cake and water by the orders of the princess.

This he was glad enough of to recruit his strength.

For two hours he was hard at work, cutting away the bars of his cage.

He only wanted to make an aperture sufficiently large to allow his body to pass through. This he succeeded in doing after great labour.

All was now quiet in the city, the inhabitants having retired to rest.

Harry passed through the streets unobserved; he left the city without attracting any attention, and ran across the plain.

Three miles off was a dense forest, in the mazy recesses of which he hoped to find safety and shelter.

Tightly he clutched his knife, for it was his only protection against the venomous reptiles and the fierce wild beasts of an African forest.

His heart almost sank as he thought of the perils he had to face.

If Jack Spencer had been with him he would not have cared.

This time he had to go through all his dangers alone and unaided, but he had strong hope of escaping death and reaching the coast.

When Harry reached the forest, it was with some misgiving that he plunged into its gloomy recesses.

He was lucky enough to find a path which had been made by hunters or wild beasts.

The jungle growth had been torn away, and the tall grass beaten down.

So far he had not been followed, and he deemed himself safe from pursuit.

There was little doubt that the revengeful Princess Matabele would have him searched for far and near.

She would not rest until she had made every effort to find him, so that she could punish him with death.

The night was clear, stars innumerable shone, with a radiance unknown in colder climes, and the moon diffused a flood of silver, which penetrated even the heart of the forest.

Every now and then the loud roaring of a lion was audible.

This would be followed by the trumpeting of an alarmed elephant.

Snakes, too, were about, as many a terrifying hiss testified.

After going about two miles, Harry came to a pool of some size, where he quenched his thirst.

Turning to look for a place to rest, he was surprised to find himself confronted by a grinning black boy, who had stolen upon him unawares.

It was Bonny, whom he had frequently seen with Peeping Tom and Knowall Dick.

"Ha! Englishman," cried Bonny.

Harry gave himself up for lost.

Surely he must have been followed, he thought.

"Beware," he exclaimed, drawing his knife, "I will not be taken alive, so I warn you not to attempt it."

Bonny looked at him in astonishment,

"Me not hurt you," he replied. "What for I do it? Me like white man berry much, yes."

"How did you find me out?"

"See you come to drink. Me watch my trap," said Bonny. "My father dig elephant trap near here. Great big hole in ground covered with boughs. Elephants come to drink, fall in hole. Once a week we come to see what we catch. Come at night, because it am cool. If got any elephant, tell father, he come and get ivory. What you do here?"

"Are you telling me the truth?"

"Cert'in'y, the whole trufe. Berry bad t'ing tell lie to friend."

"You have no one with you?"

"Me all alone, swear dat. Why you come?"

"I have run away. I thought you and some soldiers had tracked me. The Princess Matabele wanted me to marry her. Because I would not she put me in the cage. I escaped, and here I am, trying to make my way to the coast."

Bonny looked profoundly amazed.

"Not marry the princess!" he exclaimed. "Why not?"

"Because I did not like her."

"She gib lot of gold to get you back," continued Bonny, thoughtfully.

"I shall be off again when day breaks," said Harry.

"Got pistol? got knife?"

"Yes, I have a knife."

"Plenty lion, plenty snake. Look out!" warned Bonny.

"I've got a stout heart," replied Harry. "That will carry a fellow a long way."

"You wait here till to-morrow. I go

back and get you food, and if you take me, I come with you."

" Will you?"

" Yes; like to see the big water once more."

" All right! I want a companion. It is horribly lonely here," said Harry.

He was very glad of this offer, and being of an unsuspicious turn of mind, he did not for a moment dream of treachery.

They were all at once alarmed by a loud roar, not many hundred yards from them.

This was followed by the trumpeting of an elephant and the crashing of the undergrowth.

Bonny put his fingers to his lips, and drew Harry behind a large tree.

" Keep quiet," he whispered. " Lion hunt elephant. See him fall in trap, p'r'aps."

" What will you do with the lion?"

" Me shoot him, bang, dead."

The noise came nearer.

It was an exciting moment.

In less than a minute a large elephant made his appearance, hotly pursued by a magnificent lion.

He was tearing and bounding towards the lake, as if he hoped to get into the water and escape the fangs of his enemy.

The pitfall, of which the black boy had spoken, lay right in his path.

With a crash he broke through the boughs which were placed over the top.

The lion was able to pull up just in time, and, squatting on its haunches, peered round curiously to see what had become of its intended prey.

Never before did an animal look so puzzled.

Bonny raised his rifle, and taking careful aim, fired.

The lion was hard hit.

Giving a prodigious spring, it bounded in the air, and fell into the pit on the top of the elephant.

Bonny laughed in a satisfied manner at this double capture.

" Yah! " he exclaimed, " that berry good business. Got 'em both now. Lion make good skin; elephant tusk give ivory."

" Does your father sell them?" asked Harry.

" Yes. Sell to caravan traders who go to Cape Coast Castle."

" What does your father do with the money?"

" Buy cloth—buy rum from traders. Get drunk for a month—drinkee, drinkee till all gone. Then he set more trap."

" You sleep," added Bonny. " Me go and get food. To-morrow you and me go to coast at Three Points."

" Are you going back at once?"

" Yes. Cool now, no sun. Come back soon. Don't swim in lake; bad snake there; bad snake in tree, too. Look out."

" What kind of snake?"

" Big thick snake, ever so much long. Man monkey, too, come along; fight with teeth and hands."

" Leave me your gun. It is not a very cheerful look-out," said Harry.

" Can't spare shoot-gun. Back quick. Me good runner," replied Bonny.

The black boy shouldered his rifle, and started off at a run.

Harry threw himself down under a tree. The lion groaned in the pit, the elephant made a fearful noise, and threw himself about in trying to get out. Over the pool the moon cast its silvery effulgence, and its beams streamed on the ground through the interstices of the tree boughs.

Harry was so tired that not even the buzz and the sting of the horrible mosquitos could keep him awake.

How long he slept he did not know.

He awoke with a dreadful feeling of oppression on his chest.

The moon was still shining, and he saw something black, with a yellow stripe here and there, in front of him.

He put out his hand to touch it.

The thing, whatever it was, moved.

With a cry of horror, he withdrew his hand from the cold, clammy substance.

He sat up and wriggled from under the incubus, which at once began to move in a rapid manner.

Rising hastily to his feet, Harry found himself confronted by a huge python, which species of serpent grows to a terrific size in the African forests.

It had coiled itself on its tail for a spring.

Swaying its ugly horrid crest to and fro, it tried to fascinate Harry with its large glittering orbs.

Dreadful angry hisses came from it, and its forked tongue darted in and out with inconceivable rapidity.

Harry trembled so violently that he could scarcely stand.

A cold sweat broke out all over him.

He knew that if he were once enveloped in those awful coils, his death would only be a matter of moments.

Rousing himself by the exercise of an heroic effort, which was born of despair, he drew his knife from his belt.

As a forlorn hope, he threw himself on the python, and by good luck managed to plunge his knife into its left eye, and through the brain.

This, however, did not destroy the muscular activity of the reptile, which cast itself into the most frightful contortions.

Its tail lashed about in every direction.

Harry ran amongst the trees for safety, and watched its struggles.

It seemed as if it were tying and untying knots in its body.

Every minute it rolled nearer to the deep dark pool.

At length, to Harry's intense satisfaction, the creature rolled off the bank into the stagnant water.

Here its struggles were more forcible than on land. It lashed the water like a harpooned whale, sending it up in showers.

This continued for some time.

It could not succeed in regaining the land, and by degrees its strength decreased; at last it sank to the bottom.

Harry offered up a prayer of thankful-ness, for he had been standing, as it were, on the verge of the grave.

For a moment he almost wished he had married the princess, but when he thought of Marian, he was willing to brave all the dangers of the forest.

A sweet little cherub, he hoped, sat up aloft to watch over his fate.

Sleep, however, for the rest of that night seemed impossible.

He could not get the python out of his mind.

His nervous system was for the time completely broken up. Shivering fits came over him, and he sat with his back against a tree, watching the waning moonbeams on the water as they died away at the break of day.

CHAPTER IX.

THE SPIES ARE SENT FOR BY ORDER OF THE KING—A DIFFICULT TASK—LUCK COMES IN THEIR WAY—THEY HIT ON THE RIGHT TRACK.

IN Africa the natives rise with the sun, and do the rest of their sleeping during the heat of the day, when it is almost impossible to work.

Consequently it was quite early in the morning when news of Harry's escape was brought to the Princess Matabele.

Her rage knew no bounds.

She had hoped all along that the punishment to which she had subjected him would bring him to his senses.

In less than twenty-four hours she fully expected that he would send a message to her suing for mercy.

To think that he had slipped through her fingers was more than she could bear.

Instantly she ran to her father's part of the palace, and found his majesty, break-fasting on rice and fowl, under a palm tree.

"The white slave I bought has run away!" she cried.

"What is that for, O my daughter?" asked King Makolo.

"I told him I wanted him to marry me."

"What honour! What condescension!"

"He did not think so. The base wretch refused. I had him put in the cage. He cut his way out and has vanished."

"Some evil spirits must have helped him."

"Find him, father. I will cut him into a thousand pieces," said the princess, who grated her teeth.

"It is easily done," said the king.

"How?"

"I have only to send for Tom the Peeper and Dick the Knower."

"True. I had forgotten that."

"Are not all things known to them? Did they not find my golden bowl, which was stolen by Abomey? Had not the priest, Nola, begged for him, he would be now in the spirit land."

"Send for them quickly."

King Makolo clapped his hands, and the treasurer, who was standing a little way off, in attendance on his royal master, came up promptly.

He thought he was going to be asked to breakfast, and he squatted down beside his majesty.

He was disagreeably disappointed.

The king raised his hand and gave him a smack on the side of the head, which sent him sprawling on his back.

He got up with a rueful countenance, rubbing his ear.

"Dog," exclaimed the king, "how dare you take such a liberty? Am I not as sacred as the sun, moon, and stars?"

"Yes, O king. You have said truly, for you are the light of the universe."

"What do you mean by sitting down by my side, then?"

"Pardon."

"You deserve to lose your vile head."

"I am but the meanest of your slaves. What is your majesty's pleasure?" asked the treasurer, humbly.

"Seek instantly Tom the Peeper and Dick the Knower. Bring them here on peril of your life!" exclaimed King Makolo.

The treasurer departed as fast as his legs could carry him. Knowing the king's temper, he did not want to offend him again. His woolly hair seemed to curl closer at the idea of losing his life.

While he was gone, the king patted his daughter's cheek, and expressed his sympathy with her.

"You are fair to look upon," he said. "Why should this white slave despise you, since he sees that he is the joy of your heart?"

"I care for him no longer."

"Then he shall die."

"Perhaps he has gone to the coast," said the princess.

"I will send runners, swift of foot, after him. If needs be, I will send an army," replied King Makolo.

Matabele kissed her father's hand.

"My father loves me. I am happy," she murmured.

The treasurer now appeared with the two spies, who looked rather anxious at being sent for in such a hurry.

They could not help thinking that there was something wrong.

What new trial was awaiting them?

"Tom the Peeper," exclaimed King Makolo, "can you see where the white slave who was brought here with you by Bonna, of infamous memory, has gone to?"

"No," replied Peeping Tom; "but I soon will."

"Dick the Knower, can you tell me?" continued the king.

"Give me a little time," answered Knowall Dick, guessing that Harry had escaped. "I am aware that he is gone from the cage."

"Ha! how do you know that?"

"A spirit told me."

The king did not dare to question this audacious statement—in fact, he firmly believed it, and trembled slightly.

"I will give you one day and one night, Tom the Peeper and Dick the Knower, to find my daughter's white slave," he said.

"No more than that?"

"If you do not tell me where he is by that time, I will have you beheaded by the sword of the executioner. Go."

The spies walked away rather dejected.

They retired to their house, where a native had got ready their breakfast.

"Fall to," said Peeping Tom.

"I've no appetite," replied Knowall Dick. "We have a nice task before us now. Of course, Harry Rawlings has bolted."

"There can't be any doubt about that.

Wouldn't he have been a fool to stay in the cage?"

"Weren't you the fool?"

"Why?"

"To give him the knife to cut his way out. You might have known we should be sent for to find him."

"I didn't think of that," answered Peeping Tom. "Oh, dear!"

"What is Harry to us? What has he ever been?" continued Knowall Dick.

"Nothing at all."

"Just so. Well, you may get us out of the scrape, if you can. I can't, and that's all about it."

They sat down on the floor, in the absence of suitable furniture, and began to pick at a bit of fish and bread, regarding one another in gloomy silence.

Twenty-four hours was all they had to find Harry in.

How were they going to do it?

In their hearts, they wished he had been dead long ago.

While they were eating their breakfast, in a half-hearted manner, the black boy, Bonny, made his appearance in their hut.

He looked tired, hungry, and thirsty.

"Got something to eat? Me starved," he exclaimed.

"Help yourself," replied Peeping Tom. "Where have you been? I haven't seen you since sunset yesterday."

"Me been to forest. Father got an elephant pit. Me go to see what in it. Long run. Tire Bonny berry much. Come in here first, before go to father. King set me to guard you."

"There's no fear of our hooking it," said Knowall Dick. "We don't know where to go. Our companion in misfortune has gone, and I should like to drop on him."

Bonny was ravenously eating the fish and bread, of which there was abundance.

He looked up curiously as Dick spoke.

"What want to know for?" he asked.

"King Makolo has ordered us to find him."

"Well," said the black boy, "if you know all, you can tell where he is."

He laughed rather maliciously, and Dick saw that he had made a mistake.

It did not do to admit before the young African that there were cases in which he and Tom were at fault.

The news would soon get about, and he could guess what the consequences would be.

If they were regarded as impostors, their career would soon be at an end.

The king and his family had none of the sentiments of humanity about them.

Only two days before, a female slave who

was fanning the queen, had the misfortune to strike her majesty on the nose. She was instantly stripped, tied to a stake, smeared with honey, and left as a prey to the mosquitos, which, in time, stung her to death, under a broiling sun.

"Of course I know!" exclaimed Dick. "He is in the forest. You don't suppose he would be such a fool as to stay here. He is where you have come from. You have seen him, and I will tell the king."

Bonny shook with fear.

"Yes," cried Peeping Tom, taking the cue from Dick, and shading his eyes with his hand, "I can see him, lying down at the foot of a big tree."

"You see him all this way off?"

"It is a gift I have got. Yes, yes; now he gets up, he stands, he sits down again. He looks expectant, as if waiting for some-one."

Bonny was quite thrown off his guard.

He was as superstitious as the rest of his race.

In his simple mind there was a rooted idea that the two white boys knew and saw everything that they wanted to see and know.

"You see in your sleep?" he asked.

"Yes; I saw you in the forest," replied Peeping Tom.

"What did I catch?"

"An elephant."

"Anything else?" inquired Bonny.

"There was something else. A wild beast of some sort."

"That was the lion. Me shoot him when standing by white boy. You are right. It is no use trying to deceive you."

Peeping Tom looked at Knowall Dick with triumph.

They had been lucky enough to succeed again.

"It is indeed useless to try and deceive us," cried Tom.

"If you hope to, you will be sadly mistaken, young ebony," said Dick.

"Confess all!" cried Tom, in a louder tone.

"Me will."

"Down on your knees."

Bonny sank upon his knees in his fright, dropping the piece of fish he was eating, and big tears ran from his eyes over his fat cheeks.

"Me see white boy who run away at the Elephant Pool. Ebberyone know where that is in the forest. He ask me to get him food and go with him to coast. Me say yes, but mean no. Don't tell King Makolo, or he kill Bonny."

Peeping Tom laughed loudly.

"I knew it all along," he replied, "but I like you, and won't mention your name in the matter."

"Bonny do anything for you."

"So you ought. Your life is in our hands, but you shall live."

Bonny sprang up and danced with great glee.

His promise to Harry was totally forgotten; he cared for himself only. What might happen to Harry was a matter of indifference to him.

"Me go to father now," said Bonny, "tell him what is in trap, and hab long good sleep."

"Don't say a word to anyone about what we have been talking of, not even to your father," exclaimed Tom, warningly.

"'Bout white slave in forest?"

"Exactly. If you do, you will get into trouble."

"All-a-right. Good-bye. Me like Englishman."

With these words, Bonny departed.

"Isn't he a little humbug?" remarked Knowall Dick.

"Awful," replied Tom.

"Go to the door and watch which way he goes."

"Right."

Peeping Tom went outside and looked all round. Bonny was running in the direction of the house where his father lived.

The spies were only afraid lest he should go to the king's palace.

As Peeping Tom was about to rejoin Dick, he took a peep round the corner of the house.

Why he did so, he did not know.

It was instinct with him.

A large shade tree grew near the aperture which served as a window, and under this he saw the figure of a man, in a crouching position.

Whoever he was, the man was evidently listening, for he had his hand to his ear, as if he wanted to catch every word which was uttered inside the hut.

Under the porch hung a long, stout wooden club.

Peeping Tom crept back and possessed himself of this.

"What are you up to?" asked Knowall Dick.

"Hush!" whispered Peeping Tom; "lie low. I know what I am about."

He retraced his steps in a stealthy manner, and suddenly faced the eavesdropper.

"Ola! Ola!" he cried.

The man gave a jump and straightened himself up.

It was the late minister, the disgraced Abomey, who had been so intently listening to what was going on.

Abomey's mouth distended with a broad grin.

"What are you doing here?" asked Tom, angrily.

"I hear all," replied Abomey. "You think you great fetish—great trick man."

"So I am."

Abomey stooped, picked up a piece of straw, put it to his mouth, and blew it into the air.

"Poof!" he said. "That for you."

What do you mean, you old chump of wood?" demanded Peeping Tom.

"You are no good. Nola say the same thing."

"Explain yourself."

"Get secret out of Bonny. Go tell king. Yah! me hear. Me go first to king and tell him white slave at Elephant Pool."

"Will you, by Jingo!"

"Yah! yah! yah!"

"I'll settle your hash first!" cried Peeping Tom.

He raised his club.

Abomey tried to run, but before he had gone far, he received a blow on the head, which stretched him upon the ground.

With a savage energy, born of the circumstances by which he was surrounded, aided by innate depravity, Tom hit him again and again.

Abomey was mortally wounded by the first blow; the others hastened his death.

He was dead when Knowall Dick came out to learn what was going on.

Peeping Tom pointed to Abomey.

"I had to do it," he said. "The old rascal had been spying, and heard all."

"Spying on us?" replied Dick.

"Yes. He said he would go to the king first and tell him where Harry is. That would never do, so I killed him."

"Good," answered Knowall Dick. "I always felt he was an enemy, after the golden bowl business; so is that priest fellow Nola."

"Do you blame me?"

"Not at all," replied Knowall Dick, whose face grew grave; "but I say, old chappie, what are we going to do with the body?"

"That's a poser," said Peeping Tom.

They were in a state of great perplexity.

What to do they knew not, yet the body could not be allowed to remain where it was.

"I have it," cried Knowall Dick, after a pause. "There is an old dry disused well a few yards farther up the wall.

"Is there? I didn't know it. How did you find it out?" asked Peeping Tom.

"By nearly falling into it one night in the dark."

"Shall we throw him in?"

"Can't do anything else that I can see. Take hold; we'll soon hide the old sinner. Make haste!"

Tom took hold of the shoulders, Dick grasped the feet, and between them they dragged Abomey, who was a heavy man, to the disused well.

They let him down head first. He fell with a thud, and a lot of disturbed rubbish and vegetation tumbled on the top of him.

"So much for Abomey," exclaimed Peeping Tom. "Now for the king."

They started off for the king's pavilion, thinking that their deed had been unobserved.

In this belief they were mistaken.

Behind some bushes, prying eyes had been watching them dispose of the dead body.

The eyes were those of the priest, Nola.

His face was puckered up into an expression of mingled rage and pleasure. The former passion was excited by the death of his friend; the latter, by the discovery of his murderers and his place of burial.

CHAPTER X.

NOLA IS BAFFLED—HARRY IS CAPTURED AND CONDEMNED TO BE CAST INTO THE DEN OF LIONS—A REMARKABLE OCCURRENCE.

UNAWARE that Nola was following them at a distance, the spies walked quickly to the pavilion of the king.

They were in high spirits.

With much more rapidity than they had dared to hope, they had discovered Harry Rawlings' hiding-place in the forest.

"It seems a shame to give the poor beggar up," remarked Dick, whose conscience pricked him a little, which was certainly an unusual occurrence.

"I don't see it," replied Peeping Tom. "He is our enemy. You should always get rid of enemies."

"He will have to marry the princess, or his head will be cut off," added Knowall Dick.

"I don't care what happens to him," said Tom, callously. "Why should you be so tender-hearted all at once? If we don't give Harry up, we shall get in for it. I call it a piece of luck to have got it all out of Bonny."

Tom's reasoning was unanswerable, and Dick held his tongue.

They found the king seated on a divan, made of the skins of wild beasts. Two attendants only were with him, and they were handing him various ripe and luscious fruits on plates of pure gold.

"Well," exclaimed King Makolo, "have you come, O Tom the Peeper and Dick the Knower, to tell me where the white slave has gone?"

"Yes, sun of the world, and light of the universe," replied Peeping Tom. "We have consulted the spirits, and rubbed our eyes with the ointment of knowledge."

"What is that?"

"I must not tell you, because it is our secret."

"Truly spoken. I am wrong to ask," said King Makolo. "It is enough for me to hear you talk. Speak."

Tom nodded to Dick as if he wanted him to begin.

Taking the hint, Dick exclaimed—

"I know that in the night, when all was still in the city, the white slave cut his way out of the cage."

"How?"

"With a knife."

"Who gave it to him?"

"An Ashantee threw it at him," answered Knowall Dick. "He then left the city unobserved, and I know that he ran across the plain towards the great forest. That is all."

Peeping Tom shaded his eyes with his hands, and looked steadily at nothing in particular.

The king appeared deeply interested.

"What can you see, O Tom the Peeper?" he asked.

"I see, O conqueror of the lions and the elephants," replied Tom, "the white slave who has insulted your illustrious daughter. He is alone in the boundless forest.

"I see close to him a pool or lake, at which elephants come down to drink. Tall, aged trees, with big vine-covered trunks, are all around."

King Makolo held up his hand.

"It is enough," he exclaimed. "That is the Elephant's Pool, where the Ashantees shoot the monarchs of the forest for their ivory tusks. You shall each have a chain of gold. Truly, it is wonderful! Some day you might teach me your art."

"Impossible!" rejoined Peeping Tom. "I should be very glad to do so, but it is a gift from the spirits."

"How is it done?"

"I cannot tell you. It comes natural."

With this enigmatical answer the king was obliged to be content, though his curious longing was far from being satisfied.

Clapping his hands, the king waited until a messenger, who was always in waiting, entered the pavilion.

In a few words, he ordered him to send the general of his army with a dozen soldiers.

When this functionary arrived, he told him where to find Harry, to use all dispatch, and bring him alive to the palace.

The soldiers went off at the double.

Poor Harry's fate was settled by the cunning of the spies, and the treachery of Bonny.

He was in blissful unconsciousness of what had happened.

If he had known or suspected, he would have plunged deeper into the forest, braving all its perils, like a true English boy, for the sake of liberty.

King Makolo was very much pleased with the spies. He was in a better temper than usual, for his supply of rum had given out, and he was daily expecting a caravan from Cape Coast Castle to bring him some more.

When he was able to indulge his appetite for drink, he became sullen, violent, and very cruel, shedding blood wantonly.

Through his intercourse with Europeans he had a thin veneer of civilisation over him, but the savage was always there.

The brute instinct was ready at any moment to assert itself.

While the king was conversing with the spies, Nola made his appearance.

"What do you want?" asked King Makolo.

"To bask in the sunshine of my ruler's presence," replied Nola.

"I did not send for you—in fact, I don't think there is anything I have to say to you."

"Will your majesty deign to listen to me?"

"About what?"

"I have a complaint to make to your high mightiness."

"Will not some other time do?"

"The blood of one whom you formerly respected and placed high in your councils and confidence is crying for vengeance."

"Ha! say you so? Who is it?" cried the king.

"Abomey. He is dead—murdered."

"By whom?"

Nola pointed to the spies, who turned pale.

For a moment they glanced nervously at each other.

Then they boldly confronted their venomous accuser, whose villainous countenance showed to what extent he hated them.

"'GOOD HEAVENS!' CRIED BLUNT, 'THIS IS AWFUL. THEY ARE DEAD!'"

"Those two fell upon him," Nola exclaimed. "I saw them knock him to the ground with a club, and when they killed him they threw him down an old disused well. Abomey is dead. Never again will he utter words of wisdom in the Council Chamber."

"If he did not deserve death you should have endeavoured to save him; but there must be more in this than appears on the surface. Tom the Peeper, Dick the Knower, I will hear you. The priest Nola has accused you. What have you to say?"

"It is true," replied Peeping Tom.

"Why did you slay Abomey?"

"Because of your majesty. Our attachment to your person is so great. Our sense of favour received is only equalled by our sense of favour to come. We want to deserve your great kindness."

"What does this mean?"

"It means that Abomey was plotting to assassinate you and place himself on the throne."

The king sprang to his feet, his face convulsed with rage.

"You saw this?—you knew this?" he cried.

"Do we not see and know all?" asked Peeping Tom.

"Yes, there is no doubt of it. With whom was Abomey plotting?" asked King Makolo.

"It was with Nola, his friend and supporter," Tom replied, with unblushing effrontery. "Nola, the snake in the grass, the lion in a sheep's skin, who wishes you dead. He cannot deny it. Look at his guilty face. I denounce him as a bloodthirsty traitor!"

"And I endorse what you say," added Knowall Dick.

The effect of this accusation on Nola was very remarkable.

It chanced to be the fact that since his disgrace, Abomey had, in the seclusion and privacy of the temple, been conspiring with the high priest.

He had been filled with a fierce desire and intention, which every day had become intensified, to take the life of Makolo.

His heart had panted for revenge.

Nola had entered into his plans, promising to support him, and they had even gone so far as to discreetly sound the general, with a view to getting the army on their side.

Nothing as yet had been fully determined on.

Owing to the wonderful things that the spies had done, Nola was fully persuaded that they had some superior fetish.

This fetish, whatever it was, enabled them to find out everything.

How else could they have told the king that he was conspiring against his life with Abomey?

Thoroughly frightened, he lost his presence of mind, and sank on his knees.

"Pardon! Mercy!" he exclaimed.

"Wretch!" said Makolo. "It is well that I have these white magicians round me. Your heart is laid bare."

"I was mad."

"Your madness would have resulted in my death," continued the king, severely. "Abomey has been properly punished. You shall share his fate. Ho, ho, guards!"

The bodyguard rushed into the pavilion at the call.

They seized Nola, by the king's orders, and bound him hand and foot.

The countenances of the spies beamed with delight while this operation was proceeding.

"I thought that Nola had got us that time," whispered Peeping Tom.

"The king will think more of us than ever," replied Knowall Dick, in the same tone.

Their remarks were cut short by the king ordering Nola to be placed upright against the door of the pavilion.

He called for a hammer and a nail, and, grasping the high priest's right ear with his own hand, nailed it to the door-post.

The priest uttered the most doleful cries.

"Stay there," said Makolo, "until I have consulted with Tom the Peeper and Dick the Knower as to what your fate shall be."

"Mercy!" cried Nola.

"I can give you none!"

"Have I not always brought rain on the earth when you and your people wanted it?"

"Why did you conspire with that hound, Abomey?"

"Have I not always given you victory over the other tribes?"

"Why did you want to kill me?"

"Pardon, O most mighty king!" pleaded Nola. "Spare me, and blessings shall fall on you like the dews from heaven!"

"Too late! The night everlasting has come for you!"

"Let me live to make your reign prosperous."

King Makolo turned from him in the coldest and most indifferent manner, and reclining again on the skins, bade the spies sit down by him.

It was now his breakfast time.

Slaves brought in various dishes, of which the spies were invited to partake. This was a great honour, and they appreciated it.

The unfortunate Nola writhed in anguish of body and mind, with his ear nailed to the door-post.

He could have put up with that; but it was the uncertainty of his fate that tortured his restless mind.

"We have various ways of putting traitors to death!" said King Makolo. "Nola must die! How would you like to see him killed? In the gardens of the palace I have a lions' den. It contains five splendid lions. They will tear him to pieces in a few minutes."

"That is more interesting than cutting his head off!" replied Peeping Tom.

"I should like to see the animals fed," observed Knowall Dick.

"There is another way," continued Makolo. "In another part of the royal garden is a pit, which is the resort of venomous reptiles. If you like I will fling him into the snake pit."

"That is a novel idea. Anything else?" asked Tom.

"We can tie him to a stake, smear him with honey, and let the flies sting him to death. We can bury him up to the neck in the ground. We can slice him to pieces with sharp knives, or put a rock on his chest till he cannot draw any more breath; or we can flog him to death with knotted whips. Which would you like best?"

"I think I would give him to the snakes," said Knowall Dick.

"The serpents are kept for the purpose of killing public offenders," answered the king. "The hole is deep; they cannot get out. My slaves have caught them, and put them there. They are fed regularly."

"Let the snakes have him!" exclaimed Peeping Tom. "He may as well die that way as any other."

"His life is forfeited! He has confessed his villainy, which you exposed!"

"Don't say anything about that; we will always watch over your welfare," replied Peeping Tom.

"I am grateful," said King Makolo. "You two shall be my adopted sons. My daughter, Matabele, will give her white slave to the lions when he is brought back from the Elephant Pool. You, Tom the Peeper, shall marry my daughter."

"What!" cried Tom.

"Do you object?"

"Oh, no," replied Peeping Tom, recovering from the shock. "I was not prepared for it; in fact, it is too much honour—I am not worthy of it."

"Say no more. I will raise you to a high dignity, and I will find someone of my family for Dick the Knower."

"Oh, Lor'!" cried Dick.

"You are lowly now, but you shall be exalted," continued the king. "I have a sister, her name is Kanoneka. She shall be your wife."

Knowall Dick made a comical grimace.

"You are too kind," he murmured.

"It is settled. I will have you both in the family. You will be looked after. Your wives will see that you do not run away like Harry."

The prospect before them was a very disagreeable one.

Both the spies wished that they were in the forest with Harry rather than in the city to face what lay in store for them.

"I think," said Makolo, after a pause, "we will dispose of this false priest without any further delay. He shall go to the snakes."

Rising, he sent for a personage who performed the functions of a town-crier.

He was told to go into the streets of the city and proclaim, to the beating of a gong, that a plot had been discovered.

Its object was the assassination of the king.

Abomey, who was at the head of it, had been killed, and his accomplice, Nola, was to be at once thrown into the pit of snakes.

All citizens were to go into their houses for the space of two hours and shut their doors.

Nola was released from the door in a rough and ready fashion, by having his ear forcibly torn from the nail.

He was then dragged to the place of execution.

Fear had given place to a stony despair. He no longer trembled or begged for mercy, because he saw that it was useless.

He seemed prepared to meet his fate.

Nothing could save him.

Only half-a-dozen soldiers, the executioner who had him in charge, the king, and the spies accompanied the culprit to the pit.

Nola chaunted a kind of hymn or death song.

When the side of the pit was reached, the snakes could be seen in dozens, and of all sizes, lying in the dust and sand.

A few stones thrown amongst them caused them to glide about and hiss in a terrifying manner.

The executioner cut the bonds which bound Nola, and placed a long rope under his arms.

Then the wretched victim was slowly lowered into the dismal pit.

It was about fifteen feet deep.

No sooner did his feet touch the bottom than he trod on a snake, which coiled and struck him. He uttered a fearful cry.

In an instant a dozen poisonous reptiles were biting him, and moaning like a dog in pain, he fell on his knees.

For a few minutes he fought madly, desperately with his assailants, in a kind of frenzy.

Then he sank on his back, quivering.

The serpents had implanted poison enough in his veins to kill a hundred men.

Gradually his body began to swell.

The spies looked on, fascinated with horror.

This dreadful fate might be theirs any day, in this country of tortures and swift executions.

There was no trial by jury, no appeal to a higher tribunal.

It was the king's word that settled the question of life or death, for any offence, whether grave or trivial.

"Thus perish all the enemies of Makolo," said the king, sententiously.

Peeping Tom and Knowall Dick turned away with a sickening feeling.

"We will go and see the lions now," added the king. "My daughter, Matabele, will feed them."

"When?" asked Peeping Tom.

"As soon as the general returns with the white slave, Harry. The lions are hers. If anyone offends her, she always feeds her lions with them."

This declaration caused another thrill of horror to run through the spies' veins.

A short walk brought them to an iron cage, built by the side of a rock.

In this cage were five splendid lions.

An iron door was secured by a chain. This gave ingress and egress. The lion-tamer and feeder alone dared to enter the cage.

When he did, he was armed with an iron bar.

The keeper of the lions was a very important personage, for he could make the animals perform a number of antics.

He frequently gave a performance of his skill when the king entertained visitors from other countries.

For anyone else to enter the den would have been sudden death.

The lions were lying down in the shade produced by some trees planted for the especial purpose, and which overhung their den.

All at once the heat had become intense. No wind blew; a solemn hush was over all.

With their tongues hanging out of their mouths, the noble animals were panting for breath.

Even the birds sat motionless on the branches of the trees, and forgot to sing.

As the king had not brought his fly-flappers or his umbrella-men with him, he was glad to get back to his pavilion.

He thanked the spies for disclosing the plot against his life, and dismissed them to their house, assuring them that they should be summoned in time to see the execution of Harry.

They retired after assuring him that he was the greatest monarch the world ever saw; the personification of all virtues, and the incarnation of heavenly justice.

When they were alone in their house, they sat down and looked hard at one another.

"The king is getting too fond of us," remarked Peeping Tom.

"It's nice to be a white slave," replied Knowall Dick, with a dismal grin.

"I daresay the old fellow is all right when you know him, but you've got to know him first," continued Tom. "Isn't it wonderful the way he gets rid of people he doesn't like."

"My dear fellow," said Knowall Dick, "life is worth nothing in this charming country."

"I don't want to marry his daughter."

"His sweet old sister has no attraction for me."

"What on earth are we to do to get out of it?" asked Peeping Tom. "He will marry us as safe as houses if we don't do something."

"Let me think what we can do to avert the impending doom," said Knowall Dick, thoughtfully.

They were sitting on the ground, as usual, in that chairless land.

Suddenly the earth heaved so violently as to shake them; the wooden walls rocked and a rush of wind hissed through the hut.

Several wide cracks were visible in the earthen floor after this earth-trembling.

"Hallo!" cried Peeping Tom, whose head knocked against Dick's. "What are you up to now?"

"I didn't do anything," was the reply.

"None of your larks."

"I swear I never moved," said Knowall Dick.

"Then it was a shock of earthquake. Just what we might expect in this lovely climate, and you can depend we shall have a few more."

"If so, we must take our chance; but, I say—"

"What?"

"I've got an idea. Let us go and tell the king that if he honours us too much something dreadful will happen."

"Good!" exclaimed Peeping Tom. "I see your drift."

"If he insists upon our marrying his distinguished relatives there will be a catastrophe."

"Dick, you are a genius. We will seek his majesty at once."

"Yes, at once, or we shall be too late. The old fool can't have gone to sleep yet."

"That depends upon how much rum he has imbibed. If he is asleep, we'll wake the old fraud up."

They ventured to go to the pavilion, although it was well-known that Makolo was not accessible at all hours.

Although the heat continued as intense as ever, no further shock of earthquake occurred.

The one that had been felt was a warning of what might happen.

There was evidently danger in the air, which might at any moment culminate in a catastrophe.

They found the king in a bad temper. News had been brought him that the people were not at all pleased when they heard of the death of Nola.

He had been a popular priest, and was considered a great rain-maker. This was an important consideration in Ashantee, where rain does not fall sometimes for months together, and the crops suffer.

Also, during his priesthood, the nation had been very lucky in battle, never once suffering defeat.

This was all put down to his influence with the spirits, who are supposed by the Ashantees to rule all earthly affairs.

There was a difficulty in finding a suitable and worthy successor to him.

It was clear to King Makolo's mind that the discontent was widespread, and he had sent for his prime minister—appointed in Abomey's place—his treasurer, and the captain of his bodyguard.

"I am busy!" he exclaimed, waving his hand impatiently when the spies appeared.

"A few words, O most transcendant of princes," cried Peeping Tom.

"Speak quickly; I want to be alone with my minister."

"We have received a warning," continued Tom. "The spirit who gives me the power of seeing things has spoken to me."

"Ha! What has it said?" asked the king.

Directly spirits were mentioned, his superstitious mind was on the alert.

"It will not be well for me and Dick the Knower to marry the Princess Matabele and the Lady Kanoneka; they are too high for us."

"If it is my will, it must not be gainsaid. I *will* have the marriages—yes, I insist upon it."

"Then a great calamity will fall upon those in the palace and in the city," replied Peeping Tom, with the air of a seer.

"How is that?"

"I see the earth tremble; the houses fall; the people die."

"It is false. You know not of what you talk. I will not give way through silly fear," shouted King Makolo, angrily.

He was getting excited.

The spies thought it prudent to withdraw.

Peeping Tom made a low bow, as did Knowall Dick.

"We have done our duty, O spice of the earth and sky!" exclaimed Tom. "You are now responsible for what may happen."

"The marriages shall take place this evening; I have sworn it," roared the king. "What! am I dirt, to be trodden under foot? Begone!"

They retired backwards until they got outside the pavilion, when they walked to their house.

They had performed a stroke of business, and if the shock of earthquake which they expected did occur, the king would no doubt be so frightened that he would rescind his determination respecting the marriages.

The heat increased momentarily, a sulphurous smell pervaded the air, and low rumblings of thunder were audible at intervals.

The spies reclined on their beds, awaiting events.

Some hours passed, but there was no repetition of the earth-tremblings which had startled them in the morning.

All at once the sound of drums and horns broke the oppressive silence.

Peeping Tom shook off his drowsiness.

"Wake up, Dick!" he cried.

"What is it?" asked Knowall Dick, gaping. "Can't you see it's my sleeping time?"

"The guards have come back with Harry, I expect."

"Poor beggar! The lions will soon have a feast."

"Serve him right," replied Tom, heartlessly.

"Which would you choose if it came to the pinch?"

"What do you mean?"

"The snake pit or the lion's den."

"Neither, thank you," answered Peeping Tom. "Don't talk about it, the very idea makes my flesh creep."

"Shall you go to—to the execution?" enquired Dick.

"Of course. I wouldn't miss it for the world. I wonder how Harry will stand it?"

"Like a brick. He's got plenty of pluck."

"We shall see. I know it would make me say my prayers, if my teeth did not chatter too much."

They emerged from the house. The king, his officers, the ladies of the Court were thronging towards the den of lions.

Princess Matabele had already been informed of the probable capture of Harry.

This unamiable savage had intimated to the king her intention of at once giving the prisoner to the beasts.

The soldiers were ordered to go to the den, and they did so, dragging Harry with them, more dead than alive.

They had found him asleep by the Elephant Pool, and made him captive without his being able to strike a blow.

Exhausted by the heat and fatigue of the journey, he looked a perfect wreck.

Still there was a defiant air about him.

Whatever his fate might be, it was clear that he meant to die like a true English boy.

As the spies wended their way to the lions' den, they felt their position acutely.

It was through them that Harry had been caught, and his bold bid for freedom nipped in the bud.

His cruel death would not be a pleasant thing for them to look back upon in after years, should their own lives be spared.

He was to be torn limb from limb by the hungry lions.

Horrible as the spectacle would be, they could not keep away.

The palace officials and high personages appeared to be making a half-holiday of it.

Nearly a hundred had flocked to the spot, and were pushing and crowding to secure good places to see the sight.

The queen mother, her daughter, the king, and the Princess Kanoneka were provided with front places.

Behind them stood the great officers of State, then the soldiers, and behind them, grouped in a semi-circle, were the members of the Court.

The executioner took possession of Harry, whom he led, unbound, to the den, at the door of which the lion-keeper was standing.

Every drop of blood seemed to have left Harry's face, and, at intervals, an uncontrollable shudder convulsed him.

This was the result of weakness and exposure rather than of fear.

Directly the lions saw the prisoner, they set up a loud roar.

Instinct and experience told them that there was a feast in store for them.

This was not the first time by a good many that they had been fed on human flesh.

The noble-looking brutes paced their cage with impatient strides.

No overture was made to Harry by Matabele.

Her face bore nothing on it but fierce, uncompromising hatred.

She had been scorned, and her woman's nature was burning for a dire revenge.

The lion-tamer let the chain fall with a clank, the door opened, and the executioner pushed the victim inside, readjusting the chain.

Expectation was now at a high pitch.

Every neck was craned forward to get a good view.

The lions were at one end of the cage, Harry leant his back against the rails at the opposite extremity.

His lips moved, as if in prayer, for a moment, then he smiled contemptuously.

The lions, contrary to general expectation, did not seem to be in a hurry to rush upon their victim.

All at once they had become tame and subdued.

Their tails did not wag; their eyes no longer sparkled truculently; their tongues lolled out of their mouths.

Of a sudden, a tremendous clap of thunder was heard overhead, followed by another and another.

The lightning, in a zigzag manner, ran along the ground.

With a hideous rumbling noise, the rock against which the cage was built was split asunder.

The ground heaved, and parted in great cracks.

Again the rock split, and the den fell to pieces.

The people were at first too frightened to move.

Seeing that they were free, the lions paid no attention to Harry, but dashed among the spectators, who scattered and fled in all directions.

Piercing shrieks arose on all sides.

The predicted earthquake had come, and at an opportune time for Harry.

Foremost among the fugitives was the king, who, however, had not gone far before his subjects knocked him down and trampled on him, in their headlong flight.

The princesses and the queen mother did not fare much better.

Peeping Tom and Knowall Dick climbed into the branches of a tree, where they thought they would be safe.

From this altitude they could watch everything.

Harry Rawlings had been saved from a cruel and violent death by a direct interposition of Providence.

No one paid the slightest attention to him now.

They were all anxious to get away from the lions, and fearful that another shock of earthquake might engulf them.

These convulsions of Nature had, on several occasions, produced fearful havoc in Ashantee.

The lions were as much frightened as the people. They did not attack anybody. Getting under the shelter of shrubs and bushes, they cowered and waited.

Harry's only idea was to make his escape.

He had nothing to expect from the clemency of the princess or from the mercy of the king. The spies hated him, and would in no way protect him. Bonny had undoubtedly betrayed him.

At that moment he was absolutely without friends.

He was determined to once more seek the forest.

A thousand times better the forest with its dangers, than the town. The guards had all fled. No one tried to stop him.

When he reached the gate, which led from the palace grounds into the city, a lion was crouching in the passage-way.

Its tongue hanging out, and it was panting with fear.

Harry passed by it without its making any effort to molest him.

Just then another shock of earthquake took place.

It was severely felt in the town.

Harry saw several houses overthrown, and was cast on his hands and knees.

In several parts smoke began to arise, showing that some of the houses had taken fire.

There was danger of a general conflagration. This was all in his favour.

While the forces of Nature were at work, the king's myrmidons would have no time to attend to him.

Men and women thronged the streets, afraid to stay indoors.

They held their idols in their hands, and prayed to them.

Most of them attributed the catastrophe to the death of Nola, and loud murmurs arose against the king.

They offered no violence to Harry.

On turning the corner, he came to the ruins of a house, and saw a boy lying under a beam of wood, groaning heavily.

He stooped and extricated him.

For anyone else he would have done the same.

To his astonishment he saw it was Bonny, fearfully crushed about the body and face.

"Oh, Massa Harry," he moaned. "I'm dying."

"I hope not. This is a fearful time, though, for everyone."

"Massa Harry, I didn't mean to betray you. Tom the Peeper and Dick the Knower get it all out ob me about you."

"Never mind; I forgive you."

"Don' go. Do somet'ing for me," pleaded Bonny.

"I really cannot," said Harry. "Good-bye."

He could not afford any more time to talk to him. His only chance of safety was in flight, and he went on.

He had scarcely stirred a dozen yards from the spot, when that portion of the house left standing fell with a crash.

Bonny was completely buried beneath the *débris*.

This time there was no chance of his being extricated alive, and Harry was obliged to admit that he had escaped narrowly.

No one made any effort to stop him, or accosted him in any way, until he reached a spot called the Square of the Temple.

It was here that the priests had their habitation. They were not a numerous body, consisting only of one head-priest and six assistants. All lived in the temple.

No one was allowed inside, except the king and his principal officers, who four times a year visited the Hall of the Sacred Fire.

This fire was never allowed to go out. It had been kept alight night and day ever since the founding of the city, which was wrapped in the shadows of the long long-ago.

A little way beyond the Square of the Temple was the Gate of Sunrise.

It was to this Harry wanted to get.

The city was walled, and had two gates—one the Gate of Sunrise, the other the Gate of Sunset.

Many people were pouring along the streets towards the Gate of Sunrise, hoping to find safety on the sandy plain.

Houses were falling on all sides of them, and they feared they would be involved in one common ruin.

Suddenly a man, who wore a white linen tunic round his body, beckoned to Harry to approach him.

He was standing on the steps which d up to the door of the temple.

His attire indicated that he was one of the priests.

"Ola!" he cried. "Approach! I would speak to thee."

With some trepidation Harry did as he was requested.

"Who are you, and what do you want of me?" he asked.

"I am El Obed, the brother of Nola, whom the king put to death in the pit of serpents."

"What has that to do with me?"

"Be patient and silent," replied El Obed. "I was in the royal gardens when you were given to the lions. I saw you in their den. You smiled. You did not once tremble, for

"HA! DO YOU DEFY ME?' CRIED THE PRINCE."

you knew you were safe. You willed that the earth should shake and the houses fall, and so it came to pass."

Harry nodded his head.

He could see that the priest believed that he was possessed of some mysterious power, and he did not undeceive him.

"How do you do it?" continued El Obed.

"That is a secret I cannot divulge,"

"Can you stop the earth trembling?"

"Yes. There shall be no more. It is all over," said Harry, whose common sense told him that the seismic wave had gone on.

While he was talking, two priests had slipped out of the temple by a side door.

They got to the back of Harry without being perceived by him.

All at once they seized him from behind, and pinioned his arms.

He was a helpless captive.

Strong arms forced him towards the temple. What was in store for him now?

CHAPTER XI.

IN THE TEMPLE—THE FETISH—THE HALL OF SACRED FIRE—A STRANGE MEETING.

A CRUEL smile came over the thick lips of El Obed.

He motioned his assistants to bring their prisoner into the temple.

Almost before he could realize his situation Harry found himself in a large vaulted room, lighted by narrow windows cut in the walls.

Some wooden idols were placed in various parts of the chamber. The presence of cups and plates on a table made the room look like a refectory. A passage led to some inner rooms, but these did not concern the captive at present.

Harry was forced into a chair; the assistant priests closed the door and withdrew along the passage.

Harry was left alone with the wily El Obed who had so cleverly outwitted him.

He bit his lips with vexation to think that he had been circumvented.

If he had pressed on without stopping to talk, he might by that time have been on his way to the forest.

Now he had nothing before him but death or a long, hopeless captivity.

The priest carelessly threw open his robe, disclosing a belt in which were a knife and a large old-fashioned pistol.

Perhaps this was intended as a hint that resistance would be useless.

"Why have you done this? I have worked you no harm," exclaimed Harry.

"I want an assistant in the temple. You can produce wonderful effects. Tell me how you do it."

Harry was in a very embarrassing position. The priest fancied he could control the hidden forces of Nature. How was he to reply?

The more he seemed reluctant to speak, the more he was pressed to do so.

"Have you a god like that?" asked El Obed, pointing to an idol. "Where is your fetish?"

A happy thought struck Harry.

On board the ship which had brought Harry out had been a sailor, who, in return for some act of kindness, had made him a present.

This was a tobacco stopper, representing Lord Nelson, cast in brass.

He held it up.

"This is my fetish," he said. "I will confess it to you, though nobody else knows anything about it."

The credulity of the priest was easily imposed upon.

"Ha!" he exclaimed, gazing in awe at the brass effigy. "Will it do all you ask of it?"

"Well, not all, but nearly all," replied Harry.

He did not like to make the fetish appear too powerful.

"Will it tell you what you desire to know?"

"Oh, yes, It speaks to me sometimes, but not always," said Harry, putting it to his ear.

"What is it saying now?" demanded El Obed, eagerly.

"It says that the panic in the city is at an end; there is no more earthquake; the lions have been killed; many people are crushed to death; the king thinks I am dead; you are not to give me up, but to take care of me and treat me well for half a moon, then you must let me go to the coast. Do this, and you will prosper."

"Will the king make me chief priest in the place of Nola?"

"He will do so, and make you presents. Makolo will take you to his heart; a collar of gold shall encircle your neck."

"Good! I like to hear that."

"You shall be great and powerful."

"Proceed—tell me more," cried El Obed.

"I cannot at present," rejoined Harry.

For awhile the crafty and ambitious priest hesitated.

Harry still held the brass image to his ear.

"You must know," began El Obed, "that Nola was conspiring with General Sangara, the head of the army."

"What for?"

"To dethrone the king and kill all his family, except the king's son, who is a boy. The people hate Makolo. Sangara will persist in his plot. Now, the question is, which side shall I have luck in taking?"

"You mean that of the general or the king?"

El Obed intimated assent.

For a brief space Harry remained silent, pretending to listen to the fetish, but in reality to gain time to think.

He had heard the Princess Matabele remark that the general was so powerful, that she was surprised the king did not cut off his head.

It was common talk in the palace that if an insurrection broke out the guards would run away.

Everyone was afraid of Sangara.

Going on this idea, and feeling sure that a rebellion would break out soon, in which the general would be successful, he resolved to advise the priest to embrace the cause of the popular leader.

"Well, has the fetish spoken?" queried El Obed.

He thought his fate depended upon the answer.

"My fetish tells me," rejoined Harry, weighing his words carefully, "that it will be best for you to join Sangara, but you must not be in too great a hurry to act."

"How long must I wait?"

"Half a moon."

"And what then?" inquired El Obed, breathlessly.

"Sangara will be lucky in his revolt. During the interval, as I said before, the king will honour you."

"He killed Nola. You are sure he will not kill me?"

"Make your mind easy on that score."

"Very good, if everything happens as you have predicted, and I have no reason to doubt it, for I mean to follow your advice."

"And join in Sangara's rebellion?" queried Harry.

"Yes. I will not be forgetful of you. What is your heart's desire?"

"To get to the coast and return to my own country."

"What a strange idea. Where can you live better than in this city? Is it not the first in the world?"

"The last, you mean," said Harry.

"Is it possible that there is a city where you can enjoy life more than you can here?"

"I should rather think so."

"That is extraordinary," remarked El Obed, reflectively, "though I have heard the same story before, and could not believe it."

"From whom?" inquired Harry.

"A slave we have in the caves to attend to the sacred fire, which is never allowed to go out night or day."

"Of what use is it?"

"We, the priests, offer up human sacrifices at times."

"Alive?" cried Harry, in horror.

"Yes. We burn the living before the king and his officers. This is when the idols are in a bad humour, and we are beaten in war, or can get no rain," answered the priest.

"It must be a horrible scene to witness," replied Harry; "but let me ask who is your slave?"

"He calls himself an Englishman. It is from him that I have learnt to speak your language. He was captured by the great slave-trader, Bonna, and sold to King Makolo, who made him a present to Nola."

"I should like to see him."

"That you can easily do, and you can stay with him while you are here. If all goes right, and Sangara beats King Makolo, I will send you with an escort to the coast. I will see General Sangara to-night. You I will conduct to the Hall of the Sacred Fire, which shall be your home."

Saying this, El Obed conducted his captive into the passage, where he lighted an oil lamp, and told him to follow.

Harry had succeeded better than he had expected.

All now depended on the success of the rebellion.

If the general was strong enough to depose the king, all would be well, for he had no reason to doubt the good faith of El Obed.

For the time everything was in a state of uncertainty; but he hoped for the best.

Perhaps he was better off in the caves of the temple than fighting his way through the forest alone and unaided, amidst wild beasts and serpents.

He wondered how this poor countryman of his had contrived to exist as the slave of the priests, shut up in the sandstone caves, attending to the sacred fire.

What a terrible life his must have been.

Threading several winding passages,

ascending and descending short flights of steps, they at length came to the Hall of the Sacred Fire.

It was a spacious vault dug out of the friable stone, open at the top to a slight extent to let out the smoke which arose from the wood and charcoal of which the fire was composed.

It was not a large fire; on the contrary, it burned within the compass of four stones placed so as to form a square.

Only when living human sacrifices were offered up was it enlarged.

The white slave's duty was to keep it burning night and day.

A man, who seemed to have grown prematurely old, for his face and body were thin, his hair and beard long and white, reclined in a corner on some grass, which served him as a bed.

For years he had not seen the flowers, or heard the birds sing. His had been a hateful, solitary confinement.

He had not enjoyed the solace of work which is given to a convict, for work keeps the body in condition, and prevents the brain from going mad.

"Englishman," cried El Obed, "I have brought you a companion."

Then he left the two together.

The slave of the sacred fire listlessly turned his head, and slowly rose to his feet.

He looked sorrowfully at Harry.

"Heaven help you!" he exclaimed. "Who are you? Where are you from? How did you come here?"

"I am from England," replied Harry. "The slave-dealers brought me here. I am to share your solitude for a time."

"For life, you mean."

"No. I have hopes that my captivity will not be of long duration, and if I am liberated, I will see that you go with me."

"Vain hope," said the old man. "I thought so once. I dreamed of going back to Three Points. I was a prosperous merchant there, but I came into the interior to buy ivory and dust from King Makolo, and was treacherously made a prisoner."

"You came from Three Points!" said Harry. "So did I."

"I was flourishing. No man could do a better business. Fortunately the negroes could not get my money. That is all banked at Cape Coast Castle."

"What is your name?"

"Robert Spencer," was the reply.

This response fairly astonished Harry, who, for a brief space, could not speak.

He saw in a moment that he had, by the merest accident, discovered the long-lost uncle of his friend Jack.

Bill Blunt had stated that the missing man had made a journey up country, and had not been heard of afterwards.

Here was an extraordinary coincidence.

"My dear friend," he cried, "it was to see you that I came to Africa with your brother and nephew."

It was now the old man's turn to be astonished.

"I have but one brother, if he be alive now," he answered.

"The Spencers, of Clare, in the county of Suffolk, I am talking about," said Harry.

"That is the family I belong to!" exclaimed the old man, showing signs of extreme agitation, "but I am in ignorance of your meaning."

"I will soon make it all clear."

"For heaven's sake, explain!"

Harry did so. It took him a long time to make matters clear, for the story was a complicated one.

At last, Robert Spencer understood how his brother had been induced to leave England and come to Africa.

What had happened since then Harry, of course, could not tell him.

"May heaven send us deliverance," said Robert Spencer.

"If the revolt against the king is successful, I will not leave here without you," replied Harry.

Spencer seized his hand.

"Boy," he cried, "I am rich—much richer than people think. My money is in an old-established bank at Cape Coast. No one can take it from me. I only want my liberty to claim it, and I will reward you."

"Never mind that."

"If you will not accept my money, heaven will reward you."

"If I can join Jack, recover your niece, marry her, and come into my own, I shall be satisfied," said Harry.

"A great load is taken off my mind; hope dawns once more in my breast. My prayers have been heard, at last," replied Robert Spencer.

A priest now came into the hall with a tray of provisions, which were ample in quantity.

That evening was a cheerful one for the captives. There was no further shocks of earthquake, and all promised well.

Still their ultimate freedom was not a certainty.

There is many a slip betwixt the cup and the lip.

CHAPTER XII.

LIFE AT THREE POINTS—NAMAQUA, THE RUNNER, ARRIVES—HE BRINGS NEWS FROM ASHANTEE.

THE heat on the coast was intense. Fortunately the earthquake wave had not touched Three Points.

No rain had fallen for several weeks, and the grass was burnt up, even the leaves on the trees drooped as if withered.

Squire Rawlings and Charlie were still in the power of those against whom they had plotted evil, and, each day, were set to work clearing the ground in the vicinity of Bill Blunt's residence, as a punishment for their villainy.

Jack was very happy in Marian's society.

As they rowed on the bay in a canoe or walked under the trees, they often talked of Harry.

If it had not been for the uncertainty as to his fate, they would have tried to get to Cape Coast Castle, and wait for a ship to take them back to England.

But this could not be done.

They were both true to Harry, and would not quit Three Points for the present.

Blunt was expecting a runner from the interior, named Namaqua.

This negro went from place to place, picking up the news, and retailing it.

He was well rewarded everywhere for his pains, because, in the absence of post and telegraph, he was the only news medium.

So Jack waited for the coming of Namaqua, hoping to hear from him some tidings of his lost friend.

One evening the brother and sister were sitting under a palm tree.

Not far off was Blunt's house, the "Trader's Rest," about which lounged some negroes who had been taking what old Bill quaintly called "suction."

Footsteps made them look up.

It was the Squire and Charlie being driven home from their work by Sambo, their negro overseer.

"Git up, dar," cried Sambo, cracking his whip.

Squire Rawlings stumbled from weakness and nearly fell.

The cruel lash of the whip descended on his back, eliciting a yell of pain, and he went forward, leaning on his son's arm.

As they passed Jack and Marian, Charlie bent a vindictive look on them.

"You enjoy this, Spencer," he remarked. "But my turn may come again. Your treatment has not killed us, and you dare not put us to death."

"You have had your day!" exclaimed Jack. "I fear you not."

"Beware!" hissed Charlie.

"Of what?"

"Retribution."

"That is the complaint you are suffering from," laughed Jack.

When they were gone Marian shivered, and clung to Jack's arm.

"It does seem hard to treat them so," she remarked.

"Why should I have any pity for those villains?" replied Jack. "Think of what they have done. You are too sentimental. What are punishments for?"

"For those who do wrong."

"That is enough. Squire Rawlings and his son would kill me if they could. What have they not done to separate you and Harry?"

Marian became silent.

She recognised the full force of his argument, and the justice of what he had been saying.

A dreamy feeling came over them in the warm still air. Jack let his arm slip round her waist, and her head sink on his shoulder.

"Darling," he whispered, "how I love you! Harry could not care for you more than I do."

"Will you always love me so?" she asked.

"To the last day I live. You are my only sister. I will die to protect you."

Then they were silent.

They were roused from their reverie by Blunt, who came into the palm-grove smoking his pipe, his honest face beaming with health and good nature.

"Sorry to disturb you, commodore!" he exclaimed.

They started, for he had approached noiselessly.

Jack withdrew his arm from Marian's waist, and her pretty face became suffused with blushes as her heart warned her that Blunt had something to tell her about Harry.

"Don't mention it, old man," said Jack. "Is supper ready? What have you got for our delectation?"

"You'll find something good. But that is not what I came to tell you."

"What is the matter? You look excited."

"The runner has come in, and was last at Ashantee."

Jack looked up anxiously.

"Has Namaqua any news?" he asked.

"Plenty of it. First of all, one of Her Majesty's gunboats is at Cape Coast Castle, and is coming here."

"Humph!" muttered Jack. "What shall we do with Squire Rawlings and Charlie?"

"I can easily keep them dark if you and the young lady want to be taken to Cape Coast," said Blunt.

"No," answered Jack; "I will not leave this continent without my friend Harry."

"I can tell you something about him."

"What? Speak!"

"There has been a terrible earthquake at Ashantee; lots of people killed; half the houses in ruins. It is supposed that one of the white slaves is dead."

"How do you know that this white slave has anything to do with Harry?"

"Bonna sold three to King Makolo. Two are called Tom the Peeper and Dick the Knower; the other one was given to the princess because he made music."

"Harry's whistle!" cried Jack.

"Precisely. Well, the Peeper and the Knower are in high favour with King Makolo, but the music-player is missing."

"That's bad news," said Jack. "Poor Harry!"

"Don't give way," continued Blunt. "Namaqua says the music-maker ran away once, and was recaptured. Maybe he has bolted again."

"I hope he may have done so. The king is a violent wretch, from all I have heard since I have been here."

"Spills blood like water," replied Blunt. "Come inside and question Namaqua yourselves."

They did so at once.

The runner replied to their questions in an intelligent and straightforward manner, but he persisted in his statement.

Harry had been missing since the earthquake, and had been searched for unsuccessfully.

They retired to rest much troubled in their minds about him.

Early in the morning they were roused by loud cries. Jack sprang out of bed to see what it was all about.

The exclamations proceeded from Sambo.

He was wringing his hands and dancing about in the yard.

"Oh, massa!" he cried, "it wasn't my fault."

"What was not?"

"They've got away."

"Who?"

"The prisoners," replied Sambo.

Jack Spencer looked blankly at the negro.

Squire Rawlings and his hopeful son had made their escape in the night.

CHAPTER XIII.

TRANQUILITY IS RESTORED IN ASHANTEE—THE KING CONSULTS THE SPIES—THEY HAVE A SURPRISE.

THE houses in King Makolo's capital being built chiefly of mud and laths, were almost as easily erected as they had been thrown down.

When the light-hearted populace recovered from the terror they had fallen into, they proceeded to do two things.

They buried their dead, and rebuilt their houses.

The king killed fifty of his own bullocks, and gave the meat away to his people.

He appointed El Obed as high priest, and expressed his intention of going in state to the sacred fire.

But this did not increase his popularity.

His subjects continued to murmur; discontent was brooding; the people wanted a change of government.

Hearing something of this from his prime minister, a crafty old knave, named Umballa, recently appointed in the room of Abomey, his majesty adopted heroic measures.

He caused ten people to be seized in each of the four quarters of the city.

This made a total of forty victims.

The executioner cut off their heads in the market place before a vast concourse of people.

It was then publicly announced that if any more grumbling or signs of discontent were heard, one hundred men and women would be buried alive.

This smothered the rebellion for a time, but the sparks smouldered, ready to burst into a blaze at any moment.

It only required General Sangara to raise the banner of revolt.

In vain the king ordered El Obed to make rain. It would not come. El Obed went to Harry and asked him to get rain out of his fetish.

Harry made an excuse that the fetish was in a bad temper, and the rain kept as far off as ever.

This was a very serious matter.

The corn, on which they depended for their sustenance during the coming year, was withering.

The wells were drying up.

Having restored order, as he thought, the king had now time to think of Harry.

The Princess Matabele wanted him to be found in order that she might wreak her vengeance upon him.

King Makolo sent for the two spies.

What was easier than to command them to inform him, within a given time, what had become of the missing slave?

Peeping Tom and Knowall Dick approached his majesty smiling.

In reality, they were somewhat nervous.

They guessed what they were wanted for, and they had been talking the matter over.

Only that morning they had decided upon a plan of action.

"O king, live for ever!" said Peeping Tom.

"Conqueror of the world, I salute thee!" exclaimed Knowall Dick.

"Have you anything new to tell me?" asked King Makolo. "What have you seen, Tom the Peeper?"

"Nothing very important. What do you want to know?"

"What has become of the music-maker whom we were going to feed to the lions?"

"He is dead!" answered Tom, boldly.

"Ha! you know that? Dick the Knower, you say so, too?"

"Yes, your mightiness; he will never trouble you more."

The king looked greatly astonished.

Tom and Dick thought they were perfectly safe in making the assertion.

It was the fourth day since the earthquake took place, and though search had been made in every direction, nothing had been seen or heard of Harry.

There was no doubt in their minds that he had, in the confusion that reigned paramount at the time, made his escape.

As he was not likely to return to the city, they had nothing to fear.

How did the music-maker die?" continued the king.

"The earth opened and swallowed him up," replied Peeping Tom.

"Is that true?"

"Oh, yes; I'll swear to that, because I saw it," replied Knowall Dick.

"Where?"

"Down at the bottom of the garden there was a big hole. I nearly fell into it myself."

"So did I!" exclaimed Peeping Tom. "The earth shut up again so rapidly that it took the heel of one of my shoes off."

"By the sun, moon and stars, this is a strange story," cried the king. "You, Tom the Peeper, and you, Dick the Knower, have witnessed the last of the music-maker. Now, I want to tell you that I have reconsidered my order that you should marry the princesses. We do not want the spirits to be angry again and shake the earth."

"We told you what would happen."

"You did; but my ears were shut to the words of wisdom," answered the king. "If anything is likely to happen, tell me at once."

"I think we are going to have a fall of rain," said Peeping Tom.

"I know we are," added Knowall Dick.

"How—why, Tom the Peeper?"

Tom shook his head.

"It comes to me from the spirits, O royal master!"

"Wonderful!" ejaculated Makolo.

Tom had hazarded this prediction because the wind had veered round suddenly in the night.

Low, dark clouds were drifting over the horizon, and the wind soughed and sighed in a peculiar manner through the trees.

In fact, there were all the indications of a change of weather.

Umballa, the minister, now appeared to talk of some matter of State.

He had chosen an unfortunate time, for the monarch was not in the humour for business.

His sable majesty had ordered an elephant to be got ready so that he might ride through the city.

He was going to the temple, according to custom, to throw a handful of gold dust on the sacred fire.

Umballa stooped to make an abject bow, and gave the king an opportunity of raising his foot.

A well-directed kick jerked him forward on to his hands and knees.

The unlucky minister got up as rapidly as possible, which gave the autocrat another opportunity.

He snatched up a musk-melon and threw it at the vizier, hitting him on the nose with such force as to knock him down.

Then the king took him by his waist-cloth and threw him out of the window.

Tom and Dick laughed immoderately, and clapped their hands.

"Did I not serve the dog right for disturbing us?" asked the king.

"Certainly," replied Peeping Tom.

"That is the idea," said Knowall Dick.

The king smiled benignantly.

"He is a dog," he replied. "He comes of a family of dogs; but I will teach him manners. Ha!"

Umballa's head appeared in the frame of the window, and his little eyes twinkled spitefully.

Close to the king's hand was the stem of a cabbage-leaf palm, which he used as a walking-stick.

On this occasion he employed it to hammer the minister's head.

Crack! A blow hit Umballa, who, with a yell, dropped out of sight.

Then all was as silent as the grave.

"I believe you have killed him, O light of the universe," exclaimed Peeping Tom.

"No," remarked Knowall Dick; "not quite so bad as that. He is only stunned."

"What if he dead?" asked Makolo, callously. "Plenty more fill his place. Was I wrong?"

"By no means," replied Tom. "The temptation was not to be resisted. You saw him bob up his head at the window, and, very properly, you gave him one for his nob."

The king went outside his pavilion to see the extent of the damage, and the spies followed him.

Umballa was on his back, breathing heavily.

King Makolo had a rough-and-ready way of doing things. He wanted to speak to his minister to ask him what he wanted, and he did not like to be kept waiting till he came to himself.

His news must have been important, or he would not have been so pertinacious.

Taking a knife he cut one of the veins in Umballa's arm. It quickly began to bleed, and thus relieved the head.

In a couple of minutes he recovered, and opened his eyes.

"Sun of suns," he exclaimed, "what am I but a worm in thy sight? Shall I tell you news?"

"Make haste about it. I am going on an elephant to the Hall of the Sacred Fire," answered Makolo.

"May your size increase, and your appetite always be good."

"Speak promptly."

"The chief of the Higazi is reported to be crossing the forest with two thousand men. He is but five days' journey from us. This is the news of two lion-hunters."

The face of Makolo lighted up with a fierce fire.

He was brave and dauntless, loving danger and fighting for their own sakes.

"I will see Sangara about that later," he exclaimed. "Let the chief of the Higazi come. He and his men will not go back again."

Finding that the king had done with them the spies went away, as they were always glad to be relieved of his presence.

He had such a capricious uncertain temper, that they never knew when they might get themselves disliked.

"I say," asked Peeping Tom, "do you remember where the temple is?"

"Very well," replied Knowall Dick. "It is just before you come to the Gate of Sunrise—the eastern gate, you know."

"And the temple is built out of a rock," continued Tom. "The top of the rock is grass covered. I've seen goats feeding there. Now I want to take in this show. Suppose we climb up to the top?"

"That is against the rules; no one is allowed up there. The black boys are put to death if they venture within the sacred precincts."

"But we are privileged. Let us risk it. The pleasure is greater when you are told you musn't do it."

Peeping Tom shared this feeling with Knowall Dick in a marked degree.

At home, if they saw "trespassers will be prosecuted," they could not keep off the premises; and they laughed at spring-guns steel traps, and bulldogs.

They were privileged to go wherever they liked, and passing the guard at the gate of the palace grounds, they walked to the temple.

The streets were full of people, who lined each side of the roadway.

Word had been sent to all parts of the city that King Makolo was going to sacrifice gold at the sacred fire.

This was to make rain and general prosperity.

The faces of the people did not wear a contented look.

Far from it.

They spoke in whispers. There was a restlessness about their movements, and men were to be seen going from place to place, speaking to certain other men, as if they were giving them instructions.

El Obed, the high priest, and Sangara were nowhere to be seen.

When the spies arrived at the temple they went to the rear, where the rock was easy enough to scale.

With the agility of mountain goats they found a foothold, and by the aid of small trees they soon got to the top.

The rock was not much higher than an ordinary house; but they had a good view of the city, the plain beyond, which grew grass for the cattle and corn for food, with the dark background of forest in the distance.

Drops of heavy thunder-rain fell now and again; but the storm which was threatening hesitated to burst.

"'I SURRENDER!' CRIED CHARLIE. 'I AM YOUR PRISONER!'"

No. 5.

Peeping Tom was not quite satisfied with the position he had taken up, and he moved a little farther on.

Suddenly his foot slipped in a hole which he had not perceived.

He lost his balance and pitched forward.

As he did so he caught hold of Knowall Dick, and they both fell together.

A wild cry broke from them.

They had not to fall very far, but the shock knocked the breath out of their bodies, and they were partially stunned.

It was fully five minutes before they opened their eyes and came to.

When they did recover, they saw a young and an old man bending over them, chafing their hands.

A fire near them was burning brightly, throwing off little or no smoke towards an aperture in the rocky roof.

This was the hole they had fallen through.

"Harry Rawlings!" said Peeping Tom.

"Oh, Lord!" groaned Knowall Dick.

They had accidentally fallen into the Hall of the Sacred Fire.

Harry was greatly disconcerted at the unexpected appearance of the spies.

He did not know that they had reasons of their own for not making his hiding-place known.

They had declared that he was dead.

How could they allow the king to know that he was living without admitting that they were impostors?

Here was a startling dilemma for them to be placed in.

"Where are we?" asked Peeping Tom, faintly.

"In the Hall of the Sacred Fire," replied Harry. "How—why did you come here? But I need not ask. You fellows go everywhere."

"The king is coming directly to sacrifice to the sacred fire," said Tom.

"If he finds you here you are lost," put in Dick.

"We climbed on the top of the cave to get a good view of the procession, and that is how we fell down this confounded hole," Tom continued.

"Say nothing about me," said Harry; "I am under the protection of the priests."

"What do you want us to do?" asked Tom.

"Leave me alone; that is all."

"Humph!" rejoined Tom. "It might be done. Oh, dear! My ribs, I think, are broken."

"My head aches frightfully, and my arm is out of joint," whined Knowall Dick.

"Shall I put you in an inner cave, where this old gentleman and I sleep, until the ceremony is over? If the priests find you here they will kill you."

"Can we get out afterwards?"

"I will see what I can do for you," added Harry, "though the coming here of a stranger is certain death if he be discovered."

"Protect us and we will do all we can for you," replied Peeping Tom. "I swear it."

"Yes; so do I," said Knowall Dick. "In an emergency like this, we must be friends."

"That is what I say," cried Harry. "Make common cause. Work together for our mutual interests."

The sound of drums and horns was heard without.

"Quick!" said Robert Spencer, "the king is coming. Remember, all our lives are at stake."

It was with difficulty that the spies rose to their feet, and then they trembled violently.

They would require a night's rest before they got over the shock of their fall.

Harry told them to follow him, and conducted them into an inner cave, in which were beds of grass and rushes.

He left them there, cautioning them to remain very quiet.

In a few minutes El Obed entered the hall.

Usually calm, impassive and devoid of emotion, he displayed great excitement.

"The king will be here in a few minutes," he exclaimed. "Events of importance are on the eve of occurring."

"Of what nature?" asked Harry.

"I have no time to explain now. Away!"

"Shall we be safe?"

"I have pledged my word. You must not be seen here. Away!"

Harry and Spencer immediately retired into the inner cave, where the spies were resting on the beds—sore, bruised and exhausted.

CHAPTER XIV.

SACRIFICING TO THE SACRED FIRE—THE REBELLION—DEATH OF KING MAKOLO—
THE PRIEST AND THE GENERAL TRIUMPHANT—RELEASE OF THE CAPTIVES.

A QUARTER of an hour elapsed.

Then the large entrance door of the temple was thrown open.

El Obed and his attendant priests stood on the steps to receive his majesty, who appeared riding on an elephant, surrounded by his guards.

The drums were beating in a discordant manner, and the horns brayed inharmoniously.

There was no attempt at any concerted music. Every musician played of his own sweet will.

The man who made the loudest noise seemed to consider himself the most accomplished player, and received the applause of the crowd.

Getting down from his exalted position on the elephant, King Makolo was received by El Obed, who bowed low, kissing the hem of the monarch's garment.

Then his majesty, with a dozen officers of the Court, was led into the hall where the sacred fire was burning.

Makolo received a handful of gold dust from an attendant and cast it upon the fire, after which the priests uttered some wild incantations.

A huge and hideous wooden idol was brought out of a corner, and the priests prostrated themselves before it.

They grovelled there for a few minutes, and the function was over.

The king quitted the temple.

Mounting the elephant, he started to return to the palace, his guards driving back the people in a brutal manner with their wooden swords and the butt-ends of their muskets.

To gain the palace it was requisite to pass through the market-place.

This was packed with people, shouting and gesticulating as only negroes can when they are labouring under great excitement.

In vain the guards knocked them about.

In their turn they were driven back and overpowered.

The king dismounted from the elephant, and bravely put himself at the head of his men, fighting with a sword.

Shots were now freely discharged by the guards, who saw that it was an organised movement.

The people had no guns, and they fell rapidly.

"Kill! kill!" shouted Makolo.

Umballa was by his side, helping to keep off the mob.

"See!" he said. "Sangara is coming with the soldiers."

"Ha," replied the king, "we are saved!"

"Rain! rain! Give us rain!" yelled the people. "Give us back Nola; he could make rain. Give us back Abomey; he was a good man. You are a bad king; you kill too much."

"I will kill all you dogs. Wait awhile," answered Makolo.

On came the general at the head of a large force of foot soldiers, armed with short swords and muskets.

The king made sure that his deliverance from the turbulent mob would speedily be accomplished.

In this idea he was destined to be signally mistaken.

The soldiers did not touch the people, who fell back at their approach.

A lane was made for them to pass through, and Sangara quickly reached the spot where the king was standing.

The ground was strewed with the dead and dying. Most of the bodyguards were killed or wounded. Umballa had his right arm nearly cut off. The people had suffered heavily also.

"Ah!" exclaimed the king, "here is my faithful general. Disperse this vile mob."

Sangara raised his sword.

Before Makolo could divine his intention, the general cut him down.

"Die, false friend—bad king—monster!" he cried.

The king sank to the ground, cleft nearly to the chin by the prodigious stroke of the sword Sangara had dealt him.

A tremendous shout arose from the assembled multitude when King Makolo fell, and no one attempted to interfere with Sangara.

The revolt had commenced, but it did not end where it began.

Makolo's body was hacked to pieces, his ministers were killed, and those of the guard who remained alive were ruthlessly put to the sword.

A raging tide of maddened human beings, in whom all the savage instinct was let loose, surged up to the palace.

Here a carnival of bloodshed was held.

The queen, the Princess Matabele, and all the members of the royal family were put to death, save the heir apparent.

It was with the utmost difficulty that Sangara saved the life of the young prince who was to be king.

Sangara intended to rule the kingdom until the boy was old enough to manage the affairs of State.

A careful observer of these deeds of violence, though taking no active part in them, was El Obed.

When he was satisfied that the sanguinary King Makolo was dead, and the city in the hands of Sangara, he re-entered the temple and sought the captives.

It was very lucky for the spies that they had tumbled into the Hall of the Sacred Fire.

Had they not done so, they would have been included in the victims of the palace massacre.

Scarcely anyone in the royal circle had been left alive, such was the fury of the populace, who had so long groaned under a fearful tyranny.

The captives knew that something of an extraordinary nature had been taking place.

Even to their subterranean cave the hoarse shouts of the howling mob, the discharge of the guns, and the shrieks of the wounded had penetrated.

When El Obed made his appearance in the inner chamber he saw, by the light of the lamp which swung from the roof, that the spies were there.

"Ha!" he exclaimed, "the king's slaves, Tom the Peeper and Dick the Knower. How did they come here? But I see how it is. The gate of the temple was open. When the revolt broke out they fled—they took refuge here. It matters not. The king is dead. I and Sangara now reign in Ashantee."

"What!" said Tom. "Is Makolo really dead?"

"Yes. You four are at liberty to depart. I do not want you here."

"You promised me a guide," observed Harry.

"I have one in readiness; his name is Chobo. He waits without."

"Are we to go now?"

"At once. You can reach the forest before nightfall. The gate of the city is near at hand. The people are sacking the palace. Take your chance."

"Food—"

"Chobo has a gun and ammunition. I can do no more for you," answered El Obed.

Events were certainly occurring with marvellous rapidity.

All were greatly surprised, especially Robert Spencer, who could scarcely believe the evidence of his senses.

Free!—free at last, after so many weary years of miserable imprisonment! He could not deem it possible.

So strong was his emotion that he burst into tears.

El Obed walked before them to the entrance to the temple, where a powerful middle-aged negro was in waiting.

No time was lost in making a start. Harry briefly thanked the priest, and the party quitted the city of the idolaters.

It was an infinite relief to all to get away.

Savage cries and frantic yells followed them for some distance.

Robert Spencer's heart was too full for words.

Everything seemed so strange to him after being confined for so many years underground. The sun dazzled him, walking was a trouble, and he almost wished himself back in the Temple of the Priests.

This feeling, however, was only transitory. It wore off in a few hours, when he got used to the external world, and remembered that he had fifty thousand pounds to his credit in a bank at Cape Coast Castle.

The spies were a little anxious to discover how Harry would treat them.

With his usual whole-souled generosity, he forgave all the evil they had done him, and as they journeyed slowly to the coast they became a friendly party.

They had, day by day, to subsist by the gun, which was not difficult, as Chobo was a good shot and an old hunter.

Their fare was of a varied, not to say motley, character.

One day they lived upon lion's flesh; the next on monkey's; then followed antelope Birds of many sorts contributed to the *menu*

On several occasions they suffered terribly from want of water.

Had it not been for the fruit and milk-nuts they must have perished.

At last a view of the sea was gained.

The coast was reached, and their sufferings were over for a time.

"Hurrah!" cried Harry; "we have struck the right part, too. I can see Three Points to the right of us."

Leaving the others to follow at their leisure, he ran forward to the verandah of the "Trader's Rest," where he found Jack Spencer and his sister.

Giving Jack one hearty squeeze of the hand, he caught Marian in his arms, and covered her face with kisses.

This happiness was more than he had dared to hope for.

He had expected to see Jack, and, perhaps, his father; but Marian he feared was in the power of Squire Rawlings and his son.

Now ensued mutual explanations.

Both Jack and Harry had a long, eventful, and interesting story to tell, and when it was all narrated, Uncle Robert Spencer stepped up to his niece and nephew.

Bill Blunt was delighted to see the old man, whom he remembered very well, and, to celebrate the happy event, set about preparing a dinner that should be for ever memorable in Three Points.

Uncle Robert declared that he would be at the expense of it.

He also called for a sheet of paper, and, in the presence of all, made his will in favour of Marian.

To her he left all his money in the bank. Blunt and Jack were witnesses, and the important document was given to Harry for safe keeping.

"That is, in case anything should happen to me," remarked Robert Spencer.

The spies walked about, or sat by themselves.

They saw there was a coldness towards them on Jack's part, and Harry was too much engaged with Marian to think of them.

Robert Spencer and Jack discussed the future together.

"Of course," said the former, "now we are united, we must take the first opportunity that offers to get back to your mother in England."

"I have been reckoning that the gunboat, which is coming here, will take us to Cape Coast Castle, where we can get a ship."

"Exactly. We must wait for her."

"There is nothing to fear," remarked Jack, carelessly. "I feel as happy as a bird let out of a cage."

"You forget one thing, my boy. Your bitter enemies are free. You should never have allowed them to escape."

"True; I had forgotten that," replied Jack.

"How did they manage to give you the slip?"

"That is a mystery, though I believe they bribed the nigger, for he has disappeared

since. If they had no money, they could cram him up with promises," said Jack.

"Yes. Now that being so, we must be continually on the lookout for the Bawlingses," replied Mr. Spencer.

Jack felt that he was right, and determined to be on his guard. Days followed one another very quickly. Mr. Spencer passed most of his time with Blunt, whose tobacco and spirits he found very comforting. Jack was nearly always with the sweethearts, Harry and Marian. He could not make friends with the spies, who were, consequently, left to their own resources.

They spent a good deal of the day in the forest. A gun had been allowed them, but they did not bring home any game, large or small. What did they do with themselves?

This thought occurred to Jack, who questioned them one evening on their return from their wanderings.

"You fellows don't seem to kill anything," he remarked.

Peeping Tom held up a beetle he had transfixed on a pin.

"What is that?" continued Jack.

"We are studying natural history."

"Going to make a collection," replied Knowall Dick. "When the gunboat comes to start us on our way home, I shall ship the collection, which will be of great value in London."

"Sell it to the British Museum for a lot of money," added Peeping Tom.

They went indoors to supper, and Jack joined Harry, to whom he communicated what the spies had said.

"It is all nonsense about making a natural history collection," exclaimed Harry.

"What do you think?"

"That there is treachery at work."

"Tell me your idea, to let me see if it coincides with mine," said Jack.

"Squire Rawlings and Charlie are hiding in the woods. The spies have found them out, and are daily in communication with them."

"Right. You have struck the nail on the head; but what are we to do?"

"Watch and wait," answered Harry.

In this recommendation Jack thoroughly concurred.

CHAPTER XV.

THE SPIES ARE ON THEIR GUARD—FLIGHT FROM THREE POINTS—OLD FRIENDS TOGETHER AGAIN—HATCHING THE PLOT.

IT was Marian Spencer's birthday, and to celebrate her anniversary, her brother and Harry determined to have a picnic at

a place a couple of miles along the seashore.

The spot selected was called Palm Rocks

Bay, because a dozen palm trees, backed by rocks, grew near an inlet in the sea.

No more delightful position could have been chosen for their purpose.

Uncle Robert was suffering from an attack of fever, and could not accompany them, and, as a matter of course, the spies were not invited.

Their room was esteemed better than their company.

But they heard of the projected excursion all the same.

There was very little that went on that they did not hear of.

Bill Blunt was packing a basket with eatables and drinkables, which was to be put in a boat, as Jack intended to row to Palm Rocks.

The spies came upon him as he was putting in a brace of birds.

"Hullo!" said Peeping Tom.

"Hullo yourself," replied Blunt.

"Has the gunboat we have been so long expecting come in, and are you preparing to cater for the officers' mess?"

"Guess again."

"Are you going to give a picnic and invite us?" enquired Knowall Dick.

"I'll invite you to carry the basket."

"Where to?"

"The boat which is to take Spencer, Rawlings and Miss Marian—bless her pretty face and heart—to Palm Rocks Bay."

"Thank you for nothing," replied Tom.

"Declined with thanks," answered Dick.

Blunt shut down the lid of the basket.

"What is the reason of this festivity?" inquired Dick.

"It is Miss Marian's birthday, and the boys are going to celebrate the happy event by a picnic at the Rocks."

"Why aren't we invited?"

"Because you are not wanted, I guess," answered Blunt, with a laugh.

Having got all the information they could from the genial host of the "Trader's Rest," the spies took their departure, and strolled along the shore.

"Let us go to the rocks and hide," said Peeping Tom.

"What for?" asked Knowall Dick.

"To hear what Jack and Harry have got to say."

"Do you think they suspect us?"

"Yes, I do. You know we have been absent in the forest a great deal lately, and it is my opinion that they guess we are in communication with Squire Rawlings and Charlie."

"Not they."

"We shall quickly find out by spying," replied Tom.

"What can they do?" inquired Dick.

"Follow us, and then we shall be in a fine scrape. They will punish us and recapture the Squire and his son, whom we have promised to help all we can."

It was quite true, as Jack suspected, that they had accidentally met Charlie and his father, who after their escape had made a camp some miles away in the forest.

They had the negro Sambo to wait on them.

It was their hope that they might be able to regain possession of Marian.

Sambo knew the road to Cape Coast Castle, and had promised to guide them.

However, Charlie obstinately refused to move unless Marian were with them.

He did not dare to show his face again in Three Points.

His recollection of recent captivity had entered like iron into his soul.

The spies had undertaken to assist them in every way in their power.

They reported everything that took place at Three Points, and Charlie was striving to invent some plan of outwitting his enemies.

This was not so easily done.

Jack placed a negro on guard outside the house every night.

This precaution precluded the possibility of a nocturnal surprise.

Peeping Tom led the way to the Palm Rocks, which were soon reached.

The spies, after a brief exploration, found a cool and shaded cave, into which they crept and hid themselves.

Its entrance looked out upon the gently undulating sea, in whose liquid depths the clear blue sky was reflected.

"This is just the place to lay off," remarked Peeping Tom, "and I should not be surprised if the picnic party pitched under that tree in front."

"If they do, we can hear nicely," replied Dick.

"The Squire must do something quickly if he wants to get Marian, as the gunboat will be here soon, and Jack will get away."

Dick was about to reply, when the splash of oars, the sound of merry laughter accompanying it, was heard.

"Here they are," added Tom. "Keep close. If we are found, we shall catch it uncommonly hot and strong."

Presently they saw a boat approach the shelving, sandy beach. Jack sprang out, followed by Harry, who assisted Marian to land.

The boys dragged the basket up the beach, and after looking round, deposited it under the identical tree that Peeping Tom had spoken of.

They unpacked it and sat down. Jack

poured out some sherry, which he handed round.

"Many happy returns of the day, Marian!" he exclaimed, emptying his glass.

Harry followed suit, and the girl's fair face flushed with pleasure.

"I hope my next birthday will be spent in dear Old England," she said. "I have had enough and to spare of Africa."

"Your hope will be fulfilled," replied Jack, "unless—"

He paused abruptly.

"I thought I heard the hiss of a snake," he added.

"Keep a lookout," said Harry; "those pests are everywhere. I killed one on my bed last night."

"What I was going to say is this," Jack resumed, "I fear we have not seen the last of Mr. Rawlings and his son Charlie."

"They are far enough away by this time," said Marian.

"My opinion is different. I believe the spies see them constantly, and we may expect some blow in the dark."

"What is to be done under the circumstances?" asked Harry.

"If I were sure of treachery, I would make captives of Peeping Tom and Knowall Dick, just to keep them out of mischief."

"Prevention is better than cure."

"Certainly; but I am not sure, and don't wish to be unjust to anybody," answered Jack.

"Watch them. Follow them," suggested Harry.

"We will; and if we do trace them to the Squire and Charlie, I will make prisoners of all the four."

"The spies have no liking for us."

"None whatever."

"It is very surprising!" said Harry, "after we have been so good to them."

"My dear fellow," Jack replied, "have you not lived long enough to know that you have only to do some people a favour to make them hate you?"

"It shows a vicious disposition."

"We must look after ourselves. I feel sure there is something impending; not that I want to be thought an alarmist."

Harry held up his hand.

"Hark!" he cried; "there it is again."

"What?"

"The noise you spoke of. The hiss of a snake."

"I did not hear it that time," said Jack.

"But I did, distinctly."

Harry was right.

The spies had, unfortunately for themselves, got into a cave which a large rock-snake had made its home.

Resenting their intrusion on its privacy, the serpent began to hiss angrily.

Peeping Tom and Knowall Dick were dreadfully frightened.

They knew not what to do in such a dilemma.

If they remained where they were they would probably be bitten; and if they emerged from their place of concealment they would be discovered.

They determined, after a brief whispered consultation, to make a bolt for safety.

Looking very sheepish and crestfallen, they rushed out of the cave.

"Ha!" cried Jack; "the two spies!"

Harry and he sprang to their feet; one seizing by the arm Peeping Tom, the other Knowall Dick.

"Confound you!" said Jack. "What do you mean by spying on us?"

"Look out for the snake," replied Tom.

"Never mind the snake. What do you mean by it?"

A sickly smile overspread Peeping Tom's features.

"Good joke, isn't it?" he asked.

"Can't see it. Spying is most despicable."

"We thought we would surprise you. Ha, ha! What fun!"

"Ha, ha, ha!" laughed Knowall Dick. "Splendid."

"Blunt told us where you were going, and we made sure you would be glad of our company, and ask us to have some of your good things," Tom went on.

"I'm jolly hungry," put in Dick. "We know what a good fellow you are, and Harry too."

"You came to listen," said Jack, "and must have heard our conversation, which concerned you."

"Not a word," answered Peeping Tom, with an air of injured innocence.

"Not a syllable," replied Knowall Dick, looking like a martyr at the stake.

"Come. No falsehoods!"

"If I am placed in such a position that I can hear what is not intended for me, I always put my fingers in my ears," said Peeping Tom.

"I've been suffering from deafness lately. Caught a cold in my head. Fact," observed Knowall Dick.

Jack stamped his foot impatiently at their unblushing effrontery.

"That is all nonsense," he exclaimed. "You have met Squire Rawlings and his son in the forest."

"Now you *do* surprise me, upon my honour."

"Answer me truly. Have you seen them?"

"Oh, dear, no! We haven't seen a soul!"

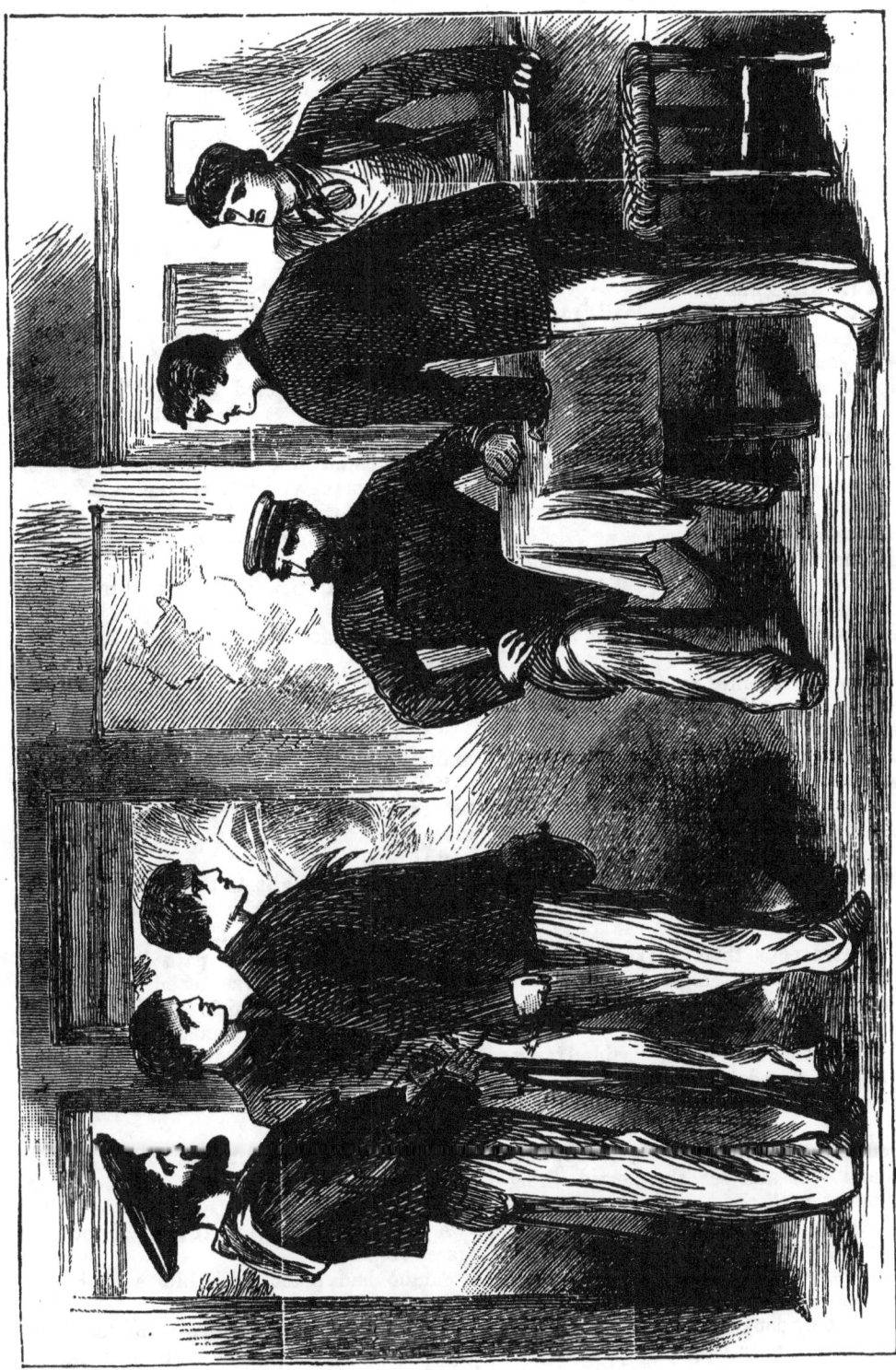

"'IF FOUND GUILTY, THEY SHALL BE PUNISHED WITH DEATH!' CRIED LIEUTENANT SMOLLEY."

cried Tom. " We have been solely engaged in the pursuit of natural history."

" Studying beetles and such like ? " said Dick.

" I don't believe a word you say."

" Don't be hard on us."

While they had been talking, the rock-snake had crawled out.

All at once it threw itself round Peeping Tom's leg, causing him to fall to the ground.

Loud yells burst from the spy.

The others fell back in alarm; but as soon as he saw what it was Jack began to laugh.

" Let him alone; it's only a rock-snake," said he.

" Help my friend ! " cried Knowall Dick.

" Not I. Help him yourself."

" Don't be so unfeeling. Will you see him die before your eyes ? "

" Will you ? "

" No," answered Knowall Dick. " I'll save him if I can ! "

With more courage than Jack or Harry had ever given him credit for possessing, Dick ran to Tom's assistance.

Bad as the spies were, they had a sincere friendship for one another.

This was the one redeeming point in their character.

Tom had got the snake's head in his hands, and Dick seized its tail, pulling at it with all his might.

It was a very comical scene.

Jack and Harry laughed till their sides ached.

The struggle between the spies and the rock-snake was a desperate one.

Perspiration ran down the faces of the boys in streams.

At length Peeping Tom managed to get out his knife, and slashed away at the reptile's neck until its head came off in his hand.

The horrid coils then relaxed, and the writhing body fell to the ground.

" Bravo ! " cried Jack. " British pluck for ever ! "

" You've done the trick," said Harry, " and deserve a medal."

Tom sat down and drew his breath more freely.

" You're a couple of nice ones," he replied, " to stand still and see the horrid thing trying to eat me."

" What ? "

" It was going to make a meal off me if Dick had not come gallantly to the rescue."

" Nonsense ! it was only a rock-snake."

" Aren't they dangerous ? "

" No; you've been long enough in Africa to know that."

" If I had I shouldn't have been in such a fright ! " replied Peeping Tom. " It has

given me a scare I sha'n't get over for a week."

" Take a walk for the benefit of your health," exclaimed Jack.

" Aren't you going to invite us to dinner ? "

" No."

" Oh ! I say, that's too bad, after all we've gone through. My nerves are thoroughly upset—entirely gone."

" So are mine," said Knowall Dick. " I tremble all over, and am almost pulseless—fact."

" Make yourselves scarce."

" Don't be mean. Let us stop," pleaded Tom.

" Your hearts are too black for us," answered Jack. " We know you, and I tell you plainly we don't want your society. Go ! "

" All right ! " replied Peeping Tom, with a vindictive look. " You might give a fellow time to get his breath."

" If I catch you playing the spy on us again, I'll make you bitterly regret it."

" Had not the snake been there you would not have caught us that time."

" Begone ! or—"

Jack picked up a stick in a threatening manner.

With considerable agility the spies ran away.

They got behind the rocks, where they were out of sight, and halted.

" What did you want to run for in that undignified manner ? " asked Knowall Dick.

" To save myself from a hiding; but I'll be revenged," answered Peeping Tom, savagely.

" How ? "

" We'll go straight to the Squire, and do anything he and Charlie tell us to."

" Good ! I'm with you."

There was no defined path through the forest. Their way was often stopped by dense jungle, round which they had to go.

It was impossible to penetrate it.

Evening was closing in, when, greatly exhausted, they reached the place where Mr. Rawlings and Charlie had taken refuge after their escape.

It was an open space, surrounded by patriarchal trees, in which birds and monkeys found a home.

A spring welled up in the middle of the grassy slope.

Sambo had taken with him a rifle, cartridges, and an axe.

With the former he killed game for their support; the latter he had found indispensable in erecting a hut for their accommodation.

He was a faithful servant.

They had promised to give him money and

take him to England with them, which pleased him greatly.

Mr. Rawlings and Charlie were seated by the cool trickling spring.

"Welcome!" shouted Charlie. "We thought our old friends would come to-day."

"We have come for good," replied Peeping Tom.

"Has anything gone wrong?"

"Jack Spencer has found us out. He is sure that you are in the forest, and we have come to put you on your guard."

"Are our enemies coming after us?" asked Charlie.

"No," exclaimed Tom; "but if we were to go back, I know we should be followed the next time we came to see you."

"Confusion!" said the Squire. "Spencer is always a thorn in my side."

"We must get rid of him," answered Charlie.

"Yes; and of Harry, too."

Peeping Tom and Knowall Dick were faint with hunger and thirst. They asked for some food, which was immediately cooked for them by Sambo over a small fire he had made.

Water they got from the spring.

"It is no use going to sleep," exclaimed the Squire. "I know you are fatigued, but I have work for you to do. Serve me, and you shall have your reward some day."

"Must we go back to Three Points?" asked Tom.

"Yes. Return to-night. Excite no suspicion. I have been plotting."

He went on to explain that he had been asking Sambo about vegetable poisons to be found in the forest.

The black had told him of a berry which had the power of sending those who partook of it into a sleep from which there was no awakening.

If the spies could put this noxious substance into the food prepared for Jack and his party, they would die.

Tom at once said that he was not afraid to do it; but it must be remembered that Marian would die, too.

The Squire replied that he had talked the matter over with Charlie, who was satisfied.

If Harry and Jack were poisoned, Marian might be also.

What he wanted was to be left in possession of his fortune without any further disturbance.

Although he loved Marian, she did not seem disposed to care for him, under any circumstances.

There were hundreds of other girls who would be glad to have him with his money.

Why should he waste his affection on Jack Spencer's sister?

This was what his father had been impressing on him for a long time past.

Charlie was content so long as Harry could not go back to England and turn him and his father out of the property they had usurped. His greed for gold was, if possible, greater than the Squire's.

The spies did not altogether like the task which was assigned to them.

There was a great deal of risk about it.

Nevertheless, they had to comply, because the Rawlingses were their friends, and they had nothing to expect from those at Three Points.

The Squire had so fully matured his plans as to have employed Sambo to collect a handful of the poison berries.

These he gave to Peeping Tom, wrapped up in a palm leaf.

"Sambo!" he exclaimed, "come here, you useful and necessary villain! I want to ask you a question."

"Yes, massa. What up now?" replied the negro.

"Are you sure this is a certain poison?"

"Sudden death, massa. Tip-top poison that—wuss than rifle which will kill at a thousand yards."

"Is there any particular taste about it?"

"No, sah. Him eat berry much like a cooked moonbeam."

"Eh! What?"

"I mean him hab no taste at all. Yah, yah, yah!"

Mr. Rawlings turned to the spies.

"You see what you have to do," he exclaimed. "When any kind of stew or soup is cooking, drop this stuff in unperceived."

"I will do it," replied Tom.

"Mind you don't eat anything from the dish."

"I'll watch it. I wasn't born yesterday," grinned Tom.

"Now be off, and luck go with you, not that I want to get rid of you, but it is a very serious crisis for us, and business must be attended to."

"Golly, massa," cried Sambo, "that berry fine kind of business. Me call it murder."

"Silence!"

"Yes, sah. Sorry me spoke."

Charlie said nothing. He was lying on his back looking up at the sky dreamily.

He had given up Marian to please his father and to suit the exigencies of the occasion, but he did not like it.

He could not forget her.

It was arranged that the spies should return to the camp after they had accomplished their dastardly work.

Then they would all make a start for Cape Coast Castle, and thence make their way in some trader to England. This was the plot.

CHAPTER XVI.

POISONED—THE ARRIVAL OF H.M. GUNBOAT "CONDOR"—THE VALUE OF A TIMELY ANTIDOTE.

On the day following the interview between Peeping Tom, Knowall Dick and Squire Rawlings, Blunt announced that a negro had brought in some little marmoset monkeys, and he was going to make a stew of them for his guests' dinner.

The spies were on the alert at once.

Here was their chance.

Although they were home late at night, Jack made no remark about their prolonged absence, but in the morning they noticed that they were followed by Chobo.

The black man shadowed them wherever they went.

Evidently he was sent to dog their footsteps. At this they chuckled.

"Take him for a walk," said Peeping Tom.

"Where to?" asked Knowall Dick.

"Into the woods, of course. Go around, and come back here in half-an-hour. While you are gone, I will slip the poison-berries into the stew."

"I'll do it.

"He is set to watch us, and I want a free hand."

"All right," answered Knowall Dick.

He at once walked off in the direction of the forest.

Chobo came up to Tom.

"Your friend going out alone, sah?" he enquired.

"What's that to do with you, ebony?" replied Tom.

"You most generally go together."

"I've got a bad head. Mind your own business. I guess I shall be down with the fever directly."

"Golly! Don't say that, massa."

"Go away," cried Peeping Tom, petulantly, as he threw himself under a tree.

So well did he act his part that Chobo was completely deceived.

Peeping Tom pretended to close his eyes, but he watched Chobo follow Knowall Dick among the trees.

When he had fully disappeared he got up.

Marian was reclining in a hammock under the verandah. Jack and Harry were on the sands, spearing land crabs with a couple of old bayonets.

In the bar of the "Trader's Rest" Blunt was busy dealing with some negroes who had come in with ivory and gold dust.

The kitchen was built away from the house, and was occupied by an old black woman, who officiated as cook.

Her name was Maum Guinea.

Peeping Tom proceeded to the kitchen, and inhaled a savory smell.

"What have you got there, mother?" he asked.

"Dat's de marmosets on fur a stew," she replied. "Clear out; you won't hab none till it's cooked, so I done gone tole you."

"I'll give you a half-dollar for a plateful."

"What's dat? A half-dollar, sure?"

"Yes; here it is."

"Wait till I go outside an' wash a plate. I've been so busy all mornin' I ain't had time to wash up."

"Make haste, then," said Peeping Tom, giving her the money.

The old woman toddled out with a plate in her hand, and during her absence Tom seized his opportunity.

He lifted the lid of the boiling pot and dropped in the poison berries which Squire Rawlings had given him.

The fatal deed was done.

Before she came back he had replaced the lid, and was looking innocently out of the window.

Maum Guinea had no suspicion of what had occurred.

She ladled out some of the stew into a basin and gave it him, whereupon he said he would eat it outside, as the kitchen was rather warm.

"I reckon you'll find that young monkey meat go down good," she remarked.

"No doubt of that," replied Tom. "It is all I shall get of it, as I sha'n't be here to dinner. I'm going into the woods.'

"Go along! you're always for everlasting in the woods. Pity you wasn't born a baboon."

Peeping Tom did not reply, as he wanted to get away, being anxious lest anyone should see him in the company of the cook.

He did not wish any suspicion to attach itself to him.

Presently he saw Knowall Dick sitting on the stump of a tree, playing with one of the ugly rough-haired dogs which swarmed about the place.

Chobo had slunk away to a distance, keeping his eyes on the spies without appearing to do so.

"What have you got there?" inquired Knowall Dick.

"Some of the monkey stew. I'll drop a

few poison berries I've got left into it and give it to the dog," replied Tom.

"What harm has the dog done you?"

"None; I am about to experiment on him in the interests of science."

The poison was put into the mess and given to the dog, who without any hesitation proceeded to lap it up.

In a minute or so there was nothing left of it.

The effect was not immediate.

For a brief space the animal frolicked round Knowall Dick.

Presently it sat down and began to yawn. Its eyes closed gradually, its head fell forward, and it had all the appearance of going to sleep.

"What do you think of that?" asked Peeping Tom.

"It will do first-rate. Now I vote we make ourselves scarce," replied Knowall Dick.

They went off among the trees, a glance over their shoulders making them conscious that the negro was at their heels.

While they amused themselves by knocking down cocoanuts, and picking fruit of various kinds and flavours, dinner was cooking at Three Points.

Bill Blunt did not dine with his guests. He laid a table for them in the verandah, where they sat by themselves.

Everyone ate heartily.

No suspicion crossed their minds that they were being foully dealt with.

They had no idea that the hidden hand of the cowardly poisoner had been at work.

"There is some left," exclaimed Marian. "If Tom and Dick come back soon, they shall have it."

"They know the hour," said Jack. "I expect they have gone to see their friends and our enemies; but Chobo is on their track."

"He will have something to tell us to-night," remarked Harry.

Uncle Robert suddenly leant forward, nodding.

"Hold up. What's the matter?" cried Jack.

"I feel so sleepy all at once," was the reply.

"You are not strong."

Mr. Spencer's head sank on the table by the side of his plate, and his eyes closed.

"I feel inclined to follow his example," exclaimed Harry.

"And I, too," remarked Marian. "It must be the heat."

"Aw!" said Jack, yawning. "I can scarcely keep my eyes open."

In a few minutes the irresistible torpor stole over them.

Their heads nodded as Robert Spencer's had done, and the four were soon unconscious of what was going on around them.

Within a few minutes of the poison taking effect on Jack Spencer and his friends, a stately ship steamed round the point.

Slackening her engines, she fired a gun.

The detonation rolled over the sea and reverberated in the forest.

A thousand times did the echoes multiply themselves.

It was the signal for a pilot.

Blunt heard the sound and rushed out on to the beach. An experienced negro got into a canoe and paddled to the gunboat through the surf.

The English flag was quickly run up to the peak.

"It is the one we have been expecting," muttered Blunt. "I will go and see Jack Spencer. He will be glad she has come."

Jack and Harry had been talking for days about the anticipated gunboat.

To her they looked for deliverance from a further stay on the shore of Africa.

Going to the verandah, where he thought to find them waving their hats and shouting with joy, he was horrified to behold the state in which they were.

He could not make it out.

Were they asleep, or what had happened?

Shaking Jack by the arm, he endeavoured to rouse him, but in vain.

He went to the others, with the same result.

"Good heaven!" he cried, "this is awful; they are dead!"

Rushing away he went into the kitchen, where Maum Guinea was washing up her culinary utensils, preparatory to having her own dinner, which was set out on the table.

It consisted of the same stew she had served to the guests.

"Have you eaten any of this?" he demanded.

"Not yet, massa," she replied. "Me only just gone done dished up, but me going to mighty quick. Dat good I assuah you."

"It has poisoned the white people."

"What dat you say?"

"They are all dead."

"Golly, massa! don't go for to say that."

"It is true. Come and look."

The old woman, trembling like a leaf, followed him to the front of the house, and began to utter loud cries.

"Oh! who hab done this?" she asked.

"You will be hanged if you are a party to it. The English gunboat has just come into the bay," said Blunt.

"Wish I may die if I did it," replied

Maum Guinea. "Why, I was going to eat some ob de bery same stuff myself."

"That doesn't look like guilt."

"No, sah, me not guilty."

She spoke so earnestly that he felt bound to believe her.

"Has anyone been in the kitchen this morning?" asked Blunt.

"Lemme see," said the cook. "Yes. Tom the Peeper, as you call him, came in."

"Did you leave him alone?"

"Yes. He ask for some ob de stew. I went out for a minute. Ah! that is the one who hab done it."

Blunt uttered a groan.

"There is not a doubt about it," he exclaimed. "He has settled his enemies, sure enough. What is to be done?"

"Gib 'em what the doctors call an emeteric."

"An emetic, you mean."

"Yes; dat is de thing. Bring de poison all up. Salt and mustard in a little hot water do de white folks good."

"Certainly. Go and get a jugful. Hurry."

Maum Guinea was off as quickly as the weight of fat she had to carry would allow her.

When she returned, Blunt poured the mixture down the throats of the sufferers, producing the desired effect on all, with one exception.

This was Robert Spencer, whose vitality had been at a very low ebb lately.

While in the course of a few minutes the others could sit up and speak faintly, he showed no sign of recovering.

Jack was the first to collect his senses.

"I have been very ill," he said. "What is it—sunstroke?"

"Poison," replied Blunt. "The meat was tampered with."

"By whom?"

"Peeping Tom."

"The villain! Have you got him? By heaven! he shall hang," cried Jack.

"Don't excite yourself, or you might have a relapse," said Blunt.

"Where is he? Produce him. I am tired of his villainies."

"So we all are."

"This shall end it. I'll put a stop to them. Bring him out."

"Unfortunately, I haven't got him," replied Blunt; "but here is Chobo coming in at a run. Perhaps he can give us some information."

"Ah, he has been watching the spies."

"Yes; by your orders."

Chobo was full of news. He rushed up to the verandah, and said that Peeping Tom and Knowall Dick had joined two white men and a negro in the forest.

An earnest conversation took place between them.

He was hiding behind a tree, and all he could make out of it was that they were going at once to Cape Coast Castle.

Indeed, the five started half-an-hour after the spies had joined their friends.

"They have slipped through our fingers," remarked Blunt; "but you are rid of them, that is one good thing."

Jack shook his head, and so did Harry.

"You can sleep in peace now," added Blunt.

"Never, so long as Charlie Rawlings lives," replied Jack.

"Is he so dangerous as that?"

"Yes; he is a cobra lurking in our path. We never know when he will strike."

"You can put a few thousand miles of sea between you."

"How?"

"Look in the bay. The gunboat's come at last."

"Bravo! that is excellent news."

They turned their eyes seaward. The vessel had come to anchor under the guidance of the pilot, and was lowering a boat.

An officer in uniform got into her, and was rowed towards the shore.

Marian was extremely weak, so the boys carried her into the parlour, placing her on a lounge, and giving her some spirit to revive her.

"What a narrow escape we have had," she remarked, "Blunt's presence of mind saved us."

"Unquestionably," replied Jack.

"I fear Uncle Robert will never wake again," said Harry. "What he went through in Ashantee completely shattered his constitution."

"I sincerely trust he may pull through," Jack answered; "but, if not, our little Marian here is his heiress."

"How can you think of that at such a time?" she asked, with a reproachful look.

It was even as Harry had dreaded.

The unfortunate man never rallied, and was stone dead ere the sun went down.

His spell of liberty had been short. His dream of enjoyment, by means of his wealth, in his native land, was an empty one.

When the boat reached the shore the officer stepped out, and was received by Blunt, who conducted him to the house, where Jack and Harry were introduced.

His name was Lieutenant Smolley. The gunboat was the "Condor," commander Sir Harding Melville, and she had come to Three Points on a special mission.

After the insurrection of El Obed, the priest, and Sangara, the general, which resulted in the death of King Makolo, the powerful Higazi tribe, under the leadership of their king Ja-Ja, arrived before the city.

No resistance was made.

Ja-Ja was accepted as king by El Obed, and he, with his wife and son, who was known as Sunday Ja-Ja, walked into the palace.

This the British would not have objected to.

But they had a strong cause of complaint against him.

All the caravans from the interior, bringing valuable articles of commerce to the coast, were obliged to pass through the Ashantee territory.

Ja-Ja was a determined robber, and immediately began stopping the caravans.

He murdered their conductors, and plundered their contents.

The "Condor" had been sent by the British authorities at Cape Coast to Three Points in order to put a stop to these reprehensible practices.

A party of blue-jackets, with a Nordenfelt gun, were to march, under Lieutenant Smolley, to the city.

All they wanted was a reliable guide.

Jack and Harry looked at one another.

"I have been a captive there, sir," exclaimed Harry, "and know the way."

"You will be well paid for your services," replied the lieutenant.

"Engage me as your guide."

"Very well; consider it settled. I have only to get the appointment ratified by the commander, which can be done when I return on board the 'Condor.'"

It was rather a rash venture of Harry's. His love of excitement prompted him to make it, and Jack was not behindhand.

He volunteered to accompany the expedition.

They felt quite content to leave Marian in the charge of Blunt, for she would, during their absence, be under the guns of the "Condor."

When Marian heard of their intention to join the expedition for the chastisement of King Ja-Ja, she was deeply grieved.

In vain she begged her brother and Harry to abandon the idea.

They had pledged their words.

Lieutenant Smolley was relying upon their services.

They assured her that they looked upon the journey in the light of a pleasure excursion.

She had her mind filled by the most gloomy forebodings.

When they took their departure she covered her face with her hands, weeping bitterly.

"I shall never see them again," she murmured.

The boys were in high spirits as they led the party of blue-jackets, which numbered twenty exclusive of the lieutenant.

They carried rifles and the Nordenfeldt gun, which was a most formidable engine of death and destruction.

In three weeks they expected to be back.

Meanwhile the "Condor" remained at Three Points.

CHAPTER XVII.

THE SPIES ARE LOST IN THE FOREST—DESTRUCTION OF THE CARAVAN— CAPTURED BY NATIVES—SOLD TO SUNDAY JA-JA.

As Chobo had reported, Peeping Tom and Knowall Dick had joined Squire Rawlings.

All felt sure that Jack Spencer and the others at Three Points were poisoned, and would never trouble anyone again.

The only anxiety of the party was to get to Cape Coast, and Sambo had assured them that he knew the way.

This assertion, however, was incorrect.

After wandering about for several days he was compelled to admit that he was helplessly lost.

It was an unwelcome confession to make, but he had to do it.

What was to be done under the circumstances?

A halt was called to enable them to come to some decision as to the route to be followed.

"Me berry sorry, massa," said Sambo, "but me clean out ob my reckoning."

"Whereabouts do you think we are?" asked the Squire.

"We ought to be on the caravan road, which passes within fifteen miles of Ashantee."

"You are a wooden-headed ass," cried Charlie, "or you would not have got us into this fix."

"Sometimes in travelling, sah, you get turned round, and then the debble himself not know where him going—yah, yah!" grinned Sambo.

"Silence!"

The black knew Charlie's fiery temper, and was silent instantly.

Peeping Tom had climbed a tree.

Knowall Dick was improving the shining hour by industriously picking and eating a luscious wild plum that grew on a tree close by.

Suddenly Tom descended the tree quickly.

"Sambo is right," he exclaimed, "about our being near the caravan route."

"How do you know?" asked Charlie.

"Because there is a large one coming in our direction. I counted no less than fifty camels."

Everybody's face lighted up.

They started with renewed vigour in the direction indicated by Peeping Tom.

Half-an-hour's walk brought them to a spot where there were half-a-dozen wells.

That the caravan would stop here was a certainty.

It was shrouded in clouds of sandy dust, but as it drew nearer they perceived that there were over one hundred carriers, with bundles on their backs, while some men, with white turbans, showed that it was owned by Arabs. Clearly it had come a long way.

When the caravan came close to them, the Squire advanced to meet it, and was kindly welcomed by an old sheik.

The Arab traders were bound for the coast, and made no objection to the white men accompanying them.

The sheik would permit only an hour's stay at the wells, because they were not far from Ashantee.

"What are you afraid of, my friend?" asked the Squire.

"King Makolo, who was an honest king, is dead," replied the sheik; "and now the biggest robber in the world has come to rule the country."

"Who is that?"

"King Ja-Ja. He is the greatest caravan robber and murderer of traders in all Africa. We have been warned that his son, who is called Sunday Ja-Ja, a bloodthirsty youth, is on the lookout for us. We are known to be richly laden. Ah, we should be a prize, indeed!"

"Perhaps the danger is exaggerated?" said Mr. Rawlings.

"Not at all. During the last five days," answered the sheik, "we have come across the mournful relics of no less than three plundered caravans."

"Of what did they consist?"

"The decaying bodies of men and camels, flocks of hideous bustards, swarms of flies."

"Then by all means press on," exclaimed the Squire. "We will not detain you, and beg to thank you for your courtesy in allowing us to join you."

The sheik, who was a venerable person, with a long white beard, bowed, and joined his partners, who were ten in number.

They were eating some dried fruits, and discussing the chances of their arriving safely at their destination, which was Cap. Palmas, on the Ivory Coast.

All were married men, having their wives and children living at this settlement, and anxiously awaiting their return.

Very enterprising men were these traders, for they had been to the foot of the Kong Mountains in Upper Guinea, to get their gold and ivory.

The carriers, none of whom were slaves, being paid a small sum for their labour, had thrown down their loads.

Now they could be seen struggling with the camels for water at the wells, chattering like monkeys, and rolling on the grass like dogs.

They were getting near home, and the consciousness of this fact always lightens the weary heart of the tired traveller.

The money earned in this trip would enable them to live comfortably for a time, unless, as Blunt said, they indulged in too much "suction." Then they would start out and work again.

The head man of the pagazi, as the porters are called, blew a horn when the camels had been well watered.

Drivers fell into their places, the porters shouldered their loads, and everything was ready for a start, when an occurrence took place which was not totally unexpected.

On the north-western side of the caravan were a quantity of trees, standing in a dense jungle of undergrowth.

All at once a hundred rifles sent their deadly bullets out of the green fringe.

Many of the camels and porters fell dead.

The others rushed away, uttering fearful cries, for they knew that Ja-Ja's dreaded men were at hand.

The Squire was standing near one of the wells. By his side was Charlie. The spies and Sambo were close by.

They were utterly dumbfounded by the suddenness of the attack.

"Down, down!" shouted Charlie. "We are attacked. Down! it is the only way to save our lives.

He fell on his side as he spoke, and his example was at once followed by Peeping Tom and Knowall Dick.

Mr. Rawlings was about to do the same, when another volley came from the bushes. He uttered a cry of pain, horror, and distress.

So did the black guide, Sambo.

Both of them were hard hit, and fell side by side groaning in deadly pain.

"BILL LEVER'S LIFE HUNG ON A THREAD."

No. 6.

PRICE ONE HALFPENNY.

[Published Every Monday.]

Though Charlie saw his father sink to the ground, he did not dare to move.

The caravan, entirely deserted, was now at the mercy of the marauders, who sprang up from their place of concealment. With wild cries and yells they rushed forward.

At the head of the natives was General Sangara, who had become one of the most trusted generals of King Ja-Ja.

On a stoutly-built horse, fifty yards off, sat a thin, vicious-looking boy of sixteen, who was naked to the waist.

His face lighted up with pleasure when he saw the havoc that had been wrought.

This was Sunday Ja-Ja, who cast his eyes upon the packages and boxes, bales and camels, as if trying to estimate the value of his capture.

The sheik and his partners had either been killed by the shots, or had run away to escape being ruthlessly butchered.

Only a few of the camels had been shot, and Sangara told his men to put the plunder on those that were left.

They could carry a double burden for a short distance, the city not being far off.

Hearing the voice of Sangara, whom they knew well, the spies jumped up, telling Charlie to do the same.

They did not think they had anything to fear from the Ashantee general, except being taken back to captivity, which was very galling, though, at the same time, better than death.

"Ha!" cried Sangara, looking closely at them, "what do I see? Tom the Peeper and Dick the Knower."

"Yes," replied Tom; "we met the caravan, and were going to the coast."

"Who is this?" added the general, pointing to Charlie. "He is not the music-maker?"

"No; he is a friend."

"What can he do?"

"Nothing."

"He shall be a slave. You shall all come back to the city. El Obed was a fool to let you go. We have a new king now. That one over there on the horse is Sunday Ja-Ja, the king's son. He will buy you from me, for you are mine."

Attracted by the white faces of the captives, Sunday Ja-Ja rode up at a gallop.

He inquired who they were, and on being told by Sangara, was much pleased, and promised to give the general anything in reason that he liked to ask for as the price of the captives.

A great deal had been said about the spies' wonderful powers since he had been in Ashantee.

It made him feel proud to think that he had got hold of them again.

They would undoubtedly be of great service to him and his father, he thought.

"Where is the old fox who led this caravan?" inquired Sunday Ja-Ja, putting his hand on a scimitar which he wore strapped to his waist.

His face became ferociously savage as he spoke.

Nobody answered his question.

"Tom the Peeper," he continued, "I am speaking to you. Where is the old Arab thief? Can you see him?"

"I must have a look round," replied Tom, who began to get hot all over.

He discovered in a moment that a youth like Sunday Ja-Ja was more difficult to deal with than a man like King Makolo.

How he bewailed his bad luck in meeting the caravan.

A thousand times better would it have been for him to continue wandering in the wilderness.

Knowall Dick hid his face in his hat and pretended to be thinking.

He had more faith in Peeping Tom's ready wit than he had in his own.

Charlie took little notice of what was going on. He knelt on the greensward and examined his father, who was unable to speak. He was bleeding to death.

"Father," said Charlie, "speak to me. Is there anything I can do for you?"

Squire Rawlings made no answer.

He turned his lack-lustre eyes on his son with an expression of affection, yet no word came from him.

The negro Sambo had been shot through the heart.

In less than a minute Peeping Tom's quick eyes had noticed a white turban dodging to and fro behind a tree.

Presently he saw a face which was undoubtedly that of the sheik, who was clearly hiding himself.

"I have it!" cried Tom. "The sheik is in that wood."

"I know it," said Dick, putting on his hat.

"Where?" asked Sunday Ja-Ja.

"Behind that big tree."

The young prince ordered half-a-dozen men to go to the spot.

Standing against the trunk the wretched leader of the caravan was discovered, seized, and dragged roughly from his place of concealment.

The old man did not tremble or show any signs of fear.

Holding his head erect, he approached the youthful tyrant.

"Hullo, old greybeard!" cried Sunday Ja-Ja. "Have you counted the moments you have to live?"

"Why should you reproach me with my old age?" replied the sheik. "You, too, will be old some day, if you live long enough."

"I have no wish to be a dotard."

"Youth should respect grey hairs, sanguinary miscreant."

"Ha! do you defy me?" cried the prince, raising his scimitar.

"You have robbed me of my hard-earned property. If you do not spare my life the brave English who protect the coast will avenge me."

"A fig for the English. You threaten me? I am a king's son. This is how I treat your insolence—so, so."

The boy struck him twice on the head with his scimitar.

He sank to the ground, streaming with blood.

No one dared to raise a hand to save him from this cruel treatment.

Raising himself upon his elbow, the shiek turned his gaze upon Sunday with a mingled expression of pity and disgust.

"Monster of iniquity," he exclaimed, "you have shed innocent blood which belongs to men who have done you no harm. Heaven will not suffer this long. Retribution is at hand!"

"Hold thy peace!" shouted Sunday.

So passionate did he become, when spoken to in a way he did not like, that his lips were flecked with white foam.

He grated his teeth together, and his snake-like eyes rolled menacingly.

The sheik was not permitted to say anything more, for the young savage dealt him a further blow, which literally cut his head off.

"Wonderful!" cried Sangara. "What a warrior he will be!"

"The old hound was insolent," replied Sunday. "I always say, 'Off with their heads!' when the rogues offend me."

"Some day the world will ring with the fame of your name."

"I will conquer all Africa," exclaimed the young tyrant, swelling with pride, "and then I will subdue the countries over the sea where the white men come from."

"All the nations shall bow the knee before Sunday Ja-Ja," said Sangara.

"Tell me, Tom the Peeper and Dick the Knower," continued the prince, "shall I one day rule the world?"

The spies did not dare to contradict him, though they despised his empty-headed vanity and pretension.

"Most decidedly you will," replied Tom. "In ten years you will be sitting on a throne cut out of a single diamond in a palace built entirely of gold and—"

Sunday stooped and gave him a blow with his hand which sent him on to his knees.

"Oh, lor! What have I done now?"

"Don't tell me any falsehoods," said Sunday. "I'm not a fool. There never was, and never will be, a diamond big enough to cut a throne out of."

Tom rubbed his head reflectively.

"Did I say a diamond?" he inquired. "If so, it was a slip of the tongue. What I meant to say was an ivory throne."

"That is as bad. As if you could make a chair out of an elephant's tusk. Take that! I don't believe you can see so far ahead."

He gave Peeping Tom another blow with his heavy open hand, which sent him rolling over. Then the boy tyrant directed his attention to Knowall Dick.

"What do you know about my future, eh, Dick the Knower?" he demanded. "Come now, tell me."

"This I know," replied Dick, "that you will succeed your father as king of a large tract of territory. You will beat all other tribes, and have a great store of gold and jewels; the white man shall be afraid of you, and—"

Sunday raised his fist again.

Before Knowall Dick could dodge out of the way, it descended on the side of his head, and over he went.

"You're another humbug," exclaimed Sunday. "You promise too much."

"Marvellous!" said Sangara, holding up his hands. "How clever he is. What wit—what wisdom. He will shine like a star of the first magnitude. Rain will always fall in his country. No pestilence shall destroy his people's cattle, no famine arise from want of corn, nor—"

"Do you want one of my blows?" interrupted Sunday. "If you don't, learn to keep a guard over your tongue. These traders generally carry some wine; go and ransack their goods till you find me some."

As Sangara departed on his errand, Sunday dismounted and walked to a tree, which afforded a grateful shade.

Here he sat down, and waited until the general returned with half-a-dozen bottles of what proved to be excellent sherry.

Sunday soon solved the question of how to draw a cork, by knocking the neck off a bottle with his scimitar.

The general stood by his side listening to his remarks; but though Sunday kept on filling the horn which served him for a glass, he gave none to his companion.

The first stage of drunkenness soon came, and he began to sing; in the second stage he got up and danced.

His third performance was to quarrel with Sangara for nothing at all, and beat him with a stick till he ran away, after which Prince Sunday drank another bottle, laughed like an idiot, and finally rolled over, and went to sleep.

Meanwhile the general had the goods carefully collected and packed, so that all should be ready for a move when the young tyrant awoke.

The spies and Charlie were guarded by two black soldiers.

Provisions were served out to them, and they were permitted to help themselves to water at the wells.

The sun had gone down before Sunday Ja-Ja awoke and gave the order to march.

First went a guard of soldiers, then came the camels and the men carrying goods, after them the three white captives, and the prince brought up the rear with more armed men.

By morning the city with which Peeping Tom and Knowall Dick were so familiar was reached.

Being conducted to the palace grounds, Sangara placed them in the very same pavilion they had occupied before.

Charlie was left with them for the present, and being fatigued with their long march, they speedily fell asleep.

At midday a slave brought them an ample supply of provisions. The man was ordered to wait on them and watch that they did not leave the palace grounds.

The spies' old easy, idle life had come back to them; but Charlie was not so fortunate.

In the afternoon the executioner came for him, saying that Sunday Ja-Ja wanted him very particularly.

"What does he want me for?" asked Charlie, trembling.

"You're to be his whipping-boy," replied the executioner.

"I don't understand you—explain that," said Charlie, whose teeth chattered like castanets.

"When Prince Sunday is in a bad temper, he sends for his whipping-boy, strips him, ties his hands to a post, and flogs him with a whip which has three leather thongs."

"Oh, lor'!" groaned Charlie. "How long does he keep on?"

"When he's tired he leaves off."

"Why doesn't he keep on with his black boy?"

"He's dead. Before he started out to destroy the caravan he gave him a whipping from which he died," said the executioner.

The spies looked sympathisingly at Charlie.

"You've tumbled into a nice thing," remarked Peeping Tom.

"You're sure to be pensioned off, if you live long enough," said Knowall Dick.

"Prince Sunday says," added the executioner, "black boy bad to whip because his skin doesn't show the marks. White boys' will."

Charlie looked wildly around as if he contemplated making a dash for freedom, but he saw the attempt would be utterly futile, and so, with a bitter groan, he followed the executioner to the king's presence.

CHAPTER XVIII.

THE WHIPPING-BOY—CHOBO BRINGS NEWS—SUNDAY JA-JA RESOLVES TO GIVE BATTLE TO THE ENGLISH.

SUNDAY JA-JA was in a very unamiable mood.

This was frequently the case with the young tyrant.

He had, in truth, a diabolical temper, which he had never been taught to keep under control.

It was a fact that he had, with his own hand, whipped several boys to death by continual and prolonged castigation.

His father, King Ja-Ja, was in a maudlin state through over-indulgence in opium smoking and rum drinking.

This threw the cares of government on Sunday's shoulders, which he did not altogether like.

When the executioner brought Charlie into his presence, he looked critically at him

"You have a good broad back," he exclaimed, "and look strong. Can you bear pain?"

"No more than you can," replied Charlie.

"We shall soon see what you are made of. If you whine and cry like a girl, I shall be all the better pleased."

"What right have you to beat me?" Charlie demanded, sulkily.

"The right of conquest. You are my slave."

"That is simply the right of the strong to oppress the weak. If my countrymen hear of this, they will make you suffer."

"Strip him!" cried Sunday Ja-Ja. "I'll have no more of his talk."

The executioner smiled grimly.

He soon had Charlie naked to the waist, and tied his hands to a stake driven into the ground.

It was impossible for him to move far.

Sunday took up a long whip with a short thick handle. It had three knotted thongs.

Giving a look at it over his shoulder, Charlie shuddered.

It was a formidable instrument.

The first cut made him tremble all over; the second caused him to clench his teeth, and the third elicted from him a sharp cry of pain.

After this each stroke compelled him to howl and beg for mercy.

Sunday was delighted.

"Ha, you white-skinned dog!" he shouted, as the blood spurted from the wounds. "How do you like that?"

"Mercy! I can't bear it!" cried Charlie. "You are killing me. Leave off!"

"I haven't half done yet. You are the best whipping-boy to holloa that I ever had. Keep it up."

"For pity's sake, don't hit so hard! Oh, oh!"

The little savage laughed till his fat sides shook.

Nothing pleased him so much as giving a fellow-creature pain.

He did not leave off till his arm ached, and Charlie's back and shoulders were scored all over.

When Sunday Ja-Ja threw down the whip, the thongs of which were clotted with blood, he made a sign to the executioner.

The latter unbound Charlie, who sank on the floor.

Uttering low moans he rolled about in agony.

"Rub his back with some ointment to get it well. I shall want to whip him again soon," said Sunday.

"White skin better to whip than black,' remarked the executioner.

"Yes. You can see what you are doing. The skin is thinner, too, and the white slaves scream more."

"It makes nice music."

"You are right. Take him away."

The executioner helped Charlie to rise, conducted him outside, rubbed his flesh with a healing ointment, and gave him his clothes.

He put them on with difficulty, for he ached and smarted terribly. His nerves seemed to be completely shattered for the time.

Choking sobs broke from him.

It was impossible for him to press back these evidences of severe suffering.

He walked to the spies' pavilion, tottering like an old man with the ague.

Peeping Tom and Knowall Dick were awaiting his coming with expectation, feeling glad that they had not been selected as the victims of Sunday Ja-Ja's spite.

"Hullo!" exclaimed Tom; "had your dose, old fellow?"

"Get it hot?" queried Dick.

"You wouldn't have cared for half of it," replied Charlie.

"He's the king's son. It is a mark of distinction," said Peeping Tom.

"Quite an honour, I'm sure," remarked Knowall Dick.

"Don't chaff me," answered Charlie, wearily.

He sank upon a heap of skins.

Peeping Tom looked out of the door.

He saw someone coming towards them.

"I say," he exclaimed, "here's old Chobo."

"You don't mean that," cried Knowall Dick.

Both guessed in a moment that he must have brought news from Three Points.

News of an important nature, too.

"Let us intercept and question him," said Tom.

"Yes, good business that," replied Dick.

They ran out and met him half-way.

"Ha! you here again?" exclaimed Chobo, in surprise.

"We have been captured by Sunday Ja-Ja."

"Strange! You are in danger for the poisoning."

"Are they all dead?"

"Only the old man. The others recovered."

"Confusion!" cried Peeping Tom. "Do they suspect us?"

"Who else? You were in the kitchen— Maum Guinea says so."

"Jack, Harry, and the girl are alive, then?"

"All three," answered Chobo. "It is a serious affair."

"Why so? We are safe here," said Peeping Tom.

"Be not too sure. Jack and Harry are marching on to Ashantee. They have a lieutenant of the gunboat, and twenty men, with a machine gun."

"Oh!" ejaculated Tom.

"That is news indeed," said Dick, making a grimace.

"The lieutenant's orders," added Chobo, "are to make King Ja-Ja and his son prisoners, bring them to the coast, and have them dealt with by the men in power."

"What have they done?"

"Robbed caravans—stopped trade. If

you are found here, so much the worse for you."

"Are you going to tell Sunday Ja-Ja this?" asked Peeping Tom.

"That is what I have come in for," replied Chobo.

"Don't say you have seen us."

"Why?"

"I have my reasons. Oblige me in this."

"Certainly. What matters it to me? I am an Ashantee, and I want to see the country properly governed."

"How many days' march are the English from here?" inquired Knowall Dick.

"Two days' only."

"That will do," exclaimed Peeping Tom. "Cut along. We shall know how to act."

Chobo left them, and they began to talk in a low and earnest tone.

The situation was becoming grave.

They had no mercy to expect from Jack Spencer or Harry Rawlings after the dastardly attempt they had made on their lives.

It was better to trust to King Ja-Ja and his son.

In time they might manage to escape.

They decided to tell Charlie the news they had heard.

Their interest was common and identical. Charlie was a clever fellow, and might advise them how to act.

It was their opinion that Sunday Ja-Ja would send for them.

They were supposed to be able to see and know everything.

Chobo had given them valuable information. How should they make use of it?

In spite of his cruel sufferings, Charlie listened with the utmost interest to what they had to tell him.

Twenty blue-jackets, with Snider rifles, and a Nordenfeldt gun, led by a naval lieutenant, were no mean antagonists.

But the Ashantees could oppose hundreds against them.

Yet the Africans were badly armed, and would be at a disadvantage when opposed to British energy, pluck, discipline and service.

If Sunday made up his mind to fight, he might win the battle; but he would have to make his soldiers throw up earthworks.

This kind of warfare they did not understand.

But they might be taught.

There was time before the arrival of the English.

Much might be done in a short space.

"The young prince is sure to send for us," exclaimed Peeping Tom. "We know everything that is going on. What shall we tell him to do?"

"Tell him to fight," replied Charlie.

"Do you think he will win?"

"He ought to."

"Perhaps he will put us in the front of the battle."

"I don't want a bullet to let the daylight into me," remarked Knowall Dick.

"The same here," said Peeping Tom.

"I don't seem to care very much what becomes of me. I'll fight," cried Charlie.

"You?"

"Yes. Why not? I may as well be dead as live to be a whipping-boy to that young brute."

The spies looked grave.

They were on the horns of a dilemma.

If they went out to fight their countrymen it would be a disgraceful thing, and they might get killed or wounded.

Supposing they stood aloof?

The English might conquer the city, and if the spies were found by Jack Spencer and Harry Rawlings, they would surely go to prison to be tried for all they had done.

"It is one of those cases in which one does not know how to act," observed Peeping Tom, anxiously.

"I wish to goodness," said Charlie, "Harry Rawlings were dead! Then I should have the property all to myself. We would get home somehow."

"We've got to get away from here first," remarked Knowall Dick.

"Can't we hide somewhere until the battle is over?" asked Charlie.

"I am afraid not."

"Well, I don't know what we can do," exclaimed Charlie, irritably. "Don't bother me. Every bone in my body aches."

He turned over on the rugs and closed his eyes, though he found sleep out of the question, lacerated as he was.

Life had lost all charms for him.

"Cheer up," replied Peeping Tom. "We have sacrificed everything for you."

"That's true," said Knowall Dick. "You have made us what we are."

"I can't help it," was Charlie's answer.

"You will have to pluck up a bit, and see us through our troubles."

"What can I do?"

"Be our leader, as you have always been," replied Peeping Tom.

"I cannot now. Leave me alone."

Tom was about to say something more to encourage him, when General Sangara made his apearance.

His face was unusually grave.

In a few words he informed the spies that Sunday Ja-Ja required their presence immediately.

Evidently Chobo had told his story of the anticipated attack on the city.

The young king knew a good deal about the British and their strength.

The news disquieted, and at the same time irritated him.

He wanted to consult the spies.

It was with some inward trepidation that they entered the presence of the young king.

Nevertheless they put on a bold front.

Sunday Ja-Ja was seated on a throne composed entirely of ivory, and in his hand he held a sceptre of pure gold.

General Sangara was by his side.

No one else was present at the audience, Chobo having gone to seek rest and refreshment.

"Tom the Peeper and Dick the Knower," exclaimed Sunday, "have you anything to tell me?"

"Yes," replied Tom, "we were coming to you if you had not sent for us."

"Speak! What do you see?"

"I see trouble coming on your kingdom, O great prince!"

"Whence does it come?"

"From the coast where the great sea washes the land. White men are marching against you."

"I know," exclaimed Dick, "that you will be attacked."

"What shall I do?"

"Fight them and win the battle. They will go down before you like corn before the knife of the reaper."

Sunday Ja-Ja clapped his hands.

"Truly," he said, "this is wonderful. If we conquer I will give you anything you ask for."

"We only want our liberty."

"You shall have it; but you must help us to fight. What do you advise us to do?"

"Dig holes in the ground and hide your soldiers in them," answered Peeping Tom. "Then the great gun the white men have will not do so much harm."

"Tell Sangara how it is done."

"Willingly, my prince," said Peeping Tom. "May your shadow never grow less; may you enjoy all the wealth in the world."

"Let no one throw dirt on your head," remarked Knowall Dick. "You are the light of the universe."

"Go with my general," cried Sunday Ja-Ja. "I have made up my mind to fight, and will do so to the death."

He did not mean his own death, but that of his subjects, for he generally kept out of the way of the deadly bullet.

The interview was at an end.

The spies departed with Sangara, who asked them how rifle pits were made. In a short time they were outside the city, and a couple of hundred men were set to work throwing up earthworks on the sandy plain.

The work only ceased when night came.

Early the next day it was recommenced with the same vigour.

Both gates of the city were strongly fortified, and the walls being thick, it would be difficult to make a breach in them.

To carry the place by assault would require a large force.

King Ja-Ja threw off his lethargy when he heard of the danger that threatened him, and went out to view the works.

"I am afraid of the English," he said to Sangara.

"Why so?" replied the general. "They are but worms."

"Not so. They are as numerous as the sands on the sea-shore. If we kill those who are coming, more will follow."

"They shall share the same fate," cried the general, valiantly. "Long live King Ja-Ja! Who can stand against him?"

In spite of his assurance, the king was ill at ease.

The spies were called, and they, too, prophesied victory complete and final.

They earnestly hoped it might be so.

It was a high stake they were playing for.

If the attacking party were defeated, Jack and Harry would most likely be killed. The spies were promised their liberty. No doubt the same privilege would be accorded to Charlie, and from him they would get their reward.

The people were not very enthusiastic, however.

They did not like King Ja-Ja any more than they had liked their late King Makolo.

Frequent murmurings were heard.

Threats of running away were indulged in.

At the end of the second day's work, when all preparations were complete, the spies sat down outside the gate.

The soldiers were standing or lounging about the earthworks.

Scouts were out in every direction.

At any moment the approach of the English contingent might be observed.

Sunday Ja-Ja had sent the spies a present of fruit, which they were eating.

He had been over the works, and expressed himself much pleased with them.

"I say, Tommy," exclaimed Knowall Dick, "there is something wrong about these Ashantee fellows."

"How's that, Dickey?"

"There is that in their manner I don't like. They won't fight, mark my words."

"Don't say that."

"'I HAVE BEEN ROBBED!' CRIED CHARLIE."

"I do, and I mean it. They do not like Ja-Ja. There is some movement on foot, though I cannot tell you what it is."

"The safest place for us will be the temple, if El Obed will allow us to hide there," remarked Peeping Tom. "He is well disposed towards us."

"I know it. We will visit him, and ask permission to seek shelter there if the Ashantees run."

"That is what I want," said Dick. "If we are caught red-handed fighting against our own countrymen, we shall fare pretty roughly."

Without losing a moment, they went to the temple, where they found El Obed.

When he heard their request, he granted it at once.

The door of the temple should be left open for them.

They also asked that Charlie might find a refuge with them, but this was objected to.

El Obed did not want the mysteries of the temple profaned by any more prying eyes.

The sacred fire was not to be gazed at by everybody.

Consequently they were obliged to leave Charlie to take his chance.

At ten o'clock the moon rose.

Half-an-hour afterwards scouts came running in from a north-westerly direction.

The British were coming.

Already they were in sight of the city.

A night attack was no doubt intended.

The utmost excitement and commotion prevailed at once, as the men took their places in the earthworks.

Sangara ran from place to place, seeing that the soldiers were at their posts, and giving out ammunition.

The spies occupied a little redoubt, not far from the gate, and awaited the onset with much anxiety.

Soon the blue-jackets could be seen advancing in a double line.

At their head were Lieutenant Smolley, Jack and Harry.

The two latter did not shirk danger.

They had volunteered for the service, and were willing to take their share of the risk.

CHAPTER XIX.

THE NIGHT ATTACK ON THE RIFLE PITS—FLIGHT OF THE ASHANTEES—OCCUPATION OF THE CITY—CAPTURE OF KING JA-JA, HIS SON, AND CHARLIE—A LEGAL ARRANGEMENT.

IT was a lovely night, and as the English advanced, they could plainly distinguish the walls of the city.

There was something else to be noticed also.

That was the earth thrown up outside the rifle pits.

Lieutenant Smolley was provided with a field-glass, through which he reconnoitred the position.

"Halt!" he cried.

The sailors instantly came to a standstill and stood at ease.

Smolley called Jack and Harry to his side.

"There is something in our front I don't like the look of," he exclaimed.

"What is it?" asked Jack.

"Do you see nothing?"

"Only a quaint African walled town."

"Have you ever been in the neighbourhood of earthworks?"

"Can't say that I ever have."

"Then I will excuse your ignorance," replied the lieutenant. "But tell me, Rawlings, when you were a captive here, did you notice those mounds in front of the gate?"

"I don't see them," replied Harry.

"Take my glass."

Harry did so.

"Ah!" he said, "now I see the mounds. The place is honeycombed with them."

"Are they new?"

"Entirely so."

"Are you sure they were not there during your stay in Ashantee?"

"Quite sure."

"Well, then, allow me to inform you that some European, having a knowledge of military engineering, has set the natives at work."

"In doing what?"

"Entrenching. There is a kind of little Plevna before us."

"Occupied?" queried Jack.

"What do you think?" replied Smolley. "Do you suppose the enemy is going to throw up earthworks and dig rifle pits for nothing? The pits, I daresay, are full of men ready to give us a hot reception."

"How did they know we were coming?"

"King Ja-Ja perhaps had scouts and runners out. It's lucky I perceived the manoeuvre."

"It is indeed. Fancy Ja-Ja preparing to give us a surprise," said Jack.

"He won't pull it off this time, though," exclaimed Smolley, setting his teeth together. "He's got an officer of the British Navy to deal with."

"Who knows a trick or two," added Jack.

"Well, I haven't qualified for acting lieutenant without picking up a wrinkle or so," replied Smolley.

He paused for a moment to settle upon his course of action.

In addition to the Nordenfeldt gun, which fired an almost incredible number of bullets every minute, he had at the last moment sent to the gunboat for a mountain howitzer.

This gun was in three pieces, and could be put together very quickly.

It was carried on the back of a mule.

"I think," he said, at length, "that we will get near enough to draw their fire."

"What for?" asked Jack.

"To make them expose their position."

"But at the same time, will not that expose us to danger?"

"We must chance that. In war there is always risk," answered Smolley.

"Why not shell them from a distance?"

"I should frighten them too soon. What I want to do is to pepper them with the Nordenfeldt."

"Of course you know best."

"Hope so. Fall in there! Quick march!"

The little column was soon again in movement, and in half-an-hour the space intervening was considerably lessened.

The enemy made no sign.

The silence of the grave reigned in the neighbourhood of the rifle pits.

Anyone would have thought that the Ashantees had, as usual, retired to rest for the night.

Fortunate, indeed, was it for Lieutenant Smolley and his men that he had surmised otherwise.

Had he not done so, he and his brave fellows would have advanced to certain death.

As they drew nearer, dusky forms could be seen gliding about from one part of the works to another.

This effectually settled the question.

There could be no longer any doubt that the rifle pits were fully manned—that every soldier was at his post, and that an effectual communication was kept up.

Lieutenant Smolley called another halt, during which the howitzer was put together and loaded.

Then they resumed their march, advancing to within five hundred yards of the formidable position of the Ashantees.

This drew their fire.

An ill-directed volley was sent at the assailants.

One man fell to the ground pressing his hand to his heart.

"Back! Retreat at the double!" shouted Smolley.

There was a retrograde movement, which took the sailors out of range of the enemy's guns.

Thinking that the English were thoroughly alarmed and demoralised, General Sangara exposed his strength.

He ordered five hundred men to get out of their cover and pursue.

This was immediately done.

A howling mob of negroes, armed with guns and spears, appeared on the plain.

They had no system of drill, nor organisation.

On they rushed, yelling like demons.

They were sure of victory.

Seeing this manœuvre the lieutenant halted his men, and formed them in two lines wide apart.

The first rank was standing, the second kneeling.

"Pick the leaders off steadily," he said. "Mr. Spencer, Mr. Rawlings, and myself will work the machine gun. Stand steady, my lads, we're in a hot corner!"

"Ay, sir," was the reply.

The men were as calm, cool, and collected as if on parade.

As for their leaders they might have been out partridge shooting in the stubble at home.

Presently a dropping fire came from the British line.

The foremost Ashantees fell to rise no more.

Yet the others pressed on as if they were anxious to embrace death.

Suddenly the sharp crack, crack of the Nordenfeldt rose on the night air, gradually increasing to a dull growl, and then an angry roar.

As the bullets scattered among the densely-packed mass of savages, they fell by scores.

Their return fire was of no avail, because they could not get near enough to hit with their old-fashioned weapons.

The sailors discharged their weapons with as much precision as if they were engaged in target practice.

In vain General Sangara tried to induce the Ashantees to continue the attack.

A panic seized them, they wavered, they broke, and fled in disorder.

Still the deadly machine gun, with its far-reaching bullets, mowed them down, until the sandy plain was dotted with heaps of slain.

Of the five hundred who went into battle, scarce two hundred returned to find refuge in the earthworks.

It was a cleverly planned and well-executed manœuvre.

"Cease firing!" cried Lieutenant Smolley.

By this time the last black-skinned rascal was sinking into his pit.

Sunday Ja-Ja had remained in the works with the spies, and he was frantic with rage.

"Who was shot just now?" continued Smolley, who always took a personal interest in those under his command.

"Abel Slater, sir."

"Poor fellow, he's lost the number of his mess; but we will avenge him. Just rig up the howitzer."

"Ay, ay, sir."

"Sight it well, and give the shell a fair wind."

The boatswain undertook this task, for he understood the working of this admirable little field-piece.

Jack and Harry looked on with interest to see the result of the firing, which was something new to them.

Their arms ached, and they were warm through the exertion of turning the handle which ground out the bullets from the machine gun.

The boatswain took his elevation, judged his distance, and applied the match.

A sullen roar followed a flash of fire.

Then the shell made a parabolic curve in the air, and with a hiss, descended in the very centre of the rifle pit.

It burst, and its contents scattered death and destruction all round.

The Ashantees were terribly frightened.

This was a new kind of warfare, which they could not understand.

It seemed as if a fiery hail were coming down from heaven to annihilate them.

Sunday Ja-Ja stole away unperceived, to hide himself in the palace.

Actuated by the same laudable ambition, Peeping Tom and Knowall Dick glided off.

They saw plainly enough that the game was up, and not caring to figure prominently in the list of killed or wounded, they made for the temple.

Scarcely had they vanished when another shell came plump among a group of blacks.

Sangara was the centre of the crowd, who were asking for advice in the crisis that had arisen.

Many were killed by the explosion.

The general miraculously escaped unharmed, though men were maimed and shattered by his side.

The question under discussion had been: was it advisable to renew the attack, stay in the pits, or retreat, yielding the field to the English?

The second shell settled it without any further debate.

Flight was decided on by all who survived, and the decision was acted upon with amazing unanimity.

There was not a single dissentient.

The general was obliging enough to lead the way.

Smolley did not deem it advisable to follow up his victory that night, concluding that it would be best to wait for morning.

He dreaded lest some ambush might be laid for him; so, setting a watch, he told the men to get a little sleep.

They were up at daybreak, and pushed on to the rifle pits, which they found deserted, but heaped up with piles of dead.

No natives appeared; they were either cowed, or had received orders not to show themselves.

Smolley marched towards the gates of the city, fully prepared to fire if he should be interfered with.

Nothing but the surrender of the city, the occupation of the palace, and the giving up of King Ja-Ja and Sunday would satisfy him.

These were his terms, of which he would not abate an iota.

Sangara, bearing a white flag, came out to meet him, and being favourably received by Smolley, proposed a capitulation.

"Is that all you want?" asked the general, in surprise, when told what the terms of the English were.

"We must stay a week in the palace, to rest and appoint a new king, who will keep order," replied the lieutenant.

"Yes, I understand."

"The instructions I have received from my Government are to restore peace to the country, and safety to the trade caravans. I must have Ja-Ja and his son given up to me to be taken as prisoners to the coast, where the Governor of Benin will punish them as they deserve."

"They are usurpers here," said Sangara. "As general of the army, I have no objection to that course."

He was overjoyed to get off so easily.

He had quite expected that the first thing the English officer would ask for would be his head.

For King Ja-Ja and Sunday he did not care.

Again there was another thing on which he congratulated himself. Ja-Ja had collected much treasure by plundering caravans, and had taken all that King Makolo had left.

As Smolley had not asked for this, the

sagacious Sungara intended to keep it for himself.

Bowing low he went on before. During the journey to the palace not a soldier showed even the butt of a rifle.

If the military mingled with the crowd, which came out to see the English, they came as civilians.

At length the palace was reached. Lieutenant Smolley, Jack and Harry were installed in the king's pavilion, the sailors, with their guns, being drawn up outside under the trees.

It was incumbent upon them to beware of treachery.

Refreshments were placed before the three leaders of the expedition.

The executioner made his appearance with his sharp wooden sword, and stood by the side of Smolley.

He had heard that the white man, with the blue naval uniform, was the conqueror, and he naturally fancied there would be some heads to cut off.

This generally was the case in Ashantee when a change of Government took place.

He had seen a few, and he understood the business.

"What do you want?" asked Smolley, who was dissecting a cold fowl with the aid of his pocket-knife.

"Me cut off head," was the answer. "Sangara gone for Ja-Ja and Sunday Ja-Ja. What you do with them? Throw them to snakes, or give them to lions?"

"Neither."

"What you do, then? Boil in oil, skin alive, bury to neck in ground, strip naked, or smear with honey and tie to trees for fly to sting to death?"

"We do not do such things in our country," answered the lieutenant. "Tell your general to confine King Ja-Ja and his son in a safe place. I will see them later on."

"Dungeon in the rock?" said the executioner. "Keep prisoners there for months and years."

"That will do so long as they do not escape."

Scarcely had the executioner left the pavilion to tell Sangara what to do with the prisoners, than Jack sprang to his feet.

He craned his neck to look out of the door.

They knew nothing about the movements of the spies and Charlie, so that Jack could scarcely believe his eyes when he saw the latter hiding behind a flowering shrub and staring in at the pavilion.

The fact was that Charlie had heard of the defeat of the Ashantees, with tremendous slaughter, by the British.

He had seen Sangara arrest King Ja-Ja and Sunday.

Wishing to know who led the victorious force, he was so imprudent as to venture to look in.

When he saw Jack and Harry he was about to run away to seek a hiding-place somewhere.

It was too late, however.

"Charlie!" cried Jack. "After him! Follow me, Harry."

Away bounded Charlie like a deer.

Before he had gone fifty yards Jack overtook him.

Turning round and standing at bay, Charlie drew a knife of which he had possessed himself.

"Back!" he shouted. "Your life or mine!"

"Yours for a thousand!" replied Jack, producing a pistol.

Charlie was placed at a disadvantage.

His knife was of no use against powder and shot.

Dropping his weapon he folded his arms.

"I surrender," he exclaimed. "I am your prisoner."

"Who would have thought of finding you here?" said Harry, coming up. "How can you explain it?"

Charlie looked very crestfallen.

"I am very sorry for all I have done," he replied. "It was my father who put me up to it, and he is dead."

"How?"

"We were trying to get to Cape Coast Castle, but got lost in the forest. Sunday Ja-Ja captured us; my father was shot. I and Peeping Tom and Knowall Dick were brought here."

"This is news," exclaimed Jack. "Where are those bright specimens of humanity?"

"I don't know. Dead perhaps! They went out to superintend the earthworks. I have not seen them since."

Harry laughed sarcastically.

"They are not dead," he exclaimed. "Those two fellows would keep out of danger, come what might."

"I declare I know nothing about them."

"They are, and always have been friends of yours," said Jack, severely.

"To serve their own purpose," replied Charlie.

"Did you not send them to poison us?"

Here Charlie saw a loophole of escape.

"Do you think I would do such a thing," he exclaimed, "when I am so fond of your sister, Marian? You must be mad, Spencer, to dream of such a thing. I knew she always dined with you. Rather than hurt her I would die a thousand deaths."

"There is something in that," remarked Harry.

"If I could only believe him."

"You may, indeed, Spencer," said Charlie, eagerly. "I may be bad, but I am not so vile as that."

"I don't know. You have not turned out trumps very often, if at all."

"Peeping Tom and Knowall Dick did it of their own accord."

"It is very easy to say so."

"I assure you that I was horrified when I heard of it," continued Charlie.

He saw he had made a favourable impression, and wanted to improve it."

This was his only chance of safety.

"Don't be hard on a poor fellow who is down on his luck," he added. "Show that you are made of noble stuff both of you."

"It is for Harry to say, not me," answered Jack.

Harry came to a sudden resolution.

"Maybe, after all," he exclaimed, "that he was ill-advised by his father."

"That's it," cried Charlie, eagerly. "Make allowance."

"As much as I can. You cannot claim the property in England, which is mine by right; but to save law business, sign a paper giving up all rights to the estate, and you can go free."

"There is no paper here."

"I carry some in my pocket."

"Where is the ink?"

"That I have also. A little bottle of ink and a pen I always carry," replied Harry.

"Lieutenant Smolley and I will be witnesses," cried Jack.

"I'll sign," exclaimed Charlie, "willingly. I have been acting unfairly towards you."

"Glad you admit it."

"Give me the chance to turn over a new leaf."

"I am going to do so."

"I will lead a better life. My past has been a miserable one. Your kindness is more than I deserve."

"No doubt about that," said Jack.

"Believe me, I am ashamed of myself," continued Charlie, who did not care what he said so long as he saved his life.

"So you ought to be."

"But," pleaded Charlie, "don't turn me adrift. How can I get home if I am left here? Take me back to England, will you?"

"No," replied Jack.

"Can't do that," answered Harry.

"I will be your servant."

Harry shook his head.

"You have proved yourself so bad that I cannot trust you," he exclaimed.

Charlie pretended to be profoundly affected.

Of course, he did not mean a word he had been saying.

His protestations of repentance, his self-accusations, and his promises of amendment were all sham.

His only desire was to share the comforts Harry would have, and to be near him so that he might take his life.

Once Harry was out of the way, there was no one else to step in and hold the property.

"Don't leave me in this barbarous place," he said. "They think nothing of killing a white man when they want to celebrate a festival or have a sacrifice."

"You must take your chance," answered Harry.

"For heaven's sake, act like a Christian."

"Have you behaved like one?"

"I admit I have not," Charlie replied, with becoming humility; "but it was all my father's fault. He wanted to keep the property for me."

"As you have made your bed you must lie upon it."

"Is there no hope for me?"

"None. The laws of the Medes and Persians were not more unalterable than is my determination," exclaimed Harry. "Come and sign the agreement, and go where you like. It is all I can do for you."

He led the way into the pavilion with Jack, and Charlie followed them.

A few words to Lieutenant Smolley explained who he was.

The deed was soon drawn up, Charlie signed it, and it was witnessed by Jack and Smolley.

"Now you can go," said Harry.

"Where?" asked Charlie, with a tinge of bitterness in his tone.

"It matters not to me. Stay here, if you choose. You seem to be at home with these savage robbers and murderers! Birds of a feather, you know, flock together."

"You turn me out into the hard, wide world a beggar!"

"Everybody cannot be rich. I am only securing my own."

"Heartless! merciless!" cried Charlie.

Harry took him by the shoulders, and pushed him rudely out of the building.

He fell on his hands and knees, but picking himself up he slunk away.

Stopping under some trees, he shook his fist and gnashed his teeth.

"Harry Rawlings!" he hissed, "you have done a bad day's work in letting me go free. I will live to be a thorn in your side, never fear, and you shall feel me, too, before long."

"That is a promising young gentleman," remarked the lieutenant, when he had gone. "If I had been you I would have held him a prisoner."

"No. I prefer to leave him to his fate," answered Harry. "Let him work out his destiny. It will not be a very brilliant one."

"Beware of him. He has a vicious look."

"Depend upon it, I shall always be on my guard."

"So will I," exclaimed Jack. "We are two to one, which reminds me that we have seen nothing of peeping Tom and Knowall Dick."

"If we can find them, let us give them a scare," said Harry.

"In what way?"

"Try them by court-martial for attempting to poison us, and sentence them to death. Two ropes can be rigged on to the branch of a tree, and we will reprieve them at the last moment when the rope is round their necks."

"Capital!" cried Jack, with a laugh.

"You will have to catch them first," remarked the lieutenant.

"We must call Sangara, the general," said Harry. "Possibly he may be able to put his hand upon them."

As he spoke the general made his appearance, and at the same time a loud howling was heard from a building a couple of hundred yards off.

"What's that noise?" inquired Smolley.

"Only King Ja-Ja and Sunday Ja-Ja," replied the general.

"Ah! what is the matter with them?"

"I have captured and lodged them in the dungeon. The executioner is beating them with sticks, according to custom. We always torture distinguished captives."

"That can't be allowed."

"Oh, he won't kill them; only half," answered Sangara, coolly, and with an air of unconcern.

The yells and shrieks of pain uttered by King Ja-Ja and Sunday were ear-piercing.

Clearly the executioner was not sparing them.

"Stop it!" cried the lieutenant, in a tone of authority. "No more of this. Go! Make the executioner desist, and come back to us."

"If it is your pleasure, but our customs ought to be respected."

"Yes, in the breach rather than the observance. Go!"

Sangara left them rather sullenly, as if disappointed.

The mighty had fallen from their high estate, and he wanted them to know it by treating them like dogs.

When Sangara returned, he reported that he had stopped the flogging.

"The executioner is an invaluable man," he added. "We never had one who knew his business better."

"I will not allow it," said Smolley.

"Your mightiness has ordered it so, and your wishes are obeyed."

"Do you know two white boys who, we are informed, are here?" asked Harry.

"Yes. Surely you mean the wonderful ones who claim to tell and see everything?"

"Those, I expect, are the ones."

"Tom the Peeper and Dick the Knower?"

"Exactly."

"They prophesied that we should beat you," exclaimed the general, "or we should not have gone out to fight. This time they were wrong. It was they who taught us to throw up earthworks and dig rifle pits."

"The young scoundrels!" ejaculated the lieutenant, his face flushing with honest indignation.

"Fancy fighting against their own countrymen," said Jack.

"By Jove! they deserve hanging," observed Harry.

"Do you know where they are?" asked Smolley.

"I have not seen them since last night. They ran away, I am told, but if you want them I will try to find them."

Sangara bowed deferentially, and went on a search for the spies.

In two hours he came back with the unsatisfactory intelligence that he could discover no trace of them.

They had left no clue whatever of their hiding-place.

He did not dream of looking in the temple for them.

The city was the abode of grief and mourning.

There were few homes into which the grim, gaunt and ghastly skeleton of death had not penetrated.

Large parties of men were out on the plain beyond the gate burying the dead.

It was a sad scene.

The air was filled with the wailing cries of women and children.

Anon it rose high, and then sank to a low, plaintive, not altogether unmusical cadence.

Such are the horrors of war.

CHAPTER XX.

THE SPIES BECOME RESTLESS—INQUISITIVENESS BRINGS ITS OWN REWARD—THE COURT-MARTIAL—TURNED OUT INTO THE WILDERNESS.

PEEPING TOM and Knowall Dick passed a good night in the temple, and laughed in the morning at their clever escape.

One of the priests, who attended to the sacred fire, brought them some food, by the orders of El Obed.

The high priest had not yet lost confidence in them, although the disaster to the Ashantee arms was complete.

He sought them after they had broken their fast, and asked them to explain the defeat.

They said that fire and lead had come down from the sky.

The shells which did so much mischief were the result of magic.

El Obed believed the story, and thanked them for the explanation.

"Ah, ah!" laughed Peeping Tom, when they were alone, "isn't he soft?"

"As putty," replied Knowall Dick. "I like to play on him. It's fun."

"Wouldn't you be pleased to have a look at Jack Spencer and Harry Rawlings?" continued Tom. "I should."

"If it was safe."

"I can't stay here all day. Don't you think we might venture into the palace grounds and take a peep round, just to see Charlie?"

"Perhaps he is hanged by this time. You know what Jack and Harry are. They are our bitter foes, and his, too."

"You are always suggesting something dreadful," exclaimed Peeping Tom. "I feel as if I had a rope round my neck already."

"Stay here if you don't want to realise the feeling."

"I can't. I must go, for I am restless."

"Well, if you are determined," replied Knowall Dick, "I suppose I must go, too."

"Oh, we sha'n't come to any grief."

"Don't be too sure of that."

"We will trust to our cleverness," exclaimed Tom, "and I am sure no harm will come to us. Have some pluck about you?"

"Why didn't you, last night, while they were shelling us? If we had put ourselves at the head of the Ashantees we might have rallied them and saved the battle. What a chance we have lost. Think of the distinction—the glory—the—"

"Stuff!" interrupted Peeping Tom. "We should have been a couple of fools to stay to be shot at."

"But the honour, my dear boy, of dying for—"

"Hold your tongue. When the Ashantees want a leader they had better come to you. I know where you would lead them."

"Where?"

"To the first hole you could find to hide in, and nothing but an earthquake would get you out of it."

Knowall Dick rubbed his hands.

"How well he knows me," he muttered.

Seeing that Tom had made up his mind to go and explore, Dick made no further objection, though he had serious misgivings.

It was a rash and venturesome undertaking.

However, Tom's nature was such that he would not have been content if he did not pry.

He was burning to know what Jack and Harry were doing.

There was a reckless disregard of consequences in his inquisitiveness.

This was what so often led him into trouble.

The priests had no orders to keep them prisoners, so they passed out of the temple as freely as El Obed himself.

From the houses the cries of mourning continued to come.

The spies were glad when they got to the palace grounds, which they entered without being challenged.

There was no guard.

Lieutenant Smolley posted his own guard round his pavilion, and the Nordenfeldt and the howitzer were both mounted, loaded and ready for use at a moment's notice.

He could sweep the approach from the town, and feared nothing.

"Look at the guns," whispered Peeping Tom, "and the sailors. That's where Jack and Harry are."

"Come away," replied Knowall Dick.

"It's the king's pavilion they've got."

"Never mind. Let us go round to our old diggings."

"What for?"

"Perhaps we shall find Charlie there."

"All right."

They glided off to the left, and soon came to the building where they used to live.

Peeping Tom looked in at the window.

Charlie was there, sitting on some mats, all alone.

"LEVER SHOOK PEEPING TOM AS A TERRIER SHAKES A RAT."

He was looking very miserable, and seemed plunged in deep thought. The fact was, he did not know whither to go, or what to do.

If he stayed in Ashantee the new ruler, whoever it was who succeeded Ja-Ja, would make him a slave.

If he attempted to reach the coast by himself it would be certain death from want of water or by wild beasts.

He could do nothing without a guide.

Dark thoughts were revolving in Charlie's brain.

He wanted to keep Harry in sight, so that he could take his life when opportunity offered.

By this means alone could he achieve independence, and live at ease for the rest of his life.

He had tasted the sweets of property, and had a deep-rooted aversion to work.

There was but one thing for him to do, and that was to remove Harry from his path.

Not a spark of gratitude did he entertain towards him for sparing his life.

His misfortunes and privations were making him desperate.

"Hullo, Charlie!" exclaimed Peeping Tom. "How are you, old boy?"

"Glad you're alive," said Knowall Dick.

Charlie looked up, and a shade of pleasure crossed his dejected countenance.

"Come into my diggings," he replied. "I was afraid you were killed in the battle last night."

"Too old a soldier for that."

"Where have you been hiding?"

"That's telling," answered Peeping Tom; "not that I have no confidence in you, but in times like these we can trust nobody."

They entered the building and sat down.

"It isn't quite safe for you fellows to be seen about," remarked Charlie.

"Why not? If the lieutenant has done nothing to you, I don't suppose he will hurt us."

"I have been before him, and on signing a deed in which I confessed I had no title to the Rawlings property, I was told to go where I liked."

"It is a wonder you linger instead of making a start," replied Tom.

"I don't know where to go. If I try to cross the wilderness, I shall be courting death in a dozen different ways."

"Not so. I don't see that. If you can reach the caravan route where we were captured by Sunday Ja-Ja, and can exist for a short time till some traders come by, you will be all right."

"I never thought of that," cried Charlie. "Will you come with me?"

"Yes," answered Peeping Tom, with decision.

"You don't imagine that we want to stay in this wretched hole?" said Knowall Dick.

"If you do, you are very foolish. However remote your hiding-place is, it is liable to be discovered, and I know that both Jack Spencer and Harry will not spare any endeavour to find you."

"How so?"

"They have been questioning me. Sangara has been sent in every direction after you."

The spies drew very long countenances on hearing this news.

"I suppose we shall be hanged or shot," observed Peeping Tom.

"It is not safe for you to stay here," said Charlie. "A slave will come with my food directly, and he will be sure to go and tell if he sees you."

"What shall we do?"

"If I were you I should go back to my hiding-place and lie low till dark, when you can meet me outside the gate, and we will go off together."

"Good!" said Tom.

"We'll do that!" exclaimed Dick.

"Be off, then. Every minute you stay here is fraught with danger."

"True; I know it. Good-bye till this evening."

The spies shook hands cordially with Charlie, feeling that they had come to a wise determination.

In the city there was no safety, but outside they might, and probably would, meet with friendly traders.

There was one imminent danger to be risked.

If they were captured by a slave-dealer's band, there was no saying what their fate would be.

Still, anything almost was better than staying in Ashantee.

When they got outside, they were about to glide off among the trees, when the form of a sailor appeared before them.

He brought his rifle to his shoulder with a sharp click.

Then he challenged them in a loud, sonorous voice, which rang out clearly

"Halt! Who goes there?'

Jack had posted a sentry outside Charlie's house, on the chance that the spies would try to communicate with their fellow prisoner.

The result showed the accuracy of his judgment.

"All right, sailor," replied Peeping Tom; "we are going on important business."

"See you later," said Knowall Dick.

"No you won't," cried the man. "If you

advance another step, I shall fire. My orders are to take you before the lieutenant commanding."

"Wh-what f-for?" stammered Tom.

"You're wanted on suspicion of being in communication with the enemy."

Seeing that they were fairly trapped, they did not waste time arguing the point with the sailor.

Telling him that they would go quietly, they accompanied him to the pavilion, where the lieutenant was still sitting with Jack and Harry.

Their surprise was great when the spies were ushered into their presence.

By this time Peeping Tom and Knowall Dick had recovered their presence of mind and their assurance.

"Ah, Spencer and Rawlings!" cried Tom. "So glad to see you. This is quite an unexpected surprise."

"Never dreampt of such a pleasure," said Dick.

"How's that?" asked Jack. "You must have known that we beat the Ashantees and captured the city."

"Bless you, no," replied Tom. "We were confined in a dark and noisome dungeon, because we wanted to go and join you."

"Fact," said Knowall Dick. "The niggers were furious because we would not fight with them."

"As if we could side against our own countrymen," added Peeping Tom.

"Rather die," said Dick.

"I apprehend you have just managed to make your escape?" remarked Harry, with a palpable sneer.

"Half-an-hour ago," answered Peeping Tom. "All night long we were digging a hole with a bar of iron."

"Big enough to get our bodies through," said Knowall Dick.

Whatever falsehood one told, the other backed up.

"And of course you at once hastened to come to us and congratulate us on our victory?"

"That's it," replied Tom.

"The ticket exactly," answered Dick.

They nodded their heads and smiled, as if they had done something wonderfully clever and were quite pleased with themselves.

"We do not believe a word of your statement," exclaimed Jack.

"Not believe us!" cried Tom.

"Not credit two old schoolfellows who always had a reputation for speaking the—ahem!—the truth?"

The word nearly choked him; perhaps it was because he so seldom used it.

"We have direct evidence to the contrary," said Harry. "You fought on Ja-Ja's side. We can prove it. You tried to poison us at Three Points. That also we can prove."

"Oh, no; not so. Some other fellows," replied Peeping Tom.

"It's a base infamous libel," answered Knowall Dick.

Lieutenant Smolley now interposed.

"They must be tried by court-martial at once," he exclaimed, "and if found guilty of the two charges preferred against them, they will be punished with death. The charges are, trying to poison, and aiding and abetting the enemy."

At this declaration the spies looked very glum.

They were afraid that their career was to be cut short, at last. No way of getting out of the difficulty presented itself.

Their ready wit was at fault this time.

Lieutenant Smolley, Jack and Harry were the members of the court-martial.

The witnesses for the prosecution were Charlie and Sangara, who were promptly sent for.

The evidence that was given against the spies was of such a condemning nature that the accused could not refute it.

When asked what they had to say, they were obliged to content themselves with a dogged denial of the allegations.

In spite of this the court found them guilty.

The lieutenant pronounced sentence of immediate death by hanging.

Two ropes were reeved over the bough of a tree by the sailors, and two stools were placed underneath.

These were for the condemned to stand upon, and when the supports were kicked away, they would be left dangling in the air.

Everything had been done so rapidly that Peeping Tom and Knowall Dick could not realize they were to die in a few minutes.

They were made to stand on the stools, and the nooses were slipped over their necks.

Then the stools were kicked away, and the spies hung in the air, struggling frantically.

They were allowed to kick and gasp and tug with their hands at the ropes for about half-a-minute.

Then Smolley ordered them to be lowered.

Directly they touched the ground the ropes were removed from their necks, and they looked round, blinking like owls.

"I say!" exclaimed Peeping Tom, "you're having some kind of a lark with us, aren't you?"

"If it's a joke, it is a ghastly one," remarked Knowall Dick.

They were both shivering violently.

"We wanted to teach you a lesson," replied Jack, "and I hope you have learnt it. You richly deserve hanging, but we give you your lives. Go where you like, but if you are found in this city to-morrow, you will be put to death."

"Then we aren't to be hanged, after all?" said Tom.

"No, not this time."

"Hurrah!"

"You have a chance of reforming. On the ruins of your evil past you can, if you like, build up a good and virtuous life."

"Doesn't Spencer talk nicely?" observed Knowall Dick, winking at Tom.

"Quite like a parson. It's as edifying as a sermon. Oh! don't I wish I was as good and clever as he is."

"And as wise and pious," said Dick.

"So handsome, too—just like Harry. What a lovely pair they are," replied Peeping Tom.

Jack rushed forward and gave each of them a kick.

"Now stop it!" he exclaimed. "I don't want any of your chaff. You two will never change. Make yourselves scarce while you have the chance."

The spies at once departed at a run in the direction of Charlie's house. Very glad were they to have escaped so well; Jack was right when he had said they would never alter.

Their hearts were not affected, nor did they feel in the least inclined to reform.

Like Charlie, all they wanted was revenge.

When they joined their confederate again he was astonished to see them, for when he saw them captured, he made sure they would be executed.

"They played you a scurvy trick," he said, when he had heard what had transpired; "but never mind, they are only preparing a rod for their own backs."

"What fools they are to let us go," laughed Peeping Tom.

"Didn't I feel queer when the rope was round my neck and I was struggling in the air," remarked Knowall Dick.

"So did I. All the blood rushed to my head, I could not breathe. It was a horrible feeling of suffocation."

"We must stick together, boys!" exclaimed Charlie. "There is plenty of money in the world. We must try to get hold of some of it. I brought you out here, and I will stick to you."

"Things have changed since then," replied Tom. "You are not much good from a money point of view."

"Union is strength," said Charlie. "United we stand; divided we fall. Recollect the fable of the bundle of sticks. Harry alone blocks my way to a fine property. We must remove him; and, independently of that, we must seize every opportuntity of making money."

"You take the lead."

"I will."

"What do you propose to do?" continued Peeping Tom.

"Don't think I am without money," remarked Charlie, confidentially. "In a secret pocket in my vest I have two thousand pounds in Bank of England notes, so that we shall be able to cut a shine at any place we come to. I will give you plenty of enjoyment when we reach Cape Coast Castle, which is the place I shall steer for."

"That is where we have been trying to get for months, but we are as far off as ever."

"I'll get you there, boys. Let us start at once."

Charlie spoke confidently, but he was far from feeling all that he tried to convey to the others.

There was a long and dangerous march before them.

Their path would be beset with savage men as well as by wild beasts.

No one attempted to stop them when they left the palace grounds. In the streets the people looked askance at them, but none offered to molest them.

At a large building, which served as an armoury, they had no difficulty in obtaining three rifles of an ancient, muzzle-loading pattern. Powder, shot and ball were also plentiful.

They took what they required.

From a shop where food was sold they requisitioned some provisions, and the keeper was too frightened to ask for payment.

The white men were terrible fellows in the eyes of the Ashantees.

They had struck terror to their hearts.

At the gate they encountered El Obed, who had been out on the plain to celebrate some mystic heathen rites over the bodies of the slain.

"Ha!" he said, addressing the spies, "you have dared to show yourselves to your white brothers?"

"Oh, yes. We don't care," replied Peeping Tom. "I could see they would not hurt us."

"And I knew it," remarked Knowall Dick, with an emphatic shake of the head.

"Where are you going?"

"To the great sea. We desire to go to our homes," said Tom; "but we have one piece of advice to give you."

"Let me hear it. I have every confidence in your judgment. You can see into the future, Tom the Peeper; you, Dick the Knower, are aware of what is happening."

"We can—we do. This is a crisis in the

affairs of your nation.   King Makolo is dead, King Ja-Ja and his son are prisoners, and for their crimes against the traders will be taken away by the British and punished."

"It is well that it should be so," said El Obed.

"Do not interfere with the English commander or his sailors, but, if you can, imprison or kill the two young white men he has with him."

"Why should I do this?"

"If you do not, they will kill you and General Sangara."

This audacious statement was implicitly believed by the high priest.

It had the effect that Tom desired to produce.

"Ha!" cried El Obed, "do you mean that?"

"Undoubtedly.   You have been very kind, and I wish to serve you.   Protect your own interests—save your life."

"Do the spirits say that it is my life or theirs?" asked El Obed, earnestly.

"You have not long to live unless you take action."

"I will.   How long will the white men stay here?"

"Half a moon; but you must act quickly."

"I thank you," replied El Obed. "You are my friend, and you shall always find one in me."

"Perhaps we shall never meet again."

"Who knows? Life is full of uncertainties."

"No," said Peeping Tom; "we part for ever. I wish you success and prosperity. Turn out of your city all the men that Ja-Ja brought with him. Elect a king of your own; live in peace and contentment; cultivate happiness. Farewell!"

El Obed was so overwhelmed with gratitude at the timely warning which Tom had given him that he seized his hand and pressed his lips to it.

"May the Great Spirit have you in his holy keeping," he remarked.

The three adventurers now passed through the gate and began to cross the sandy plain towards the dense forest, by the skirt of which the great caravans went.

They were in high spirits at having obtained the privilege of leaving the city, which they hoped fervently never to see again.

"I think," observed Peeping Tom, "that I deserve a vote of thanks."

"What for?" inquired Charlie.

"Getting it up so prettily with El Obed for Jack and Harry. The priest believes all I tell him."

"Do you think he will try to kill them?"

"I am sure of it.   Like all his countrymen, El Obed is awfully superstitious."

"They are well guarded."

"That is nothing to a cunning savage."

Walking quickly, they arrived by nightfall at the edge of the forest, and determined to camp for the night.

A glorious sense of freedom pervaded their breasts.

No matter what perils they had to face they enjoyed their liberty, and were not subject to the petty caprices of a tyrant like Sunday Ja-Ja.

There were marks in the sandy waste, outside the forest, of camels' feet, showing that they were in the track of the caravans.

A shady spot was selected, they put their bags of provisions on the ground under a tree, and then arose the great question of the tropics. This was water.

Where were they to find any?

Already they were parched with thirst, and their sufferings would be intolerable if they had to pass the night without this essential necessary of life.

Loading their guns with ball, they started through the forest to find a spring.

They had heard from the natives that there were two or three in the neighbourhood, and that the hunters had dug wells to retain the water.

This made the vicinity dangerous, because it attracted the wild beasts.

It was now growing dark.

The forest looked very gloomy and forbidding.

As they penetrated farther into it, loud roars were heard on all sides, indicating that the lions were abroad.

It was necessary to exercise the utmost vigilance.

At length they came to some wells.

Their delight, however, was damped by seeing two gleaming eyes in front of them.

"Hold!" whispered Charlie. "It is a lion."

He darted behind a large tree.

His example was promptly imitated by Peeping Tom and Knowall Dick.

CHAPTER XXI.

EL OBED AND SANGARA—THE PLOT—A NARROW ESCAPE—EL OBED'S CONFESSION—THE VOW OF VENGEANCE.

THE high priest remained at the gate long after the white men had gone away, brooding over what Peeping Tom had told him.

The warning had sunk deep into his mind.

While he was ruminating, Sangara came in.

"What news, O Sangara?" asked El Obed. "My heart is heavy within me."

"Why should it be so? The white conquerors have agreed that King Makolo's son shall rule over the land. He is but a youth. The government will be in your hands and mine. That is what we have been wishing for."

"The heart of the leader is good," said El Obed, "but the two white young men he has with him are not to be trusted."

"How?" inquired Sangara.

"My life is threatened by them."

"Who told you that?"

"Tom the Peeper, who knows everything. If I do not kill them, they will undoubtedly have my life."

"Ha! is it so?" cried Sangara. "Apart from the friendship I have for you, I should regard your death as a public misfortune at this crisis of our country. It must not be. Your enemies shall die."

"It would not be difficult if we could separate them from their party," mused El Obed.

"Is that all you require?" replied Sangara, with a smile.

"You speak as if it were easy of accomplishment."

"And with reason. I heard them say just now that they were going into the forest early to-morrow to shoot big game, such as elephants and lions. That will be your opportunity. Follow them, and shoot at them from behind a tree."

"Good. Will you accompany me?"

"I cannot. My absence would occasion comment. You are seldom seen in public; it will be thought that you are attending on the sacred fire."

El Obed recognised the force of this objection, and determined to go alone.

"Do they take anybody with them?" he asked.

"But two men—one to act as guide, the other to carry provisions," answered Sangara.

That was enough for El Obed. He thanked the general for his information, and returned to the temple.

One of the priests was posted at the gate to tell him when the hunters left the city.

He passed the night by the sacred fire, uttering weird incantations to the idols for good fortune.

At dawn the watchman came running in.

"The white men have passed out," he said.

El Obed snatched up his gun, and made his way to the gate.

The forms of Jack and Harry, with their two sable attendants, could be seen about a mile distant.

El Obed followed the boys at a safe distance.

A long walk brought Harry and Jack to the confines of the forest.

They disappeared within its dense and mazy depths.

The priest now quickened his pace.

He entered the forest at least half-an-hour after them.

It was easy to trace their progress by the way in which the grass and wild flowers had been trodden down.

In some places, too, they had cut their way through the jungle with their knives.

All at once the report of a rifle echoed through the forest.

This was followed by a loud roar and another shot.

A lion had been encountered by the hunters, who had fired upon the king of beasts.

El Obed smiled in a ghastly manner, and passed on, grasping his gun tighter.

His enemies were not far off.

In a few minutes he saw them standing over the dead body of a noble lion, as they slipped fresh cartridges into their weapons.

He took careful aim at Harry, and fired.

As soon as he had done so, he ran away, intending to reload and shoot at Jack when he got another opportunity.

But he came to a full stop before he had gone far.

His progress was barred by a lion of enormous size.

Trembling in every limb, the wretched assassin knew not what to do.

To advance was certain death, to retreat was to invite capture.

It was an embarrassing dilemma, which he had been far from anticipating.

Harry uttered a cry, staggered, and put

his hand to the side of his head, withdrawing it covered with blood.

"Good heaven!" cried Jack; "you are hit. What vile coward has done this?"

He looked closely at him with great anxiety.

He saw that the bullet had grazed his ear, carrying away a portion of it.

A little nearer, and it would have crashed into his brain.

"You are not seriously hurt. I will see if I can find the dastard who fired the shot," said Jack.

"Upon my word, this is a horrible place to live in," replied Harry.

"You are right," replied Jack. "A man's life is not safe for a day in this wretched country."

He walked in the direction whence the shot had come.

A few strides brought him within sight of El Obed.

The high priest's face was distorted with a fear he could not conceal.

Lashing its flanks with its tail, the lioness gave a blood-curdling roar, and prepared to spring upon its helpless prey.

It was the mate of the one which Jack and Harry had slain.

Having cubs in the vicinity, it was rendered peculiarly savage.

The maternal instinct told her that there was danger about.

El Obed turned to fly.

This was the signal for the lioness to spring, which she did, flying through the air and alighting on El Obed's back.

He was borne to the earth, and a sickening crunching of bones ensued.

Jack put his rifle to his shoulder, and fired at the struggling mass on the sward.

Brief as the look he had of him was, he had recognised the high priest.

That he was the would-be assassin he was quite sure.

A bullet sped towards the lioness, and entering her body under the left fore-leg, reached the heart.

The animal uttered a low growl, followed by a series of moans, and rolled over in her death agonies.

El Obed did not move.

Harry came running up at this moment.

"Why," he exclaimed, "it is El Obed!"

The priest half turned his head.

His right arm and shoulder were horribly torn and bitten, the bone being crushed.

"Come," he said, faintly, "come nearer. I would speak."

The boys approached him to hear what he had to say.

It was evident that El Obed was dying fast.

"I am going to the land of the spirits," he said. "I am called, and have not long to stay."

"Why did you want to kill me?" asked Harry.

"I will tell you."

His voice was faint, and his eyes were becoming glazed.

"No lie shall pass my lips," continued he. "I am going fast. Tom the Peeper, who sees everything, and Dick the Knower, told me that you intended to have my life."

"I?" ejaculated Harry.

"Yes; and if I did not kill you, my blood would flow. You had the city, you were in power. What could I do? Can you blame me?"

"You should not have listened to him."

"But he is the Knower."

"Just as much as I am."

"What! have I been deceived?"

"Grossly!" replied Harry.

El Obed closed his eyes and spoke no more.

Slowly but surely his life blood ebbed away.

Harry and Jack saw that they could do nothing to save him or alleviate his sufferings.

They retraced their steps towards the city.

"The spies," said Jack, "have no sense of gratitude. We must hunt them down, and Charlie, too."

"I would have let them alone," replied Harry, "if they had not interfered again with us."

"It must be a war of extermination."

"I fear so, or we shall never be safe," exclaimed Harry. "Heaven knows I am soft-hearted enough, but I vow I will have revenge on them for their perfidy."

"What can we do?" asked Jack.

"Follow them up. We shall hear of them on the coast somewhere."

"If they ever reach there."

"Bah! Those fellows are bound to land on their feet. If I do not follow them, they will me. We must have it out."

"I begin to think it best, after all, not to be too severe on them. If you do meet with Charlie, why not make terms with him?" suggested Jack.

"How can I?"

"Give him an allowance of so much a year."

"That would only make him want more; besides, there is Marian."

"True. I had forgotten that."

"The spies would not attempt to injure us, unless they were egged on by Charlie. Though the Squire is dead, Charlie has all his father's bad points."

"And his own, too," said Jack,

"We must curb him somehow," continued Harry; "but how, I cannot tell. Time will show us how to act. He is a thorn in my side, and always will be until he closes his eyes in death. If we go back to England I shall always go in dread of him—he will persecute me."

"You cannot kill him."

"Did I hint at such a thing?"

"I fully sympathise with your feelings, but I should advise you to buy him off!" exclaimed Jack.

Harry reflected for a moment.

"Perhaps you are right," he answered.

"I am sure so. Cancel your vow of revenge. That kind of thing does no good. Try kindness and liberality."

"By Jove, Jack!" cried Harry, "you are a noble-minded fellow, and a good counsellor. I will be advised by you."

"To act kindly?"

"Yes."

"Good. You will find it the best policy in the end," said Jack. "However bad a human being may be, there is always some good points in him. You want to find this out and touch the proper chord."

"I will do all I can," said Harry, "to place Charlie above the pangs of poverty, so that he shall have no excuse for not leading a respectable life."

"That is the way to take the sting out of him," replied Jack.

"As they proceeded homeward, Harry thought a good deal about this new mode of dealing with an enemy.

He hoped it would succeed, though he had his doubts and misgivings.

Charlie was not very promising material to work upon.

They stayed only a few days longer in the city. Lieutenant Smolley allowed Sangara to make Makolo's son Prince of Ashantee, and himself regent.

The general undertook to put down slavery as well as he could, to treat all white men well, and to protect traders.

Ja-Ja and Sunday Ja-Ja were taken to the coast, put on board the gunboat, conducted to Cape Coast Castle, and imprisoned for their misdeeds.

Jack, Harry and Marian took leave of Bill Blunt, and were accorded a passage to the same place.

Here they stopped at a comfortable hotel, questioning all the traders that came in with merchandize about Charlie.

No one had seen anything of him or the spies.

Marian established her claim to the money left her by her uncle.

She was now an heiress, which was very convenient, as she was able to supply Jack and Harry with money, the latter being precluded from getting any until he arrived in England and proved his right.

A steamer came to Cape Coast once a month. They could have returned to the Old Country had they chosen to do so.

Harry, however, insisted upon lingering in this torrid spot on the chance of ascertaining the fate of Charlie.

Weeks passed by.

Several caravans, richly laden with costly bales, came in, but none of the traders had seen or heard anything of three young white men lost in the interior.

What could have become of them?

Life in Cape Coast was pleasant enough. The English Consul invited them to his house, and his wife was very kind to Marian.

Still, they soon grew tired of staying there.

At last Harry declared that if they received no news in another month they would give up waiting.

The first ship should take them home.

They had not been out quite six months, yet they had seen and gone through a great deal.

Events had succeeded one another with remarkable rapidity.

Mr. Spencer and his brother were dead; so was Squire Rawlings.

What would be the next scene in the strange drama of real life?

The month elapsed, and still no news was received of the missing boys.

It was concluded that they had perished miserably in the wilderness, either falling a prey to wild beasts or dying of thirst.

A ship came into the harbour.

She was not going to England but was going along the coast to the Cape of Good Hope.

"Before we go home let us see a little more of Africa," said Jack.

"I have no objection, if Marian will supply the money," replied Harry.

"Of course. You can have what you like," exclaimed Marian, generously.

It was arranged that she should draw out of the bank a thousand pounds, which they deemed would be enough for their adventure.

The remainder of the fortune left her by her uncle she ordered to be sent over to her credit at the Bank of England in London.

Full of expectation of enjoying new pleasures, they embarked on the steamer and started for the Cape.

The land of Kaffirs, Zulus, Boers, ostriches, diamond fields, and romance was before them.

CHAPTER XXII.

MEETING A CARAVAN—TREACHERY IN THE CAMP—BILL LEVER—ARRIVAL AT CALABAR—A START FOR ALGOA BAY—THE DIAMOND MINES.

CHARLIE, with all his faults, was brave.

He was not afraid of the lion that was glaring at him and the spies, but the latter were. They fell flat on their faces; he raised his rifle and took aim.

The bullet struck the lion in a vital part, yet it did not stop the brute's spring.

Seeing the infuriated animal launch itself in the air, Charlie followed the example of the spies, and threw himself down.

He was just in time.

The mighty beast jumped clean over him.

Then the spies rose and fired at the lion, putting the finishing touch to his death.

"Bravo!" cried Peeping Tom. "We have saved your life, Charlie. What an awful brute that lion is."

"Look at him kicking now," said Knowall Dick.

"Saved me!" exclaimed Charlie. "You cowards did nothing worth speaking of."

"Didn't we settle him?" asked Tom.

"We gave him what the French call the *coup de grace*, come now!" cried Dick.

"It's no use quarrelling over it. The beast is dead. That's all we care about. Now for a drink."

Saying this, Charlie went to the well, and kneeling down, put his mouth to the water and quenched his raging thirst.

The spies followed his example.

Suddenly they heard the sound of footsteps and voices, accompanied by the snapping of dry sticks and the breaking of twigs that were in the way.

Someone was approaching.

Who could it be in that vast solitude?

"Hide," whispered Charlie, running behind a big tree.

The spies imitated him without a word.

As silently as possible they reloaded their weapons, so as to have them ready should an emergency arise.

They could not help trembling with expectation.

This was such an unusual occurrence.

In a few minutes they saw a tall, thin white man, with a keen but, withal, good-humoured expression of countenance, advancing towards the wells. He was apparently about forty years of age.

He was accompanied by two negroes—one old, the other young.

"Ingami," he said to one, "have you got the brandy?"

"Yes, massa," was the reply.

"And have you the glass, Monkey Tricks?"

"It am right here, massa."

"Very good. I see the water, and I will have a drink. Your African water wants qualifying."

"Me know, sah; me find de wells!" exclaimed the one addressed as Ingami.

"We have been a long time without water," said Monkey Tricks. "My tongue am awfully dry."

They quickened their pace, and were soon drinking heartily.

"You like dat, Massa Bill Lever?" asked Ingami.

"So much so that I will take another horn. Put more brandy in it; I'm dead beat."

"Why not lie down, sah?"

"I will. If I sleep, don't let me lie more than two hours. Our men will have to come here to-night with the caravan camels."

"Orright, sah."

"Keep a sharp look out. Lions come to these wells, and the Ashantees have been making raids lately."

"Me keep one, two, eyes open, massa," answered Ingami.

"Me do dat also," said Monkey Tricks.

Bill Lever, as the negroes called him, drank again, lighted a cigar, and threw himself down under a tree.

In less than ten minutes he was fast asleep.

Charlie judged that Lever was a trader, with a small caravan, who had engaged pagazis, or carriers, and bought camels to go into the interior for the purchase of ivory and gold-dust.

Ingami and the young negro called Monkey Tricks were his trusted servants.

"When Lever was snoring, the two negroes sat down and helped themselves to some brandy and water."

"Good chance now," said Ingami.

"What for?" asked Monday Tricks.

"Kill massa. Get all in caravan. Say him die ob de fever."

"Yah, yah! Dat good."

Monkey Tricks rubbed his hands.

"S'pose we club him to deff?" continued Ingami.

"No; knife."

"Or use little shoot-gun. Him got two in um belt."

" Make too much noise."

" Who here?   Yah! you fool nigger," said Ingami.

" Who you's calling names?   I'll hab you to understand me no fool.   When we get to Calabar me not speak to you."

" Orright.   I take it back.   You clebber man, same's me.   Now, talk sense.   How we kill de boss?"

" Stab him."

" You?"

" No; you," said Monkey Tricks.

" Well, you see, I's tired," replied Ingami.

" And I's got a ache in my arm."

" Oh! you one big fraud," cried Ingami. " You's always wantin' me to do ebbery t'ing."

" Why not?   You de eldest."

Ingami rose and drew his knife.

It was a formidable-looking weapon.

" S'pose I's got to do it," he said, with a yawn.   " That comes ob trabelling wid a boy and putting confidence in him.   We're both in it, though.   You can't say not'ing 'bout me."

" Who wants to?"

" You hab a queer way of talking sometimes.   Massa prop'ly call you Monkey Tricks.   You more like monkey than man."

" What you call yourself—baboon?"

" Me man."

" Gorilla!"

" Hush! or I'll lose my temper and stab you instead o' massa.   Me man, I say!"

Monkey Tricks held his peace.

He did not like the attitude Ingami assumed, and fancied he had provoked him far enough.

Charlie knew nothing about Bill Lever. He had never seen him in his life before, but here was a countryman in difficulties.

There was a plot on foot among his African servants to murder him.

This must be prevented at all hazards.

He clutched his gun tightly, and waited for a forward movement.

Ingami fell on his hands and knees, put his knife between his teeth, and glided like a snake towards his victim.

Monkey Tricks eagerly watched the movements of his companion.   Slowly Ingami approached the white trader.

He raised himself and held up the knife, pausing for a while as if searching for the spot where the heart was.

Bill Lever's life hung on a thread.

" Fire!" said Peeping Tom, in a low tone.

" Watch the young one," replied Charlie.

" He shan't get away."

" Good!   Here goes!"

Charlie discharged his gun.   Ingami fell back and rolled over.   Lever sprang up, and Monkey Tricks attempted to escape.

Peeping Tom was after him.

Before he had gone far, he seized him by his short woolly hair, and dragging him to the ground, pounded him with a stone till he was nearly senseless.

Lever rubbed his eyes and stared at Charlie.

Knowall Dick had gone to the assistance of Tom, should he require any.

" Hullo!   what's up?" asked Lever, in astonishment.

" Attempted murder," replied Charlie.

" What have you been doing to my servants?"

" I and my two friends have been made slaves in the city of Ashantee.   We escaped, and took refuge in the forest.   We sought the wells, and concealed ourselves when we heard your approach.   Your men plotted to murder you.   Ingami has his knife tightly clenched in his hand now.   I shot him. My friend has floored the young black rascal."

" Good," said Lever.

" It would have been all over with you had we not been here."

Lever held out his hand, and Charlie clasped it.

" I'm Bill Lever," continued the man. " Everybody knows me on the coast.   I've been trading in gold dust and ivory for five years, but after this experience I reckon I'll quit it."

" The niggers are treacherous," remarked Charlie.

" That's no name for it.   They are incarnate fiends.   I didn't take much stock in Monkey Tricks, as I call him, yet I did think Ingami was solid."

" Are you English?"

" To the backbone.   I'm a Londoner, and have been pretty near everything, except a diamond miner, and now I think I'll go to South Africa and look after stones."

Ingami tried to speak, but a rush of blood to his mouth choked his utterance.

There was no hope for him.

In a few words Charlie told Mr. Lever that he and the spies had come out as midshipmen in a vessel which had been wrecked off Three Points.

They had been saved, he said, but the slavers made a raid, carried them off, and sold them in Ashantee.

He did not say a word more.

" I've been to Three Points," replied Lever, " but I don't trade there.   It is a poor place.   My caravan is bound for Calabar."

Charlie breathed more freely.

So did Peeping Tom and Knowall Dick.

They had been afraid that Lever was going to Three Points, in which case Bill

Blunt would have had something to say about their true character, even if they did not meet Jack Spencer and Harry Rawlings.

They were greatly relieved.

"I like you, my lad," continued Lever, "and I'll be your friend."

"Thank you, sir," replied Charlie. "I want one."

"I have to thank you for saving my life. I'm rough and ready, straight up and down, but people who know me will tell you that Bill Lever is not a bad sort."

"I'm sure of that."

"You and your friends shall go with me to Calabar, if you like."

"Willingly."

"I'll sell my camels and we'll go to the diamond-fields."

"That would just suit me."

"Have you any dust?"

"A little," replied Charlie. "I could chip in to buy a claim."

"Good enough. It's a bargain."

Charlie and the spies could scarcely believe in their good fortune.

They did not care whither they went.

A little adventurous life in the diamond-fields of South Africa would just suit them.

Perhaps they would make their fortunes there.

Charlie introduced Peeping Tom and Knowall Dick to Mr. Lever, and told him how they had befooled the natives in Ashantee.

"If you two can only see and know about the diamonds," said Lever, "we shall soon double-discount all the others who are in the same business."

By this time Monkey Tricks had recovered his senses.

He got up, and seeing that Ingami was dying, held up his hands for pardon.

How the other white men had come there he did not know.

All he did know was that he was in a bad fix.

"Mercy, massa, mercy!" he cried.

"You rascal," said Lever. "Why did you want to kill me after my kindness to you?"

"Him do it all. Ingami the bad man."

"You lying little wretch."

"No, sah, not me. Nebber touch a hair ob your head."

"I won't give you the chance."

"Le me go 'way, massa," pleaded Monkey Tricks.

"Yes; you may go where the bad niggers go."

"Where dat, sah?"

"Down below."

Lever took a pistol from his belt and levelled it at Monkey Tricks.

"Mercy, massa, don't shoot," yelled the negro.

"You hound," replied Lever, "I wouldn't spare you on any account. A life for a life. You wanted to kill me. Now it's my turn."

There was a sharp crack.

Monkey Tricks threw up his arms, and fell forward—a corpse.

"I'm a dead shot," said Lever, complacently.

"That bullet was beautifully put in," remarked Charlie.

"I reckon I can drill a hole as well as anyone."

"By Jove! I should not like to stand up against you."

Bill Lever looked straight at him,

"Don't give me cause, my boy," he said, "and there will be no need. I'm a good true friend, but a bitter enemy."

"The niggers got what they deserved."

"Yes. But let's get out of this. My caravan isn't far off. I'll make you boys welcome, and take you on to Calabar, where my market is. Then, ho! for South Africa and the diamond-fields, eh?"

"That's it," said Charlie.

"I applaud the sentiment," observed Peeping Tom.

"And I respect the proposer of such a glorious expedition," remarked Knowall Dick.

As they walked to the spot where the caravan had stopped, Lever asked the boys a variety of questions about themselves.

They adhered to the story that they had been sent to sea by their parents and wrecked.

According to their own account, they would be an acquisition to any party.

Their respectability could be vouched for by dozens of people, if they were only at home.

It came out casually, in the course of conversation, that the spies were called Peeping Tom and Knowall Dick.

"What are they called that for?" inquired Lever.

"Because of their prying propensities. They must know everything," replied Charlie.

"That's a bad habit," said Lever, frowning. "You'd better not try to find out anything about me."

He looked very much displeased.

This disclosure about the spies had evidently annoyed him.

"We sha'n't go out of our way to do that, sir," replied Peeping Tom.

"It always comes to us," said Knowall Dick.

"How?"

"Comes natural like."

"None of your nonsense," cried Lever, crossly. "You can't humbug me like that. You poke your noses into other people's affairs, or you wouldn't have got those nicknames, I'll warrant."

"No, sir—" began Peeping Tom.

"If ever I catch you trying to find out things about me," interrupted Lever, "I'll give you a hiding you'll remember to your dying day—I will, or my name isn't Bill Lever."

"What things?"

"I didn't say anything in particular. I'm warning you, that's all, my lads."

After that he put his arm through Charlie's and talked to him as if he had the intention of making him his friend.

To the spies he had taken a dislike.

They fell behind, and conversed in a low tone.

"I don't like that man," said Peeping Tom.

"Nor I," rejoined Knowall Dick. "He's not genuine."

"Not at all. He wears a mask."

"Yes," replied Tom, "and I'll bet anything he has a secret."

"Of what kind?"

"Some terrible kind; but we'll find it out. We will make it our business to do so."

"Certainly," chuckled Knowall Dick. "That will just suit us, eh?"

"Of course. It's what we live for," replied Peeping Tom. "When we get a bit older we ought to become detectives."

"Just the very thing nature created us for," cried Dick, raising his voice. "Wouldn't it be fun to hunt a murderer to his doom."

He spoke so loud that the wind carried the words to Lever's ears.

"What's that you say?" he demanded.

In an instant he turned fiercely.

"Nothing sir," responded Dick.

"You said something about hunting a murderer. My ears never deceive me," thundered Lever.

"Oh, yes," exclaimed Dick, carelessly. "I merely remarked that if any criminal got into this pathless forest, it would not be easy work to track and catch him."

"That's foolish talk; a bloodhound would do it; but a man of that kind is safer in a city than he is in a forest."

With this curious remark, Lever resumed his walk with Charlie, and took no more notice of the spies.

The latter were more than ever convinced that he had a secret.

He was a man of mystery.

Perhaps a murderer himself.

When the encampment was reached, Lever told his men where they would find water, and informed them of the treachery of Ingami and Monkey Tricks.

They expressed great aversion to and detestation of such a dastardly treacherous act.

To show their allegiance they knelt down, each one in turn putting Lever's right foot on his head.

This was to prove their loyalty and devotion.

After a good supper, Charlie and the spies slept well, and the next day started for Calabar.

Lever informed them that they might ride on one of the camels, if they liked, though he preferred walking.

They tried the experiment, and quite agreed with him.

A more disagreeable mode of locomotion than camel riding cannot well be imagined.

It took them some time to reach Calabar, and when they did, Lever quickly disposed of his camels and merchandize.

A ship was loading in the harbour; they engaged a passage, and were soon leaving the equator behind them.

The more Lever saw of Charlie, the more he seemed to like him, but his antipathy to the spies increased.

At last Algoa Bay was reached, and they started in a waggon drawn by six bullocks to go to some diamond fields lately opened.

These were situated at Beerfontein, a hundred miles from the coast.

The bullock driver, an intelligent Dutchman, stated that some good finds were being made, and that the town was full of ruffians from all parts of the world.

In fact, the scum of the earth had resorted thither.

Charlie offered to put a hundred pounds to the same sum of Lever's to buy a claim.

This was at once agreed to.

The spies were to have no share in the claim, but were to receive so much a day for working the mine.

There would be plenty of digging and washing to do.

This was settled on the first night of the journey up country, when the Dutchman had outspanned his bullocks and the party were having supper.

Charlie rather imprudently displayed his bundle of bank-notes when he took some out to pay Lever his share of the purchase money.

In a moment Lever noticed them.

"Ha!" he cried, "where did you get all that money?"

Charlie looked somewhat confused.

"Where did I get this money?" he replied. "Why, I earned it and saved it."

"I'm glad to hear it," said Lever.

"A fellow does not come out to Africa for nothing; you didn't."

"On, no! I admire you for it. Stick to the money, my boy. Some chaps at Beerfontein would rob you, if they knew of it."

"That they never shall."

"You shouldn't flash it."

"Thank you for your advice. I don't intend to do so."

It being nearly time to turn in, the conversation dropped ; but Charlie could not help thinking that there was a dangerous gleam in his new friend's eyes.

It denoted avarice.

Nothing more was said the next day about the money, and Lever was, if possible, more friendly than ever with Charlie.

The road to the diamond fields was an uninteresting, undulating plain, covered with rank grass and granite rocks.

It was a weary, uneventful journey.

Everyone was delighted when the town of Beerfontein was reached.

A stream flowed by the mines supplying the inhabitants with water for drinking purposes and for washing the earth in which the diamonds were found.

There were nearly five hundred rough men of all nations, living in wooden houses rudely knocked together.

No women were to be seen, however.

A tavern or hotel, called the "Republic," was the principal hostelry in the town.

At the door of this the driver halted his bullock team.

The name of the proprietor, written on the wall, was Dalbiac.

Directly the waggon stopped, the hotel-keeper, a stout middle-aged man, with a foreign cast of countenance, came out.

"Ha !" cried he, looking at Lever, "is it possible that we meet again ? "

Lever turned pale under his bronzed skin.

"You ? " he ejaculated.

"Why, yes."

"I thought you dead."

"And I fancied you were being taken care of under lock and key. Ha, ha! you are a clever fellow, Bill—"

"Lever," the addressed hastened to say.

"Oh, is that it ? Well, I am still Dalbiac. It is a long time since we met in our dear Paris."

"Five years."

"Time flies," replied Dalbiac. "So you have come to try your luck in the diamond fields ? "

"I and my young friends."

"You are welcome. Stop at my house. You shall not find my charges too high."

"It is a bargain. Believe me, I am very glad to have met you."

Dalbiac led the way into the house, and was followed by Charlie and Lever.

The spies had listened attentively to the conversation which had taken place.

"I say," exclaimed Peeping Tom, "the landlord knows something about Lever."

"Rather more than he would like told," replied Knowall Dick.

"We must watch. There is money to be made."

"In heaps," said Knowall Dick; "and I should like to have Lever under our thumbs, because he does not like us, and has taken no pains to conceal his bad feeling."

They now went into the house and approached the bar.

Here a fresh surprise awaited them.

CHAPTER XXIII.

MEETING AN OLD FRIEND—SPYING—LEVER'S SECRET—A BIG STONE OF PRICE—THE SHOOTING AFFRAY.

A TALL, well-made young man, whose face was tanned by the fierce South African sun, was standing in the bar.

"Hullo !" he cried, when he saw the spies. "By Jingo! this is a strange meeting."

"Bully Warner!" exclaimed Peeping Tom.

"What next ? " said Knowall Dick.

"Yes, boys, it is your old friend Warner," was the reply. "I knew you had gone to sea in Squire Rawlings' yacht, but I little expected to meet you."

"Same here. The Squire is dead."

"Ah !"

"Killed by the natives on the Gold Coast," said Peeping Tom; "but Charlie is with us."

"I suppose you have had your ups and downs ? " remarked Warner.

"Plenty of them."

"I have had mine."

"We are only too glad to think we are alive, and should not be sorry to get back to the old spot in Suffolk."

"We are not going through until we have made our pile ; but, I say, old chum, tell us how you got here."

"In a ship."

"Well, I don't suppose you swam the

Atlantic Ocean," exclaimed Peeping Tom. "What made you come?"

"The force of circumstances, one of which was my father's boot."

"How?"

"My dad, you know, is a passionate man, and won't stand too much nonsense. When you fellows went away, after old Dobby was drowned, Doctor Birchoften gave up school keeping."

"Retired?"

"Exactly. He and Miss Martha rent that old house with the large garden in the town, which is called 'The Dahlias.'"

"I know it," exclaimed Peeping Tom. "Many a time have I climbed the garden wall in fruit and nut time."

Knowall Dick made a grimace.

"I've been there earlier than that. Unripe apple time," he said.

"Somehow," continued bully Warner. "I got wild when the school closed, and was always in trouble. So father sent me to sea. I didn't like it. When we reached Port Elizabeth, on our way to India, I bolted, and got up here to the diamond mines at Beerfontein. I had the luck to please old Dalbiac, and he made me his bar-tender."

"How do you like it?"

"First-class," answered Warner. "Plenty to do at night, but it's an easy life in the daytime."

"Why don't you mine for diamonds?" inquired Tom.

"Too much hard work. I've no money to buy a claim. If you find a diamond, you must give it to your master."

"Can't you sell it?"

"No. That is what they call I. D. B., or illicit diamond buying. It's a crime out here, and if anyone buys a diamond without its whole pedigree being known, he gets imprisoned."

"Where?"

"Oh, he's sent down in custody to Petermaritzburg."

"What kind of a man is your governor?" asked Knowall Dick.

"A hard case. If you offend him, look out," rejoined Warner.

"Do you have any rows here?"

"Sometimes they shoot. When that happens, take my advice and run. This is a rare gambling saloon, and if a man is full of drink and loses his money, he is apt to lose his temper, too."

"I understand."

"Now," added Warner, "what will you have? I'll stand treat, for I don't suppose you are overburdened with cash."

"You've struck it the first time," replied Peeping Tom, grinning.

"Dry as a chip," said Knowall Dick. "Hungry as a hunter, and as poor as a beggar."

"On that table we always set a free lunch. Help yourself amd nominate your poison."

"Thank you," exclaimed Tom. "What drink do you recommend here?"

"Dutch beer—lager. No spirits, unless you're hardened, or don't mind dying suddenly. The whisky is to be avoided."

"Is it so bad as that?"

"Benzine is nothing to it," replied Warner. "I've seen dozens of the men, who've acquired the whisky appetite, drop out and die quicker than lightning. My boss does his own cellar work, but how he makes his whisky is an awful secret."

While the spies were partaking of the free lunch, which was agreeably washed down by a glass of tolerable lager, Warner asked who Lever was, and where they had met him.

Peeping Tom informed him of all the particulars.

He had just finished, when Charlie made his appearance. He was as much surprised to meet Warner as the spies had been.

"Three of the old school!" he exclaimed. "I'm only an outsider, or I'd say four."

"You are one of us now," replied Tom.

"We'll stick together," cried Charlie. "If you work for me and Lever, Tom and Dick, we'll reward you liberally."

"When you have got a claim, start us on the work," answered Tom.

"That will be to-morrow."

"So soon?"

"Yes. Dalbiac, who is a first-rate fellow when you know him, has told Lever of a claim for sale."

"Are you going to buy it?"

"Right away, or we shall lose the chance. A lot of fellows are after it, but the owner holds out for his price. I shall be back in a couple of hours. The boss has ordered dinner at six."

"We shall be all right with Warner—bully Warner, as Jack Spencer and Harry Rawlings used to call him," said Peeping Tom.

"I can't stay to chatter. I'm all business," cried Charlie, running off.

Warner drew some more beer out of the keg.

"Did you ever see anything of Jack and Harry after you left school?" he asked.

"Yes," replied Tom. "We met them on the Gold Coast. They are on this continent now somewhere, I fancy; but we don't want to talk about them. They are not our friends."

Warner yawned.

"It's my sleepy time," he observed. "I generally take an hour's nap in the afternoon in that big chair of mine you see in the corner of the bar."

"Good idea!"

"The governor generally relieves me, but he is engaged at present with your boss. I can hear the champagne corks popping in the private room."

"Can I help you?" asked Peeping Tom.

"If you like to you can mind the bar for an hour. It isn't likely anyone will come in, because the population is at work. Still, some loafer might knock off, and then he would require to be served."

"We will see to it. Take your nap. Leave all to us."

"Call me if anyone enters," said Warner.

They promised to do so, and Warner went to sleep in the chair he had indicated.

"We seem to have tumbled into comfortable quarters," remarked Knowall Dick.

"Fairly so," replied Peeping Tom. "Warner is our friend, but we shall have to work at so much a day, mining, for Lever and Charlie."

"They have the capital."

"We ought to have a share in the profits."

"Certainly, but we shall not get it. They are not going to work on shares."

"If I find a big stone, I shall stick to it," said Tom.

"You know what Warner told you. Beware of I. D. B. Who will dare to buy the diamond unless you prove your right and title to it?"

"That's a shame."

"Of course it is; yet how can we help ourselves? We are not capitalists."

"Then we have to work and sweat in the dirt and sun, for a paltry weekly wage, to enrich others?"

"That," said Knowall Dick, "my dear fellow, is precisely what the toiling millions in this world are doing at this moment, and if they did not they could not exist. The whole fabric of society is based on the principle of the many working for the few."

"Wait till I find a valuable diamond," said Tom, sulkily.

"You've got to find it first. When you do, we'll discuss the matter. At present I'm off."

"Where to?"

"Mind the bar for Warner. I am going to kneel down at the keyhole of the private room where Dalbiac and Lever are."

"What for?"

"Can you ask? I want to listen. Perhaps I shall get an inkling into Mr. Bill Lever's secret, and if we put the screw

on him he may be more civil to us," answered Knowall Dick.

"Capital. I'll keep watch."

Bully Warner, tired out, was sleeping soundly. No one was to be seen in the street, and the hotel was silent.

Knowall Dick stepped on tiptoe into the passage, and sinking on his knees outside the door of the private room, put his ear to the keyhole.

Every word that was uttered in the private room was audible to him.

"Ha, ha!" he heard Dalbiac say, "we have landed on our feet; but how on earth did you get out of that scrape in the Rue Morgue?"

"You mean when I robbed the miser?" replied Lever.

"And murdered him."

"Oh! that was only a detail. The fellow wanted to make a noise when he saw me walking off with his cash-box, and I tapped him on the head.

"It was rather a hard knock, I admit, but what can a man do under such trying circumstances?"

"True. You were Mr. Barnes at that time, now you are Lever."

"I've been a leaver ever since."

"Ha, ha! a good joke."

"I cannot afford to stay long in one place."

"You were arrested for killing—I beg pardon—for tapping the miser, if I remember rightly?"

"You do."

"How did you get out of the toils of the law," asked Dalbiac, "if it is not an impertinent question?"

"By no means. I had money. I put in bail and never surrendered to it. In fact, with what I had left I went to Africa, on the Gold Coast, and became a trader. I have made money, which—"

He paused a moment, and broke out into a laugh.

"Don't look at me like that," he added. "I have banked it at Algoa Bay. You don't suppose I was such a fool as to bring here with me more than I required?"

"Bravo! Still the same," replied Dalbiac.

"And you? Now tell me about yourself. You were the prince of pickpockets," cried Lever.

Dalbiac grinned hideously.

"So I am now," he answered. "Just give me a chance. Men come in here to my saloon, get drunk, and are cleared out. What puzzles them is how it's done and who does it?"

"They don't suspect you?"

"Not for a moment. If they did, I should soon be a dead man."

"'SPARE MY LIFE!' CRIED CHARLIE. 'I MAKE NO RESISTANCE!'"

No. 8.

PRICE ONE HALFPENNY.

[Published Every Monday.]

"Have you a hard crowd here?" inquired Lever.

"The scum of creation," answered Dalbiac; "but, *ma foi*, I skin them to the last shilling."

"You are doing well, then?"

"Never better."

"That young fellow, Charlie, who has gone to inquire about the claim you spoke of, has got a pile of money."

"Is he not your friend?"

"No. I picked him up on the Gold Coast. Our friendship does not amount to a row of pins. If you, the prince of pickpockets, like to try your hand at relieving him of his wealth, and give me half, I sha'n't holloa."

"Good."

"Is it a bargain?" asked Lever.

"My dear Barnes—"

"Don't call me by that name. It revives unpleasant memories."

"Does it remind you of the old miser you robbed and put to death in the Rue Morgue in Paris?"

"The wretch haunts me sometimes when I have had too much whisky! But, I say, have you never taken life?"

"*Sacré bleu!*" growled Dalbiac, "I have killed my man."

"How did you escape being sent to New Caledonia?"

"The same way you did. I cut and run. Ha, ha! Fill up your glass. I'll open another bottle. There is plenty where that came from."

"Well, well, we are friends."

"To the death."

Dalbiac held out his hand, which Lever shook heartily.

"Having heard enough, Knowall Dick crept away, and rejoining Peeping Tom, told him all.

It was clear that Charlie was to be robbed, but that did not matter to the spies, as they cared only for themselves.

It would not do for them to warn Charlie, because they might incur the displeasure of Lever.

They had to bide their time and watch the course of events.

At six o'clock they sat down to a substantial dinner, and at night they were provided with good beds.

In the morning a man named Bob Burnet came to the hotel to see Lever and Charlie. He was the person to whom Dalbiac had sent Charlie on the previous day. He had a claim which he wished to sell for two hundred pounds.

It was considered a good claim because other men who had mines around it had been doing very well.

Bob Burnet had not worked it more than three or four yards from the surface. He was known as an idle, lazy, drunken, swaggering fellow. He had no money to pay labourers to dig and wash for him, and he did not care to work more than one day in the week.

He was a gambler, and a frequenter of all the drinking and the card-playing saloons in town.

Always ripe and ready for a quarrel, standing six feet, with a strong burly frame, he was more feared than liked.

Dalbiac took him into his private room, where they were soon joined by Charlie and Lever, who were anxious to complete the bargain and set to work on the claim.

Burnet put a small uncut diamond on the table.

"There's a stone I dug out yesterday," he said, "from my claim I'm going to sell you, so you can be sure there something in it."

All pressed forward to look at it.

Dalbiac was by Charlie's side, and while the young fellow was engaged in examining the diamond, the Frenchman slipped his hand dexterously into his pocket, and drew out the wallet in which he kept his money.

It was all in Bank of England notes. What gold and silver he possessed was in his trousers pocket, and this amounted to only about twelve pounds.

No one saw the deed done, nor did anyone notice the thief put the stolen money into a drawer in the table.

"Now," continued Burnet, "I'm willing to sell, if you're ready to buy, for two hundred pounds. Here is the deed of conveyance, as I got it when I purchased the claim."

"We've only got to pay the money," said Lever. "My partner pays one half, and I plank down the other. There's my share."

He counted out the sum of one hundred pounds.

Charlie felt in his pockets for his wallet.

A look of blank dismay came over his countenance.

"Hang it!" he faltered. "I have been robbed! My wallet's gone!"

"That's bad," replied Lever. "When did you see it last?"

"Yesterday afternoon it was all right, because I took out a ten-pound note to pay the waggoner. I have not thought of it since."

"Were you in the bar last night?" asked Dalbiac.

"For about an hour. I had two or three drinks while I was taking stock of the miners."

"That settles it," exclaimed Dalbiac. "We have some light-fingered gentry around this section."

"What can I do? It is all my fortune! I'm ruined!"

He looked the very image of despair.

"Am I fooled?" asked Burnet. "Ain't you chaps going to buy this 'ere mine?"

"Yes; I'll complete the purchase, anyhow," answered Lever.

Charlie sat down and buried his face in his hands.

"Cheer up!" cried Lever. "I'll give you work. You sha'n't starve. It's bad luck, but it can't be helped."

Charlie looked at him with a pallid face. He had tears in his eyes, and trembled.

"I had hoped to make a fortune," he rejoined, in a broken voice; "and now, what am I? Nothing but a day labourer—a toiling slave. I wanted to work for myself."

"Never mind. You shall work for me. We will start on it to-day. Call Tom and Dick."

Some wine was ordered. Tom and Dick were invited to join in the merry-making, and all were gay except Charlie.

He had received a blow from which he found it difficult to recover.

"You'll find all the plant you want at the mine," said Burnet. "There are pick-axes, shovels, rope pulleys, baskets and wheel-barrows."

"Come on, boys, we will begin mining to-day," cried Lever. "You'll all three have to do something for your living. I can't afford to keep you for nothing. Now then, Charlie, wake up! Work's the word. If you are not ornamental, you must be useful."

"And dig diamonds for you?" asked Charlie, bitterly.

"Certainly. Why not?"

"When I had my money I was a gentleman, and you did not talk like that."

"Circumstances alter cases."

"I'd rather go into the show business again."

"Do what you like. I offer you a chance, and you are a fool not to take it."

"Anyhow," said Charlie, in an obstinate tone, "I'm not going to work for you. I've got a pound or two left, and I'll look round. If I find out the villain who took my money, I'll have his life."

Saying this, he strode out of the room, left the house, and walked up the street.

"Poor chap!" observed Dalbiac, with a hypocritical leer, "he does take his loss to heart."

"He'll come to his senses when his bit of cash is spent," replied Lever. "I don't intend to be bad friends with him. Go on, you two. I'll follow directly. The claim is marked No.5, a little way down B. Street, turning out of the Second Avenue."

Peeping Tom and Knowall Dick at once departed, feeling rather uncomfortable at the prospect of having to work hard.

Lever guessed that Dalbiac had robbed Charlie as he had suggested, and he waited to receive his share.

Bob Burnet soon went into the bar and left them alone.

"Part up!" said Lever, curtly.

"With all the pleasure in life," answered Dalbiac. "Didn't I do it cleverly?"

"When did you do it?"

"While you were looking at the stone."

Dalbiac opened the drawer, took out the wallet, and divided the money in equal shares.

Both men were highly satisfied.

"I am afraid I shall have trouble with that loafer, Burnet," remarked Dalbiac. "I wish you luck with your new claim."

"Do you think I shall meet with any?" asked Lever.

"That's my opinion. Burnet's been too lazy to tap the lode. Some of the men alongside in B. Street have struck it rich."

"Then there are diamonds lying about loose?"

"Yes, in a manner of speaking. It was only a few weeks ago that a man from Cape Town took out a stone in the next claim to yours which will weigh thirty carats when it is cut."

"Why does Burnet sell out, if that's so?"

"Didn't I tell you he'd rather drink and smoke and gamble than work?" answered Dalbiac.

"Well, I mean to make my boys work, if I don't do so myself. I'll go and start them, and come back for a bit of dinner with you at one."

Dalbiac promised that the dinner should be ready at the time specified, and Lever went to visit the claim he had bought.

The spies, stripped to their shirt-sleeves, had commenced. Peeping Tom was in the hole digging out the earth, which he shovelled into a basket.

Knowall Dick hauled it up by means of the pulley rope, and emptied it into a wheelbarrow.

When the barrow was full they would have to wheel it to the stream—which was a quarter of a mile off—and wash it.

If they found any diamonds, they were to give them to their employer at the end of the day's work.

The sun was shining fiercely, and the boys were bathed in perspiration. Their heads were protected by broad-brimmed straw hats, but they suffered a great deal.

Lever watched them for some time, and saw the first barrow load washed.

There was nothing in it.

He gave them some money to buy food, telling them to go when they were hungry to an eating-house.

Then he left them to return to the " Republic."

" This is warm work," remarked Peeping Tom.

" I'd rather look on and see it done," replied Knowall Dick. " Can't we get a better berth?"

" Not here. There is only one kind of industry."

" What fools we were to come."

" Oh! we shall get used to it in time. Wait till we find a good stone. If we do, we'll sell it in spite of what Warner told us."

" Don't be too sure."

At one o'clock they had some dinner.

In an hour they resumed their toil.

The ground was hard and dry, but it crumbled easily after it was broken up.

Digging and hauling was the worst part of the business. The washing of the dirt was cooler and easier.

The second lot, like the first, yielded nothing.

In the third barrow load, however, they were destined to find something to reward their unremitting efforts.

Knowall Dick wheeled the barrow to the stream, and Tom took off his boots and socks, turned up his trousers to his knees, and went into the water, holding the riddle or sieve, into which Dick shovelled the earth.

He put the riddle in the water and shook it vigorously.

Some large stones remained in it.

One of these attracted his attention.

He scraped the dirt off with his knife and it revealed a brilliant surface, which flashed in the sun's rays.

" Hurrah! " he cried, " I've got a diamond this time."

" Are you sure? " asked Knowall Dick, greatly excited.

" I don't think there can be a doubt about it. What a size it is! I feel certain it is worth a lot of money."

" Shall you give it up?"

" No," replied Peeping Tom; " we'll sell it. I don't care about the penalty. We'll chance that."

" Suppose we get imprisoned? " said Dick, nervously.

" We must keep our secret. The man who buys the stone is not likely to betray us, for his own sake. This work under a hot sun is killing. If we get some money to live upon we can get down to the coast, and ship to England. I have had enough of Africa."

" So have I. Who do you think will buy the stone?"

" I saw a shop at dinner time on Second Avenue. The name was Van Hysen, diamond buyer. We will go to him."

Knowall Dick made no objection. He was a little nervous about the transaction, but at the same time willing to run a risk to escape from the servitude they were in.

Dressing themselves, they left off work, and proceded to the shop of Van Hysen.

He was an old, attenuated Jew, and the best judge of diamonds in the town.

They found him in his office, working at a stone, the beauties of which he was developing in a skilful way.

" Goot day, my poys," he exclaimed. " Do you come to puy or shell?"

" You are a buyer of diamonds," replied Tom.

" Vy, certainly. I pay monish for anything goot."

" What do you think of this?"

Tom handed him the stone, which he examined critically under a microscope, and weighed in his scales.

He then cut it on one side.

" It was a very fine diamond," he exclaimed.

" What is it worth?"

" A thousand pounds," replied Van Hysen.

Peeping Tom could scarcely contain his delight at the magnitude of this sum.

It was a fortune.

" You shall have it. Hand over the money," he cried, joyfully.

The jew looked up through his spectacles, and a smile played round the corners of his mouth.

" Stop! " he exclaimed. " Not so fast, my friend. I said the stone was worth all that amount, but I did not say I would give it."

" What do you mean?"

" There is such a law as the I. D. B. You ever heard that, eh?"

Peeping Tom's countenance fell.

He saw that there was going to be some trouble.

Disposing of the diamond was not to be such an easy matter as he had expected.

The Jew was cunning in the extreme.

" Yes," he replied, " I know all about it."

" Illicit diamond puying is punished by imprisonment. Many a man is doing five years on the breakwater for puying or selling a stone to which he had no right or title."

" But I dug up this stone myself."

" Where is the deed of your mine? " asked Van Hysen.

" I have not got it," answered Tom.

" That is enough for me," said the Jew.

" You are working as a hired labourer for somepody else. This stone you have stolen, for it was your duty to give it to your master at once."

Peeping Tom felt his legs tremble, and Knowall Dick was inclined to cry.

They had got themselves into a scrape.

" I could go to the police," continued Van Hysen, " and have you locked up. Then how would you look ? "

" Please don't do that, sir," pleaded Tom.

" We will give the stone to our employer," said Dick, in an agony of fear. " Don't say anything about it. No harm is done."

" You was a couple of young thieves."

" We're awfully sorry, sir," continued Tom.

" Father Abraham ! what two pad poys, to be sure," the Jew went on. " How long have you peen here ? Who is your employer ? "

In a few words Tom told him.

" Ha ! you are strangers," Van Hysen resumed, " and your master is a greenhorn. You think to hoodwink him. If you had money you would run away."

" We should," answered Tom.

" Does anypody know you found this stone ? "

" Not a living soul."

" You have spoken to no one, and were not seen to come in here ? "

Tom shook his head.

" Vell, I will have pity on you," exclaimed Van Hysen. " This stone I keep, and I give you twenty-five pounds."

" Is that all ? "

" See what a risk I run. It is enough for you," replied the crafty old Jew. " My word ! you get off easily. Take the monish and go."

The spies were sadly disappointed at receiving no more, but, after all, it was better than being locked up.

They took the twenty-five sovereigns, which he counted out, and began to breathe more freely.

Fearful lest they might be remarked coming out of his shop, the Jew took them through the back way.

He did not want to excite suspicion in anybody's mind, for he was as liable to punishment as they were.

The bargain he had made was a magnificent one, for when cut and polished the diamond would be worth a great deal more than he had estimated.

" I say," remarked Peeping Tom, as they walked towards the hotel, " that was a close shave."

" Rather," replied Knowall Dick, " I thought we were in for it. The Jew has got the bargain, but we can't grumble."

" No. I am satisfied."

When they entered the bar of the " Republic," Warner was behind it, as usual, and Burnet was sitting with his back against the wall in a drunken slumber.

" Fix us up a drink," said Tom.

" Champagne ? "

" Yes."

While they were drinking their wine, Charlie came in.

" Hullo ! " he exclaimed. " I did not expect to see you fellows here."

" Why not ? " asked Peeping Tom.

" I was strolling about the town, and saw you go into Van Hysen's; the diamond buyer, and though I waited a long while, I did not see you come out."

Tom reddened, and then turned pale.

" Quite a mistake, I assure you," he replied. " I don't know the name."

" Never heard it before," said Dick.

" Oh, that's all nonsense ! " answered Charlie. " I suppose I can believe my own eyes ? "

" We were at work all day, and finding it did not agree with our health, we came straight back here."

" No, you didn't."

" All right ! Have your way. I sha'n't quarrel with you, but I must repeat that you are mixing us up with somebody else."

" Is it likely ? "

" I deny it."

At this moment the door opened again, and Lever walked in, his face flushed with the drink he had taken during the day.

He heard the words uttered by Peeping Tom.

" Deny what ? " he demanded. " But wait a moment; how comes it that you boys are back so early ? "

" Do you want to know ? " asked Tom, rudely.

" If I didn't I shouldn't enquire."

" We don't mean to work any more. It's a dog's life. Send us back to England."

" I did not bring you out here," said Lever. " Get back the best way you can. If you won't work for me, how are you going to live ? "

" That's our business."

" Be careful how you address me. What were they doing, Charlie ? There is something up, I can see," exclaimed Lever, " and I mean to get at the bottom of it."

" I saw them go into a diamond buyer's."

" Ha ! who was that ? "

" A Jew of the name of Van Hysen."

" That looks strange. What did you do that for ? "

" It is not true," said Peeping Tom.

" I call it a deliberate falsehood," cried Knowall Dick.

"Come, come, that won't do," exclaimed Lever. "It looks to me very much like a case of I. D. B. I shall inquire into it. You have found a diamond and sold it to Van Hysen. That is why you don't want to work any more."

"Nothing of the kind," replied Tom.

"I have been robbed."

"You have not."

"Turn out your pockets, both of you. This morning you had no money. If you have any now, it is proof positive that you found a stone and sold it. Turn out!"

"I sha'n't."

"You young hound, I'll make you," shouted Lever.

"Don't touch me," said Tom. "If you do you will repent it."

Lever lost his temper at once.

Seizing Peeping Tom by the arms, he shook him as a terrier shakes a rat.

The sovereigns in his pocket chinked.

Three or four fell out.

"By heaven!" he yelled, "there is the proof of what I alleged. I have been robbed! The thieves have found a diamond and traded it off with Van Hysen. Go to the police, someone. I'll have them all up before the judge for I. D. B."

Again he shook Tom.

In vain the latter struggled to escape from his clutches.

He held him in a vice-like grip.

Knowall Dick, who was always loyal and true to his friend, seized a chair.

Going behind Bill Lever, he gave him a blow on the back, which caused him to release Tom and face his assailant.

Before Dick could strike him a second time, Lever hit out with his clenched hand.

The blow caught him on the forehead.

He rolled against the sleeping miner.

The shock roused him from his drunken stupor.

"What in thunder is this?" he cried.

His bloodshot eyes glared around the barroom, and his hand sought the butt of his pistol, which was stuck in his belt.

"Don't shoot," said Knowall Dick. "It wasn't my fault."

"You knocked up against me."

"I was hit by Lever. He is the one you ought to blame."

This explanation turned Burnet's wrath in Lever's direction.

"What did you want to hurt the boy for?" he demanded. "If you are on for a fight, tackle a man."

"I've no quarrel with you," replied Lever.

"I'll make you have one. Draw your pistol. We'll see who is the best shot. Come on!"

Are you mad?"

"No more than you are."

Saying this, Burnet cocked a revolver and fired at Lever.

The bullet missed him very narrowly.

There was an insane, murderous glare in the fellow's eye.

Before he could fire again, Warner courageously sprang over the bar, and tried to wrest the weapon from him.

His orders from Dalbiac were always to disarm men who began to shoot.

A struggle ensued between them.

"Let it go. I mean to have it," exclaimed Warner.

"You'll have it where you don't want, if you don't look out," answered the drunken ruffian.

"Nonsense! You wouldn't hurt me."

"Wouldn't I? Don't you fool with me, young man. Go back behind the bar and attend to your business."

"Not until you give up the pistol," persisted Warner.

The struggle continued, and Burnet, uttering a fierce oath, pointed the revolver deliberately at his opponent.

In a moment of madness he pulled the trigger.

With a heartrending cry Warner threw up his arms and sank to the ground.

The spies and Charlie were horrified.

Not satisfied with what he had done, Burnet laughed fiendishly, and pointed his revolver at Lever again.

"It's your blood I want, and I mean to have it," he shouted.

At this threat Lever became alarmed.

He could see that the man was not responsible for his actions.

"I've done you no harm," he said.

"Yes, you have."

"It's a mistake," continued Lever. "You are thinking of the man with the knife behind your back."

"What man?" asked Burnet.

"That tall, dark fellow right behind you."

Burnet, alarmed and surprised, turned to look.

Of course there was no one behind his back holding a knife.

It was only a ruse of Lever's to divert his attention, and prevent him from shooting.

Taking advantage of his being off his guard, Lever shot him through the heart.

With a dull thud the burly form of Burnet fell upon the sanded floor.

Hearing the firing, Dalbiac was roused, and rushed into the bar to ascertain the cause.

He was astonished to see two bodies stretched out in the throes of death.

"What's up?" he asked,

"I had to do it," exclaimed Lever. "He brought it on himself."

"That's true enough," said Charlie. "He fired at Lever first, and killed Warner for trying to disarm him."

"The chap was mad drunk," continued Lever, "and started shooting free. I tell you I was forced to drop him."

It was found on examination that Burnet was quite dead; but though mortally wounded, Warner was able to speak.

Tom and Dick put him on a bed in a little room adjoining the bar, and tried to soothe his last moments.

The bar-room was soon filled with people, for the news of the shooting affray spread like wildfire, and the miners quitted their work.

Lever went to the police office and gave himself up, but on explaining the affair was allowed to go.

It was considered in that wild community that he had acted with commendable discretion.

Such accidents, as they called them, were of frequent occurrence.

Great sympathy was expressed for Warner, but the general verdict respecting Burnet was that it served him right.

His body was dragged into an outhouse, and Dalbiac sold more liquor that night than he had done in a week.

Lever was treated by everyone, the result being that he speedily collapsed, and was carried to his room speechless.

Meanwhile Warner's life was fast ebbing away.

It was a strange thing that his two old school chums should be with him at his death-bed in that far-off land.

He was bleeding internally, and now and then a rush of blood would come to his throat and nearly choke him.

The pain he suffered he bore bravely, but his mind was ill at ease.

"I'm going to die early," he exclaimed, "and I'm afraid."

"What have you got to fear?" asked Peeping Tom.

Knowall Dick stood at the foot of the bed and listened.

A terrified expression came over Warner's countenance.

"I keep on thinking of Kennedy," he replied. "You remember little Kennedy when we were at school?"

"Yes, quite well."

"I killed him," continued Warner. "It is true that I didn't mean to do it, but I was an awful bully, and led him a dreadful life. I am sorry I killed him."

"If you are sorry for a sin, you will be forgiven," said Peeping Tom.

"I wish I could think so. When I close my eyes I fancy I can see Kennedy in a white robe, but a spirit stands by him holding a black robe, and keeps beckoning to me."

"It's a funny fancy," remarked Tom.

"I am not going to the same place that Kennedy is in," added Warner, shutting his eyes.

There was a pause for a brief space.

Suddenly he opened his eyes with a wild cry of anguish.

Feebly grasping Peeping Tom's hand, he said, in a terrified whisper—

"Oh, Tom, it's quite true."

"What's true?" inquired Tom, who began to tremble at the strange expression which had distorted the face of the dying youth.

"About the place where the wicked go. I saw the flames surrounding the unhappy wretches whom Satan holds in his power."

"You saw it?"

"Oh, so plainly. That is where I am doomed to go. I heard the mocking laughter of the fallen angels. Take warning by me. Promise."

"I will," replied Tom.

"And you too, Dick."

"Yes, I'll try to be a better fellow," said Knowall Dick, whose teeth chattered.

They were both greatly impressed by this singular death-bed scene.

As the end drew near, Warner's dread of the phantoms his mind had conjured up increased.

He shuddered and crouched as if already in the flames.

Yells of agony broke from his livid lips.

These were mingled with prayers for mercy.

At length a flow of blood choked his utterance, and in a horrible spasm he passed away. It was a dreadful end.

"Poor fellow!" remarked Peeping Tom. "I hope I sha'n't die like that."

"He had Kennedy's death on his mind," replied Knowall Dick.

"It just shows how it must have impressed him. He has not lived so very long after his victim," added Tom.

"I call it awful. Let's go," said Dick, who felt the atmosphere of the room oppressive.

He was not easily impressed, but this death had affected him as he had never been affected before.

In the bar-room they found Charlie, who had been looking for them.

"Where have you chaps been?" he inquired.

"Staying by Warner till he died," answered Peeping Tom.

"Is he only just dead? I thought he was killed at once."

"It was a sad scene. Where is Lever?" said Tom, wishing to change the subject.

"Carried upstairs, tipsy," replied Charlie. "I'm sorry I spoke about seeing you come out of Van Hysen's."

"So you ought to be," exclaimed Tom, reproachfully.

"I didn't think for a moment it would get you into a row."

"You might have known it would. What did Lever say before he was taken upstairs?"

"He was telling the men here that he intended to have you and the Jew arrested for I. D. B.," rejoined Charlie.

"Do you think he meant it?" asked Peeping Tom, nervously.

"I'm sure he did, and he will do it, too. That's what I wanted to warn you about."

"What shall we do?" asked Knowall Dick, in perplexity. "You are a friend of ours, and a good fellow. Advise us."

"I say, leave the place," replied Charlie.

"But where can we go?"

"To-morrow early the bullock team leaves for Algoa Bay. Book your seats in the waggon, and I'll go, too."

"Will you really go with us?"

"Like a shot. I am not going to stay here. What's the good of it without money? Capital is wanted in this place," replied Charlie. "My mind is bent on getting back to England."

"Are you still thinking of Harry?"

"Yes; and if I can get a shot at him from behind a hedge on a dark night, I mean to do it."

Charlie spoke so savagely that there was no mistaking his earnestness.

Yet Harry wanted to forgive him and mend his character.

It was rather a hopeless prospect.

"Let that drop, though," he added. "You know I've got a few pounds left—enough for my own use. How much have you got?"

"We ought not to admit—" began Tom.

"That's all rubbish! I know you found a stone and sold it. What did the old Dutch Jew give you for it?"

"Twenty-five pounds; but I dropped some of the money when Lever shook me. I have only a score left."

"That's better than nothing. Give it to me. I'll book our places in the waggon, and at daybreak we will be off."

"Thank you, old fellow," cried Peeping Tom.

"You are very kind," said Knowall Dick.

To what extent they were indebted to him they found out afterwards.

Tom gave up his money most willingly.

It was received and pocketed by Charlie with a bland air.

He looked the very picture of honesty and genial good nature.

"You are all right until Lever wakes up," he exclaimed. "He will have to swear an information before you can be arrested."

"Ha, ha!" laughed Peeping Tom; "we shall be far away by that time."

"There is only one danger," mused Charlie.

He seemed to be talking to himself.

"What is that?" asked Tom, anxiously.

"They say Captain Moonlight is about this section."

"Who is he?"

"A notorious and daring robber. He has a band of men with him like a brigand chief, and robs mails, waggons, and private houses," replied Charlie.

"I don't expect he will interfere with us," said Dick.

"He may."

"Why do you imagine that?"

"Because the waggon takes out a large parcel of diamonds, consigned to Algoa Bay."

"Ah! I see. It is a tempting prize."

"Now you two can turn in. I'll get the seats in the waggon, and don't forget daybreak to-morrow."

"Not we," answered Peeping Tom. "I shall never forget your kindness—never."

"That's all right, old fellow; don't mention it," replied Charlie, who went away to secure the seats.

The express office was only over the way. The waggon started from the door. They watched him into the place, and then retired to rest, their nerves being somewhat shaken by the events of the day.

Their window looked out on the street, and with a last fond look at the express office, they tumbled into bed.

Just as the grey dawn was breaking they awoke, and their faces beamed with delight at the idea of leaving.

They were already tired of the diamond mines.

What a lovely day it promised to be, and how they would enjoy breakfasting on the road in a few hours' time.

There they would get a little springbok shooting, and perhaps bowl over an ostrich.

The prospect was simply enchanting.

Never had the spies been in higher spirits.

They were soon dressed, and when he had his coat on, Peeping Tom ran to the window.

"Hurrah!" he cried; "the waggon is there with a span of twelve bullocks."

"It is on time," said Knowall Dick. "We must not delay."

"I am ready now. Ha! there is Charlie taking his seat."

"He is punctual."

"Yes. Three cheers for Charlie! He's the kind of friend to have!"

"We will give the cheers on the road. If we make a noise now we may wake Lever."

"I should like to wake him in the Irish sense," replied Peeping Tom.

"So would I. Lever had Charlie's money."

"Either he or Dalbiac. They stood in with each other. Now, are you ready?"

"Almost. I just want to lace up this boot," said Knowall Dick.

Tom waved his hand to Charlie.

The latter took no notice of him.

It seemed strange that he did not make any sign of recognition.

All at once there was a loud knocking at their bedroom door.

The spies turned ghastly pale.

"Oh, good Lord! What's that?" gasped Peeping Tom, with his mouth open.

Dick opened the door. A man with a pistol in each hand walked in.

Two other men were behind him.

"What do you want?" asked Tom.

"I am Simpson, the sheriff of Beerfontein," was the reply, "and you will do well to surrender, as I have a warrant for your arrest on a charge of I. D. B."

"Illicit diamond buying? Oh, dear!" groaned Tom.

"It is not true," said Dick.

"You will have to prove that. Van Hysen is already in custody for buying; we want you for selling."

"Who makes the charge?"

"Your master, Mr. Lever, will prosecute, but the information was laid last night by a young man named Charlie Rawlings," answered Simpson.

The spies sat down on the bed.

This information completely paralysed them.

Charlie had betrayed them, and was going off with their money.

What conduct could be more traitorous or dishonourable?

Words failed them to express their feelings.

CHAPTER XXIV.

SENT FOR TRIAL—THE ATTACK ON THE WAGGON BY CAPTAIN MOONLIGHT— THE TABLES TURNED—CHARLIE'S PUNISHMENT.

THERE was a resident magistrate at the diamond fields, who dealt with cases of assault and petty larceny, the prisoners being sent to a wooden building called by courtesy the gaol, where the sheriff resided.

But all charges of a serious kind, such as murder, arson, or illicit diamond buying, were heard at Algoa Bay, whither the culprits were conveyed on a warrant.

A short conversation between Peeping Tom and the sheriff elicited the fact that Van Hysen when arrested had confessed.

He had tried to make all the amends in his power by giving up the stolen diamond.

This had been restored to Lever, who was roused from his bed for that purpose.

The Jew's confession, however, availed him little.

He was manacled and placed in the waggon which was about to start for Algoa Bay.

Charlie had already taken his seat.

He was far from imagining that the victims of his treachery would be his companions to the coast.

Yet it was so arranged by the authorities.

The spies were handcuffed, and informed by the sheriff that they would be forwarded under the escort of two policemen, who were then in the room, in the bullock waggon, to be tried in a superior colonial court.

They felt dreadfully ashamed of themselves when they had the handcuffs on.

"How long imprisonment shall we get, sir?" asked Peeping Tom.

"Five or ten years," replied the sheriff; "perhaps the former. The Jew is sure of ten."

"It's very hard."

"They'll put you on the breakwater, which is being made with convict labour. It's healthy work, you know."

"Oh, dear!" moaned Knowall Dick. "I wish I'd never come here."

"It's all through Charlie betraying us," said Tom. "What a contemptible trick. I should like to trounce him for it."

"We were fools to trust him with our secret."

"It was stupid to come out to Africa with him in the first instance."

"I'll send you up a bit of breakfast," exclaimed the sheriff. "You are now in custody of these two constables, who are responsible for your safety as far as Algoa

Bay. I'm sorry for you, my lads, but you knew what you were about when you stole the stone, and you must put up with the consequences. If every labourer here kept the diamonds he found, where would the masters be?"

Saying this, he left them. Their feelings were bitter, but they deserved what they would receive.

After all, Van Hysen was worse than they.

If there were no receivers of stolen goods there would be no thieves.

He was to blame for buying from them, and the ridiculously small price he gave showed that he was a bad man.

Presently some bread and butter and coffee were brought them, which they managed to partake of, in spite of their downheartedness.

Scarcely had they finished when Lever entered the room.

"So you two are in custody?" he exclaimed, grinning. "Serves you right. Oh! aren't you a cunning pair?"

"Please try and get us off," said Peeping Tom.

"Not me. It's out of my hands. What a beautiful stone it is! I showed it to Dalbiac, and he says there is a small fortune in it."

"We're very sorry, sir."

"You'll be sorrier soon. It wasn't good enough for you to work for me. How will you like to toil on the breakwater and wear Government clothes?"

"Oh, dear!"

"I don't want to rub it in, so I won't say any more, except I'm surprised your friend sold you," remarked Lever.

"I'm not. He's bad enough for anything," replied Peeping Tom.

"Well, you know him best."

"We are thoroughly deceived in him; but time has its revenges," answered Tom.

"Ah! we may get even," said Dick.

"What would you do to a chap like that, eh?"

"I'd like to tear his heart out," rejoined Tom.

"You'll travel together in the same waggon; but, watched and ironed, you are not likely to do him much harm."

"Our turn may come."

"The sky may fall, and then you will catch larks," laughed Lever.

"Unexpected things happen," continued Peeping Tom. "You are very merry just now."

"Haven't I a right to be? I'm in luck and doing well here?"

"You're only a criminal, after all, and a fugitive from justice."

"Ha! what do you mean?" cried Lever, blanching.

"We overheard your conversation with Dalbiac, who is as bad as you. Beware!"

"You venomous young cub. But never mind! You cannot hurt me. I shall soon be rich if I find some more diamonds in my mine."

"Beware, I say!" repeated Peeping Tom.

"Bah! I laugh at your threats and predictions," exclaimed Lever, turning on his heel.

The stairs which led to the saloon below were narrow and steep, being imperfectly lighted.

On the the top stair he missed his footing.

Plunging headlong down, he tried to grasp the banister. It broke in halves, and with a loud cry he fell to the bottom.

With a dull thud he reached the mat.

Roused by the noise and the cry, Dalbiac rushed out of his room.

He picked the man up, but dropped him again in affright.

His neck was broken.

Bill Lever was dead.

The policemen and the spies came down and gazed, horrified, at the sight.

The constables could not resist commenting on this strange accident.

"That's quick work," said one named Martin.

"There's a curse on this house," remarked the other, who was called Holden. "Let's get out of it. Last night the bar-tender and Bob Burnet were shot."

"It was Bill Lever who killed Bob," replied Dalbiac.

"I know; and now he's called away. It's odd," answered Martin. "Come on, you boys, we'll get into the waggon."

The spies followed them out of the house and across the street. The only passengers were Charlie, the three prisoners, and the two policemen. The waggon was laden with several iron safes, containing packages of diamonds consigned by the miners to bankers and dealers in Algoa Bay.

Charlie had received an intimation from the driver that the I. D. B. prisoners would be taken with them.

This news did not disconcert him.

He was not afraid of the reproaches with which he expected the spies would greet him.

Still he would rather have travelled without them.

The police carried rifles and pistols, the driver was also armed.

Van Hysen was not so cast down as might have been expected.

There was a cunning half-smile on his face.

When the spies got into the waggon, a large crowd had assembled to have a look at them.

There was some groaning and hissing.

I. D. B was held to be a great crime in this little community.

Charlie turned his back and took no notice of his former companions.

The Jew wished them "good day," in a friendly manner.

He knew it was not to them he had to attribute his fallen fortunes and present desperate condition.

"Ve are friends in misfortune," was all he said.

The driver cracked his long whip, and the bullocks drew the waggon out of the town.

Charlie had secured a book and a mattress. He reclined comfortably, reading and smoking.

It was a very warm day, but the inmates of the waggon were protected by an awning.

Scarcely a breath of air relieved the heat.

They carried provisions and water with them, and there were stations on the road where they could replenish their supplies.

A halt was made for dinner at mid-day, and at six o'clock in the evening they outspanned for the night.

Peeping Tom and Knowall Dick had been too miserable all day to utter more than a few words.

The Jew had been equally silent, and the two policemen did nothing but play cards.

While supper was being prepared by the driver, the spies and Van Hysen were allowed to walk about the grass-grown plain together.

If they had strayed far, a shot from their warders would have reminded them of the fact very quickly.

They were narrowly watched.

As they were prisoners, their fare was only bread and water; but Charlie, who had money, was able to buy canned provisions from the waggoner, and whisky, if he wanted it.

"My poys," said Van Hysen, "you should hold up your heads a little higher."

"What is there to induce us to do so?" asked Peeping Tom.

"T'ings may not be so pad as you t'ink."

"I wish I could see a ray of light."

"Can I trust you not to say a vord?" said the Jew, eyeing him keenly.

"Certainly," answered Peeping Tom; "we will be as silent as the tomb. But what have we to hope for, save a long imprisonment?"

"Let me tell you a story."

"Proceed."

"Two years ago I vas travelling on horseback from the mines to Petermaritzburg," continued the Jew. "On the vay I saw a man lying on the ground half dead. Vell, I vas the goot Samaritan. I found on examination he had been speared by a Kaffir. I bound up his wound; I fed him; I gave him drink. He got vell after I had stayed by him three days."

"That was charitable."

"Ah! you not see the drift of my story?"

"Not yet."

"This man vas a robber—vat you call a freebooter—by name Captain Moonlight."

"Ha!" cried Peeping Tom, "we have heard of him."

"Ya! he shall rob the stages—the waggons."

"Yes!"

"He stops all travellers."

"What has that to do with us?"

"A lot," answered the Jew. "Vait, my young friend, I tell you. He promised to be my help if I ever vant him. Two days ago I received a letter from him, telling me not to send any diamonds by this bullock waggon, for he vas going to rob it two days out from Beerfontein."

"Oh!" ejaculated Tom.

"You see now?"

"Rather."

"Ve shall not have to vork ten years on the breakwater. Ven Captain Moonlight shall attack, ve vill drop down in the vaggon, and the bullets vill not hurt us. Leave all of the rest to me."

"Splendid," said Peeping Tom.

"Keep it secret. Ve shall see," added Van Hysen. "They not got us yet. Oh, no!"

The spirits of the spies rose at this news.

If Captain Moonlight—this dreaded and mysterious robber of South Africa—attacked the waggon, the chances were he would be successful.

He had never failed yet.

Though many attempts had been made to capture him they had been unavailing.

He rode on a coal-black horse, and wore a mask of the same coloured crape.

No one accompanied him—his nefarious work was done alone and unaided.

Where he lived was a dark and impenetrable mystery.

Martin, the head constable in charge, blew his whistle.

This was a signal to the prisoners to return.

They did so immediately.

To enable them to have their meals, the handcuffs were removed.

Charlie held a tin of salmon in one hand, and another of corned beef in the other.

"Will you have some?" he asked.

"I want nothing from you," replied Peeping Tom.

"You are welcome."

"After what you have got up for us," cried Tom, "I wonder you have the assurance to speak."

"I don't like dishonesty," answered Charlie.

"Oh, no! you never did," said Knowall Dick, sarcastically. "What did your father and you do to Harry Rawlings?"

"He is an impostor."

"You are a rank humbug, and that's all about it. What did you betray us for?"

"I. D. B. is a very serious thing. The interests of a diamond mining community must be protected."

"Rubbish!" exclaimed Peeping Tom.

"Will you have salmon or corned beef?"

"Neither at your expense."

"Leave it alone, then. It is your loss, not mine. Some people are so perverse. No doubt you will be glad of it some day. When I want to be charitable and make friends, you will not allow me. I think it is very hard, for I have always been a good friend to you."

Peeping Tom was unable to resist laughing aloud at this statement.

"Don't you believe me?" asked Charlie. "I assure you I have regarded you as brothers, and it cuts me to the heart to see you in this position."

"What's the use of all this hypocrisy?" said Peeping Tom. "You put us in this hole. We have only you to thank for it."

"It was a duty I owed to society. You see, I am very conscientious. Really, when I get home I think I shall study to be a parson. 'Faith, hope and charity' is my motto. What a glorious thing is charity! Have some of this tinned salmon?"

"No. I won't be under any obligation to you."

"Try the corned beef, then."

Peeping Tom raised his hand, knocked the tin out of his grasp, and sent the salmon flying after it.

Then he doubled his hands, and gave Charlie a blow which upset his equilibrium, and caused him to roll against a wheel of the waggon.

His head was cut, and he became insensible.

"Bravo!" cried Knowall Dick. "My fingers have been itching to punch the humbug. If you hadn't done it, I should."

"I couldn't stand his chaff any longer."

The policemen laughed, but said nothing. They were eating their supper in a leisurely way.

The driver was giving his bullocks some water, and Van Hysen had crept into the waggon as if tired.

The backs of the policemen were turned towards him, consequently they did not see the old Jew making signs to the spies.

He was moving his fingers and winking his eyes, and he tried to attract their attention by coughing.

His excitement was intense.

It was a calm still evening, with just a little wind blowing over the plain. Not a tree was to be seen. The herbage was scant, the bullocks having trouble to get enough to eat.

Suddenly Peeping Tom caught sight of Van Hysen, and nudged Dick.

"What's the old image winking at?" inquired Tom.

"Blest if I can tell. He'll shake his head off if he isn't careful," replied Dick, smiling.

"Seems to me he's beckoning us."

"Perhaps he's sat down on a snake, and does not feel comfortable. They do get into waggons sometimes."

"He evidently means business," exclaimed Tom, finishing a biscuit, and drinking a mug of water with as much relish as if it was nectar.

"We must go to him," said Dick.

They got up and walked to the waggon.

The policemen had begun to play cards.

They nevertheless perceived the movement.

"Where are you chaps off to?" cried Martin.

"We were only going to the waggon to have a chat with the Jew," answered Peeping Tom.

"All right! I'll attend to you presently."

He held up and clanked the steel handcuffs.

All this time Charlie was lying insensible on the ground.

No one thought it worth while to take any notice of him, he being despised as a common informer.

"What's up?" asked Tom, softly.

"Hush!" replied the Jew, in a whisper. "Come into the cart. Quick! It is of great importance."

They climbed in.

"Ah! maybe your life is safe now," continued Van Hysen. "It vas not so outside."

"Why not?"

"Captain Moonlight is coming. I saw a man on horseback on the verge of the horizon, and I know ve shall be attacked to-night, and before long, too. If you vas outside, you might get a bullet in your head."

"I thank you for calling us," said Peeping Tom.

"Did I not tell you that ve vas companions in distress, and I vould help you? Lie low. Pretend you vas ashleep."

This advice was too good to be neglected. They leant against the side of the waggon, and let their heads droop upon their breasts.

It was growing rapidly dark. The policemen could scarcely see their cards. The waggoner had staked his cattle so that they should not stray, and Charlie, having come to, was rubbing his eyes and trying to remember what had happened to him.

All at once a dark form, which had approached without being noticed, arrived within a few yards of the driver.

He raised a pistol and fired.

The unfortunate man sank to the ground weltering in blood.

Startled by the report, the policemen sprang to their feet, and snatched up their rifles.

The stranger sent a rifle bullet at Martin, and shattered his right shoulder.

Holden, the other constable, saw a tall figure pointing a gun at him, and he fired at it.

The ball flew wide of the mark.

Quick as lightning the compliment was returned.

Holden fell by the side of his fellow officer, and never spoke again, for he was shot through the heart.

As for Martin, his groans of pain were heartrending.

Charlie got up quite bewildered.

He saw before him a tall man, whose face was covered with a mask of black crape, through which his eyes glared like live coals.

This strange and awe-inspiring being held a pistol at the youthful villain's head.

"Wh—what's the matter?" stammered Charlie.

"Who are you?" demanded the stranger.

"A passenger to Algoa Bay. But wh—who are you? That's m—more like the question."

"I am Captain Moonlight, at your service," was the answer as the stranger politely took off his broad-brimmed hat.

Charlie sank on his knees and held up his hands.

"Spare my life, good kind sir," he said. "My rifle is in the waggon, and here is my pistol. I make no resistance."

"Hand them over, with any money you may have about you."

"Yes, sir—certainly, sir."

"Deceive me, and you die!"

Tremblingly, Charlie hastened to do as he was ordered. His pistol, his knife, his precious money were all given up to the dreaded robber of the plains.

Many were the queer, almost uncanny, stories that were told about this remarkable man.

Some declared that he was the son of an English nobleman, others that he was an escaped convict.

"Now," said Captain Moonlight, "where are the prisoners for I. D. B. I hear you have with you?"

"Oh! you know that?" cried Charlie, tremulously. "There are three. Who told you about them?"

"No one," answered the robber; "and yet I am aware that Van Hysen the Jew and two youths are here."

"How did you find out?"

"In the simplest manner possible. I was in Beerfontein last night and this morning."

"Were you not afraid to venture there?"

"My disguises are as numerous as they are perfect. I can speak six languages. Now I am an English Colonist; in an hour I would be a Frenchman, a Dutchman, or an Italian.

"There is a price upon your head of one thousand pounds, I have heard," said Charlie, reflectively.

"And you would be just the one to claim it if you had the chance," replied the highwayman, sharply.

"I, sir? What makes you say that?"

"Because I have been told that you were the informer in this I. D. B. case. You shall be attended to presently. Hullo!"

He raised his voice.

"You in the waggon," he added, "come out. There is no danger now."

The spies and the Jew had been listening, but were afraid to move until ordered to.

Gladly they sprang out of the waggon, for they felt that they were safe and free.

There would be no trial, no prison, no slavery on the breakwater now.

"My old friend," said the robber, "I am glad to be able to return your kindness to me. You are free to seek a home in some other town. You and your friends, too, can travel with me for a hundred miles south. Then we must part company."

"I accept your offer," replied the Jew. "Put, alas! I have no capital to start afresh with."

"I'll see to that. There are packages of stones in this waggon enough to enrich both of us."

"Ah! you are a prince. Vat a man!" cried Van Hysen, in ecstasy.

It did not matter to him where he lived; and if in time he could communicate with his wife, and tell her to rejoin him, he would be happy.

The spies looked at the bodies. The driver and one of the constables were quite dead, but the second constable was suffering terribly.

He was filling the air with his cries and piteous supplications.

"For heaven's sake, kill me right out!" he moaned. "I can't bear this. Put an end to me."

Captain Moonlight went up to him.

"Do you really want to die?" he asked. "Is there no chance of your being able to get back to Beerfontein?"

"I'm done for. Settle me, and I will forgive you," was the answer.

"It is a pity. You are a fine fellow. I am sorry I had to shoot you, but I will do all in my power to oblige you now."

Taking a revolver from his pocket, he pointed it at the man's ear.

Then he fired deliberately.

"Very unpleasant these things," remarked the robber. "I hate to have to shed blood."

He resumed his conversation with Van Hysen, and they went to the waggon to examine the packages of diamonds, which they could easily do, as the moon had by this time risen.

"They vas all very fine shtones," said the Jew, who was husky with excitement.

"We need not open the packages here," answered the robber.

"How you carry them? Do you shtop here to-night?"

"By no means. We shall march at once. My horse has two saddle bags; they suffice to hold my plunder and provisions. I never stop long in one place. They will be hunting for me here in a day or two, but I shall be two or three hundred miles away."

"I hope meinself they never catch you," exclaimed Van Hysen. "You vas the best man that vas ever let live."

"I can echo that wish," said Captain Moonlight, with a smile.

He whistled through his fingers.

In a few minutes a coal black steed came trotting up to him.

This was his favourite horse, on whose back he went everywhere, and which had learnt to obey every intonation of his voice.

The saddle-bags of which he had spoken were capacious, and could contain a good deal of property.

Taking the diamonds from the boxes in which they had been stowed for safety, Captain Moonlight placed them in the bags.

Van Hysen assisted him.

"What are you going to do with the informer?" inquired the robber. "I have heard all about your story."

"You vas meaning dot poy Sharlie? Vell, I know not. He can't come along vith us, and he can't be let go back to Beerfontein."

"Shoot him, eh?"

"Vell, I vill see. Vhere is Tom—Dick? Hi!"

The spies were not far off, having been engaged in the pleasant pastime of ransacking the pockets of the dead men.

They were rewarded by finding some money, which they appropriated to themselves.

"What do you want, captain?" asked Peeping Tom.

"Where's the informer about the I. D. B.?"

The spies looked round for Charlie.

He was not to be seen anywhere near the waggon.

"Blest if I know, sir," replied Tom. "I rather imagine the beggar has bolted."

"After him—after him!" shouted Captain Moonlight. "We must have the fellow, dead or alive."

Charlie had been pondering over the remarks made by the robber. He saw that he was not wanted, and fearful that he would be ill-treated, if not killed, he determined upon running away.

That the spies would not spare him, he was positive.

Peeping Tom saw him in the distance making off as hard as he could, and, calling to Dick to follow him, gave chase.

They had not an easy task, for Charlie ran for about two miles before he was overtaken and captured.

He was weak from the blood he had lost when he had fallen against the cart wheel, and offered no resistance.

"Ha! ha!" laughed Peeping Tom, as he laid hold of one arm, while Knowall Dick took the other, "we've got you."

They led him along between them.

"It's a strange world," said Knowall Dick. "We're down to-day and up to-morrow."

"Let me go," pleaded Charlie. "I will never interfere with you again."

"You won't have the chance. Don't ask me to release you," replied Tom. "I'm only flesh and blood, and it's more than I can do."

"I am sorry for what I did, but I had been robbed of my money, and was half mad."

"No excuse will avail you. Come along, my beauty. You are settled this time, and I wish Harry Rawlings was here to see it."

"And Jack Spencer, too," said Dick.

They soon regained the waggon. Captain Moonlight and Van Hysen were awaiting them; the former held a coil of rope in his hand, the latter had a stick.

"Place him against the off-hind wheel of the waggon," exclaimed the robber. "I'll tie him there. If he gets rescued, so much the better for him. If no one comes along here in twenty-four hours, the thirst and the heat will settle his business."

In a few minutes Charlie was securely fastened up.

He was bound to the wheel like Ixion.

"Blitzen," cried Van Hysen, "I thought he vas to be shot. Vell, I give him one goot rap on the head. So."

He raised his stick, and dealt the hapless prisoner a vicious blow.

The spies looked jeeringly at Charlie.

It was the hour of their triumph, and they could not refrain from enjoying it.

As for Charlie, he looked terribly cast down and dejected.

His reverse of fortune was all the more bitter to bear because it was so totally unexpected.

"Ha, ha!" laughed Peeping Tom; "you are rightly punished, my boy, for your treachery."

"We are up now, and you are down," remarked Knowall Dick.

"Never for to rise no more," cried Van Hysen. "You one dirty humbug. You give us avay to the tarn bolice. If it vas not for my friend the captain I should be on my vay to vork on the breakwater."

The Jew was greatly excited.

At every word he spoke, he worked himself up more and more, until he danced before Charlie.

He even went so far as to pull his nose.

"There," he went on, "that vas for you! Tweak, tweak! How you vas liking that? Oh, you t'ief!"

Van Hysen was destined to find out that it is possible to go a little too far.

Irritated by having his nose pulled, Charlie managed to get one hand loose.

He had no sooner extricated it than he made a grab at the Dutchman's belt.

Van Hysen had taken up the revolver of one of the dead policemen.

To possess himself of it was for Charlie the work of a moment.

No sooner had he got it than he pointed it at the breast of the old diamond merchant, and fired.

The spies started, and ran behind the waggon for protection.

Captain Moonlight had got on his horse, and was ready to make a start.

Seeing what had happened, he galloped up, and with the butt of his pistol struck Charlie a blow on the head, which stunned him.

"Deuce take such a fellow," exclaimed the robber. "Are you much hurt, Van?"

The Jew had fallen on his side, and was clutching at the grass with agonised movements.

"I am dying fast," he groaned.

It was so indeed.

He was growing weaker every moment.

"Gott in Himmel!" continued Van Hysen, "I did not think it was possible to suffer so much pain. Oh, my money! my diamonds! Why cannot I take you with me?"

A ghastly pallor came over his face, he trembled violently, and shrieked aloud as his agony became unbearable.

It was impossible to offer him any assistance or to alleviate his sufferings.

"Poor chap! he is done for," said Captain Moonlight, riding up to the spies, who were crouching in the rear of the waggon. "Your friend Charlie is a dangerous customer."

"You never know where to have him," replied Peeping Tom.

"Nor where he is going to have you," laughed Knowall Dick.

"It is a singular thing," remarked the robber, gravely. "I have seen his face in my dreams."

"Bad ones, I should imagine."

"Very bad indeed. In my dreams he is always betraying me to the police. I am seized, and I awake shivering."

"I don't think he will have much chance of injuring you," said Tom "after that crack you gave him."

"No. Hunger, thirst, and the heat of the sun will soon settle him," answered the captain.

"What shall you do with the Dutchman?"

"Leave him to fight it out with death. We can do him no good, and I can't bear to see him suffer. In an hour it will be all over. Come!"

He walked his horse to accommodate his pace to that of the spies.

For some distance they could hear the terrifying cries of the dying Dutchman.

He was fighting hard with the grim destroyer.

They travelled all night, and found some rock-sheltered spot, or cool ravine in which to sleep during the day.

The springboks were numerous, and they lived on those they shot.

Several broad rivers intercepted their course, compelling them to swim over.

Captain Moonlight took off his crape mask, and was revealed as a handsome middle-aged man.

After they had been travelling for three days and nights, the captain, on the morning of the fourth day, said, abruptly—

"After a few hours' sleep we m t separate."

"What shall we do, sir?" asked Peeping Tom, in alarm.

"'WHO AM I?' DEMANDED THE INTRUDER."

No. 9.

"Ten miles from here, due north, is the City of Colesberg, which is about two hundred miles from the sea. You have a little money to live upon for a time, and no doubt you will soon succeed in getting employment when you get there."

"Shall we not see you again?" inquired Knowall Dick.

"Never. Ere to-morrow's sun sets I shall be far away. I will say good-bye now, for I may be gone before you wake."

He held out his hand to each of them, they thanked him for his kindness, and all sought rest under some trees.

The country was now getting well wooded. Streams irrigated the ground, which produced an abundant crop of rich heavy grass.

Flocks of sheep and herds of cattle were to be met with; and they passed several large farms.

These Captain Moonlight had carefully avoided, as if desirous of not being seen.

When the spies awoke from their slumber, the robber was gone.

The sun was still riding high in the heavens, so they knew they had not slept very long.

"He's taken his departure," exclaimed Peeping Tom, looking round. "What if there is no city, and he has left us here to starve!"

"I think there is," replied Knowall Dick. "The farms and the cattle look like it. Isn't he an extraordinary man? He shaves close, as a rule, for he had not much hair on his face."

"That is the better to disguise himself. Do you recollect the night you and he went after a springbok while I minded the horse?"

"Yes, certainly."

"I looked into his saddle bags, and found three wigs, a couple of false beards, and whiskers of different colours, and I made bold to take a package of—"

"Don't say diamonds," cried Dick. "I have had enough of them."

"It was gold, my boy. Six rolls of sovereigns. Twenty-five in each roll."

"That's good! Go up one," exclaimed Knowall Dick, rubbing his hands. "But, I say, you were talking of disguises."

"What of it?"

"Just this. I could tell Captain Moonlight under whatever disguise I might meet him," replied Dick, confidently.

"How would you do that?" asked Peeping Tom, curiously. "I'll bet he can make up as well as any actor."

"No matter. I would know him."

"Tell us how," said Tom.

"Look at the wrist of his left hand," replied Knowall Dick. "It is frightfully scarred from a severe cut; all the muscles are contracted."

"That is important. I notice one thing, and you another. We ought to be detectives."

"What shall we say when we get into town?" observed Dick. "It won't do to let out about the I. D. B. business, or mention Captain Moonlight's name."

"Say we have been tramping up country, looking after work."

During their conversation they had commenced their walk to Colesberg. With the money they had recovered from Charlie, and that which they had taken from the dead policeman, and driver, and the captain, they were possessed of nearly two hundred pounds.

Before sunset they entered the town of Colesberg, a prosperous community, the prominent members of which were Dutchmen.

Peeping Tom inquired of a burgher for a good hotel, and was directed to the "Hoffman House."

It was kept by an Englishman, named Sutton, and was famous for its cooking, combined with reasonable charges.

They went inside, and were received by the landlady, a handsome woman.

Peeping Tom placed seven sovereigns on the table.

"For a week's board for two," he said, "paid in advance."

"Very good," replied Mrs. Sutton. "Will you have a double-bedded room? If so, it is No. 15 on the first floor. Dinner will be ready in ten minutes."

"That will do first-rate," answered Tom. "I am sharp set."

He went upstairs with Dick, and they had a wash, and smoothed their hair with their hands as well as they could.

"We must get some new clothes," said Tom.

"Yes; we want a rig out badly," rejoined Dick.

"I think we have struck pleasant quarters."

"It is about time. I have had enough of camping out."

A bell rang as a signal for dinner, and they descended to the dining-room. There were about twenty guests in the hotel.

Mrs. Sutton presided at one end of the table, her husband facing her.

He was a pleasant-looking man, with a long beard and whiskers.

The spies sat close to him.

Mr. Sutton looked curiously at them, and then chatted agreeably, asking how far they had come and what they thought of doing.

To these questions Peeping Tom gave general answers.

"Are you capitalists?" inquired the landlord.

"In a small way," replied Tom. "Nothing very big, you know."

"Do you intend to buy cattle, hides or wool or ostrich feathers?"

"Oh! we are not at all particular."

"Let me advise you to be careful about buying diamonds without a certificate."

"That is not in our line."

"I am glad to hear it. So many people get into trouble about diamonds up here."

Peeping Tom thought there was a curious look in Sutton's eyes as he spoke.

"Is there any place of amusement in your town in the evening?" he asked.

"There's a sing-song down the street, but it doesn't amount to much," was the reply. "It is called the Meister Singers. Most of the songs are Dutch."

When dinner was over, the spies decided on going to the music hall, and rose from the table. The landlord pointed out through the open window the direction of the place.

"Turn to the left when you get out," he said. "It is a few doors down."

"Thanks, very much," replied Tom.

Knowall Dick said nothing.

His face assumed a grave expression, and plucking Tom by the sleeve, he seemed anxious to get out of the room.

"What's the matter?" queried Tom, when they reached the street.

"I am puzzled," was the reply. "When the landlord raised his hand to indicate the way, I saw his wrist."

"What of that?"

"Have you forgotten what I told you about Captain Moonlight? The wrist was frightfully scarred, like that of the famous robber."

"But this man has a beard and whiskers. His complexion is not so dark. I don't see any resemblance," said Peeping Tom.

"It's a disguise."

"Then you mean to say that Sutton, the landlord of the 'Hoffman House,' is—"

"Captain Moonlight. Yes!"

The spies became silent. Reaching the hall they paid and went in. A Dutchman was singing a ditty about a girl called Gretchen, who could make sauerkraut and liver sausage better than anyone else.

The hall was not full, and taking a seat near the orchestra, they ordered some lager beer.

Presently they began to speak again about the subject which was uppermost in their minds.

"Do you think he suspects that we have penetrated his disguise?" said Tom.

"No," replied Knowall Dick. "I could tell from his manner that he did not think so for a moment."

"He is a dangerous man. We must mind what we are about. He would kill us without the slightest scruple."

"Keep dark. That is all we have to do."

They were both agreed on this point.

When the artist had finished his song, some acrobats came on, calling themselves "The Bounding Brothers of the Mountains of the Moon."

These men had been all over the world. They were growing old, and from starving in New York, London and Paris, they were making a precarious living in South Africa.

Several times they missed their tips, which showed that their joints were getting set and rusty.

At last they got on a high rope, from which one man suspended himself by his feet, and the other hung on to his hands.

Suddenly there was a cry of terror among the audience.

The second man had slipped from the nerveless hold of the first.

Down through the air he rushed like a comet.

With a crash he struck the hard wooden floor, and remained senseless, with the blood streaming from his nose and mouth.

The management was too poor to provide a netting in case of accidents.

With a choking sob the brother slid down a rope, and kneeling, bent over the inanimate man.

"I knew this would happen," he said, in a broken voice. "We ought to have given up the business long ago, but we could not afford it."

A voice behind the spies exclaimed—

"He will climb no more."

They turned round, and to their astonishment beheld Sutton, the landlord of the "Hoffman House."

How long had he been there?

Had he overheard their remarks?

These were questions which agitated their minds, but which they had no means of answering.

"You here?" observed Peeping Tom.

"I thought I would drop in for an hour," was the reply "and I took a seat behind you; but I would not interrupt you as you seemed so much interested in the performance. I am sorry I came now."

"Why so?"

"On account of the sad accident. I can't bear suffering and bloodshed. It is lucky I did not bring my dear children. They are so tender-hearted that they would never have got over such a scene."

His tone was certainly not that of a sanguinary robber.

"I shall go now," he added, after a pause.

Giving them a friendly nod, he retired.

"I say," whispered Peeping Tom, nervously, "do you think he was listening?"

"Yes," replied Knowall Dick; "he followed us for that purpose."

"We are in a nice fix now."

They looked gloomily at one another.

Two attendants now came in and carried off the injured man.

Some sawdust was thrown over the blood.

A tall lady, whose face was covered with paint and powder, came to the footlights and sang "The Watch on the Rhine."

Everyone was delighted at the stirring melody.

The sad disaster was forgotten amid the vocal strains and the music of the orchestra, the members of which blew and scraped with a will.

Yet the poor acrobat died during the night.

The spies waited until the performance was over, and returned to the hotel, proceeding at once to their bedroom.

They had no weapons to defend themselves with in the event of being attacked in the night.

Not to have thought of a pistol or a knife was an oversight.

They had foolishly wasted the evening in the pursuit of pleasure.

To secure themselves from interruption, Peeping Tom proposed that they should lock the door. He went to it for that purpose.

To his dismay he found the key was gone.

"Shove the drawers up against the door," said Knowall Dick. "I'll help you."

The drawers were a heavy piece of furniture of substantial make, and it was with difficulty they were moved.

With some exertion they were placed against the door.

It would not be very easy for anyone to enter now.

They would have to make a great noise first, which would awake the heaviest sleeper.

After some deliberation the spies decided that they would lie down in their clothes.

Owing to nervous apprehension it was some time before they went to sleep.

In the middle of the night Peeping Tom was roused by a noise as of someone trying to push the drawers aside.

He listened intently.

The room was in pitchy darkness.

He felt a hot breath on his cheek.

"Did you not hear something?" whispered a voice.

It was that of Knowall Dick.

He, too, had been awakened by the suspicious and mysterious sound.

"Yes," answered Tom, in the same tone. "Keep quiet! Listen!"

They were both in a state of extreme anxiety.

Who could it be outside, if not the landlord of the hotel?

Their hearts beat so quickly that they could almost hear them thump.

For a brief space all was still.

Then they heard the noise again.

The door creaked, and the drawers moved.

CHAPTER XXV.

CHARLIE MEETS WITH UNEXPECTED LUCK—ENEMIES BECOME FRIENDS— THE PURSUIT OF CAPTAIN MOONLIGHT.

IT was about eight o'clock in the morning when Charlie recovered consciousness, and the sun, bright in the clear blue sky, was streaming down with tropical severity on his unprotected head.

His sufferings from thirst were intense.

He was faint from a considerable loss of blood, and the sand flies tormented him almost beyond endurance.

Some birds of prey were picking the bodies of the two policemen, the driver, and Van Hysen.

Charlie shuddered when he thought this would probably be his fate before the breath was out of his body.

Bound as he was, he had no means of protecting himself against their savage attacks.

At present they had enough food to satisfy their voracious hunger.

He gave himself up for lost.

From what quarter could he expect any help on that desolate part of the globe?

All his wickedness rose up before him, and he wished he had led a better life.

His sufferings continued without any diminution until midday. His eyes were bleared and bloodshot.

His lips were parched and livid, and his black swollen tongue protruded from his mouth.

The heat seemed to set his brain on fire, and he feared he would die raving mad.

He attempted to cry out for help, but he could scarcely articulate.

All at once he heard the sound of a cheery voice saying, "Hullo! are you dead?" and opening his lack-lustre eyes, he looked up.

Close by was a bullock waggon, which had halted.

The driver and two young men were standing by, and a girl was looking out at the back of the waggon from under the awning.

Did his eyes deceive him?

Was it a delusion, or were the two young men Jack Spencer and Harry Rawlings, and the girl Marian?

He was not long kept in doubt.

One advanced to him and exclaimed—

"Why, Charlie, is it you? Do we meet again like this, old fellow?"

The tone was kindly and indicative of friendship rather than of hostility.

He had expected that if ever they did meet he would be overwhelmed with reproaches, which his conscience told him were well deserved.

What had he done to deserve friendship or consideration at their hands?

He had acted the part of a villain all through.

There was no mistake, however. It was Jack, Harry and Marian. They had reached that part of Africa, and hired a bullock waggon and a guide to drive, for the purpose of shooting springbok and ostriches.

A capital time they had enjoyed, and their success and love of sport had led them to go farther than they had first intended.

By a mere accident they had come across Charlie.

They were just in time to save his life.

He could not have lasted out the night had he not received relief.

"Water! water!" he moaned, feebly.

Jack and Harry had a good supply of stores of all kinds in their waggon, as well as kegs of water.

They gave him some brandy and water, which revived him greatly, and then they cut him loose.

"More!" he said. "I want more!"

"Not yet. Give that time to go down," replied Jack. "I can see you have had some trouble. What is it all about? The dead bodies tell a tale, so does that crack you have got on the head. It is a fearful cut."

"Tell the truth," exclaimed Harry.

Marian had got out of the waggon, and lighted a spirit lamp, over which she put a tin saucepan, into which she emptied a glass of water.

"I will make you some beef tea, in which you can soak some biscuits," she said, very kindly.

"You are all too good to me," he replied.

"We are taught to forgive our enemies," Jack replied.

"Can you really forgive me?"

"Willingly. Try and act better."

"I will never be bad again," cried Charlie, the tears coming to his eyes. "You are a couple of good fellows, and Marian is an angel."

"Far from that, I'm afraid," answered she, smiling.

He had some more drink, and then the beef tea and biscuits, which renewed his waning strength.

When he was able he told them all that had happened since he left King Makolo's capital with the two spies.

In return they informed him of their adventures, and their resolve to forgive and reform him if they met.

Charlie could scarcely believe in his good luck.

Marian had become an excellent cook, and she made a tasty stew of some springbok meat they had killed that morning.

Jack opened a bottle of champagne, and they were very merry over their dinner.

"You did not expect such good fare," he remarked.

"No indeed," replied Charlie.

"Peeping Tom and Knowall Dick ought to be here," observed Marian.

"Let us follow up their tracks," exclaimed Harry. "This Captain Moonlight will perhaps make robbers of them, and, if so, they are sure to be hanged."

"A good idea," answered Jack. "They are old schoolfellows, and bad as they have been, we must do our best for them. We can follow them by the marks of the horse's hoofs, and have plenty of shooting as we go along."

"There is a price on Captain Moonlight's head," said Charlie.

"Of how much?"

"One thousand pounds, dead or alive."

"We will have it, save Peeping Tom and Knowall Dick, and rid the country of a pest at the same time," cried Jack.

He was always ready for any adventure.

That Captain Moonlight was a desperate man he did not doubt for a moment, but he did not fear him.

Marian acted like a ministering angel to Charlie. She bathed his head, fully believing in his penitence.

"When we return to England," she said —"which will be shortly—Harry will give you a start in life; so that if you cannot be the Squire, you can get on honestly and respectably."

Charlie shook his head sadly.

"I don't want the property, and I mean to be honest," he replied; "but I fear I shall never see England again."

"What induces you to say that?"

"It is my belief I shall die in this horrid country."

"Why, how?" she asked.

"As a punishment for bringing you here. I had such strange fancies this morning before you came up."

"Perhaps you were delirious at times."

"Very likely; but I saw my own grave," said Charlie, "and read the inscription on the headstone."

"What was it?"

"'Sacred to the memory of Charles Rawlings. Erected by his friends, Jack and Harry,'" replied he.

"Let us hope it will not be so," she said, encouragingly.

They were interrupted by the cracking of the driver's whip. He was an old Kaffir, who knew the country well, and he was in-spanning.

He belaboured the bullocks unmercifully, having names for all six, which they quite understood.

"Come up, Dutchman," he shouted. "Where you going to, Englishman? You no good. Hi! Frenchman. Now then, Johnny. Hi! Diamond. Want me to cut your hide off? Zug, Zug! Get in there. Me pay you."

Jack helped Marian into the waggon, and came up to Charlie.

"You can ride," he said. "Harry is spreading a mattress for you. I know you are far from strong."

"Thank you. I am as weak as water," was the reply. "How can I repay your kindness?"

"By trying to be a man, and redeem the past."

"Am I not too bad?"

"Nonsense!" cried Jack. "It is never too late to mend. Look at our nigger, Usibepu. He is lashing the cattle. He is always swearing at them or something. A clever fellow, but a very sour one. He's so sour that we call him the vinegar merchant."

"That's good. Ha, ha!" laughed Charlie.

The arrangements were soon complete.

Marian made him comfortable, and gave him a fan to keep off the flies.

Going on in front, Jack and Harry traced the way Captain Moonlight had gone by his horse's footmarks.

These were plainly visible in the sandy soil.

The robber had not got a very long start of them.

It was their intention to catch the rascal at all hazards, and hand him over to justice.

CHAPTER XXVI.

THROWING OFF THE MASK—THE COINERS' RETREAT—IMPRISONED FOR LIFE.

IT was a peculiarity of the curiosity of the spies, that it nearly always got them into trouble.

This occasion was no exception to the rule.

While they were deliberating as to what they should do, the drawers moved again slightly.

The doors opened sufficiently to permit of a man entering the room.

They were not at all surprised to see Sutton.

Nor were they astonished to find that in one hand he held a revolver, and in the other a candle.

The bland smile that he could call into existence at will had vanished.

His face was rigidly stern, and the corners of his mouth were drawn down, showing that he was in a determined mood.

He shut the door behind him, replacing the chest of drawers, and looked angrily at Peeping Tom and Knowall Dick.

"Who am I?" he demanded, abruptly.

"Please, sir," replied Peeping Tom, who was in a great fright, "your name is Sutton, and you keep this hotel."

"Everybody says he is a highly respectable man," put in Knowall Dick.

Sutton grinned sardonically.

"You did not say so in the music hall this evening," he exclaimed. "You put me down as somebody quite different."

"Who was that, sir?" asked Tom, innocently.

"Captain Moonlight, the robber."

"Quite a fancied resemblance, I assure you," replied Tom.

Sutton took a black crape mask from his pocket and put it on his face.

"Now you know me," he cried.

The spies were silent—

"But," added Sutton, "unfortunately for you, it is possible to know too much. No one has ever penetrated my secret but you. Yes, you are the first to do it."

He went on to admit that he had led a dual existence.

In the town of Colesberg he was the well-known and highly respected citizen who kept the hotel; when he was a masked and armed rider on the plains he was the redoubtable Captain Moonlight.

The land was ringing with his audacious robberies.

Police were hunting for him in every direction.

Yet, strange to say, his wife even had no suspicion of his being a robber.

She thought that his journeys were all undertaken on business.

"It would have been better for you two," said Sutton, "if you had not been so smart in finding me out."

"We won't mention it to anyone, sir," answered Peeping Tom, shaking in his shoes.

"Oh, no, you would not! Of course, you are not the kind of boys to do such a thing," replied Sutton, sarcastically.

"Too much the gentlemen," remarked Knowall Dick, who was ghastly pale.

They expected every moment to be shot or stabbed.

"You would not denounce me to the police and get the reward! Oh, no! I shouldn't like to give you the chance. I must cut your claws."

The spies fell on their knees.

"Please spare our lives," they cried, in chorus.

"I do not intend to kill you, because I think you will be more useful to me alive than dead."

"Thank you," said Tom.

"Not so fast. Wait a bit. You're in too much of a hurry," resumed Sutton. "I was about to inform you that you would never see the light of day again."

"Wh—what?" stammered Tom.

"You don't mean it?" cried Dick.

"That is the sentence I pass upon you. A vault at the bottom of this house will be your future home. Come, let us descend."

He went to the wall, and pressing his finger against a knob, which looked like a brass-headed nail, a cunningly concealed door opened outward.

This revealed a flight of steps, spirally constructed.

"Descend, I say," he repeated, in a voice of command.

The spies saw that he was in grim and terrible earnest.

He had pronounced their doom, and was losing no time in carrying out the soul-deadening sentence.

"No, no!" said Peeping Tom. "We are too young to be penned up in a dungeon. I want the air—the world—freedom."

"It is hateful," Knowall Dick sobbed, in an agony of terror. "I shall die in the dark! Give me light!"

Relentlessly Sutton pushed them towards the spiral staircase, which he compelled them to descend by pricking them with a knife.

As they went along they cried aloud, so affected were they by their position.

For the remainder of their lives they were to be buried alive, perhaps to be some day forgotten and starved to death.

They did not know that they were to have companions.

But so it was.

After descending several flights of stairs, they traversed a passage, at the end of which was a spacious vault.

A lamp hung from the roof; it was covered by a shade, which cast down the light on a table.

Seated at this table, opposite one another, were two men, who had piles of glittering coins, both gold and silver, before them.

These they were taking out of dies, carefully examining them to see if they had any defect.

Sutton was a coiner as well as a robber.

These men, named Fanshaw and Potter, were his confederates, and they knew about his connection with Captain Moonlight.

Sometimes they accompanied him on his very dangerous expeditions, in fact they were partners in villainy.

They had an extensive apparatus for coining, and turned out a large amount of spurious money.

But they never attempted to pass any in Colesberg, it being their custom to go two and even three hundred miles for the purpose.

Fanshaw and Potter were well educated, gentlemanly-looking men. They came from England, one having been a clergyman, the other a schoolmaster.

Offences against the law had compelled them to fly their native land.

For nearly a year they had been connected with Sutton, carrying out their evil schemes without detection.

The fire was just dying away. Crucibles full of molten metal were on the hob.

Placed on a side table were cold meat, ham and fowls, bottled ale, wines, and spirits, as well as a box of choice cigars.

The coiners did not neglect their creature comforts.

Two comfortable beds were at their service, for sometimes they remained in the vault a week at a time.

When they appeared in the hotel they gave out that they had been in the country prospecting for gold and diamonds.

"Good evening, gentlemen," exclaimed Sutton.

They started to their feet, looking in alarm at the spies.

"I have brought you two slaves," he proceeded. "They have made themselves dangerous to me, so I have condemned them to imprisonment for life in this vault. They will work for you like convicts in the Siberian mines, and you are at liberty to beat them as much as you like."

Potter, who had been the schoolmaster, replied—

"I like beating boys. You could not have made me a better present."

"And I like to look on and hear them scream and see them squirm while they are being thrashed," said Fanshaw.

It was he who had been the clergyman, but his idea of Christian charity was rather limited.

Sutton suggested that they should leave off work and partake of supper, to which the three men sat down.

The spies were left, standing alone, bewildered at the strange sights they saw around them.

There was only one door to the vault, the one by which they had entered.

It was strongly bound with iron.

Sutton had opened it with a silver key of peculiar workmanship.

The chance of escaping from the coiners' den was small.

Their hearts sank, for they fancied that the vault would prove their tomb as well as their prison.

The light of the lamp fell upon the schoolmaster's face, and Peeping Tom could not help thinking he had seen him before.

"Boy," said Potter, "get a corkscrew and open some bottles of beer—either of you or both."

Peeping Tom did so, and Knowall Dick handed round the glasses.

"Were you ever in Suffolk, sir?" he asked, "for you are very much like a gentleman at our school."

"What was the name of your head master?" replied Potter.

"Doctor Birchoften. There was Mr. Dobby, second master, and—"

"Whom do I resemble?"

"Mr. Caner, the third master, sir."

"Right! That's who I am; and now I can see that you two are the spies of the school, Peeping Tom and Knowall Dick."

Sutton laughed at this mutual recognition.

"By George! they are well named," he exclaimed; "but do not show them any kindness or foolish forbearance for the sake of old times."

"Not I. They were friends of Dobby's, not mine. I always hated them for their prying disposition," replied Caner.

No more was said, though Caner might have added that when he left the school it was with the doctor's cash-box in his possession.

Sutton did not stay long.

He talked a little in French to his companions, so as not to be understood by the spies, and departed as he had come.

The coiners threw Tom and Dick a blanket each, which they wrapped round them, and went to sleep on the floor.

Caner called them up next morning and ordered them to light the fire, prepare breakfast and clean up the place, which had a lavatory with water laid on, a cellar for coal, and all conveniences, including a sink.

It was not like a cave in the wilderness.

After a refreshing wash, the coiners indulged in brandy and soda, which seemed to get into Caner's head, making him vicious.

The spies were watching the kettle boil. Caner thought they were purposely slow. He picked up a walking cane, and seizing Tom, thrashed him soundly as if he had been back at school.

Knowall Dick was the next victim of his spleen, and the howls of the two filled the vaulted chamber.

"Let them have it," said Fanshaw. "Keep it up."

Caner did so until his strength gave out, when he sat down and laughed as the boys rubbed their backs and legs.

This was not an isolated case. They were frequently treated like this without commiting any offence.

Their time was passed in waiting upon the coiners, doing such work as was constantly required.

They were cuffed, kicked, caned and indifferently fed, so that they were veritable slaves.

Once more their lives were rendered a misery and a burden to them.

It was all through seeing and knowing too much.

In a few days it was announced to them that the coiners were going a journey of some distance for the purpose of getting rid of the money they had made.

They anticipated that they would be gone about a fortnight.

Provisions were supplied to the spies, who were glad of being alone, with the prospect of nothing to do.

Here they were disappointed.

Caner procured an arithmetic book, pens, ink and paper. He marked off a large number of sums of all kinds for each of them.

"There is a holiday task for you," he exclaimed, with a grin. "If it is not done, and done correctly, when we return, I'll kill you."

"It is such a lot, sir," remarked Tom.

"I don't care. You can do it, and you shall, or I'll make you suffer."

"We'll do our best," said Dick; "but it is rather hard on us. We are out of practice."

"Get in again, then. Ha, ha! Thought you were going to lie about and do nothing, did you?" cried Caner, tauntingly. "Now pay attention."

"Yes, sir."

"For every sum that is not worked out correctly I shall give you twenty cuts with the cane, so look out."

With these words he quitted the vault with his companion in crime, leaving the spies a prey to their reflections.

Bitter thoughts surged through their minds.

They heard the key turn in the lock with a sharp click, and their hearts sank.

If the coiners were captured and sentenced, and all three of them refused to say anything about the vault, the captives would be starved.

No sound from them could reach the outer world.

They were separted from that by yards of thick inpenetrable concrete.

"Don't be cast down," exclaimed Peeping Tom, who saw a tear in Knowall Dick's eye. "What's the use of crying?"

"I'm always piping my eye now, though I'm glad those fellows have gone. What a beast Caner is!"

"Awful; but don't bother about him now. Have some of this food they have left. Pitch in!"

Peeping Tom suited the action to the word. He and Dick were soon busily engaged in attacking the viands.

Although they enjoyed themselves, their eyes occasionally sought the door. They felt their imprisonment keenly.

The future was black and dismal.

They had no chance of getting away from their cruel and chilling servitude.

CHAPTER XXVII.

M'COY'S HOTEL—A TALK WITH A STRANGER—THE WOLF IN SHEEP'S CLOTHING.

AFTER a long, but on the whole, pleasant journey, Jack Spencer and his party arrived within fifteen miles of Colesberg.

They had tracked the horse of Captain Moonlight as far as this, but owing to a heavy night's rain, all marks were obliterated.

Towards the close of a summer's evening, they came to a roadside house, which bore the sign of "M'Coy's Hotel."

Here they halted the waggon.

The house stood alone, no other building being in sight. Mr. M'Coy, an elderly Scotchman, came out and bade them welcome.

"We want a good dinner and beds," exclaimed Jack.

"Varra weel," replied the cautious Scotchman. "You can have a' that, if you've got the siller to pay for it. Ye ken, we trust nobody in these parts."

Harry put his hand in his pocket and showed him a quantity of sovereigns.

"Will that do for you?" he asked.

"Weel enough. Come intil the parlour. I have wines, lager and speerits. There is mutton in the larder, and I'll kill some chickens to broil. The gude woman has aye been a prime hand at cooking."

They followed him into a spacious, well-lighted room, while Usibepu out-spanned the oxen.

"Are we near any town?" inquired Jack.

"There's the bonny town of Colesberg within six hours' ride wi' your bullock waggon. Are you traders?"

"We are travelling partly for sport and partly for another purpose."

"What may that be, if it is not unbecoming in me to ask? You see I'm not a curious chiel, for I never interfere in onybody's business, but I like to know for information," said M'Coy.

Jack was about to reply, when a man drew up on a coal-black horse, and hitching him to a post, walked into the house.

M'Coy met him in the passage.

"Aweel!" cried he, "it never rains but it pours. Step inside, Mister Sutton. I've but one room for guests, and there is a waggon party there. Ye'll not mind them, puir creatures, they're all young."

"I am going a journey," replied Sutton. "All I require of you, my friend, is some refreshment."

"Mebbe the party will let you dine with them. I'm ganging to cook a haunch of mutton, with et cæteras."

"You're a canny Scot. Arrange it as

you like," said Sutton. "Anything will suit me."

M'Coy led him into the room.

Marian had taken off her hat. Her long flaxen hair was streaming over her shoulders. Charlie was looking out of the window at the black horse, and Jack and Harry were lighting some cigarettes.

"This gentleman," said M'Coy, "is one of the leading citizens in Colesberg. He keeps the best hotel, and has been mayor twice. Sutton's his name."

"Glad to know him, I'm sure," replied Jack. "My name is Spencer. The lady is my sister. My friend is Harry Rawlings. The other is Charlie."

Sutton started as he recognised the last-named.

He quickly controlled his emotion, however. His dress was that of a substantial farmer. He wore no hair on his face. The false beard and whiskers he only put on when farther from home.

Charlie turned round, but did not recognise the robber.

Still, he thought he had seen the horse before.

"Bring in some wine at my expense," exclaimed Sutton. "We will make merry while we can. I must be off after dinner."

"That's richt," answered M'Coy. "It's a puir heart, mon, that never rejoices. That's my opinion."

He bustled off, presently returning with a couple of bottles of champagne, which he served out to the company.

"Will you have any objection to our dining together, Mr. Spencer," asked Sutton, "as our host's resources are rather limited?"

"None at all," rejoined Jack. "We shall be pleased with your company. For some time we have been wandering about deprived of any society."

"Have you come far?"

"From Algoa. We have been shooting bok, seeing the country, and enjoying ourselves."

"You have money?"

"Oh, yes; we are independent. My sister is an heiress, and my friend Rawlings has a large property in England."

"It is well to be you. What brings you to these parts?"

"A romantic idea," said Jack. "We have undertaken to rid the country of a dangerous robber."

"Indeed!" ejaculated Sutton.

He raised his eyebrows a little superciliously.

"We mean to capture Captain Moonlight—if we can."

"That is well added."

"You have heard of him?"

"Who has not? He is described as being here, there and everywhere—a regular will-o'-the-wisp—here to-day and gone to-morrow. He has baffled the constabulary for years."

"But he won't baffle us."

"Do not be too sure of that, my friend."

"We have tracked him as far as this. It was only this morning we lost the scent, owing to the rain. He is not far off."

"Why have you set yourselves this task," asked Sutton—"this phantom chase, I may call it? Has he injured you?"

"He allowed an outrage to be committed on Charlie, whom he left to die."

"How was that?"

Jack related the story.

"According to your account your friend was not much deserving of sympathy," said Sutton.

"That makes no difference. It is a novelty to hunt down a robber. I rather like the excitement of the thing," Jack answered.

"There is no accounting for taste," replied Sutton. "I would prefer to let this Captain Moonlight alone, or some fine night he may let the moonlight into your body."

He shrugged his shoulders and drank his wine.

"You seem to take a strange interest in this fellow," exclaimed Charlie.

"I? Not at all," said Sutton.

"He's a villain and deserves hunting down. He rode a coal-black horse just like yours outside."

Sutton laughed at this remark.

"I suppose there are other black horses besides his?" he responded. "Perhaps I am like him."

"He was just about your height and build, but he had bushy whiskers, beard and moustache, with a crape mask over the upper part of his face," said Charlie.

"Do you want to insult me by comparing me to a robber?" cried Sutton. "I am a respectable man."

"No," rejoined Charlie; "I did not mean in that way."

He left the room, and the conversation was adroitly changed by Jack and Harry.

It was evident, however to the most superficial observer that Sutton was ill at ease.

He bit his lips and fidgeted with his hands, as if he wanted to be far away.

That Charlie suspected him he was sure.

Suddenly the door opened, and Charlie rushed into the room.

He held in his hand a crape mask.

"Look!" he cried. "I found this in

one of the saddle bags of this man's horse."

Sutton's face darkened.

Clearly the latent demon was aroused in his breast.

"This is singular," said Jack. "How do you account for it, Mr. Sutton?"

"I don't know how it got there," was the reply. "What right has he to search my bags?"

"It is suspicious."

Sutton moved towards the door.

"No, you don't," exclaimed Charlie. "I believe you are the man we want."

"Whom do you mean?"

"Captain Moonlight," replied Charlie, putting his back against the door.

Sutton immediately produced a revolver.

Jack and Harry searched their pockets for their own.

A look of dismay crossed their faces.

They had left their weapons in the waggon, and were defenceless.

"Stand back!" shouted Sutton.

"Not I!" replied Charlie. "Fall on him, Jack! Floor him Harry, while you have the chance. I will swear to him. It's the famous robber—Captain Moonlight!"

"Look out!" said Jack. "We do not meet on equal terms. We are not armed. Take care of yourself.

"You have brought this on yourselves," exclaimed Sutton. "I will shoot everyone in this room, by heaven!"

Charlie rushed upon Sutton, seizing him by the throat with both hands, and tried to drag him to the ground.

It was a desperate and foolhardy act.

Sutton placed his pistol to Charlie's ear and fired.

The wretched young man fell to the ground a quivering corpse.

Marian uttered a shriek, and sank to the floor in a dead faint.

"Fly for the pistols," cried Jack. "I am after you."

"The window?" queried Harry.

"Yes; it is open."

Harry put his hand on the sill, and vaulted out into the road.

"Die!" shouted Sutton.

He fired at Jack, but missed, though the bullet went perilously near to the young fellow's head.

Like a harlequin in a pantomime, Jack sprang after Harry.

He did not think that Marian was in any danger.

In this conjecture he was grievously mistaken.

Hearing the shots, M'Coy ran to the door.

"Hech, mon, what's to pay now?" he asked. "Has the de'il and all his imps broken loose?"

Sutton replied by dashing his fist into his face.

M'Coy fell at full length in the passage, stunned by the blow.

In an instant Sutton rushed to Marian, snatched her up in his arms and hastened from the house.

He unhitched the black horse.

Jumping on to his back, he placed Marian on the saddle before him, and striking the horse with his heels, dashed away like the wind.

The noble steed went like an arrow from a bow, being trained to these perilous occurrences.

It was growing dark, as the sun had set.

When Jack and Harry emerged from the waggon with their pistols he was out of range. In vain they fired after him.

"The rifle! Quick, quick!" cried Jack.

Harry clambered on the wheel, got the rifle, and gave it him.

It would kill at a thousand yards.

Sinking on one knee, Jack took aim carefully and fired.

Anxiously they awaited the result of the shot with straining eyes.

It seemed as if the horse staggered for a moment, but if this was so, he was not seriously injured.

He galloped on, and the robber was soon out of sight.

"Gone!" said Jack. "Here is an adventure. Charlie dead!"

"Let us see to Marian," replied Harry, with a sweetheart's misgivings.

"Yes; I saw her fall in a faint."

They hastened back into the house.

M'Coy was sitting up rubbing his head, looking dazed.

Passing him they walked into the room, stepping over the body of Charlie.

Of course, Marian was nowhere to be seen.

In a state of wild excitement they went over the house.

Every room was ransacked, and then they searched outside, with the same melancholy result.

They returned to the front room, where M'Coy and his wife were examining Charlie.

"This is a sad thing," exclaimed the Scotchman. "I wad nae have believed it of Sutton. The puir body must hae gane clean daft, and he sae respected, too."

"Didn't you hear who he is?" asked Jack.

"Never a word."

"Captain Moonlight, the robber! He shot my friend because he denounced him, and would have killed me."

"Hoot awa', mon," exclaimed M'Coy. "How can that be, when he's Sutton, the hotel keeper o' Colesberg?"

"He has two characters. People have not found him out. At home he is respectable; out, he is a bandit, murderer, thief; but I will find him, and rescue my sister. He has taken her for revenge."

"I have heard he's awa' a good deal; but he has a wife and two bairns."

"It is a great blow to think he has escaped with Marian," said Harry. "What is his idea?"

"We shall see before long," replied Jack.

Harry let his head fall on his hands, Jack paced the room, Mrs. M'Coy retired to the kitchen and went into hysterics, while her husband carried Charlie into a shed and covered him over with some sacking.

After some delay M'Coy produced lights, and brought in the dinner, with some more wine.

"Take a bite and sup," he said. "Ye'll stand in need o' it. Grief is a saer wearer of the body. Act like men. Ye'll find the leddy, I hope."

"Right!" replied Jack. "We must eat to live. Wake up, Harry."

"I want to go after Marian," answered Harry. "Cannot we get horses?"

"I know a game worth two of that."

"How! Explain it!"

"We will go to Sutton's hotel. Not a word shall be said. McCoy must keep all things dark. To-morrow we bury Charlie here, then go on to Colesberg."

"What use is that?"

"Sutton dare not return, unless disguised, but he will communicate with his wife. That is a sure thing. I will watch night and day. We will trap the wily villain, trust me."

"I wish I could think so."

"Take my view of the case," replied Jack.

"But Marian—my whole thoughts run on her."

"He will keep her secretly somewhere and not far off. She will be his last card to play. If we will not let him and his wife and children go free, we shall never see Marian again. That will be his threat. For that reason he knows we shall not put the police on his track. She is safe."

M'Coy agreed with Jack, and promised to say nothing about the outrage. The Kaffir Usibepu was similarly cautioned, and told that he would remain at the inn, while Jack and Harry walked on to Colesberg.

The next day a grave was dug, and Charlie was buried.

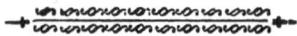

CHAPTER XXVIII.

ON THE WATCH—RETURN OF THE COINERS—THE CONFLICT IN THE VAULT.

WITHOUT loss of time Jack Spencer and Harry Rawlings walked on to Colesberg, and engaged a room at the hotel kept by Sutton.

By a singular coincidence the wife gave them the apartment which had been occupied by Peeping Tom and Knowall Dick.

It had remained vacant since their imprisonment in the coiners' vault.

Mrs. Sutton went about her business as usual, not seeming to have any care on her mind.

The day after their arrival Harry had a bad attack of fever and ague, which compelled him to take to his bed.

Jack pulled down the blinds to darken the room, and left him by himself.

For a couple of hours he sat in the reading-room, watching the entrance to the hotel.

No one at all resembling Sutton appeared, and he began to fancy that the robber had gone farther afield than he had anticipated.

If so, what had he done with Marian?

He could not ride any great distance with his fair captive.

The situation was becoming complicated, and he knew not how best to act in the interests of his sister.

He went back to the bedroom to see if he could be of any service to Harry.

The latter was very weak, but quite conscious.

"How are you, old fellow?" inquired Jack.

"I am afraid my head is going wrong," replied Harry.

He looked nervously round the apartment

"What do you mean?" asked Jack.

"I see strange things."

"Don't alarm yourself; you will be all right when the fever leaves you, to-morrow or next day."

"I have not been asleep."

"What did you see?"

"All at once," replied Harry, "about ten minutes after you had left me, I fancied I saw the door open."

"Of this room?"

"Yes; two men entered cautiously, shut the door, and walked to the wall near the chest of drawers."

"What next?"

"Now comes the wonder. They went through the wall."

"Ha, ha!" laughed Jack.

"That's right. I knew you would laugh," said Harry, smiling; "but I was wide awake recollect, and not dreaming."

"Two phantoms going through the wall, eh?"

"Conjured up by my excited brain," continued Harry. "It was awfully real and life-like, though."

Jack sat by his side fanning him until he went to sleep.

Then he walked to the wall through which the two strange men were supposed to have disappeared.

A slight examination showed him that the paper had been cut through.

Following up this discovery, he made out the line of a door.

Harry, perhaps, had not been deceived, after all.

A little more investigation showed Jack the secret spring, which he pressed, with the result of opening the door.

That he was on the verge of some strange discovery he did not doubt, though what it was he was at a loss to conjecture.

He might have obtained assistance, but he preferred to solve the mystery unaided.

With a pistol in one hand, and a light in the other, he began the descent of the private staircase.

Very cautiously he proceeded until he came to the passage, at the end of which was the door leading to the vault.

This had a little while before been unlocked by Fanshaw and Caner, and was standing open.

These were the two ghosts Harry had seen going through the wall, as he thought.

They had fancied the room was empty.

No one had told them it was let.

Owing to the darkness they had failed to notice Harry lying in bed.

Going along on tiptoe, Jack blew out his light and approached the vault.

Standing still in the shadow of the door he beheld the coiners seated at a table, with bottles and glasses before them.

To his surprise Peeping Tom and Knowall Dick were waiting upon them.

The spies were looking very pale and ill from the effects of their confinement.

It was a most unhealthy place to be cooped up in.

"What have you been doing during our absence?" asked Fanshaw.

"We tried to make false money, like you," replied Peeping Tom.

"If you have spoilt our moulds I'll kill you," said Caner.

"The metal got stuck in one," said Knowall Dick. "There was no grease in the mould; but there is no damage done."

"That's lucky for you, my bucks," cried Fanshaw. "Has the governor been down here since we went away?"

"No, sir."

"You've been all alone?"

"Rather too much so, sir," said Dick.

"Sutton told me," remarked Caner, "that if we wanted him we should hear of him at Brand's."

"Oh, is that the direction he has gone in this time?" answered Fanshaw.

Jack made a mental note of this piece of information, though he had not the remotest idea who Brand was, or where he lived.

It was something to go upon, however.

Like a little scrap of paper, which often enables the detective to trace out a crime, it might lead him to his sister.

"If I were the guv'nor," Caner went on, "I should turn the robber business up altogether."

"Bless your soul," replied Fanshaw, "he can't. That fellow loves danger and daring exploits."

"He'll be hanged," remarked Caner.

"I won't go so far as to say that," answered Fanshaw, "though it is possible. One thing is sure: he will die in his boots."

"And the best way to die," laughed Caner. "It is quickly over then. No mock sympathy, or sham sorrowing of hypocritical relations."

"Hullo!" suddenly cried Fanshaw.

"What's the matter now?"

"There is something or somebody at the door. Look out."

"Are you going to fire?"

"Yes, by heaven!"

Saying this, Fanshaw levelled his pistol at Jack, whose figure, dimly outlined, his sharp eye had noticed.

"Mind what you are about; it may be the governor," cried Caner.

"Not it."

Instantly Fanshaw fired.

The bullet flattened itself against the wall just above Jack's head.

It would have killed him if he had not ducked in time to avoid it.

As Fanshaw had provoked hostilities, it was only fair to retaliate, which Jack did in a prompt manner.

As soon as the smoke had curled upwards sufficiently to permit him seeing his man, he returned the shot.

True as a die was his aim.

The bullet of death flew straight to the heart.

Throwing up his arms with a sharp cry, Fanshaw sank onto the floor.

Caner was terribly alarmed.

He did not attempt to shoot. Blowing out the lamp he put the vault in total darkness.

Then he rushed to the passage, and collided with Jack so forcibly as to knock him down.

He stepped over his body.

His only hope was to get out into the street and fly from the city.

It mattered little who had discovered the secret of the vault. It was known, and to linger in Colesberg was no longer safe.

In short, it would have been madness to do so.

The spies had, at the first shot, crawled under a table, fearful lest they should get hurt in the affray.

Jack lost no time in relighting his lamp.

He advanced fearlessly into the vault, for he had seen Fanshaw fall, and knew that his confederate had made his escape.

The only danger was that the spies might take him for an enemy.

To avoid this, he shouted out—

"Tom, Dick, come forth. I am Jack Spencer!"

In a moment the two boys emerged from their place of concealment.

They were so overjoyed to see him that they could hardly speak at first.

His presence and bold behaviour had liberated them from bitter slavery, which had begun to appear an endless chain to them. They had lost heart, energy, hope.

"This is just what I can enjoy," exclaimed Peeping Tom. "I meet a dear old friend and schoolfellow, whom I thought at the other end of Africa, or at home, and he brings me freedom."

"Don't lay it on too thick," said Jack.

"He can't lay it on thick enough. You're a regular brick," cried Knowall Dick, "and, like the good fairy in the story books, you contrive to turn up just in the nick of time."

"Have you been badly treated?"

"Shamefully. The average dog leads a far better life."

"How did you get here?"

"We came with Captain Moonlight; but let me tell you the story. It wants a lot of explanation."

So it did. Jack, however, had heard the best part of it from Charlie, and it came to him like a twice-told tale.

It was the turn of the spies to be astonished when Jack related his own story.

"What!" exclaimed Peeping Tom, "Charlie dead? Really dead, at last!"

"Poor beggar!" said Knowall Dick; "but I always knew he would come to a bad end."

"I saw it from the first," replied Tom.

"He was a bad lot," continued Jack. "I must admit that, though I do not like to talk against the dead. You two did not care much for him, or you would not have left him tied to the waggon. If I had not come up when I did he would not have lasted out the day."

"Look how treacherously he acted towards us," remonstrated Peeping Tom.

"He made use of us on all occasions, and we did not get much for it," observed Knowall Dick.

"It serves you right for having such a bad master. Harry and I are willing to forget and forgive the past. We will take you back to England with us."

"Hurrah!" cried Tom. "You are one in a thousand!"

"I must find my sister, and hunt down Captain Moonlight," added Jack. "Then we will start for home."

"Home," repeated Tom, "sweet home! The very name makes me long for it again."

"I'd rather have our little village than all this continent," replied Dick. "It's rather mean, though, to return without any money. We had some, but these coining rogues robbed us of it."

"Is there anything you want from here?" asked Jack. "If not, let us get upstairs. Harry has a chill, but he will be glad to see you."

"Shall we say anything about the coining and Captain Moonlight?" asked Peeping Tom.

"Not a word till I give you permission. I want to work out my plan in my own way."

"All right," said Tom. "You have only to give us your orders, and we will obey them."

Leaving the dead man in the vault, they shut the door and went up the stairs.

When they reached the bedroom, Jack drew up the blind and let in the sun upon Harry, which awoke him.

He felt much refreshed by his sleep, and listened with great interest to all he was told.

The spies he greeted as old friends, forgetting, as if it had never happened, that they had tried to do him an injury.

"So," he said, "I was not deceived, after all. My men going through the wall were real men and not phantoms."

"Very real," replied Jack. "So much so, that one of them nearly put an ounce of lead into me."

"Who do you think the one who escaped is?" asked Peeping Tom.

"We forgot to tell you that bit," said Knowall Dick. "It is our old master at Dr. Birchoften's, Mr. Caner."

"How strange!" replied Harry. "I never thought much of him. He was sly and deep."

"Well," exclaimed Jack, "you fellows can have a chat. I am going to pursue my investigations, as the police say."

He left the spies sitting by the side of Harry's bed, and talking to him about their adventures.

The bar-room of a South African hotel is always the place to pick up any news or hear the latest gossip.

It was to this place that Jack went.

A man who looked like a substantial farmer was drinking some beer and conversing with the bar-keeper.

He was stout, and had a profusion of red hair, and withal his appearance was prepossessing.

Jack approached, called for a glass of wine, and made a casual remark about the weather.

"There has been a deal of rain up the country," replied the man.

"Ah! you are from the country, not a townsman?" said Jack.

"A farmer. I came in to-day to sell some wheat; as I passed the high part of the town I noticed the reservoir which supplies you with water. It is swollen, and does not look particularly safe."

"That has often struck me," remarked the barman.

"If it was to burst, it would swamp and ruin all your town," continued the farmer. "There would not be many left alive."

"Let us hope there is no danger of that," said Jack. "By the way, do you know anyone named Brand in your part of the country?"

The farmer looked curiously at him.

"Why, yes," he rejoined, "very well indeed, seeing that he is a neighbour of mine."

"I have business with him," replied Jack.

"His house is only about eight leagues from here, and, if you like, I will drive you to it."

"Really you are very kind."

"The road is good, and there is plenty of room in the waggon."

"It is a bargain, Mr.—"

"Joubest, that's me. Drink up, and we'll be off, or I sha'n't get home till long after dark."

Taking up a demijohn of whisky, the red-headed farmer proceeded to the yard, followed by Jack.

Two horses were hitched to the waggon.

They got in and drove off, Jack feeling rather proud to think that he had so soon got on the track of Brand.

Through him he should be able to track Captain Moonlight.

Already he fancied the famous robber was in his power.

Joubest did not talk much. He lighted a big meerschaum, and smoked with stolid satisfaction, and Jack followed his example.

"What kind of a place has Brand got?" inquired Jack.

"A house and an old mill. He's a miller, you know," was the rejoinder. "What's your business with him?"

"It's of a private nature."

"Oh! sorry I spoke. No offence, I hope? None meant."

"Neither is any taken."

The waggon went on, climbing a road which wound up a hill.

Colesberg was built in a valley, one side of which was beautifully sheltered by hills.

It was at the top of one of these that the reservoir of which Joubest had spoken was built.

In a few minutes they passed it.

It was much fuller of water than usual, and if it burst its banks catastrophe must follow.

It would descend like a flood on the town, sweeping away churches, banks, hotels, offices, and all the pride of its masonry.

"There's the death-trap," remarked Joubest.

"Do you think it dangerous?" asked Jack.

"I have always thought so. Suppose some rascal was to put a bag of gunpowder against the wall and light it?"

"It would blow a hole in it, and let the water into the town," replied Jack. "But who would be such a dastard?"

"A madman might do it for fun; an injured man for revenge; a thief for the purpose of robbery," said Joubest.

Again he became silent, and the road now being level, they went on at a better pace than before.

Although the road was good, it was destitute of trees, and the want of shade made the glare of the sun very unpleasant.

Suddenly Joubest pulled up the team sharply.

He pointed to the sandy road in front of them.

A large black snake was lying asleep, coiled up.

"Lend me your shooter," he exclaimed.

Jack took his pistol from his pocket and handed it to the farmer, being entirely unsuspicious of any plot.

"'I WILL SHOOT EVERYONE IN THIS ROOM!' CRIED SUTTON."

No. 10

Why should Joubest harbour any sinister design against him?

Instead of firing at the snake, the farmer presented the muzzle of the weapon at Jack's head.

"Dare to move, and you are a dead man!" he cried.

There was a change in his voice.

Before, he had drawled out his words; now, he spoke in an authoritative tone of command.

Jack was amazed.

He could do nothing, however.

By giving up his revolver he had rendered himself defenceless.

Joubest passed a strong leather strap round the upper part of Jack's body and buckled it tightly behind his back.

This rendered it impossible for him to use his arms.

"What is the meaning of this outrage?" he demanded."

Joubest took off his coat and divested himself of half-a-dozen waistcoats.

These had given him his burly appearance.

Then he removed his broad-brimmed hat and dashed a red wig on the bottom of the waggon.

"Sutton!" ejaculated Jack.

The mystery was out now, and he looked very crestfallen at being imposed upon so easily.

He had forgotten that Captain Moonlight was a man of infinite disguises.

"By Jove!" said he, "you are too clever for me."

"When I heard you speak about Brand, I felt that you knew too much, and determined to have you," replied Sutton.

"What will you do with me?"

"Lock you up for the present with your sister at the old mill."

"Is she unharmed?"

"I have not touched a hair of her head. She is safe under lock and key in a room in the mill. Mrs. Brand attends to her wants; but how did you hear of Brand?"

Jack related what had happened in the vault.

It was now the robber's turn to be astonished.

"Fanshaw killed?" he exclaimed.

"Yes; but the other escaped."

"We shall overtake him, I expect," said Sutton. "He is sure to make for the old mill, as I told him I should be heard of there. What did you want to find me for?"

"To make terms for the release of my sister," replied Jack.

"You have said nothing to anybody at present?"

"Absolutely nothing. I might have denounced you to the police, and had your wife arrested."

"Had you done so, you would have signed your sister's death warrant."

"How so?"

"If my secret had been blurted out, and my wife locked up as an accomplice, I would have shot your sister and thrown her in the river."

"I was afraid of that."

"Let me understand the situation," Sutton went on. "Your friend Harry is in bed with a chill; Tom and Dick are with him?"

"That is so."

"The three know that I (Sutton) am Captain Moonlight, the notorious robber, who has been laughing for years at the South African constabulary?"

"They do."

"Can we trust them to say nothing?"

"I strictly enjoined them not to do so," said Jack, "and I have no reason to think they will disobey my orders."

"If so, all will be well. I will start you and your friends on the way to the coast. You must drive your bullocks."

"I have a waggoner, old Usibepu we called him," exclaimed Jack.

"You had."

"Why speak in the past tense?"

"An outrage was committed at McCoy's last night. The Kaffir was killed, and McCoy and his wife were found dead in their bed."

"Is this true?"

"As gospel," answered the robber.

Jack could not repress a shudder of horror.

He could tell in a moment whose hand had done the awful deed.

The McCoys and the Kaffir had known too much.

It would have been inconvenient for Sutton if they began to talk.

Jack regarded the man by his side as an incarnate fiend.

"When you are gone," continued Sutton, "I shall sell out and move with my wife and children."

"Where to?"

"Australia. I have made money enough, and am tired of the life I have been leading. If you can understand such a paradox, I want to be a good citizen."

"Does your wife know that you and Captain Moonlight are identical?" asked Jack.

"Not for a moment. She has not the slightest idea of it," replied Sutton.

"That is strange."

"I love my wife and children too dearly

ever to let them hear of my disgraceful actions."

"Then they only know you as the loving husband, affectionate father, and man of business?"

"Just so—that's all."

"What will you do with your coiner accomplice, Caner? Will you trust him?"

"Not further than I can see him. I shall—"

Here he significantly touched the butt of his revolver.

"Kill him?" queried Jack.

"Certainly; dead men can't speak," answered Sutton. "I won't injure you. I shall send Caner into Colesberg to bring out your friends to-morrow morning, and start you off as quick as possible. I must keep you a prisoner to-night."

"What for?"

"I cannot run risks. All will be well if your friends keep their tongues quiet."

"As for Harry Rawlings, I can answer for him," replied Jack.

"Are you sure he is no chatterer?"

"No more than I am."

Sutton stroked his chin thoughtfully.

"I distrust Tom and Dick. They can't keep out of mischief," he observed.

"They never could," replied Jack. "We did not nickname them the Spies of the School for nothing."

"Well, well," cried Sutton, quickly. "Your fate and your sister's depend on the discretion of your friends."

"How do you mean?" asked Jack, anxiously.

"Simply this: If anything happens to my wife, by heaven! I'll kill all of you."

"But—"

"It is useless to argue the matter. Sit still. I'm going to whip the horses up. We are close to a roadside house. Caner ought to be there."

As Sutton went on with the waggon, one wheel went over the black snake, which had been the cause of Jack losing his pistol.

It uttered a terrifying hiss, and tried to hurl itself at the wheel, but its back was broken.

Sutton gave it a cut with his whip which made it fall in halves.

"Poor fool!" he muttered. "Thus will I destroy all my enemies."

A drive of about two miles brought them to a roadside tavern, which was prettily embowered with trees.

Here, as he had expected, he saw Caner seated in an arbour, covered with roses and creepers, with a bottle of wine before him.

"What has happened?" asked Caner, jumping up.

Sutton explained how he had met Jack and made him a prisoner.

"I know all," he added, "and I want you to go back to the town for me."

"That will be attended with danger," replied Caner.

"Not it. No one knows you."

"But the boys?"

"You must bring them with you to Brand's."

"Oh! that is the plan."

"Start at once. I must send them all off to the coast as soon as possible," exclaimed Sutton. "The one who is in bed has only got a chill. Hire a conveyance if necessary. You will have to travel all night."

"Very well. It shall be done," answered Caner.

"Do not let the grass grow under your feet."

"No fear of that."

Caner finished his wine.

"Any message for the wife?" he asked.

"Not a word. I will attend to her. She thinks I am on a journey."

Caner lighted his pipe, and at once retraced his steps to Colesberg.

He knew that Sutton was a man of action and not to be trifled with.

After half-an-hour's rest, Sutton and Jack resumed their journey to Brand's old mill.

Jack was hopeful that his troubles were nearly over.

He was extremely anxious to get out of Africa.

His only apprehension was that Peeping Tom and Knowall Dick might get them into some scrape, from which it would be extremely difficult to extricate themselves.

CHAPTER XXIX.

THE SPIES MEDDLE AS USUAL—ARREST OF MRS. SUTTON—AN UNEXPECTED DEATH—RAGE OF THE ROBBER.

AFTER Jack's departure Harry Rawlings felt so much better that he got up and sat in a chair.

The fever was leaving him.

"I won't be so selfish as to ask you fellows to stay with me," he exclaimed.

"Go and look round. Amuse yourselves. You must want it after being shut up in a vault for so long a time."

"In reality, I do feel rather brain-foggy," replied Peeping Tom, "but I do not like to leave you."

"That would not be the correct thing," said Knowall Dick.

"Cut along; don't mind me."

"If you insist upon it—"

"I do. When you come back we will see about dinner. Jack may not return until very late."

"All right," answered Peeping Tom. "We will take a walk."

"Certainly, as it is Harry's wish," said Knowall Dick.

They were only too glad to get away, as the confinement had told upon their constitutions.

Telling Harry they would not be long gone, they went downstairs and left the hotel.

Once in the street, breathing the fresh air again and seeing the shops, their spirits rose wonderfully.

"We are well out of that hole," remarked Peeping Tom. "I could not have lived very long in the vault."

"Nor I; but, I say," observed Knowall Dick, sagely, "we have no money. If Harry takes us back to England, which I suppose he will do, we shall land without a penny."

"Harry is rich."

"No matter; we cannot expect anything from him. Charlie was our friend, and the goose that would have laid the golden eggs is dead."

"Jack means to get the thousand pounds reward for Captain Moonlight's capture, and we shall have nothing," replied Peeping Tom.

Dick looked cunningly at his friend.

"You have struck the right key," he answered. "Why can't we get it ourselves? It would be a nice little sum to divide."

"Where did the coiners say he could be found?" asked Tom.

"Bother it! I forget."

"So do I."

They were at a deadlock here, for the name of Brand had utterly escaped their memories.

"Try and think," said Knowall Dick.

"It's no use. My mind is a blank. The shooting did it," replied Tom. "But if we go to the captain of the police, and tell him all we know, he will find Captain Moonlight and pay us the reward."

"I will do it if you will," was the answer.

"What will Jack Spencer say?"

"I don't care. We shall be perfectly independent when we get the money," said Knowall Dick. "Why should we be left out in the cold? Come along. I don't want to go back to England penniless."

They had wandered up Main Street while talking, and were now in front of the police station.

A constable stood on the steps.

"Do you want anything here?" he asked.

"Who is the boss?" inquired Peeping Tom. "I should like to have a word or two with him on very important business."

"Captain Kruger is at the head of the constabulary in this town," was the answer. "He is inside. You can see him."

"Good enough," said Tom.

"Show us in without delay," added Dick.

"You look as if you were in a particular hurry," remarked the constable. "Can't you tell me your business?"

"Couldn't think of it," answered Tom.

"Utterly impossible," said Dick. "It is an affair of State, and we could not communicate it to a—ahem, a subordinate."

"Step inside," rejoined the man. "I guess you have been to the music hall and had your watch and chain stolen."

"You are a good fisher, but you'll have to wait to find out what I have come here about."

Baffled in his attempt to extract information, the officer showed them into the private room of the chief of the constabulary.

Captain Kruger was a man of only forty years of age—tall, quick, athletic, with an eye like an eagle's.

"How can I serve you?" he asked, looking up from his newspaper.

"By arresting the greatest criminal in South Africa," replied Peeping Tom.

"The hugest scoundrel that ever—" began Knowall Dick.

"Do you mean Captain Moonlight?" interrupted the captain of the police, trying to conceal the interest he was beginning to feel.

"That is the identical person."

"What do you know about him more than anybody else does, may I inquire?"

"If we give you information which will lead to his arrest, shall we be entitled to the reward? That is what we want," continued Peeping Tom.

"Certainly; I will pay it you myself."

"When? That's the question."

"As soon as we clap our hands on his shoulder," rejoined Kruger.

"I am satisfied with your promise," exclaimed Tom. "You will be surprised when I tell you that the robber is a highly respected townsman of yours."

"Indeed! What is his name?"

"Sutton, of the 'Hoffman House' in Main Street."

"Ha!" cried Kruger. "I should never have suspected him. What proof have you of the truth of your allegation?"

"Ample. Listen to me," replied Peeping Tom.

He related how he met Sutton in the first instance, but he was too cunning to say anything about illicit diamond buying. He declared that he and some others were travelling to the coast when Captain Moonlight attacked the waggon, killing all except themselves, whom he brought to Colesberg.

The police captain was somewhat startled when Tom detailed how he had discovered Sutton's identity with the robber, and his subsequent incarceration in the coiners' den.

"Humph!" said Kruger, as he concluded, "you have done well to come to me. Where is your deliverer, Jack Spencer?"

"Hunting up the robber," replied Peeping Tom.

"Can you not recollect the name of the party at whose house the coiner said he was to be heard of?"

"I am sorry to say that I cannot. Wish I could."

The police captain rose and accompanied them to the hotel, where he was shown the vault with all its appliances for making base coin.

He looked at Fanshaw's face.

"That fellow has been in prison," he remarked. "I know him. This plant is quite enough to arrest Sutton and his wife. I'll have her at once."

He quitted the vault, and sought the private room in which the books were kept.

Mrs. Sutton was there with her children, pretty, happy, neatly dressed, and an elderly lady, her aunt, who assisted her with her accounts when her husband was absent on one of his journeys.

The spies stood outside.

They were compelled by instinct to listen to and see what was going on.

Though they did not know why, they began to fancy that they had been a little hasty.

"Good-day, Mr. Kruger," said Mrs. Sutton, genially. "What can I do for you this fine morning?"

"Is your husband at home?" asked the police captain.

"He is travelling."

"In what direction, may I inquire?"

"That he did not tell me. He never informs me of his movements, or as to the nature of his business."

"I regret that I have a very unpleasant duty to perform," exclaimed Kruger.

"Is there anybody staying in the hotel you want?" she asked.

"Only you."

"Me?"

"Yes. We have discovered a very extensive coining plant in one of your cellars, and we can prove that Sutton is no other than the notorious robber, Captain Moonlight, who has terrorised the country for years."

Mrs. Sutton gasped for breath.

Her eyes rolled wildly.

Kruger was not the kind of man to allow himself to be deceived, however.

The aunt, whose name was Blyth, was horrified; at the same time she was very indignant.

"How dare you bring such an infamous accusation against an innocent man?" she asked.

"I wish he was innocent, for your sakes," replied Kruger.

"Why do you talk of arresting this lady?"

"Because I am sure she knows all about her husband's villainy."

Mrs. Sutton, white as a sheet, trembling all over, pressed her hand to her side.

Her face was contorted, as if she were suffering acute pain.

"I swear, as heaven is my witness, that I know nothing," she answered.

Her solemn look, the intensity of feeling with which she spoke, would have convinced anyone but a police officer.

On Kruger it had no effect.

He was accustomed to acting of all sorts.

"You are my prisoner," he said.

"My children!" cried the unhappy mother. "Must I leave you?"

"This good lady will mind them," replied Kruger, pointing to Mrs. Blyth. "You need not close the house, but I must send two of my men here."

"If this is true of my husband, let me die."

"Do not make a scene, madam."

"I have no wish to live. My heart is broken, and my happiness fled for ever. Alas! that I should have ever loved him; but we have been so happy."

Her tears fell fast.

The children began to cry also, and clung to their mother's dress.

"Do not take her away," pleaded the aunt. "If it is necessary to put her under restraint, let it be done here."

"The matter is too serious," replied Kruger.

"For pity's sake, do as I beg of you."

Kruger shook his head sadly, but firmly.

Again the look of suffering crossed Mrs. Sutton's features.

She gasped for breath.

Suddenly she fell to the floor, clutching wildly at the carpet.

"Heaven," screamed Mrs. Blyth, "she is dying! Help! help!"

There could be little doubt that she was right.

Looking out of the door, Kruger saw the spies.

"Run for a doctor, quick!" he cried.

They did so, and in less than five minutes came back with a medical man.

It was too late, however.

Mrs. Sutton was no more.

The spies were alarmed at the course events were taking.

They went upstairs to Harry, and told him what they had done.

Also how death had robbed Kruger of his prisoner.

Harry was immensely annoyed at their conduct.

"You have made fools of yourselves, as usual," he exclaimed. "Why couldn't you consult me before you acted?"

"We wanted to get the money," replied Peeping Tom, sheepishly.

"It was a smart stroke to get the cash reward," said Knowall Dick.

"I wish Jack was here," replied Harry, with a puzzled air.

He knew not what to do.

"Will Jack be angry?" asked Tom.

"Undoubtedly. He told us to keep things secret, and his back is no sooner turned than you let them out."

"Sutton won't like it either," remarked Dick. "You have made a nice affair of it, I must say."

"Suppose we go out and have a look for Jack?" added Knowall Dick. "Are you strong enough to walk?"

"Not far, though the fever has left me; but I will come," replied Harry.

They went into the hall, where, coming from the private room, was heard the sound of weeping.

It was the little children mourning for their dead mother.

Passing out of the house, the three boys walked up Main Street, looking everywhere for Jack.

By accident they took the road which led to the reservoir.

One side of it was lined with leafy trees.

This shade, aided by the cool air rising from the water, made the spot an agreeable resting-place.

Harry was growing tired, and he pro-posed a rest, which the spies gladly assented to.

Throwing themselves on the dry grass under the trees, they indulged in the pastime of throwing stones into the water.

After a time they felt drowsy and went to sleep.

While they were in this state, Caner passed by them, having been sent, as we know, by Sutton, to bring the boys to him.

Little did he guess what had taken place.

Caner descended the hill, and walked up the street, towards the hotel, intending to seek Harry in the first instance.

At the door he was surprised to behold a crowd of people.

Two policemen in the hall kept them back.

The greatest excitement was exhibited on all sides.

Most extraordinary rumours were flying about, but the fact was known to everyone that Sutton was a coiner and robber.

Everyone felt sorry for the awfully sudden death of Mrs. Sutton.

She had been deservedly popular and respected.

Caner saw in a moment that something very much out of the common had happened.

He was acquainted with the hotel porter, who was standing on the edge of the crowd.

To him he appealed for information.

This was promptly forthcoming.

The porter had frequently seen Caner, but had no idea that he was connected with the coining.

"You see," he exclaimed, "the boss has been carrying on awful."

"What has he been doing?" asked Caner.

"He had a full-fledged coining place in the basement. That's found out."

"Is it?"

"Oh, yes. The police are in possession. Then the guv'nor is Captain Moonlight; that's found out, too."

"Who would have thought it?" observed Caner.

"No one; that's what folks are saying," replied the porter. "But the worst of it is, the missis was in it."

"I can't credit that."

"Oh, yes. She was just as bad as the master. Police-captain Kruger came to arrest her, and she fell down dead."

"What!" cried Caner.

This was extraordinary news.

What its effect upon Sutton would be he did not like to think.

"She's inside there with her aunt," continued the porter, "and the children, poor little things, crying their hearts out for their mother. Go and look, if you don't believe me."

"How on earth did Captain Kruger find it all out?" queried Caner.

"That is the best bit out," answered the porter with a grin. "Two youths were staying here, and they found out all about the governor."

"Two youths, do you say?"

"That's what they call them, but I think they are little old men."

"What makes you think so?"

"Oh! they must be Government detectives to be so clever as they have proved themselves," the porter replied.

"Where are they now?"

"I saw them go out of the hotel about a couple of hours ago, in company with another young fellow."

"Which road did they take?"

"They went up Main Street, as if they were going towards the reservoir. Anything else you want to know?"

"No, thank you," said Caner.

He was nearly wild with excitement at the news he had heard.

Sutton's only chance of safety was in immediate flight.

Chase would be made for him without delay.

As the spies were directly responsible for this state of things, Caner did not think it would do them any good to take them to Brand's, even if he could find them.

Sutton would be very likely to wreak his vengeance on them.

As he passed by the reservoir on his return journey, he heard voices among the trees.

These he recognised as those of the spies.

"I shall sleep at the police station to-night," remarked Peeping Tom, "for I can see what is coming."

"I know," replied Knowall Dick. "Sutton will swear to have our lives when he hears what we are responsible for."

"He must not catch us."

Caner pushed aside the branches of the trees.

"You here!" cried Peeping Tom.

"Make no noise. I will shoot the first who attempts to betray me," replied Caner. "I have news for you. Sutton has captured Jack Spencer. He and his sister Marian are safe at present about twenty miles from here. I was sent to take you there to Sutton. You were to be sent to the coast on taking a vow of secrecy. What has happened has altered all that, and you will do best to keep away until I see how the wind blows."

"You have heard, then?" asked Knowall Dick.

"Haven't I just come from the hotel? The people are standing round the door as thick as flies."

"It is a sad affair," said Peeping Tom.

"You should have known better. However, you can journey with me to within a few miles of the house where Sutton is, and I will come and tell you what is best to be done," replied Caner.

They were all glad of this proposal.

It was with difficulty that Harry walked the distance, but he did succeed in reaching an old barn.

This was five miles from Brand's mill. In it was plenty of dry straw.

Here Caner left his companions to recruit themselves by a rest, while he went on to Sutton. His mind was full of doubt.

It was impossible to tell how the robber would take the doleful news he had to tell him.

He did not mean to let him know where he had hidden the spies and Harry.

The fugitive's first impulse might be to go and kill them.

Sutton was pacing up and down a small lawn or grass plot in front of the old mill.

To the left of him was the farm-house, to the right the little river which turned the moss-covered mill wheel.

"Back at last," exclaimed Sutton. "You have been a long time."

"I have had a lot to do," replied Caner. "It is a long walk, mind you."

"Where are the boys?"

"I have not been able to see them."

"Why not? What has occurred? There is something wrong. I see it in your face. Speak, speak! and quickly."

"Calm yourself," said Caner. "The fact is Peeping Tom and Knowall Dick have been to the police for the reward and told everything. Kruger came to arrest your wife, and the shock killed her!"

Sutton staggered as if he had been shot.

"Oh, heaven!" he cried. "Dead! My Alice dead!"

"There is no doubt about it."

"You dare to bring me this news? Oh! you shall suffer for it. They shall all suffer. I will kill them everyone."

"I have done nothing."

"You have. I'll strangle you. This is more than I can bear. All known! My wife dead! Oh! my brain reels."

The blood rushed to his head, and his face became purple.

With a hoarse cry, half sob, half yell, he threw himself upon Caner.

The unfortunate ex-schoolmaster was borne to the ground.

Sutton fell on him, and seizing him by the throat, carried out his threat.

Not satisfied with reducing him to a corpse, he stabbed him half-a-dozen times with his knife.

Sutton's appearance was that of a madman.

For a few minutes he seemed undecided how to act.

Then he went to a stable at the rear of the house, and hastily saddled a horse.

Springing onto its back, he rode off like the wind in the direction of Colesberg.

His lips were compressed with a savage earnestness, and his eyes flashed with a vindictive fire.

He galloped the horse at its utmost speed over the sandy road.

Clouds of dust rose behind him.

The wind began to blow and rain to fall heavily.

Thunder crashed and lightning flashed, forked and vivid.

What cared he for the war of the elements?

His hat fell off, and he rode bare-headed in the fearful storm that was now raging.

When within a mile of the town, his horse stumbled and fell, throwing him heavily to the ground.

He was not much hurt, and with a cry of rage he got up.

The horse was too much exhausted and injured to move.

Cursing the animal for his immobility, he proceeded on foot.

In a short time he came to the reservoir.

The storm had passed over, and the stars began to shine again.

There was no one to be seen in any direction.

The silence of the grave reigned supreme in the stilly night.

Selecting the side of the reservoir nearest the town, he made a hole in the wall, and placed in it a can of gunpowder, with which he had provided himself.

In his eyes was the light of insanity.

"Ha, ha!" he laughed, "there shall be an awakening to-night. It shall sound like the last trump on the Judgment Day. My poor wife shall be avenged."

He supposed that the spies were in the town.

The destruction he hoped to send to everyone, he expected would overwhelm them.

There was a fuse attached to the powder.

Striking a match he lighted it.

One thing he had forgotten, and that was to calculate the time properly.

Before he could retreat, the explosion took place.

The report was heard for miles.

In an instant the wall of the reservoir was rent in twain.

A stone was hurled at Sutton, which struck him on the forehead, killing him on the spot.

Then the huge volume of water rushed out like a flood.

A large part of the wall succumbed to the pressure.

The raging tide caught up the body of the infamous Captain Moonlight, and bore it along like a cork.

Down the hill it went with its ghastly burden.

Although he had destroyed the town, he had killed himself.

The explosion caused many houses to fall, people were drowned by hundreds, and the once flourishing place was a heap of ruins.

It was an awful tragedy.

The survivors never knew how the catastrophe happened.

It was a secret that no one could divulge, for nobody had seen the fell deed done.

CHAPTER XXX.

THE morning broke fair and sunny. The spies and Harry were early roused from their slumber in the barn by the songs of birds.

"I say," cried Peeping Tom, "where is that fellow Caner? He ought to have turned up before now according to promise."

"Perhaps he has betrayed us," remarked Knowall Dick.

They walked out of the barn. Two hundred yards off was the gliding river' and moored to a stake was a boat.

"Let us get in the boat and go down the river," exclaimed Harry. "We shall get to the mill we have heard of, and see what we shall see."

"That's very oracular," answered Tom. "But is it safe?"

"Why not?"

"Captain Moonlight may pay us a little delicate attention we do not require."

"I dreamt he was dead!"

"Dreams are all nonsense."

"So they may be," said Harry. "It is a fact nevertheless that I fancied Caner came to me saying he had been shot, and that Sutton was drowned."

"That is more likely to be our fate," laughed Peeping Tom.

"So I think," assented Knowall Dick. "However, I'll go in the boat."

"And I," said Tom.

Accordingly they walked to the river side and got into the boat. Tom and Dick took the oars, while Harry steered.

The river was not broad, but it wound through the flat country in a serpentine manner.

A couple of hours' pulling brought them within sight of the old mill.

At a top window overlooking the water was a face.

The window was small and protected by thick iron bars.

"Hi! help! hi!" cried a voice.

The boys in the boat looked up.

"By Jingo!" exclaimed Harry, "it looks to me like—yes—like Jack Spencer."

"It is, too," replied Peeping Tom.

"Marian is behind him," said Knowall Dick. We must rescue them; but how?"

That was the question.

As they drew nearer they saw a door nearly flush with the water.

It was only secured by means of a padlock.

They rowed to it, and Harry attacked it with his knife and wrenched out the staple.

Brand and his wife had not yet risen.

Jack and Marian recognised their friends, and encouraged them in their efforts.

In a few minutes Harry was on the floor of the barn, the spies remaining in the boat.

He ran up a flight of wooden stairs.

To batter down the door of the room in which Jack and Marian were confined did not take him long, with the aid of a bar of iron he found ready to his hand.

Marian sank into his arms, and he covered her face with kisses.

"At last I have found you, my dear girl," he said.

"I thought our doom was sealed," she replied.

"How did you get here?" asked Jack.

It was no time for explanations.

Harry urged them to come down and get into the boat at once, which they did.

Then they started back for Colesberg as hard as the spies could row.

There was plenty of talk then, but they did not know all until they landed near the road and met some men.

These told them of the bursting of the reservoir, and the finding among the *débris* the dead body of Sutton.

When the boys heard of this they breathed more freely.

The inhabitants of the ill-fated town had fled from the lower part to the upper—that is, such of them as survived.

Happening as it did in the night, when the people were asleep in their beds, the catastrophe had resulted in a tremendous loss of life.

The bell in the principal church was tolling all day long as the dead bodies were got out of the ruins and carried to a place of sepulture.

Jack Spencer and his friends did not know whither to go or what to do.

Some enterprising men had erected large tents, where people could get something to eat and drink, and sleep on the ground.

In one of these, on the high ground near the now empty reservoir, kept by a man named Dawkins, Jack found a temporary refuge.

Going inside, he procured a tolerably good dinner.

The tent was crowded with people who were crushed, heartbroken, crying for lost relatives and ruined homes.

"Oh!" said Marian, "it is dreadful to hear the poor creatures. How long shall we have to stay here?"

"Until we can find a waggon to take us to the coast," replied Jack.

"We certainly can't tramp it," remarked Harry.

"Brand has a waggon," said Jack. "He goes to the coast sometimes. I fancy Sutton meant to send you and Tom and Dick with him."

"Brand is Sutton's accomplice. I should not like to trust him," replied Harry.

"Oh! he's all right."

"What kind of a fellow is he?"

"Pretty good for a Dutchman. He hates the English, of course, and thinks that South Africa was made for the Mynheers."

"We have money," said Harry. "A conveyance will be obtainable soon. We are all right so long as we can pay our way."

The spies, as usual, were restless. They could not sit still, and rising, went outside, with their hands in their pockets.

At some distance on the left of the plateau was a cemetery. The bell kept on tolling in a melancholy manner.

Funeral after funeral wound along the road to the gate, and the air was filled with the cries and lamentations of the mourners.

A man in a cart drove up to the entrance to the tent.

He got down and went to the bar, which was just inside, and called for some refreshment.

"I wonder what he has got in his cart," said Knowall Dick.

"It looks like a farmer's cart. I'll peep," replied Tom. "Watch the man and if he comes out suddenly, cry 'care!'"

"All right."

Climbing up on the wheel, Tom looked over the side and saw something covered with a strip of coarse canvas.

Leaning over, Peeping Tom drew aside the covering, and a cry of horror escaped his lips.

He saw before him a horribly bruised, battered and mutilated corpse, one of the arms being entirely torn away from the body.

At such a time there was nothing extraordinary in seeing a dead body.

Such ghastly relics of mortality were lying about in all directions.

What filled him with astonishment was to recognise in the dead man no other than Sutton.

The man to whom the cart belonged was evidently a friend of the late Captain Moonlight, and had at considerable pains and risk to himself recovered the remains.

His intention, no doubt, was to give him decent burial, which the authorities would not have done.

Who could this kind friend be but Brand?

Neither of the spies had seen this man of whom they had heard so much.

But he was well known to Marian and Jack.

Hastily dropping from the cart wheel, Peeping Tom went up to Knowall Dick with a white face.

"You look as if you had seen a ghost," remarked Dick.

"Worse than that. Sutton's dead body is in that cart."

"Oh!" cried Dick, "we must look out. Who's rescued it, do you think?"

"Most likely Brand, his old time friend."

Knowall Dick looked at the body of the cart.

A name was written on it.

It was just what he had suspected.

"Brand, Lonely Farm, Vreeberg Road."

"If Brand gets to know that we are here, we may expect no mercy at his hands," exclaimed Peeping Tom.

"None," replied Knowall Dick. "He is sure to have heard in the town all about our betraying Captain Moonlight, and perhaps he'll try to kill us both."

"Oh, dear!" groaned Tom; "there is always some fresh trouble cropping up for us."

They could not or would not see that it was all their own fault.

"We may stick here for a week or more before we obtain a bullock waggon to take us down to the coast," observed Knowall Dick.

"Well," said Peeping Tom, with the air of a philosopher, "we've got to chance it.

I'm not going to leave Colesberg until I have got the reward offered for Sutton."

"Certainly not. We earned it, and we'll have it, even if it is what they call blood money."

There was a brief pause.

"I've heard," said Tom, "that blood money is unlucky. Anyhow, we'll take it, won't we?"

"Rather! Look here: go into the tent and see what Brand is doing. Take a quiet peep."

Tom nodded, and crept noiselessly into the tent.

To his surprise he saw Brand standing at Jack's table, talking earnestly to him and Marian.

He crept a little nearer and listened.

"I'm sorry for what I did to you," Brand said; "but you must know that Sutton and I had been acquainted for years. I never went with him on any of his expeditions, though I knew well enough what he did. He gave me the money to buy my farm with. My wife and I owe everything to him. He would come and stay for a week at a time with us. He and I were like brothers; to think of his death distracts me."

"You should not have harboured such a man," replied Jack.

"Ah! you do not know what friendship is."

"The police would like to get hold of you, Mister Brand," said Jack.

"They could do nothing to me. I was the friend of a criminal. That is all."

"You should have given him up."

"Never! Sooner would I have cut off my right hand. Listen: I have been into the town. I have found his body. It is in my cart outside."

"Sutton's body?"

"Ya," replied the Dutchman. "It is there right enough."

"What are you going to do with it?"

"He was mein friend, I tell you. I shall dig a grave in my garden. I will bury him there, and each day I will cover that grave with flowers."

Brand brushed away a tear which came unbidden to his eye.

An idea struck Jack.

"You have a waggon and a team of six bullocks with which you track to the coast sometimes?" he said.

"Ya, that is so."

"If you will take me and my party to the nearest seaport we will pay you well for your trouble, and I will say nothing to the police about your connection with Sutton."

"What will you pay?"

"The usual rates," replied Jack.

Brand closed with the offer.

"Come on to my house at once," he said. "You will do better than stopping here. You need not fear me now. The lady will be cared for by my wife."

"What do you think of the proposal, Marian?" asked Jack.

"I don't care for this place," she replied. "There are dozens of people here now, and at night it will be crowded. We shall all be sleeping on the floor."

"Then we will go. Expect us to-night before dark, and have supper ready. How long before you can hitch up your team and start?"

"Two days. I have work to do to-morrow."

"Of what kind?"

"Revenge!" replied Brand, in a hissing tone. "Sutton was my friend. I will avenge his death."

Shaking his fist in the air, he hurried away, having a wild, scared, half-mad look on his face.

Soon afterwards his cart was heard rattling over the hard road.

"Whom does he want to be revenged upon?" asked Harry.

"That's a mystery," replied Jack.

Peeping Tom stepped forward.

"I have heard all," he exclaimed, "and there is no doubt in my mind that the fellow is after me and Dick."

"How should he know that you betrayed Sutton?" inquired Jack.

"He could easily pick up that bit of intelligence."

"It doesn't matter. We will look after you."

"I shall go and claim the reward, and place myself under police protection," replied Peeping Tom.

"So shall I," added Dick, who had joined the group. "If we don't, we shall be murdered by that cranky Dutchman."

"Come with us."

"No ; not for worlds," cried Peeping Tom.

"Not for all the diamonds in Africa," chimed in Knowall Dick.

"It is a pity to separate," said Harry.

"I know my book. Good-bye," answered Tom. "Come on, Dick. We'll go where we can be safe."

Jack, Harry and Marian urged them to stay, but nothing could induce them to do so.

They linked their arms together, and walked quickly away into the ruined town to go to the police station.

Both had every confidence that they would obtain the reward which they had fairly earned.

It would make them independent of everybody, and they could go home when they liked.

"Ha, ha!" laughed Jack, "it does not take much to frighten them, after all. Perhaps we are just as well off without as with them."

"I never could bear those boys," remarked Marian. "Really, I hope I am not uncharitable, but they are my pet aversion."

"When I extended the right hand of fellowship to them," exclaimed Harry, "it was through a feeling of charity, and little else. I remembered that they were old schoolfellows, and that they were friendless in a foreign land."

"Well," said Jack, "they have left us of their own accord. I can't help it."

By this time they had finished their repast.

Rising, they paid for the accommodation they had received, and commenced their journey.

Brand's Lonely Farm, as it was called, was reached before sunset, and the Dutchman and his wife had prepared an excellent meal.

A large mound in the garden indicated that Brand had consigned Sutton's remains to the grave.

After dinner Marian and Mrs. Brand retired. The Dutchman produced long pipes, tobacco, and a flask of Hollands.

"Will you take some schnaps?" he asked.

Jack and Harry made no objection to a little drop, and they were soon comfortably seated near the open window, through which the cool night air entered freely.

"I will give you blankets," added Brand, "and you shall sleep down here. We have only two beds. One is mine and mein frau's, and the other is for your little lady."

"We are old campaigners," said Jack; "please do not put yourself out of the way on our account."

"You must keep your pistols ready. This is a lonely place, and after the inundation there will be hungry tramps about. If you hear me moving early do not be alarmed. I shall go out before daylight."

"May I ask what for?" inquired Jack.

"To seek revenge for the betrayal of my poor friend Sutton," replied Brand.

"Upon whom?"

"Two boys who were staying in the hotel. I have the description of them so good that I would know them anywhere."

"What will you do to them?"

"Shoot—put bullets in their hearts," said the Dutchman, fiercely. "I shall sleep for three, four hours, then go out to seek these rascals in the town. Most men would be tired with what I have done. Not me; I am iron. My blood is boiling—my head on fire. I rest not till I get revenge for the death of my friend Sutton."

"I'd think better of it if I were you," exclaimed Harry.

"No, no! Never!"

"Revenge is a bad passion. It recoils on the head of the man who seeks it."

"Death to the betrayers!" shouted Brand. "Check me not! I have sworn it!"

Waving his hands wildly in the air, he went to a press, took out some blankets, threw them on the floor, and rushed away.

They could hear the tramp of his heavy boots as he ascended the uncarpeted wooden stairs.

Jack and Harry looked anxiously at one another.

"That man is mad," remarked Harry. "He has gone crazy thinking about Sutton's death, and that of his wife, and the destruction of the town."

"If so, he is sane and solid on one point," replied Jack. "He's heard the whole story, and has got his knife into Peeping Tom and Knowall Dick, and fully intends to kill them."

"Yes; it is lucky for them they did not come here with us. What ought we do in the matter?"

"I don't know," Jack said, in perplexity.

"If we were to go and try to find them we do not know where to look for them; besides, I am too dog tired to walk all that way," observed Harry.

"That is out of the question. They don't deserve it, either."

"True. We are helpless in the matter," replied Harry.

"They must take their chance. Let us lie down. I can't hold up my head," exclaimed Jack, yawning.

It was very warm. They spread out the blankets, and closed the windows to keep out the night dews and malaria.

Then they reclined on the blankets and tried to rest.

Harry soon went off, for he had undergone a great deal of fatigue; but Jack was unable to sleep.

They had left the oil lamp burning, turned halfway down. Their pistols were by their sides, and they were ready for any surprise.

The door of the room was open, so that they could hear anything that went on upstairs.

All was still as the grave, barring the heavy snoring of the Dutchman and the everlasting buzz of the mosquitoes.

Though he closed his eyes, and tried to think of dear Old England only, Jack could not get to sleep.

If he sank off into a half-doze he awoke with a start, dreaming of savage men fighting.

At last he gave it up in despair, arose, sat on a chair, and lighted a pipe.

He had not been smoking long before he heard a tap, tap at the window.

Starting, he seized a pistol and listened attentively.

In a few seconds the tapping was repeated.

Going to Harry, he shook him by the shoulder and made him awake.

"Anything wrong?" asked Harry, who was wide-awake in a moment and ready for action.

His experiences in Africa had taught him self-reliance and given him presence of mind, if they had not done anything else.

"There is somebody outside," replied Jack.

"Call the Dutchman."

"Not till I know what it is. I'm not so easily scared. Take your shooter, and we will investigate."

"Get shot perhaps."

"I don't think so," said Jack, advancing to the window.

The curtain was drawn across. Without pushing it back, he asked who was there.

"Thank heaven! it is Spencer's voice," he heard someone say.

"I thought we had struck the right shop," exclaimed another person.

Instantly Jack recognised the speakers as Peeping Tom and Knowall Dick.

He was apprehensive for their safety.

They had strayed into the lion's den, as it were, and stood in peril of their lives if Brand saw them.

Throwing back the curtain, he flung open the window, which was level with the ground, and the spies stepped in.

They looked very dejected, thoroughly fatigued, and altogether discouraged and disheartened.

"What has happened so quickly to bring you here?" asked Jack.

"We knew you would give us shelter," replied Tom.

"And protection," added Dick.

"I thought you were going to seek that at the police station," observed Harry.

"We tried to," said Peeping Tom. "Oh! this is an awful country."

"Something cruel," cried Knowall Dick.

"Tell us all about it," exclaimed Jack. "What has occurred to upset your plans, and bring you here, of all places in the world?"

"My dear fellow, we have been shamefully treated," cried Peeping Tom, in a state of great excitement.

"How so?"

"We went to see the captain of the police, Kruger. We asked him for the reward, and what do you think?"

"I can see he didn't give it you."

"Not he. We were ignominiously kicked out. He swore that he alone found out Sutton's secret, that we had nothing to do with running the criminal to earth, the reward was his, and if we were seen again within ten miles of Colesberg, he would run us in for twelve months on a charge of trying to extort money by false pretences."

"Did he kick you?"

"Didn't he! I'm sore all over," rejoined Peeping Tom.

"So am I. Oh, dear! this is a horrid country. All the people are frauds," whined Knowall Dick.

"Except you two," remarked Jack, with a half-smile. "It just serves you right for meddling. However, this matter can be referred to the Governor, and smart as Mr. Kruger thinks he is, I don't imagine for a moment he will be able to keep the reward."

"Certainly not," observed Harry. "We can help them to prove their case at headquarters."

The spies' long faces relaxed a little.

This was better news than they had expected to hear.

They did not so much mind being kicked, but they did decidedly object to losing the money they had reckoned on.

"Will you take care of us here, and protect us?" asked Tom. "For heaven's sake, don't leave us in the lurch. I believe Brand is as much down on us as the police captain."

"You are right there," replied Jack. "Only just now he was vowing vengeance against you for betraying his friend Sutton."

"He has got your description, and means to start out after you at daybreak," said Harry. "He has sworn to have your lives!"

The knees of the spies knocked together, and their faces blanched.

"You are joking," stammered Peeping Tom.

"Having a lark with us," said Knowall Dick.

"Indeed," answered Jack, "we were never more serious in our lives. Brand has sworn to shoot you on sight."

"What shall we do?" asked Tom. "I —I don't want to be shot."

"I—I can do without it," said Dick, shivering.

Two more miserable specimens of humanity could scarcely be imagined.

Just as they thought they were out of all their troubles, and going happily home, a new one threatened them.

Suddenly a heavy step was heard on the stairs.

Every eye was turned towards the door.

"Hide, hide!" said Jack Spencer, in a loud whisper.

The spies were too terrified to move.

"Hide!" continued Jack, angrily.

They attempted to crawl under the table, but they were too late.

Their opportunity was gone.

Brand stood in the doorway, with a light in his hand, and he uttered a cry of joy.

"Ha!" he cried, "the flies have come into the net. I heard the tapping at the window, and I have also heard your talk. Down on your knees and prepare to die."

Peeping Tom and Knowall Dick, paralyzed with fear, knelt down.

"Mercy!" said Tom. "I've done nothing to you. Jack, help us."

Knowall Dick lost his head altogether.

"Help! Murder! Fire! Thieves! Police!" he yelled, rolling on his back.

Brand levelled a pistol at him.

He was preparing to fire.

At this moment, which was so critical in the career of the spies, Jack thought it about time to interfere.

"No, you don't," he exclaimed. "Two can play at that game."

"What have you got to do with it?" asked Brand, pausing.

"Everything. They are my friends."

"So was Sutton mine."

Jack stepped boldly forward.

"Stand back!" cried the Dutchman; "or you, as well as they, shall die."

Jack's only reply was to fire at Brand.

He aimed at his leg, and shattered the bone above the knee, causing him to fall in an agony of pain.

His pistol exploded harmlessly in the air, injuring no one, and Harry promptly took it away from him, so that he could do no more mischief.

His imprecations, in Dutch and English, rang through the house.

"I'm sorry for it," remarked Jack, "but I had to do it. His leg may be mended, but he could not have given back to Tom and Dick their lives, if he had once taken them, as he said he would."

Roused by the noise, Mrs. Brand and Marian hastily attired themselves, and came downstairs.

Brand fainted from loss of blood, and the pain of his wound.

All the attention possible under the

circumstances was paid to him, and the wound was bound, after which he was carried upstairs, where his wife sat by his side.

She could not speak a word of English, and was utterly unable to understand who was to blame.

Jack and his party sat in the parlour, snatching a few hours' sleep as best they could.

No further danger was to be apprehended from Brand.

The spies overwhelmed Jack with thanks. Dick even went so far as to hug him round the neck.

At last the morning came.

After eating some breakfast, Jack undertook to walk to the town and ascertain if any waggons were likely to start soon for the sea.

CHAPTER XXXI.

JACK SPENCER DETERMINES TO HELP THE SPIES TO GET THEIR REWARD.

BEFORE he started, Jack went into the garden and smoked a cigarette.

He thought his troubles were over now, and that he would soon be back in dear Old England.

His adventures in South and West Africa had been quite enough for him.

Like many a wanderer, he longed to get back to the Old Country.

To his mind there was no place like the land of his birth.

While he was walking to and fro, Peeping Tom came up to him.

"I say, Spencer," he exclaimed, "can I speak a few words to you?"

"What about?" asked Jack.

"Excuse me. I won't detain you very long."

"Wire in, then, and get your name up."

"The fact is," said Tom, "we—that is, Dick and I—have been talking this morning, and it seems a mortal shame that we should be done out of the reward for the detection of Sutton, by that Dutch hound, Kruger."

"So I think."

"You do?" asked Tom, joyfully.

"Kruger is like all these insolent Boers," answered Jack. "He wants to make money anyhow, and despises the English. They live on the memory of Majuba Hill and Laing's Neck, where, by accident, they defeated our troops."

"If you are going to the town, will you see Kruger, and see if you can get the money for us?"

"I will—with pleasure."

"We are not rich. Our parents are poor."

"I know that."

"It would give us a start in life."

"I will make it my business," said Jack Spencer, "to call on Kruger, and do the best I can for you."

"A thousand thanks."

"I am not in a hurry to get away from here," continued Jack. "All danger is over now. Brand is shot through the leg, and is not likely to be able to move out of his bedroom for weeks to come."

"You will help us?"

"Certainly. You only ask for what is right and just."

"Kruger would not dare to kick you out as he did us."

"He might try, but I would be equal with him. The worst of it is, these Dutchmen do not like us."

"The Governor of the State would see us righted."

"He is in Prætoria. How can we get at him? The Transvaal is broad, and travelling takes time and money."

"I heard that he was coming to Colesberg."

"When? where?" asked Jack.

"Some fellows were talking in Dawkins' tent yesterday," replied Peeping Tom, "and they stated that the Governor of the Republic was expected in the town to do what he could to relieve the sufferers from the inundation caused by the bursting of the reservoir."

"Very likely."

"President Joubert is our man. See him, and Kruger will not dare to refuse payment of the reward."

"I will do all I can for you."

"True and honest?"

"Trust me," replied Jack Spencer.

"You are a brick."

"Flatter me. Lay it on thick," said Jack, smiling.

"A regular trump, I call you."

"I'm off. Tell Harry Rawlings and Marian what I am going to do, and if I do not come back for a few days, they need not be alarmed."

"Hadn't I better come with you?" asked Peeping Tom.

"What for? To take care of me?"

"Not that exactly."

"I don't want a nurse. I'm out of leading strings," said Jack Spencer.

"Of course, you are, I know that; but, at the same time, you might be glad of a little advice or assistance."

"I like your cheek."

"Let me come with you," pleaded Peeping Tom.

"Well, I don't mind," said Jack, after a moment's reflection; "but I can't take Knowall Dick, too."

"Certainly not. Let him stay with Harry Rawlings and your sister Marian."

"All right."

"They will not come to any harm while Dick is with them."

"We will go and tell them," said Jack Spencer.

They walked into the house together.

What with her household duties and nursing her wounded husband, Mrs. Brand had scarcely a moment to speak to anybody.

Marian rendered her what assistance she could.

For this help the woman seemed grateful.

Brand preserved a sullen silent demeanour, as if he were nursing his wrath and cherishing vengeance.

He could do nothing at present.

No infant child could have been more helpless, for his injured leg prevented him from moving.

If Marian brought him a basin of broth, smoothed his pillows, or read something to amuse him, he never thanked her.

His eye flashed like that of a basilisk, and he frowned darkly.

She was the sister of Jack Spencer who had shot him.

The spies had betrayed his friend Sutton to death.

It was easy for those who could read between the lines to see that he was the enemy of all who were harbouring in his house.

But as we have said, he could do nothing to hurt them until he got better.

The vicious old Boer was compelled to bide his time.

Marian had noticed his malignant glances, and they rather disturbed her serenity.

She was afraid of Brand.

When Jack and Peeping Tom entered the sitting room, Dick was playing a game of dominoes with Harry Rawlings.

Marian was industriously mending a rent in her dress. It had been torn and mended a good many times, and she was longing for the time when she could buy a new one.

"I am going into the town, as I told you, to enquire about the tracking towards the sea," he exclaimed. "Tom is coming with me, and we may be away for some time."

"What for?" asked Marian, in surprise.

"Are you in a hurry to depart?" enquired Jack.

"Indeed, I am; and so would you be if you saw the looks the old Dutchman gives me, when I go into his room."

"Are you afraid of him?"

"Not now. I shall be, though, when he gets well and strong enough to walk about."

"That will be some time."

"Of course, but when he can stand, look out! That's all. He would murder the lot of us in our beds," said Marian.

"He won't have the chance," answered Jack. "We will be off before that happens."

"Do not linger. Delays are dangerous."

"I must have a few days," continued Jack Spencer. "Dick and Tom have honestly earned the reward offered for Sutton's capture or death. It is theirs by right."

"That is so," remarked Harry Rawlings.

"It is a shame that Herr Kruger should appropriate it," observed Marian.

"He shall not be allowed to do so," replied Jack.

"How are you going to prevent it?" queried Harry Rawlings.

"I shall seek the Governor of the Free State, acquaint him with the full particulars of the case, and demand justice."

"Do you know where to find him?"

"Joubert—that is his name—is reported to be coming to Colesberg to see what he can do to help the victims of the recent disaster," rejoined Jack.

"That is lucky," said Harry. "I have heard that President Joubert is a rattling, downright, jolly good fellow."

"So have I. While, according to the common talk, Kruger is just the opposite."

"I don't like him a little bit. He's ordinarily civil to your face, but there is an undercurrent of duplicity and brutality."

"Anyone can see that."

"Beware of him."

"Pshaw! He can't hurt me. I shall leave you, Harry and Dick, to look after Marian," exclaimed Jack.

"I don't want telling to do that," replied Harry, smiling. If anyone dares to attempt to touch a hair of my precious girl's head, I'll—I'll spiflicate him."

"How is that operation performed?" asked Jack, laughing.

"It's double Dutch for lamming the life out of a fellow."

"Ain't you rather warlike to-day?"

"I always am when there is a possibility of danger befalling my little maid, Marian."

"'DARE TO MOVE AND YOU ARE A DEAD MAN!' CRIED JOUBEST."

The young lady blushed at this speech, but she nevertheless felt proud of her lover.

Girls always like brave boys and men.

They hate cowards and sneaks.

Hero worship has always been a cult among English women.

It is as strong to-day, when they talk of Havelock or Gordon, as it was in the days of the Crusades.

"You see, I leave you in good hands," said Jack.

"I wish Harry would not talk so much," replied Marian. "He must be fond of hearing his own voice."

"He does not mean any harm."

"No more does the animal with the long ears, that brays, yet he makes plenty of noise."

Jack and the spies roared with laughter.

"Marian has a good opinion of you," cried Jack.

Harry Rawlings assumed a lugubrious aspect.

"I'm done for," he replied, "when the girl of my heart goes back on me. She has compared me to a donkey, a creature that eats thistles, and brays. She says that my eloquence is nothing better than the braying of an ass. Therefore, everything I say must be asinine. Boohoo! I shall never get over it."

"Can't you stand a little chaff?" asked Marian.

"Not from you."

"You'll have to. It is about time you began to learn to endure it."

"You're an awful tease when you like."

"Every girl is. What's the use of a sweetheart if you can't tease him sometimes, and make him feel mean and miserable?"

"Oh, that's it, is it!" said Harry.

"Of course. Courtship can't be all honey and sweet. It would not do to let a man think too much of himself."

"Why not?"

"If a woman did, he'd think himself better than her," answered Marian, with a pout on her pretty lips.

Jack looked at his watch.

It was already eight o'clock in the morning.

"I guess I'll be off, boys," he said. "Keep a sharp look out."

"You just bet we will," replied Knowall Dick.

"Possibly you will have people coming here from Colesberg who have been washed out of their homes by the inundation."

"How shall we treat them?" asked Harry.

"Civilly and kindly. Never be rough on a weary starving man," answered Jack.

"I understand. Good-bye."

"Wish you luck," said Knowall Dick. "I'm glad, though, it ain't me going with you, Spencer."

"Why so?" enquired Jack.

"Old Kruger knows how to use his right leg, he does, and I've no particular wish to be booted again, though it may suit some people, especially my pal Tommy."

"I like your style," cried Peeping Tom.

Knowall Dick winked his eye and put his tongue in his cheek.

These were favourite little tricks of his.

"I shall take precious good care to keep out of his way," remarked Peeping Tom. "Oh, my! I'm sore yet; sitting down's no pleasure to me."

"Same here," rejoined Dick.

"Since Spencer has been kind enough to champion my cause, he will have to do the talking. I'll stand behind him and use him as a buffer."

"Go on," said Dick, "you're like a sheep's head."

"How's that?" asked Tom.

"All jaw. Ha, ha!"

"Get your hair cut!" cried Tom, as he followed Jack Spencer from the room.

They took the centre of the road, for there were no trees to shade it, and the middle provided better walking than the side.

The heat of the sun did not trouble them much now, for they had been in Africa long enough to get used to it.

They were both of them in high spirits.

Jack Spencer was jubilant because, as far as he could see, his troubles were over, and he would soon be on the way home.

With Peeping Tom, the source of pleasant reflections arose from avarice.

He made sure that Spencer would procure the reward for him, and he was revolving in his mind how he could swindle Knowall Dick out of his share.

Tom wanted to keep it all to himself.

He was very fond of money, and young as he was, wanted to start in business for himself.

What that business was to be, he had not quite made up his mind.

His inclination, however, was to be established as a private detective, and keep an agency.

This is a very good paying sort of enterprise, requires little outlay, and was just suited to his tastes and capabilites.

A few hours' walking brought them to the top of the hill which overlooked the town of Colesberg.

How strangely altered it was.

Innumerable houses had been swept away, and nearly all was wreck and ruin.

The people dispossessed of their homes were still camping out on the hillside.

There was a hopeless crushed air about them, as if they had lost their all, and were afraid to begin the world again.

Arriving at the tent kept by Dawkins, where they had halted the day before, Jack and Peeping Tom went in.

They wanted some refreshment, and a brief rest.

Sitting down at a table, they ordered some cold meat, bread and beer from a waiter.

While they were eating, Dawkins, whose acquaintance they had previously made, came up and shook hands with them.

"Back again, gentlemen," he said; "glad to see you."

"We are staying at Lonely Farm," replied Jack, "but we have business in the town."

"He's a queer kind of old Dutchman. I never took much stock in him."

"How was that?"

"I don't know. Instinct, I suppose. He's a Boer and I'm an Englishman."

A fine specimen of his country he was, too.

Fully six feet high, and stout in proportion.

An athlete, every inch of him.

"You don't like the Boers," said Jack.

"Not I. They put on too much side, and are as grasping as misers; besides, they are an ignorant lot, knowing nothing of the world outside their Free State.

"Brand was a friend of Sutton, *alias* Captain Moonlight."

"I'm not surprised to hear it. He was always regarded as a shady lot."

"Have a glass with me?" asked Jack.

"No; you'll drink at my expense. Hans!"

He held up his hand to a waiter.

"Ya," replied the fat sleepy-looking Dutchman.

"*Ein, zwei, drei, vier bier*—four beers, and look sharp."

"Ya," again said the waiter.

"They are a lazy lot. It's difficult to move them," continued Dawkins. "I wish I'd stopped in Cape Town, and never come out to the Transvaal."

"What made you do it?"

"It was a little trouble about I. D. B."

Jack gave a shrill whistle.

He had heard a good deal about the law respecting illicit diamond buying, or I. D. B. as it is called at the Cape.

The natives employed at the diamond mines often conceal stones about their persons.

They sell them for a small price.

Anyone detected in buying a diamond in this manner, is sure to be sentenced to a long term of imprisonment.

"I kept a saloon in Cape Town," continued Dawkins, "and was doing well. One day a Zulu came in for a drop of square-face, as they call the Dutch gin."

"And he offered you a stone."

"Exactly. I was fool enough to buy it. Some of my customers witnessed the transaction; they warned me that if the police heard of it, I should be arrested, so I skipped to Petermaritsburg, and came on here."

The waiter brought the four glasses of beer and deposited them on the table.

They chinked the glasses together.

At this moment a man entered the marquee and took a seat at a table behind them.

None of them noticed him.

It would have been better for them if they had, for it was no other than Kruger.

The chief of the Colesberg police eyed them keenly.

"This has been a great calamity for the town," remarked Jack.

"Awful!" replied Dawkins.

"The houses were all of wood, so I suppose it will not take long to build them up again."

"That will soon be done. It's the loss of life I'm thinking of," Dawkins answered. "People quickly rebuild towns. Look at the damage that is often done by fire and war. In a few months all traces of the devastation are wiped out. But I say!"

"What now?"

"You didn't tell me what business you are on. If I can help you, I will gladly do so."

"Thank you very much."

"An Englishman ought always to help another if he is able to do so," added Dawkins.

"The fact is," replied Jack Spencer, "that I want to see justice done to my friend here."

"Has he been robbed?"

"Shamefully. He is entitled to the reward offered for the capture or death of Sutton."

"Really? I didn't know that. Why can't he get it? Has he asked Kruger?"

"Yes; and not only been refused, but kicked out of the police headquarters."

"Well," said Dawkins, "it ain't exactly safe to speak your mind in these confounded Dutch towns, for you never know who may be listening and sneaking; but that is just what you might expect from that chap Kruger."

"He won't pay up."

"Wants to collar the lot, eh?"

"Every cent of it, and what can the boy do? If he has no help he will be done. I mean to assist him all I can."

"That's really kind of you," Dawkins

said. "It shows that you have a good heart."

"I hope so," replied Jack. "I am too young to be mean."

"Kruger is a hard nut to crack."

"I know it; and for that reason, if he does not stump up the reward when I ask him for it, I shall go direct to the President of the State."

"He's a fair man. I reckon he'll see the lad righted."

Just then, Peeping Tom happened to turn round.

He caught sight of the police superintendent.

It would have been odd if Peeping Tom had not discovered him.

Squeezing Jack Spencer's arm, he whispered in his ear—

"Behind you. Look out!"

"For what, or whom?" asked Jack.

"Kruger."

Jack sprang up, and without the slightest fear, faced the head of the police.

He was rather pleased than otherwise to be confronted with him.

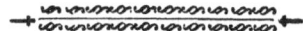

CHAPTER XXXII.

KRUGER'S STRATEGY.

NOTHING daunted at being discovered in such close proximity to the three speakers, Herr Kruger coolly returned Jack Spencer's look.

"Good-day," he exclaimed, raising a glass of beer, which had just been brought him, to his lips.

"Glad to meet you," replied Jack.

"*Gesundheit besser nor krankheit.*"

This in German means—

"Good health. It is better than bad health."

This salutation is usual among the Teutons.

"Have you been listening long?" asked Jack.

"Long enough to know what your game is," was the answer.

"It is an old saying that listeners never hear any good of themselves."

"What your opinion of me may be, is a matter of supreme indifference to me."

"You know this boy by my side?"

"Yes, I have seen him and his companion," replied Kruger. "Yesterday, I had the satisfaction of kicking them."

"What for?"

"They demanded the reward for Sutton's capture, which they are not entitled to."

"I beg your pardon, they are!" said Jack, warmly.

"I deny it!" retorted Kruger.

"On what grounds?"

"I tracked this man to his lair, and ran him to earth without any assistance from anybody."

"Oh, what a crammer!" cried Peeping Tom.

"Hold your tongue," exclaimed Jack. "I'm doing this business. Leave this lying Dutchman to me."

Kruger got red in the face.

He brought his fist down on the table with a bang.

"Look here," he said. "If you insult me I will run you in."

"You can't do it for mere words," replied Jack.

"Can't I! Just learn that I'm the boss here, and can do as I please."

"The President, Herr Joubert, is over you, and I will appeal to him."

"You can't," retorted Kruger.

"Why can't I?"

"Because you will not be able to get at him. It was reported that he was here, but he is not, and will not be until to-morrow."

"He has left Pretoria."

"I know that; but he has not arrived here. Therefore you cannot go and see him, and I can do as I like. You shall not see him. If you do not clear out of this town within an hour, I will have you taken out and left on the road to Capetown."

Jack Spencer allowed his lip to curl with a smile.

"You think you are very big, Mr. Kruger," he said; "but I am not afraid of you."

"I'll make you sing very small before I have done with you."

"No, you won't."

"Wait and see," said Kruger, defiantly.

He took out his watch and looked at it.

"Three o'clock in the afternoon," he continued. "At four—that is within one hour—you will clear out, or, as your countrymen say, be chucked out. You understand what I mean."

"I shall not go unless you pay the money to this boy, who is fairly entitled to it."

"He won't get a shilling, or you either," cried Kruger. "I believe you are an illicit diamond buyer, and Dawkins will have to give me an account of himself, if he takes your part. If the town has been flooded and half ruined, I have plenty of policemen about, and I am master here."

"Until the President comes."

"I'll settle you before that. *Du bist fericht mein kint.*"

In his low Dutch language, as they call it in the Netherlands, this meant. "You are mad, my child."

This speech did not in any way abash Jack.

He was determined to be as firm and uncompromising as Kruger himself.

"Do you mean to pay up?" he asked.

"Not a single solitary pfennig," replied Kruger. "The money representing the reward for Sutton's capture has been in my hands for months, and it is going to remain there."

"But you did not earn it."

"I say I did, and you can't prove the contrary. Anyhow, I don't want to argue the point with you. I am going down town, and I will give you just sixty minutes by the clock—that's one hour—to take yourself out of Colesberg."

"Suppose I don't choose to go? Is there any law to compel me?"

"Yes. The law respecting bad characters."

"How do I come under that?"

"I suspicion you to be B. C.—that's bad character; and I am empowered, by the Act of the States Legislature, to run such out of my jurisdiction, without applying to a judge, or giving any reason for it."

"I shall refuse to go," said Jack.

"We will see," answered Kruger. "If you are violent, we shall repel force by force. Good morning."

Bestowing a malignant look upon the three, he strode from the tent, with all the arrogance of a jumped-up Jack in office.

He was resolved to exert his power, to enable him to retain the reward money in his pocket.

Being naturally avaricious, he was also unscrupulous; and it is not exaggerating to say that justice was often bought and sold in the Free State.

Kruger was never above accepting a bribe, and was reported to have lined his nest well.

"What are you going to do about it?" asked Dawkins.

"Show fight," replied Jack.

"You'll find it hard lines to kick against Kruger. He's a terror when he starts."

"You seem afraid of him all at once," said Jack.

"I'll allow that I am; that's a fact. I own up to it."

"Then I can't expect any help from you."

"Not now, after what he's said," answered Dawkins. "You see, I've got to live here, and make an income. He could take away my licence, and levy blackmail on me. He'd ruin me in less nor a week. I should give in if I were you. Clear out."

"From your point of view that may be all right. I am only sorry I cannot accept your advice."

"I shall have to ask you to leave my marquee, then."

"What for? Am I doing any harm?"

"Not in the least degree," said Dawkins; "but, at the present moment, I've got about fifty customers in my tent, and an hour later, a lot will be coming in for teas. Any scene would do me harm."

"All right; don't be alarmed. I'll go. Thank you for nothing, Mr. Dawkins. I thought you were a very different kind of fellow."

"Everyone for himself, is the motto in these days."

"It looks like it with such chaps as you."

"Come, don't cut up rough. It ain't my fault."

As he spoke he offered his hand, which Jack Spencer refused to take.

Brushing brusquely past him, followed by Peeping Tom, he quitted the marquee, and going out into the road, sat down at the side.

It was fine and warm.

The homeless people were scattered about on the grass, some sitting, some lying down.

The weather being so cheerful and hot, both day and night, they did not appear to suffer much.

Most of them had money, and those who had not, borrowed from those who were better off.

Men like Dawkins had been able to erect tents and procure a supply of meat, beer, spirits, and bread.

As soon as the President arrived, they expected he would open a relief fund, to lend them money to rebuild their homes.

"Don't you think, Spencer," remarked Tom, "that you had better turn this job up?"

"I sha'n't," replied Jack, doggedly. "If Kruger's chaps run me out, I'll walk in again."

"Perhaps they will club you."

The Transvaal police were rumoured to be very handy with their truncheons, or clubs as they were called.

"If they do, I'll shoot."

"That will bring us into trouble," said Peeping Tom, doubtfully.

"Don't you fret," cried Jack. "I am fighting your battle, but I do not ask you to run any risk."

CHAPTER XVI.

HOW CRAMMER APPEARS IN THE ACADEMY, AND HOW MARY SAVES HER CHARACTER AND HER PLACE.

THRASHAM was utterly dumbfounded at the scene on which he gazed.

Not so his scholars.

They laughed till the tears ran down their cheeks.

"What can this mean?" echoed the master.

As the question was addressed more to himself than to his scholars, none vouchsafed a reply.

"The girl's in a fit," continued her master; "but what right has she up at this hour? Jane, Jane!"

Mr. Thrasham stooped over the housemaid, and took her hand.

Jane slightly recovered.

Only just enough, however, to fasten her nails in the back of her master's hand.

Thrasham winced with pain.

"Confound her," he muttered, tearing his hand roughly away.

"I'll tear your eyes out!" shrieked Jane. "Oh, you vile wretch!"

Thrasham leaped back.

This language to him, and from one of his servants.

"What could it mean?"

He asked this question aloud.

Ralph Towers took upon himself to reply.

"Touched, sir, a little, I think, in her head."

"Never heard of her being subject to such things as this," mused Thrasham.

"Shall we lift her up, sir?" asked one of the boys.

"Yes, and sit her on a chair."

This was done.

"Bathe her face with a little cold water," said Thrasham. "She is coming round, and then she will explain, perhaps, what all this means."

Ralph Towers bathed the face and hands of Jane, and tried to arouse her.

The tones of the brave lad, soft and pitiful as they were, had the desired effect.

Jane looked bewilderedly around upon the assembled throng, as if in search of some-one, and then, finding that person was not there, she covered her face with her hands and burst into tears.

Thrasham and his pupils looked on in silence.

At length the master of the academy asked—

"Jane, what does this mean?"

Jane did not reply to this question.

All she did was to sob heavily.

Mrs. Thrasham now appeared on the scene.

"Send these boys to bed, Mr. Thrasham, and I will see what is wanted here," said the lady.

"Now, boys, to bed," said Thrasham.

The boys turned to obey the mandate.

Mrs. Thrasham placed her hand on Jane's shoulder.

Thrasham looked at the wrecked crockery on the floor, and shook his head sorrowfully.

The boys paused, the lady let fall her hand, and the master raised his eyes.

"What's that?" was the exclamation of one and all.

It was a scream in a female voice.

They listened.

Then another sound came to their ears.

The tones were thick and husky.

"Keep quiet, I tell you," were the words he used. "I tell you I want to speak to you."

"Go away. Oh, do go away!"

This was in the voice of the cook.

"I shan't. You put your arms round my neck and said you loved me, and I won't go away."

Thrasham looked at his wife.

The lady glanced at her husband.

Jane rose to her feet, and glared fiercely at the door.

"Oh, do for goodness sake, go away," said the cook in a whisper, but so loud that it was heard.

"I tell you I shan't go away. Fetch that little man out here. I've got something to say to him."

"Come to-morrow," pleaded Mary.

"I've got to go to prison to-morrow," said the man.

"I know that voice. Jane, can you explain this?" said Thrasham.

Jane did not reply.

She had caught sight of a policeman's hat in the garden beyond the kitchen.

More than this—she saw, by the moon's faint light, the cook in the arms of the man.

The sight roused her.

She clenched her teeth and her hands.

"It's—it's——" she gasped. "Oh it's him and her!"

"Boys," cried Thrasham, "see what this means!"

Ralph Towers sprang into the garden, followed by Hugh Tempest, Dolf Edwards, and several others.

On seeing them, Crammer, for he it was, released his hold of Mary the cook.

In turn the boys laid their hands on the public schoolmaster.

"What does this mean?" yelled the intoxicated man.

"Come and see," said Ralph.

And without further remark, they dragged Crammer into the kitchen.

Jane, when she perceived that it was not the individual she had suspected him to be, sank into a chair.

Thrasham held up the candle to the face of Crammer.

Crammer looked at the light then at Thrasham.

Raising his fist he dashed the candle from the hands of the little man.

The other lights having been extinguished when the table was overturned, all were now plunged into profound darkness.

"Want to set fire to my whiskers, do you?" yelled Crammer.

"How dare you, sir, be upon my premises?" cried Thrasham.

"Get a light! oh, get a light!" exclaimed Mrs. Thrasham.

She was fearful for her husband, and, womanlike, placed herself before him.

"I came to pull your nose," said Crammer.

And thrusting out his hand in the dark, he seized the frill of Mrs. Thrasham's cap, and tore it completely off.

A light was procured, and Crammer was seen standing with her lace in his hand, and the policeman's helmet over his eyes.

"I've been assaulted and insulted," hiccupped Crammer, "and I'm not a man to submit to such treatment quietly. Get away from that little rascal, and let me annihilate him."

But Mrs. Thrasham pushed him back as he staggeringly made up to her husband.

The blow was very slight.

It was, however, quite heavy enough for the inebriated form of the public schoolmaster.

Down he went into a sitting position.

Off rolled the helmet to the floor.

The hair of Crammer falling over his face, and his head drooping on one side, he now presented anything but a very flattering appearance.

"How came you on my premises, sir?" cried Thrasham. "And pray, sir, why should I not send for the police, and give you into custody?"

"What do you say, you mannikin?" stammered Crammer, making an effort to rise.

It was, however, unsuccessful.

Down he went again.

And there he sat among the fallen dishes, glaring out of his bleared eyes at those around him.

"How came you here, sir? Are you in league with my servants to injure or rob me? I think I ought to give you, and my cook and housemaid, into custody

"I'm not so brave as you, and if I run, you won't think it mean of me. I really couldn't stand up against a lot of police."

"Don't say any more. Your help would be of no use to me."

"I am delighted to hear it, because I should not like you to have a bad opinion of me. My heart's good."

"Do you suppose I don't know what you are?" exclaimed Jack. "Nature has made you a humbug and a sneak."

"Oh, don't say that, Spencer," whined Tom, deprecatingly.

"I do say it, and I'll stick to it. You're no good in a fight—no one could rely on you—but you're artful."

"If you get into a scrape, my cunning may do you more good than my fists would."

"Let us hope it may."

"If I only had Knowall Dick here, I shouldn't care."

"What possible use could he be to us?"

"He's jolly artful as well as I. When we are together, we generally manage to pull a thing off," replied Peeping Tom.

Suddenly Kruger appeared in front of them.

He was followed by two policemen in uniform, and seemed to be walking up the road on business.

Not the slightest attention did he condescend to bestow upon Jack and Peeping Tom.

But after proceeding a few yards he halted, pointed to them, and said a few words in a whisper to his officers.

Then he passed on, leaving the two men behind him.

"Now for it," thought Jack.

The time had come.

Kruger intended to keep his word.

The sudden approach of danger made Peeping Tom tremble.

"I must have been born nervous," he observed. "I do feel so bad."

"Cut along. I have told you that I don't want you to stay," Jack replied.

"I'll retire to a distance, but I'll keep an eye on the proceedings."

"You needn't unless you like."

"It's my duty. You are doing so much for me and Dick, that I must do something for you. If those men hurt you, I'll make them regret it."

Jack gave him a push, which was intended to convey his sense of weariness at listening to him.

"I'm going. You've no call to shove a chap, especially a harmless little chap like me."

"I don't want to hear your bald-headed talk."

"Then I won't inflict it on you any further."

"You can cut, I tell you. Wait up the road somewhere."

"I won't be far off."

"If anything happens to me, you had better tell Harry Rawlings," continued Jack.

"I'll hide up a tree I see over there, and if you get licked, I will foot it back to Brand's farm as hard as I can," replied Peeping Tom.

"That's the ticket."

Scarcely had Jack Spencer spoken these words than the officers advanced quickly towards them.

One made for Tom, the other approached Jack.

Peeping Tom saw that his design was to capture him, and promptly picked up a stone.

It was a large-sized one. He threw it at him with all his force, hitting him on the forehead.

The policeman reeled and sank to the ground, stunned and bleeding.

"I've scored," said Tom; "he won't arrest this child, but I am afraid I shall have to run for it. The police will have a grudge against me. Hullo! here comes old Kruger."

He was right.

Kruger had been hiding behind a stone wall, while his men approached Jack.

Seeing one fall he revealed himself, determining to come to the rescue if he was wanted.

Rather alarmed at the presence of the chief of the police, Peeping Tom ran to a tree.

No heed was taken of his movements.

He succeeded in reaching the tree, into the branches of which he climbed.

Here he was effectually hidden.

But he could see all that passed beneath him.

The second policeman had, by this time, reached Jack Spencer, who looked indignantly at him.

Kruger was fifty yards in the distance, watching the course of events.

"What do you want with me?" inquired Jack, his eyes flashing fire.

"I have orders from my chief to conduct you out of the city, and to warn you that if you return, you will be shot on sight," was the reply.

"Shot! you daren't do it. I am a British subject."

"In the state of affairs at present existing in this city you would not be missed."

"I defy you to touch me!" cried Jack.

"Look here," said the constable, "it's no

use for you to play the fool with me. I have told you what my orders are, and must do my duty."

"Go away and leave me alone."

"I must take you out of the city limits. If you resist I shall lock you up."

"On what charge?"

"I don't know. You'll find all that out."

"But there is nothing against me."

"You've offended the chief, and he will soon formulate a charge. I'll bet, if you don't take a fool's advice, young man, and make yourself scarce, he will railroad you to the penitentiary in less than forty-eight hours."

"He can't do it," replied Jack.

"Pshaw! He's done it before, and will do it again. Are you coming or not?"

Jack folded his arms.

There was a look of stern determination on his face.

"No," he said, emphatically.

"You'd better think different," said the policeman.

"Touch me if you dare!"

Peeping Tom was growing momentarily more and more excited.

"Here's a lark," he muttered. "There will be ructions presently."

The policeman stretched out his hand, attempting to seize Jack Spencer by the arm.

This the latter resisted, and a violent struggle ensued.

Jack fought hard with his fists.

The constable used his club, and hit Jack several blows on the head.

He began to stream with blood.

"Give it him!" cried Kruger. "Let him have it!"

"All right. I'll fix him," was the reply.

Jack began to feel giddy, and was growing tired of the unequal contest.

"Leave off clubbing me, you brute!" he exclaimed. "I'll shoot if you touch me again."

"Look out for yourself," continued Kruger. "He says he'll shoot. Floor him. Gott in Himmel! Settle him!"

Again the policeman raised his club.

Rendered desperate by the unmerited punishment he was receiving, Jack drew his revolver.

He had become reckless.

His blood was up, and he did not seem to care what happened.

Aiming at the man, he was about to fire, when his arm was knocked up.

The bullet flew harmlessly through branches of a neighbouring tree.

It was Kruger, who rushed forward and saved his officer.

The next moment the latter struck Jack again on the head.

This blow settled the matter.

Jack rolled over like a log, uttered a groan, and lost his senses.

At this moment, the policeman who had been rendered unconscious by the stone thrown at him by Peeping Tom, came to himself.

He ran to the assistance of his mate.

"Where is the other one?" asked Kruger.

"Bolted, sir. He bowled me over with a stone and cut away. I didn't see which way he went," was the reply.

"Get a stretcher," continued Kruger. "We will lock this young man up. The surgeon had better strap his head up. I will see what is to be done with him to-morrow."

"He was going to fire on me," said the first officer. "You saved me."

"It is a grave offence. The judge will give him a long term of imprisonment," answered Kruger.

A large crowd, attracted by the report of the pistol, had assembled.

But nobody attempted to interfere.

Jack was a stranger in the town, and everyone knew that it was dangerous to meddle with Kruger.

The policemen went for a stretcher, while Kruger stood over the prostrate form of Jack Spencer.

In a short time they returned, and placing him upon the stretcher, conveyed him to the Central Police Station.

"He shall be tried to-morrow, and I will take care that for some years he will languish in prison. The reward is mine. He was a fool to interfere with me," exclaimed Kruger.

With a smile of satisfaction he strode away.

Peeping Tom was afraid to come down from his airy perch in the tree.

He determined to wait until it was dark.

CHAPTER XXXIII.

PEEPING TOM COMES TO THE RESCUE.

HALF-AN-HOUR passed, and Tom was beginning to feel cramped in his elevated position.

He had a strong inclination to get down and chance detection.

The crowd had dispersed.

There was no policeman to be seen anywhere about.

All at once he noticed two rough-looking men, who were attired like miners, coming towards the tree.

They stopped when they came underneath it.

"We can talk here, Bill," said one.

"Ay, Jim," replied the other, "there is no one to hear what we say."

"The question is, shall we do it?" continued Bill.

"Of course, we will do it. Isn't it a fine chance of making a splendid haul?"

"Are you sure your information is correct?"

"Certain sure," said Jim. "President Joubert is on his way here with only one attendant. They are riding, and are expected at the hotel to-night at nine. The road goes through the wood three miles from here. In a couple of hours' time they will be in the midst of the trees. It is reported that Joubert brings a bag full of gold for the relief of the sufferers."

"It will amount to a good sum," remarked the one called Bill, thoughtfully.

"Hundreds of pounds, I should imagine."

"We ought to have it."

"We will," cried Jim. "It is worth making a bold bid for. All we have to do is to stop the President and his attendant in the woods. When they see themselves covered by our pistols, they will soon hand over the gold, and we will tramp on to Kimberley."

"Yes. Colesberg will be too hot to hold us."

"Is it agreed?" asked Jim.

"I'm on," answered Bill.

"Then let us start at once."

They lighted their pipes, took a sip out of a flask of whisky, and trudged off.

Peeping Tom at once conceived the bold idea of following them.

The President of the State had supreme power.

If Tom could save him from the two villains who intended to rob him, he would establish a claim to his gratitude.

He would be able to ask him for the reward for exposing Captain Moonlight.

In addition to that, he could ask him to interfere on behalf of Jack Spencer.

It was a magnificent opportunity.

He would have been cowardly and foolish if he had neglected to take advantage of it.

Getting down from the tree, he followed the ruffians at a safe distance.

It would not do to excite their suspicions.

Evidently they were scoundrels of the deepest dye.

Men who would not hesitate to commit any crime.

For three miles he kept them in sight.

Then they entered the wood, through which the main road ran.

After going half-way through it, they halted and hid themselves behind a large tree.

Tom also got into the wood and noiselessly drew up to within a few feet of them.

He saw them cock their pistols and get in readiness for the intended attack.

It was a cunningly devised ambush.

Satisfying himself of the precise position taken up by the rascals, Tom cautiously made a circuit.

He got half-a-mile ahead of the men.

Then he went into the road.

Scarcely had he done so when he saw a gentleman, followed by an attendant, approaching on horseback.

It occurred to him at once that this was the President of the Free State.

The sun was declining in the west.

Sombre shadows were cast by the patriarchal trees.

Running up the road he waved his hand.

"Stop, if you please," he cried.

"What do you want, boy?" demanded the leader.

"Are you the President, sir?" asked Peeping Tom.

"You have divined rightly. I am," was the reply.

"Have you a sum of money in a bag?"

"That is a strange question to put, but I may say that I have."

"Well, sir, I have come to warn you that you are to be robbed and, perhaps, murdered."

"How? When? Where?" he queried.

"A little farther up the road, sir."

"How do you know? Come nearer and tell me all about it, my lad."

Tom did so without any hesitation.

The President listened to him with the most lively interest, as did his companion.

Tom did not omit to mention the reward and the brutal treatment of Jack Spencer by Kruger.

"You have rendered me a great service," said Joubert. "I will not fail to see that justice is done to you and your friend Spencer."

"Thank you, sir. It is all I ask," replied Tom.

"Now you must do me and my companion another service."

"You have only to name it."

"We will tie our horses to the branch of a tree. We three will enter the wood on foot. You can conduct us to the rear of these two men, and we will shoot them down before they can fire upon us. Do you understand?"

"Perfectly."

Lead on, then, and be as noiseless as possible," said Joubert.

He dismounted, as did his attendant.

They made their horses fast and followed Peeping Tom into the wood.

Conducting them to the spot where the robbers were waiting, Tom pointed them out.

They were facing the road, intently watching for their prey.

Not the least idea had they that they were out-manœuvred and surprised.

Each had a pistol in his hand.

The President singled out one, the attendant the other.

Both fired at once.

Loud reports followed, echoing through the wood.

The robbers fell forward.

Both were shot through the back.

They uttered terrible groans, yells, and imprecations.

Two more shots were fired at them, and they became still for ever.

Bill and his friend Jim were dead.

Joubert advanced, and turning the bodies face upward, looked at them.

"I don't know them," he remarked. "They are not personal enemies, possibly sufferers from the inundation, actuated by greed."

In this opinion the attendant fully concurred.

The journey to Colesberg was continued without any delay.

Peeping Tom walked by the side of the President's horse.

He did not deem it prudent to quit his new friend and protector.

If Kruger got hold of him, he would no doubt treat him as cruelly as he had done Jack Spencer.

Perhaps he would kill him outright.

Joubert was well acquainted with the town, and though wearied and hungry after his journey, determined, after a brief consultation with his companion, to postpone going to the hotel until he had seen Kruger.

His wish was to have justice done at once.

He could wait to gratify his own comfort.

It was dark when they entered Colesberg.

The town presented a desolate appearance without any gas, the works having been injured by the water.

They made their way, without accident, to the headquarters of the police.

On asking for Kruger, they were informed that he was in his private room.

The President sent in his name.

Kruger came out and welcomed him heartily.

He took him by the hand, conducting him into the room, where he offered him and his attendant some refreshment.

It was accepted.

Peeping Tom had also entered the room.

He stood in the shadow of a book-case.

Kruger did not remark his presence.

Had he done so, he would not have been so much at his ease.

He smiled, and appeared to be greatly delighted.

"We have been visited by a great calamity," he remarked.

"You have, indeed—thanks to th wickedness of Sutton," replied the President.

"Your presence is a great honour, and will reassure the citizens. I am told you also bring money."

"We will go into the question of relief presently. I wish to talk to you about a matter that concerns yourself."

"Indeed! What may that be?"

"Who captured Sutton?"

"He was detected and exposed only."

"Who gave you the information that led to this result? Was it not two English boys?"

Kruger hesitated.

The President beckoned to Tom.

"Step forward," he continued.

Peeping Tom did so.

"You know that the reward offered was won by, and is due to, these boys. Hand it over, or I will disgrace you, and put another in your place."

"Pardon," said Kruger.

"It is more than you deserve."

Kruger went to a safe, and took out a bag of gold.

This he handed to Tom.

"So far, so good," exclaimed Joubert. "Now produce your prisoner Spencer."

"You know everything."

"It's my province to do so."

Reluctantly, Kruger left the room.

In a few minutes he returned with Jack.

The latter's head was strapped up with plaster and surgical bandages.

He appeared to be weak, but held himself erect.

"This gentleman is the President," cried Tom. "I met him, and he's doing justice."

"I thank him for considering me," said Jack.

"You have been badly treated," remarked Joubert.

"He drew his pistol on an officer," pleaded Kruger.

"Had it not been for that," answered the President, "I should have dismissed you from your post."

"You pardon me?"

"I do."

After a few more words, the President and his attendant left for their hotel.

Jack and Peeping Tom followed them out of the station.

They went up the hill to Dawkins' refreshment tent.

There was nothing to fear from Kruger now.

They had a powerful friend in Joubert.

That night they slept in the open air.

The following day, after breakfast, he heard that a team was going to the coast.

He proceeded to the spot.

To his great gratification he found that a caravan of six waggons was being got ready that day.

A number of citizens wanted to leave the ill-fated town for ever.

He at once secured seats and accommodation for five.

The road to the coast passed Brand's house.

At four o'clock that afternoon, Jack, Harry, Marian and the spies were comfortably seated in a waggon.

A thick awning kept off the scorching rays of the sun.

Their journey was a pleasant and uneventful one.

At Cape Town Harry married Marian, and took first-class saloon passages for all, on board one of the Union Line steamers for England.

The spies were advised to enter the detective business.

That was a line especially suited to them.

Jack found his mother nearly heartbroken at his long absence, and her grief at her husband's untimely death was great.

Harry took his wife to the Hall, no one now objecting to his title, since the Squire and Charlie were dead.

He made Jack a present of the farm.

*　*　*　*

Harry Rawlings and Jack Spencer are near neighbours and good friends.

Jack has determined not to marry until his mother dies, and finds plenty of enjoyment in being a gentleman farmer.

The spies have turned over a new leaf, and are devoting themselves to business and money-making, some very difficult cases having been put into their hands, and brought to a successful conclusion by their sagacity.

They are still Peeping Tom and Knowall Dick, but instead of being the Spies of the School, or the Spies Abroad, they are the SPIES OF LONDON.

THE END.

On Monday Next, August 30th,

WILL BE PUBLISHED

Nos. 1 and 2 of the Famous Story,

THE RIVAL SCHOOLS, THEIR FUN, FEUDS, and FROLICS.

With the First Issue will be presented Gratis a Tinted Picture for binding when complete, and the whole enclosed in an Attractive Wrapper.

Order your Newsagent at once to reserve you a copy every week of

THE RIVAL SCHOOLS,

and read the Amusing Incidents occasioned by Conflicts with the Boys of the Rival Establishments.

SPREAD THE NEWS TO YOUR FRIENDS.

Nos. 1 and 2 on MONDAY NEXT,

ONE HALFPENNY ONLY.

OFFICE: 173, FLEET STREET, LONDON, E.C.